# TERROR
## IN 16-BITS

MUZZLELAND PRESS
GOLDEN, COLORADO

ISBN-10: 0-9970803-4-5
ISBN-13: 978-0-9970803-4-6

THESE STORIES ARE WORKS OF FICTION. ANY SIMILARITIES TO REAL PEOPLE, PLACES, OR EVENTS ARE PURELY COINCIDENTAL.

EDITING AND LAYOUT BY JONATHAN RAAB
PROOFREADING BY JESSICA RAAB
COVER ART BY PETER LAZARSKI

JOYSTIX MONOSPACE FONT BY TYPODERMIC.

WWW.MUZZLELANDPRESS.COM
TWITTER & INSTAGRAM: @MUZZLELANDPRESS
EDITOR@MUZZLELANDPRESS.COM
FACEBOOK.COM/MUZZLELANDPRESS

# STAGE SELECT

**TPK**
by Adrean Messmer...................................................................1

**CENTRALIA**
by Sean M. Thompson.............................................................28

**SAIRENS**
by Julie K. Godard..................................................................47

**DR. COAGULANT'S SPLATTER LAB**
by Jonathan Raab.....................................................................70

**A LUMP AND HIS BOY**
by Richard Wolley...................................................................109

**I'M A GOOD PERSON, I MEAN WELL,
AND I DESERVE BETTER**
by J.R. Hamantaschen............................................................127

**RESET**
by William Tea......................................................................181

**ONEIROVISION**
by Brian O'Connell................................................................203

**LEEDS 2600**
by Matthew M. Bartlett.........................................................226

**THE OWLS OF UNDERHILL**
by Amberle L. Husbands.......................................................253

**THREE DAYS AS MR. MCGREGOR**
by Jack Burgos......................................................................280

**ANGELS' ARMAGEDDON**
by Amber Fallon....................................................................306

**TERROR FROM THE 50-YARD LINE**
by Thomas C. Mavroudis.......................................................323

**SNOW RIVER**
by Alex Smith.......................................................................338

**THE DRUNKARD'S DREAM**
by Orrin Grey........................................................................371

**ABOUT THE DEVELOPERS**....................................406

# TPK
## BY ADREAN MESSMER

The location is the Valentine Manor. Opulent, decadent luxury from a time long past. It has watched the years go by from its perch on the rotten ait in the middle of the split river. Before the land was settled, the soil was so sour even the water refused to touch it.

The players are friends masquerading as strangers. Or maybe it's the other way around. The setting is a failed night. A class reunion. A coming storm. Friendships that fell apart. Languished. Decayed. Being pulled back from the grave. They are trying to reconnect. To find that spark to light the friendly hearth. Retrace those paths that lead to long talks, inside jokes, and eventual heartbreak.

Desperation drives them down that road. Willful ignorance makes them forget where it leads. Over the rickety, truss bridge, grey water flowing in stormy fits just a few feet below. The walls enveloping them like a hand. Or a cage. They ignore the gathering gloom in the west. They follow the spider of temptation that whispers sweet promises to the fly. They believe they are not the fly.

*The old road is cracked and crumbled. A tangle of branches blocks out the waning sunlight. Trees forever, all they can see. The bridge was maybe just a nightmare and the road ahead is a deep and verdant dream. And then it shatters in bright white, the sun breaking through the clouds, the car breaking through the trees.*

*There it is. The childhood dare.*

*They get out of the car, wary and excited in equal measure. Playing at being scientists, explorers, friends. Believing they will go home as better people, their love rekindled.*

*The keys, the egress, the end.*

Maria continued to walk with purpose. Claire followed behind her in a daze. The large pipe was heavy and her shoulder ached from carrying it for so long. She ran her other hand along the walls, thinking about the way the torn wallpaper felt under her fingers rather than how Maria was them leading deeper into the house instead of out. Claire touched the splintered frame of every crooked picture, squinting to see them in the darkness. Even if there had been windows, it wouldn't have helped much. The storm outside had turned the afternoon to premature evening. She hadn't felt a doorframe in a while and this hallway was becoming impossibly long.

"Maria, I changed my mind," she said.

Maria didn't stop. She didn't even look back. Her long ponytail swayed with each step. Her slim figure only visible because of her white sweater, fading out where the bloodstains made it blend in with the darkness.

"Maria, can you hear me?"

"What do you want to do, Claire? Go back and sit in your car? The bridge is washed out. Nothing but rain. You could drown out there."

"You're freaking me out." She shivered and crossed her arms. The fabric of her hood was cold and heavy with rain water. Her own dark hair was plastered around her shoulders and face. Maria wasn't wrong. There was nothing out there but rain. But in here, her friends were dead.

"They're not your friends," Maria said.

Claire stopped. "What did you say?"

"They never were." Maria's voice was like an echo, detached and not quite coming from her. Around the edges of the sound, there was whispering static.

Claire's blood ran cold. She wanted to run, but found herself reaching out to Maria and touching her arm. Maria's sweater was soft and dry, but her body radiated cold through the fabric. She turned and Claire held her breath. She wasn't sure what she'd expected, but Maria looked fine. Tired, with a haunted look in her dark eyes, but fine. Claire bit her lip, trying to calm herself down.

"What did you say?" she asked again when she could finally find the air to do so.

Maria looked down at her closed fist. Blood seeped through her fingers. She must have cut her hand on the glass key.

"I don't think we're getting out of here again," Maria said. "It let us go once, but I think we were too young to understand this place then."

"What are you talking about?"

"You know, it was after Max made us come here that

everything went wrong."

Claire nodded. "Sure, but that's because Max was an asshole."

"But he wasn't. Remember? He was fine before that night."

It was true in the way that any memory is true. Claire could remember a version of Max that she'd fallen in love with. But that version crumpled under the weight of more recent memories. The ones that Maria and Josh hadn't been there for.

"No. I don't remember," Claire said. Anger crept up like bile in her throat. She'd called Josh a thousand times—Maria even more. Neither of them ever answered. She closed her eyes and tried to calm down. To remind herself that they were entitled to their own lives and—it didn't matter now. The image of Josh's body flashed across the backs of her eyelids like lightning. "I'm sorry. I just…" Her voice faltered. "I want to get out of here."

Maria's hand was cold as it enveloped Claire's. "You're never getting away from him again, Claire." Her voice took on that nightmare, static-laced quality.

Claire sobbed and pulled free. She ran. None of this was on any of the floor plans she'd looked up earlier. *I have the internet.* Lot of good that did her, here, in this place.

She ran until the air smelled like rain and she thought that meant she was close to an exit. But the next turn brought her back to Maria.

Maria was in front of a large silver door with strange, arcane symbols embossed on the surface. There were three slots, one under each symbol. The vague outline of a man, a fist shaped object with a rusty stain running down from it, and an oval filled with wavy lines.

Maria turned to Claire. The veins in her eyes were black and spreading down her cheeks like tears. Claire held the pipe in both hands. Maria put her hand out and opened her fingers one by one, displaying the keys.

"Open the door," Maria said, her voice like unraveling webs.

Claire shook her head. "I don't want to do that."

Maria smiled. "What makes you think you can start saying 'no' now?"

"Shit." Claire wiped her eyes with the back of her hand, leaving big black smears of mascara under her eyes. "I just want to go home."

"This is the only way out."

Claire wasn't sure this was the kind of *out* she wanted, but she stepped forward and let Maria drop the keys into her hand. Maria moved to the side and Claire took her place in front of the door. One by one, she slipped the keys into the locks.

Bright light shone from around the edges of the door as it opened. Claire closed her eyes. Maria started to cry. It was a high, whining sound.

She opened her eyes.

First, she saw Max, too tall and looking down on her. He moved closer, his body swaying and lurching like he was on a boat. Claire stepped back, running into Maria. Maria's arms went around her, holding her tight. The pipe hit in her the shin, sending a spike of pain like a splash of cold water that forced her out of shock. But she held on.

"I'm sorry, Claire," Maria said. "We should have been there for you. Maybe we wouldn't be here now if we had been."

Light flashed and danced off the surface of eight mirrors. Claire blinked, trying to understand why they were there and moving. Max's body ended at his torso, into the cephalothorax of an arachnid. Gnashing pedipalps extended from his groin. Instead of legs, he had the jagged-edged glass, each one clicking against the ground, leaving large gashes in the wood floor.

Claire raised the pipe and aimed for his stupid, smirking mouth.

*The heart, the body, the soul.*

Claire was in the foyer, dripping wet and halfway to the door, digging her keys out of her pocket when Maria came pounding down the stairs. The torrential sound of rain was all around them, making the house feel almost safe.

Maria grabbed her by the wrist. Claire's hand was bloody, with something gripped tightly in her pale fingers.

"What are you doing?"

"I don't know." She was fighting back tears. "I tried to call 911. But they said the storm made the river flood, so the bridge is a no-go." The tears broke free. "But, Jesus, I can't stay here. This place is so fucked up. I can't even tell what's real."

Maria nodded. "Yeah. Yeah. I know. But I think I know how we can get out."

"How?"

"We need to find Josh and Max." Maria pulled an old key,

the bow carved into a simple eye, out of her pocket and showed it to Claire.

"Where did you get that?"

"Upstairs. I think the house is trying to tell us something."

Claire stared silently at Maria for a few moments.

"It's a house. What the fuck." It wasn't a question. She pulled away and Maria let go.

"You're right." Maria shook her head. "I'm sorry. I don't… This place is messing me up."

Claire bit her lip and looked to the door. There was nothing out there for her. Her car, sure, but no bridge. No road out of here. "It's fine," she said and opened her hand, showing Maria her own key. It was identical to Maria's except the bow looked like a small, sleeping baby. "What do we do now?"

Maria took the key from her.

"We find Josh and Max."

Maria walked with purpose, to the double doors behind the large staircase. The hiss of rain quieted as they went deeper into the Victorian mansion. The old floor creaked under them. The house's rooms and halls were dark beyond where the pale light from tall windows failed to reach. Claire tried counting doors, comparing it to her memory of the map. She tested a few doors as they went, each one stuck or locked.

Shivering, she pulled her hood up, hoping it would warm her, even though it was wet, too. She wanted to disappear. To find the safety she felt as a child, hiding from the boogeyman under the covers and knowing it couldn't get to her. But she didn't have a blanket and it was still midday.

None of this should have been happening. Maria's certainty was almost as terrifying as everything else.

Her shoes were wet and squelching, but something felt suddenly *off*. She looked down, fishing her phone out of her pocket. She turned on the flashlight and her phone beeped. *Low battery.* It illuminated the floor long enough for her to see sticky red liquid on the warped wood, staining the white rubber of her sneakers.

"Maria," she started.

But Maria was pushing the door open. Claire didn't look away fast enough. There was a body leaning against the wall. She closed her eyes, trying not to remember that Josh had been wearing a grey dress shirt just like that one. The smell of cold blood hit her and she gagged.

"Maria, wait," she begged.

Maria knelt down and looked over Josh like he was a puzzle box. Something to be solved. Broken glass from the mirror above clung to him like glitter. His fist was closed tightly around something. She pulled his fingers open one by one.

Lying in his palm was a shard of broken glass. One end was a jagged heart. The other had the hills and valleys of a finely cut key. Maria picked it up gingerly and looked to Claire.

"We've got them."

Claire covered her mouth. "Got what?"

"The keys." Maria added Josh's to the others in her hand. Each one had the bow carved in a different shape—a heart, a baby, and an eye.

Claire furrowed her brow, wanting to cry again but so tired of doing that.

"Keys to what, Maria?"
"Let's find out."

*The past, the blood, the teeth.*

Maria walked down the dark hallway, running her hand along the wall. The tattered wallpaper was soft and feathery on her fingertips.

"Claire?" she called out again.

She thought she'd seen Claire go up the stairs. Which seemed stupid at the time and even stupider now.

"Claire, listen, it's dark and creepy up here and I just want to go. But I can't because it's your car. So, come on." She fumbled in her pocket for her phone and used it as a flashlight. "Let's go find the boys and get out of here, yeah?"

She forced herself to keep breathing in the stale air and listened for an answer. None came. She continued down the hallway toward the light from a small window at the end. It was an anemic little window, with iron bars that wanted to be decorative but the scratches around the base belied the truth. Rainwater, leaking in through the old seams, ran down the inside of the glass.

Outside, the clouds were almost black, pouring down fat drops of rain. The trees were epileptic in the wind. Claire was out there, running up the hill, away from the hedge maze and toward the house like something was chasing her. Maria cursed softly and turned to go back the way she came. She was halfway down the hall when she heard something from one of the rooms. Whispering, like insects skittering over paper. A chill started at the base of her skull and went all the way down to her toes. She paused and looked toward the sound, wondering if the light had been on in that room before.

"Josh? Max?" She pushed the door open.

The room was smoky and silvered, making it difficult to focus on anything for too long. The images blurred and slipped away. The furniture was faded and old, just like everything else. A woman stood in the corner, cowering. The hem of her long skirt was wet and heavy, soaking up blood that pooled around her. A man stood above her, his knuckles white and scratched.

He took a swing at the woman, catching her in the jaw. Her head hit the wall. Something glittered in her mouth. Maybe just blood catching the light. He hit her in the stomach and she slipped and crumpled to the ground. Maria thought she recognized the man. Louis Valentine. But the scene was more familiar than that.

She could see Claire and Max like that. She'd spent a long time ignoring the rumors and not answering Claire's phone calls. She told herself she was busy and she would call back. But then she heard about what was happening. Rumors and secrets. *Did you hear about Claire? Poor thing. Lost the baby.* She'd wondered then if it was Max's fault. But she didn't know what to say, so she never called back.

The man bent over to hit the woman again. Teeth and blood spilled across the hardwood floor. The woman sobbed silently and they both vanished in a flash of wormy mist. But the teeth and blood remained, glinting in the light.

Maria looked over her shoulder. The light coming splashing across the stairs looked warm and inviting. But she went into the room and crouched by the mess. Mixed in with the teeth, covered in blood, was a key. Trying to avoid the viscera, she picked it up.

Downstairs, the sound of rain and wind got louder for just a moment. A door slammed closed.

"Claire?" Maria said, jumping to her feet.

Max stood in the doorway, blocking her path. He held onto the doorframe, leaning in and smiling wolfishly. Blood leaked between his fingers.

"What to do with a problem like Maria?" he said.

Maria hid her hand in her pocket, not sure why, but thinking he shouldn't know about the key. "Excuse me?"

He crossed the room to her in long, heavy steps. She tried to stand her ground, but cringed when he got within arm's reach and backed away until she hit the wall.

"Are you afraid of me?" His breath was hot against her face.

"No," she lied.

His fist caught her in the jaw. Her teeth snapped together, catching the end of her tongue. Her mouth filled with blood. Through the rushing sound in her ears, she could hear Claire calling for her and Josh.

*The mirror, the glass, the aberrant reflection.*

Josh thought that he might die in this room. The floor was covered with a deep, matted carpet with a smell that was two parts dust and three parts mold. Lumpy blankets and rotting pillows covered the large bed in the center.

Mirrors hung on every wall, most of them spider-webbed with cracks. Long, sharp shards of glass littered the floor, glittering in the half-light filtering in through the decaying velvet and lace curtains. All of them bouncing their reflections back and forth, from one to the other. It made him a little dizzy.

He hadn't planned to be in here. *In here* was deeper into the house and farther from the car. He'd meant to leave. To go out the front, back to the car, and drive away. To safety. But he'd lost Claire in the twisting hallways and the rain outside was threatening to turn the driveway into a muddy river. So, back inside he'd gone, looking for her. She had the car keys.

Half-burned candles stood on the dresser. Some in holders, some standing and stuck with their own wax. He found a pack of old matches in one of the drawers and lit a few candles for light. Picking up one stuck in an old beer bottle, he went to the wall behind the desiccated settee sofa. It didn't take too long to find the ghost of the message they'd left. Maria's big heart, drawn in red marker, stood out the most on the feathery wallpaper. Their names inside had almost faded away. Claire and Maria had written their names at the top. Below that was Josh and Max, with a plus sign between them. He'd known he shouldn't do it even then. He couldn't remember what he'd hoped for, but Max saw it just before they left. He swore he wouldn't tell anyone, but the next day everyone knew. Including Claire. They hadn't talked much after that.

Josh picked at the paint until it chipped away, leaving an awkwardly large space between the two. That felt right.

"Hey, Gorrister," Max's voice cut through the silence.

Josh gasped and jumped, hitting his shoulder on the sofa. It moved a few inches before catching in a hole in the carpet. Max laughed, the sound echoing off the walls.

"Fuck you." Josh rubbed at the tender spot on his arm.

"I'm sorry, man. That was—" he paused, looking at Josh for a little too long. "Shitty. I'm sorry. I shouldn't have snuck up on you."

Josh leaned back against the wall. Max had already stabbed him in the back. It seemed prudent to not let it happen again.

"What do you want?"

Max shrugged. "I don't know. The girls went off somewhere else. I thought maybe none of us should be alone. And I thought we could talk."

Josh laughed.

Max kicked at the broken glass on the ground. "Are you going to be mad at me forever?"

"Yeah, that's the plan. You outed me to everyone."

Something moved along the jagged edge of the mirror.

"Come on. It was ten years ago," Max said, a whining lilt to his voice.

"Shut up."

"You know what? Fuck you. This is—"

Josh put up a hand, cutting him off. "No, seriously. Just be quiet for a second. I thought I saw something."

Max froze, watching Josh's face. "What is it?"

A ripple that was maybe just shadows passed through the mirrors. Josh blinked hard. In the mirrors, the room's colors shifted from the faded blues and greys of abandonment to the warm hues of nostalgia. The bed was plush and soft. The carpet thick and warm. The candlelight shimmered on the gold leaf in the wallpaper.

Josh shook his head. When he looked up again, Max was standing closer to him, waving his hand in front of his face.

"Hey, where'd you go?" Max asked.

Josh gritted his teeth and pressed himself harder against the wall. "Don't touch me."

"Jesus. I'm not. But you're acting weird."

"Do you see that?" Josh asked, pointing to the mirror at the head of the bed.

Max followed Josh's gaze, looking over his shoulder.

"See wha—what's that?"

They watched the reflections in the mirror. Max, not facing the mirrors, but Josh. Not moving closer to the glass, but pining Josh to the wall, running his hands through Josh's hair. Josh touched his lips, swearing he could feel Max's breath on his face.

"Stop it," Josh hissed.

"I'm not doing anything."

Josh touched the mirror, tracing the aberrant reflections. "How did you do this?" He pulled the mirror away from the wall, looking behind it. "Did Claire help you set this up? Is this some kind of payback?"

"I told you," Max said evenly. "I'm not doing anything."

Josh pressed his fists against his eyes. Bright flashes of white sparked and bloomed along his eyelids. He leaned back on the wall, nudging a mirror with his shoulder. It fell, hitting the floor with a crack and the tinkling of broken glass.

"Whatever," Josh opened his eyes and looked at Max. "It's not going to work."

Max crouched on the ground, looking at the pieces of broken glass. His reflection was still looking at Josh. The

Max reflection stood up and walked across the room, smiling warmly.

"You know, we keep doing this. Going back and forth with each other. Coming back to this house." Josh couldn't tell if it was Max or his reflection speaking.

"What are you talking about? I've never been back here."

Max's reflection nodded and laughed. "Right. I guess that was just me."

The reflection stopped inches from Josh's. Josh thought he could feel Max's breath on his face again, smell the cheap, happy hour martini Max had before they left. He wanted to back away, but he was already against the wall.

"Back off, Max."

And then Josh really did feel Max on top of him. His hand on his shoulder. Pressing him harder against the wall. The peeling wallpaper tickling the back of his neck. He opened his eyes. Max was still across the room, watching him. But in the mirror, their reflections were face to face.

"Get off me, Max." Josh tried to push him back.

The Max reflection grinned, his teeth flashing.

"Isn't this what you want?"

"No. Not for a long time."

Heat blossomed over his chest, cooling quickly. Like spilled coffee. There was a hitch in his lung. He breathed in fast and deep to clear it, but the pain only intensified. He coughed out a yell. Hot phlegm coated his tongue.

The real Max backed up, looking at his hands. A deep, dark cut ran across his left palm.

Josh laughed again.

"Fuck. At least it wasn't the back this time." He raised his hand up to the shard of glass pinning his shirt to his sternum. Each heartbeat was sharp agony.

Max smiled at him a little sadly.

"Yeah. Like a true friend this time. Right in the chest." He turned and walked out the door, leaving as Josh slipped to the floor.

Josh pulled the shard of glass out of his chest. In the half-light of the room, it flashed silver and cold. Like a key.

*The garden, the dogs, the empty grave.*

Claire slammed through the door, the hinges screaming. The rain hit her like razor blades, cold and lethal in the wind. She stumbled and slipped down the hills, past the garden full of soggy, dead flowers, the twisted, overgrown hedge maze, and across the large expanse of slick green grass, until the smell of wet dogs stopped her.

She was at the kennels. She remembered the stories about Louis Valentine and his dogs. How, after Emily killed him and then herself in the master bedroom, the dogs had been left out there alone and hungry. The ones kept together eventually attacked, ready to eat anything, even each other. The ones alone wasted away, howling into the empty night.

The smell was thick and overwhelming, even in the rain. Or especially in the rain. Drifts of mangy, dirty fur were gathered in the corners like snow. Tufts of it caught in the bars of the windows and kennel doors. Claire couldn't figure out why it would still be there at all, decades later.

From the woods, something howled. High, whining, and hungry. Claire stood under the awning of the kennels, her breath coming in ragged gasps. Something close to a sob. She closed her eyes and counted until her heart slowed down.

"Jesus Christ," she said to no one.

She looked back up at the house, all the way up the hill. It hadn't felt so steep on the way down. She almost laughed at herself. Her fear was melting away, leaving her feeling silly. It was hard to even think about—like a dream. Whatever had happened inside the atrium, it couldn't have been real. Just her imagination and stress and not enough sleep.

She squinted through the sheets of rain, trying to see her friends through the dark windows, but it was a watery blur. Pushing herself off the wall took more effort than she liked and she started the trek back up, the smell of dog still clinging to her. The thing in the woods howled again, but closer. Claire glanced at the trees and pulled the sleeves of her wet hoodie over her hands, a chill running down her spine and settling in her stomach as heavy, cold weight. She tried to jog, but it only lasted a few seconds before she slipped and felt silly again.

"Get it together." She forced herself to laugh. It made her feel better until she saw the black shape loping out of the tree line toward her.

She shot to her feet. In a panicked, hesitating moment, she turned to run from it, back toward the kennels before thinking better of the decision and going for the house. She kept falling on the wet grass. Her feet finally found friction on the stone path in the garden. For a moment, she could make herself believe there was an echo under the sound of the raindrops, but it wasn't true. The sound behind her was the rushed click of long claws on the path, getting closer.

Another shape appeared on the path in front of her. It was as big as a Great Dane, but stockier. The water around it ran downhill, staining her muddy shoes red. At first, she couldn't make sense of the dog's color. Then she realized it was because the dog didn't appear to have any fur. It was pink and white. Shiny and deep, arterial red. When it breathed, flecks of blood puffed out of its nose like dragon's smoke.

One behind and one in front, she could go right or left. Left would lead her toward the woods. She dove right into the hedge maze, crashing through the thin branches that tried to grow over the entrance.

Vines snaked across the cracked flagstones, growing thickest where the rainwater collected. Behind her, the dog-things slipped around the corner, their paws splashing in the puddles. She turned left, then right, then right again. Tripping on twigs and slipping on wet leaves. The rain ran into her eyes. Cold drops slinking down her back. Her clothes were heavy and saturated.

Then she ran into a solid wall of branches. They scratched at her face and tangled in her hair. Dead end.

She turned to face the dogs, but they were gone. A small, raised garden stood in the middle of the cul-de-sac. The plants were tossed aside, roots naked and washed clean by the rain. The dirt, freshly dug, was piled back into place. She could hear something whimpering under the dirt, the sound just barely audible over the pounding of the rain. Something between a puppy's whine and baby's cry.

She stepped up onto the raised brick wall and started digging. The dirt was cold and slimy in her hands. Every time she pulled a handful aside, the rain washed half of it back down, through her fingers. The crying grew louder as she dug. Her fingers brushed rough wood and something inside scratched urgently.

The dogs barked somewhere in the maze, not too distant. But Claire couldn't pull herself away. The crying inside sounded like her own. The scratching of her nails echoed on the inside. She cleared the dirt away, revealing a small, hinged box. Blood ran down the front of it, like it had been filled with the liquid until it spilled out the seams. Her hands shook as she opened it.

A golden key.

*The switch, the lights, the hanged woman.*

"Oh, wow." Claire turned in place. "This room is bigger than my apartment."

The incoming clouds made the day preternaturally dark. The foyer was indecently large, with a double staircase swirling up to the second-floor landing. Everything was faded cream and gold and covered in a thin layer of brown dust. Maria found the light switch and flipped it up and down a few times.

"It's not going to work," Max said.

"You know," Maria said as she pushed the door open, making the rusted hinges groan. "I don't remember you being so intolerable."

Claire moved to let Max go past her. "He always was. He just used to be better at hiding it."

Josh laughed. "Yeah, that's true."

"What am I even doing here if you guys hate me so much?" Max asked.

Josh patted Max's arm. "That's a good question."

Their footsteps echoed on the stained marble floor. Mold traveled up the cracks in the old wood paneling and clung to the velvet swirls of the peeling wallpaper. The wind screamed around the corners of the house, sneaking in through the cracks and broken windows, making the crystal chandelier swing. The prisms tinkled together.

"The house has a generator." Claire said, looking at her phone. "We could probably get the lights on. It's in the basement. Wait, no. It used to be. During renovations, they moved it to the atrium." She glanced up and around. "That's, uh, down the hall. To the east. I think."

"Do we want the lights on? I'm not sure I want to see this place lit up." Josh turned his pack of cigarettes over in his hands. "I'm pretty sure that's toxic mold. I don't need to see my death while I breathe it."

The hallway was claustrophobic compared to the foyer. They walked single file, Maria leading with a small flashlight she had pulled out of her purse, Claire following while watching her phone screen, and Josh and Max uncomfortably close, neither one really wanting the other behind them.

The atrium was a semicircle cathedral of glass and greenery. Near the top of the iron gridwork, rainwater dribbled down the inside of the glass, sneaking in through cracks. The plants were deflated and brown and it smelled of wet decay. They stepped over thick, ropey roots and vines.

Maria found a closet buried under a wall of English ivy.

A large, rusted metal switch plate was mostly hidden behind the half-dead leaves, next to the door. She brushed them aside. There was a long, empty slot in the middle of it.

"Guys!" she called out. "I think I found something."

Claire trotted over from a copse of dead trees, their trunks trained to spiral up like a unicorn horn. She squinted at the plate. "Congratulations. You found a switch without a switch."

"What do we do?"

"Maria, come on. Do you need a quest giver?"

"A what?"

"Nothing."

Claire pulled at the door, snapping vines. The rusted hinges groaned as Maria joined in to help. They got the door open enough to slip in one at a time. Maria shone her flashlight around the small room. Broken-handled shovels and cracked watering pails were stacked along the perimeter. They searched the splintered, wooden shelves for the switch. Every item moved intensified the wet smell of mildew.

"Is this it?" Maria held up a splintered wooden square with a long piece of metal coming off one end.

Claire considered it for a bit before nodding.

"I mean, probably? I'm not super versed in old timey electrician practices. But let's try it."

Max was leaning on the wall with his arms crossed when they came out. Claire was careful to stay an arm's length away from him. He watched them heft the large switch up to the plate, and cooperatively try to jam it into the slot. It took them a couple of tries before it clicked and locked into place.

Claire clapped her hands. "We did it!"

Max frowned at them. "Like it's rocket science."

Maria flashed him a glare as she pushed the switch up. An electric hum filled the silence. For a moment, it seemed as if the whole house was vibrating. Then, with a soft pop, light after light came on, filling the atrium with soft, yellow light.

Josh came over, brushing wet brown leaves off his shirt. "The lights came on. No one told me I was a mess."

Max leaned on the wall. "Did anyone really need to? I thought it was obvious."

Claire fiddled with the headphones around her neck, wanting to put them on to block out the fight, but thought it might be rude.

Maria stood up suddenly, looking up at the apex of the glass ceiling. "What's that?"

The lights flickered in and out as everyone looked to where Maria pointed.

"Lightning?" Claire asked.

"No, *mira*." Maria stepped away from the shed and pointed more emphatically.

Flash on, there it was. A dark spot. Off, and it was gone. From somewhere, maybe all around them, came the sound of creaking rope. It was more echo than real and they wondered, after it was gone, if they'd heard it all. Claire inhaled to ask about it, but before the words came out, there was a snap. A flash of lightning and the lights went out. When they came back on moments later, the broken body of a woman lay in the center of the group.

"Oh, what the fuck…" Claire stepped back.

The woman arched, bones cracked, angles going the

wrong way. Josh dropped his cigarettes. The woman stood. Her black, starched skirts and tightly laced corset seemed to be holding her together. A noose was wrapped around her throat, digging into the bloodless skin. The rope trailed behind her. Her face was mangled, with ruined teeth coming through her lips. When she moved, the sandpaper sound of bones grinding together echoed off the glass.

Max smiled, eyes wide and unbelieving. "Is this happening?"

Maria shook her head. Like she was trying to will the woman back into non-existence.

But the woman didn't disappear. She took a jerky, unnatural step toward Claire. And another. One more and Claire and turned and ran, slipping on the wet corpses of plants.

"Claire!" Maria called. She glanced at the woman one more time, then ran after her friend.

The woman turned her attention to Josh. She reached out with her crooked fingers, brushing the soft cotton of his shirt. He fell back and scrambled away. He felt cartoonish — trying to get to his feet while still crawling backwards. The knees of his pants soaked through with the dirty rainwater. The door to the atrium felt stiff and stuck but he shoved through it, pain shooting through his shoulder.

Claire. He had to get to Claire. They came in her car. She had the keys. He ran down the narrow hallway they'd followed to get here, back to the foyer and through the front door that was still ajar. But the car sat empty. Rain came down in a steady, grey drizzle. He didn't want to go back inside, but he needed those car keys.

*The door, the storm, the key.*

Claire rattled the domed, double doors. "It's locked."

"There's a fix for that." Max picked up a rock and tossed it in the air a couple of times.

"Oh, man," Claire shook her head, moving away from the door and its stained-glass windows. "I dunno. I don't think we should break—"

Max threw it hard past Claire's head. She flinched back, but it bounced off the glass and hit her in the side of the head anyway.

Maria jumped the cracked stone stairs to Claire. "Asshole. What the hell?" She pushed Claire's messy hair back, checking for injury. "No blood."

Claire smiled, nervous and twitchy. "Hooray," she said, deadpan and giving half-hearted jazz hands.

"I didn't mean to hit her with it. It should have broken the glass." Max made his way up the porch steps to stand beside them. He tapped the cold glass, shifting it in its seat. "It's not even that stable."

He picked up the rock again. Claire flinched as he pulled back and slammed it into the glass. He yelped and dropped the rock, shaking his hand. "Fuck!"

"Oh, did that hurt?" Claire asked, rubbing her head.

"Maybe, shut up," he snapped.

Maria stood up straight between them, forcing him to back up. He stumbled down the shallow stairs.

"Maybe don't talk to her like that," she said.

Watching them from next to the car, Josh considered

getting back inside and taking a nap. He lit another cigarette and took in a deep drag. The day was chilly and grey and only getting more so as it went on. He closed his eyes, breathing in the wet air and smoke, ignoring their argument. It always smelled vaguely rotten near the river. And being on a small island in the center of it didn't help.

Thunder rumbled in the distance. Josh looked that way just in time to see lightning arc across the clouds. The sudden light reflected on something in the grass.

"Glass breaks, okay?" Max said. "That didn't break. I'm just saying it's weird."

"Maybe I can pick it." Claire crouched in front of the door and dug something out of her bag.

Maria crossed her arms, watching. "You know how to pick locks?"

Claire smiled up at her. "I mean, I have the internet. I know how to do a lot of things."

"Guys," Josh said. "Maybe we should go. It looks like there's a storm."

Maria stepped off the porch and looked in one direction, then the other. "Dammit."

"Is it in the east or west?" Claire asked.

Maria furrowed her brow. "East, I think?"

"We should be fine." Claire pulled the sleeves of her big hoodie over her hands. "Storms go west to east."

Maria gave her a look.

Claire shrugged. "I told you, I have the internet." The thin rod she was using to pick the lock snapped in half. "Shit."

"And nothing else." Max kicked the rock off the small porch.

Lightning lit up the sky again. The thing in the grass flashed. Josh tossed his cigarette as he stepped into the thick grass. His foot sunk into the soft earth. He bent down and parted the cool blades with his fingers, combing through them until he found a brass key. He held it up by the old, rotting ribbon tied through the hole in the top. It glimmered in the grey light.

"Maybe this'll help." He trotted over to them and handed it to Maria.

She slipped it into the lock with a loud click. "Yeah. Looks like."

Claire sat back on her heels. "How did that fit? My pick is in there."

The door jumped open. Like it had been waiting.

# AUTHOR'S NOTE

THIS WAS SO HARD TO WRITE OMG.

I've always found the puzzles in video games—especially survival horror—to be really weird. Like, who made them, and why? That was the first thing I wanted to play with. I wanted to capture the weird, esoteric quality of them.

I just finished a run-through of *Until Dawn* and really liked the storytelling style there—how each character would give you a little piece of the story until they all finally came together at the end.

*Silent Hill* has been one of my favorite franchises. No sin goes unpunished, even if the sin was only committed in your mind. You could do nothing wrong and still end up there and totally screwed because all of us think we are guilty of something.

Many of the characters are named for some of my favorites. Josh from *Until Dawn*, Maria from *Silent Hill*, and Claire from *Resident Evil*. It might cheating a little, but Josh's last name is Gorrister. I never played the *I Have No Mouth, and I Must Scream* game, but I read the book a lot. I figured it was close enough that Jonathan wouldn't mind too much.

# CENTRALIA
## BY SEAN M. THOMPSON

A crack split the road leading into Centralia wide and sharp. If John hadn't done his research, he could have easily shredded a tire, lost his muffler, or worse.

In the interest of preserving his car's health, he decided to park by an abandoned cemetery, about a mile back from town. The "Graffiti Highway" lived up to the moniker bestowed upon it by the haunted travel website; it was covered in multicolored names, spray-painted on every possible surface of asphalt. The site certainly hadn't led them astray: this abandoned town in Pennsylvania was just as creepy as advertised. A light smoke blanketed the landscape, caused by active fires in the mines beneath the town.

John and Erin were stiff from the drive, a six-hour slog from Connecticut to Pennsylvania. The trip wound them through steep mountain roads, past lonely farms, and mile after mile of plowed field. As they got closer to Centralia, John couldn't help but wonder if anyone actually *lived* in any of the towns they passed. They'd only seen five people in the last hour: two big guys at one farm, collecting hay with pitchforks; a man and a woman sitting smoking cigarettes on a porch at another house; most haunting of all, a young woman, standing in an otherwise-empty field, staring up at the sky.

As they walked, Erin stretched her arms over her head and yawned. John was tired too, thankful for the coffee he'd had on the last leg of the trip. Although he was excited to see Centralia, he'd be more excited to get to the hotel after they were finished.

There was only one house next to this part of the Graffiti Highway. The rest was dense wilderness, the abandoned cemetery, and the town further on ahead. If it weren't for the distinctive road, the only way they'd have known they'd arrived at the right place would have been the GPS. The smoke obscured everything else, lending a classic Hollywood vibe to the town.

Centralia had a stillness to it. John couldn't get over the feeling that the town in the distance was watching them. The trees—with leaves that rustled in the light chill wind—seemed to be wholly aware of their presence. A large SUV was parked in the driveway to the nearby house, and a sign on the fence out front read "No trespassing, violators will be shot."

There was a certain threat to the place—like a coyote poised, waiting to strike. A beautiful area, certainly, but eerie. Of course, wasn't that why they'd traveled so far? To play the game in a creepy, abandoned town. What better setting for a horror game?

"You excited to play?" Erin asked.

"It does seem super futuristic, huh?" John said.

Erin fished her cell out of her back pocket and smiled.

The week before, Hideo Kanata—creator of the *Quiet Mountain* video game franchise—had announced and simultaneously released a virtual version of *Quiet Mountain* for mobile devices. The buzz was amazing, and within days people were screaming on the street, scared by the nightmarish creatures which popped onto their cell phone screens. The first game in the series had been released some twenty-odd years ago for the PlayStation and Nintendo 64 systems. Both John and Erin had played every game in the series since, and their love of the mythology of the game in part led to their courtship, having met on a forum for *Quiet Mountain* seven years ago.

Erin gasped.

"Do you think they'll have Skinny Men here?! Oh my god, do you think they'll have Barry the Bear?!"

"Calm down honey, I'm sure they'll have all of them."

John was exhausted. He wasn't crazy about wandering around in an abandoned coal-mining town, with active fires still raging below it. He couldn't imagine exploring around here was the safest. Yet, he knew enough about Erin to understand she would have gone alone, and he wouldn't be able to live with himself if something happened to her in the middle of nowhere, Pennsylvania.

John had to admit he was curious about Centralia. What made a Japanese software developer decide to model an award-winning, multiple decade-spanning game franchise off of a random town in America? Oh, the story was creepy, sure. A mysterious fire spreads out of control and sends the residents fleeing, then continues to burn below in the coal mines for decades. But there were other creepy towns in

America, too. The abandoned Dudleytown in John's home state of Connecticut—referred to as "the village of the damned,"—which was supposedly cursed. Or Animas Forks, Colorado, another ghost town located near haunted mines.

"Are you going to play with me or what? Come on, turn on your phone," Erin said, slapping him on the shoulders, jogging in place.

"All right."

He took out his phone and navigated to the *Quiet Mountain* app. As the game loaded, an air raid siren rang out, one of the classic parts of the game's score. A squealing noise— what he'd found out was the sound of a metal pipe scraping against a cheese grater—emanated from the speakers of his cell: an audio cue that meant one of the game's many terrifying creatures was about to attack.

"You logged on?" John asked.

"You better believe it, baby," Erin said.

"Then let's do this."

They walked into town as a chilling soundtrack of groans and aberrant noises played from their phones, which were synced up perfectly. The game featured location tracking to link you with the other players in your immediate area. John was armed with a big scimitar on his screen, while Erin wielded a sawed-off shotgun. The game essentially auto-generated monsters, which it then threw at you, based on your real-world location. And it had never been officially substantiated, but they had heard many rumors that if you played the game *in* Centralia, the experience was scarier than anywhere else in the world. Of course, that rumor proved irresistible to Erin.

They passed a sign welcoming them to Centralia, and John decided that when they came back tomorrow, he'd take pictures of all this stuff to show to his friends. That was, if he could get anything useable, what with all the smoke.

Strangely, they were able to walk all the way into town without anything popping out at them.

"Where are all the monsters?" Erin asked, her disappointment obvious.

"I'm sure we'll get some, hon. It probably just needs a bit to load. The service isn't great around here, remember?"

"I hope so," Erin said.

John gave her a kiss on the cheek.

"We could always just do it," he said, and winked.

"In your dreams. I'm not even taking my sweatshirt off around here. This place gives me the creeps."

"I'm with you on that."

Demonic giggling bubbled from his phone's speakers. He turned around and held his phone in his line of sight, the image of the road behind them no longer empty. On the screen, standing right where they had just traveled, was a Skinny Man—one of the gaunt, skinless attackers ubiquitous to the game. John yelled, and thrust his phone forward, the blade on the screen stabbing through the Skinny Man's stomach. The creature screeched in pain and its pixelated guts fell to the road. Then the thing blurred out of existence.

"Awesome!" Erin shouted.

*"You shouldn't be here."*

"What?"

John turned around to fight whatever new monster had spawned. The voice was feminine, insistent. Perhaps it was a new creature he hadn't encountered before.

There was nothing on the screen. He turned again, scanning the environment through his phone.

Still nothing, save for the ever-present smoke.

"Did you hear that?" John said.

"Hear what?" Erin replied.

"It was a spooky sounding lady whispering *'you shouldn't be here.'*"

"No, I wish I heard that!" Erin said. "Let's keep moving, maybe she's farther up."

"Yeah," he said, his voice faltering.

He'd never heard that voice before in any of the older games, and definitely not in this new one. There were occasionally other human characters you'd find, sure. Flashbacks, or ghosts, there to give you clues about puzzles you had to solve to continue. But this was a whole new game, the first one in the series that used cell phones and "augmented reality," and who knows, maybe it had a glitch or two that caused a voice to spawn without a person or a monster showing up. Or, more likely, it was an environmental effect meant to creep players the fuck out. If that was the case, yeah, mission accomplished.

They reached the town center and passed a dilapidated gas station. The red lettering atop the main storefront of the station had long since faded out, a barely legible "Centralia Gas" above the decrepit storefront. Remnants of shelving remained inside, visible through stained plate glass windows. John couldn't help but wonder what the place had looked like in its prime.

On both sides of the street stood empty storefronts, with broken front windows and doors on busted hinges leaning drunkenly, creaking in the breeze. The wind lightly shifted the smoke around the long-forgotten businesses. Trash from other explorers, empty beer cans, and fast food wrappers crinkled underfoot. Graffiti of stick figures fucking—and flames engulfing more stick figure people—was on the sidewalk that ran in front of the town library. A crumbling, concrete statue of the Madonna, the top of her head missing above the nose, stood in the overgrown grass. Shrubs once kept trimmed and neat now grew wild in front of a playground that was home to rusted swings and a rocking horse with the paint worn away. And always the stillness, which seemed so artificial, like walking into a room where people instantly got quiet.

"Why is there a statue of Mary in front of the library?" John wondered aloud.

"Heard it was a religious town when people still lived here," Erin said. "Lot of good it did them."

A metallic, squealing noise seemed to come from the playground. Expecting to see something on his cell, John readied himself to stab another monster. He found nothing on the screen however, save for the playground and the rocking horse, tilting with an odd rhythm. The noise continued. He looked over his phone. On the playground— on the actual playground, not the version he saw through his phone—he saw a small naked boy. The boy's skin was burnt black, peeling in places. The child sat atop the rocking horse, smiling wide. He rocked back and forth, a metronome of charred flesh.

*The Old Church needs a new congregation*, the boy said, the words not audible, but somehow manifesting in John's mind. He was too frightened to move. Even breathing seemed out of his depth. His chest constricted. Panic seized him in a crushing hug.

"Do you see that?" he managed.

"What, are there Faceless Women?"

"No, the boy. On the playground."

"Huh?"

He shut his eyes tight. When he opened them, the boy was gone.

"I think we should get going pretty soon," John said.

"Bullshit we should. Let's give it another hour. We drove all the way here, why are you being like this?"

"Because I'm not sure how safe it is out here."

"Oh come on, you're just scared. That's the point! We are playing a *scary* phone game in a *scary* abandoned town. Come on, let's keep playing. If you really want to go after another twenty minutes, you can go wait in the car, and I'll come back when it gets dark."

"I definitely don't want to do that," John said.

On their screens, a bloody arm plopped onto one of the swings, with its index finger pointing towards the library. A note like wind rushing through metal chirped.

"Ooh, a puzzle!" Erin said, and ran off towards the entrance to the library.

John knew that a puzzle in the game was usually either a lock with a combination you had to discover hidden somewhere close by, or some other type of brainteaser; sometimes you had to find a radio, which gave you a clue as to how to advance.

"Wait!" He ran after her.

Erin wrenched open the front door and ran inside. He followed her into the darkness. John held up his phone, peering into the game's other world. To his left, a severed head, its eyes missing, smiled at him from atop the main desk.

"Ah!"

"Follow the bloody arrows to the puzzle," it hissed.

"Ha, you screamed," Erin said.

"I did not scream. I yelped. There's a difference..."

"Whatever you big baby. Come on, let's go find this puzzle."

Sure enough, along the center aisle of the library leading to the empty book shelves—likewise covered in graffiti and trash—there were bloody arrows leading them deeper into the shadows.

"Have fun, John," the decapitated head yelled after him, his phone's speakers producing the sound as distant and echoing.

"How does it know my name?"

"What? Oh, you've never had them call you your name before? We're logged in. The game knows your name from that."

"Have they ever called you by your name?"

"Yeah, I had a Knife Possum screech it at me one time. Before I blew its head off."

Between the shelves, he could barely see his way forward. Erin seemed to have the same problem, and turned on the in-game flashlight, which activated her phone's flash. The beam of light tracked over the shelves and along the ground to the bloody arrows, which pointed further into the library. The flashlight beam moved over to the next shelf, where a Skinny Man's face scowled at them, his body behind the shelf, head poking through. They both cried out.

"Crap!" Erin said, aiming her phone in the creature's

direction.

She fired her sawed-off at the screeching Skinny Man, whose head exploded in a mass of red pulp, before its body faded away.

"Okay, that one got me, woo, damn," Erin gasped, breathing heavy.

"You want to take a break for a bit?" John said, not willing to outright ask his girlfriend if they could just stop.

John was not entirely sure he wasn't having some kind of psychotic break. The game had never quite affected him this way before, but then again, they were in the town the game was based on. The designers had amped up the experience, but whether that was the case—or just his own mind playing tricks on him—he couldn't be sure. He thought about Erin out here alone in the dark, and pushed the thoughts of heading back to the car aside. Besides, at least here he was with her. Back at the car he'd be alone, and that was nearly as scary as being in the center of Centralia.

*Keep going,* the charred boy whispered.

"Oh, please tell me you heard that," John said.

"Yeah, a voice said 'keep going.' I think it was that severed head at the front."

"Oh. Thank God."

Erin's flashlight beam led them out of the stacks. They followed more bloody arrows to a backdoor with a large lock over it. John looked away from the screen of his phone, and saw the lock wasn't really there: it was a part of the game, a piece of the puzzle they had to solve.

"Great, so now we have to guess a lock combo. How the heck are we going to do that?" John said.

Something *thumped*. John held up his camera and turned

to see a shape shambling out of the darkness towards them. A Faceless Woman, eyeless and noseless, her pale grey body worming along the ground. Her worm-like maw stretched open to reveal multiple rows of sharp teeth. He sliced his sword through her head, and the two bisected halves slumped to the floor, black blood pumping out. Teeth clinked to the wood. He waited to see if the creature was dead. He was about to kick the Faceless Woman's body when he remembered that, right, she wasn't really there.

This time, the corpse didn't disappear, even though he was sure she was dead. He turned his own flashlight on, and aimed it at the body. Something metallic gleamed from within the ruined meat of her throat. John leaned in closer. A license plate sat wedged inside the Faceless Woman's chest.

"Gross," he said.

"Allow me," Erin offered.

A well-aimed shotgun blast, and the rest of the corpse exploded in a black and grey rain of flesh and fluid. That did it, and the gore faded away, leaving just the license plate, which only had six numbers on it.

"I'm not sure how much of a puzzle that was. We kind of just had to kill a thing."

"So? It's a new event, far as I can tell," Erin said. "Read that back to me."

"3-4-5-8-9-2."

She entered the numbers onto the lock on the screen of her phone, thumb maneuvering the combination into place. Both phones offered up a satisfying *click*, the lock opened, and in true video game fashion, immediately disappeared.

"We only have another half hour or so of daylight. Let's

keep going," Erin said, pushing open the door.

A Snake Demon lunged at them, John screamed, and sliced forward with his sword, while Erin fired a blast from both barrels. Snake Demons were powerful foes, and he had to slice a second and third time as Erin fired one more blast from her shotgun before the thing went down in a mass of striking snake heads, horns, and scaly green skin.

"I hate those fucking things," John said.

"I think they're pretty rad," Erin said.

They exited the library, pushing through the big wooden door, hearing it creak on its old hinges. There appeared to be nothing behind the library, save for an empty field and the woods beyond. Only, now that he could focus on their surroundings, John noted a small dirt footpath leading through the field to the forest.

He scanned to the left and right, but there were only sorry-looking trees and underbrush. The sun was already starting to sink below the tree line. The ever-present smoke left visibility low.

Dusk would be upon them soon.

"I think we should head back," John said.

"Oh, come on baby, we came all this way. Let's just head to that church first. It's super creepy."

"What church?"

He looked up from his phone. The church looked to be carved from dark stone. Its bell tower loomed above the pines and oaks. Stray rays of sunlight illuminated the outer walls and foundation.

He couldn't describe why he should feel so against this journey. Why every instinct in him told him to turn tail and flee. They'd driven very far to get to Centralia, and he loved this game. Under normal circumstances, he should have been having a blast. It was more than just nerves and the spooky setting, more than just being in an isolated place. He didn't believe in ESP, nothing like that, yet this strong aversion to playing the game here coursed through his veins like a poison.

"Come on, John, just five minutes inside. It looks like it'll take us like ten minutes to walk there. Then we can go to the hotel, and I'll—"

What she whispered in his ear made him bark with laughter. Even with what she'd just told him she'd do, John still desperately wanted to leave. The terror he'd felt was compounded by seeing that church. The angle the stone tower stood at was *off*, or maybe it just looked that way from where they were standing.

"Let's go check it out," Erin said, and ran off along the dirt path, staring at her phone's glowing screen the whole time.

He ran after her, leaving his phone up, but staring over it for the most part, all too aware they were now wandering into the woods with only twenty minutes or so of daylight left. As he ran among the trees, he heard laughter, and had to keep telling himself it was just from the game. The screaming was only a part of *Quiet Mountain*'s ambient soundtrack, of course.

The more he stared at the church, the more it didn't seem to be real—blurry, indistinct—as if it should be an image in the game, not in real life. It looked to be very, very old, with certain parts of the roof collapsed inward, and big chunks of stone masonry along its sides and parapet crumbling or missing. At the top of the domed cupola, only a jagged piece of metal stood, the cross torn down long ago.

He looked at the church through his cell screen, and noted dark clouds behind the tower and cupola. In-game, the cross remained. He looked back at the church sans phone, and the same clouds were there. He could have sworn the sky was lighter and free of clouds just a moment before.

Erin dashed off to the left and he followed after her. She was running so fast, and he didn't want to lose her. He tried to ignore the pain of anxiety in his guts.

"Slow down!" he yelled.

"Catch up!" she yelled in turn.

He swore, heard things running after him, and had to keep repeating in his head that this was just a game, they'd get to the church, and then they could head back, go to the hotel. Erin laughed, just out of sight, and he used the last of his energy to try to close the gap between them.

Somehow, they'd skipped dusk altogether.

Honest night closed in around them, the time of nocturnal hunters and haunting things. John imagined he felt the hot breath of something steam against his neck. He had to run; run as fast as he could, or be forced to get a good look at the landscape around him, and everything therein. He'd grab glances through the phone frequently enough that he knew there was nothing in the game chasing him. If the creatures were from *Quiet Mountain*, he'd have seen a bloody arrow as a hint on the screen. The screen was empty, save for the trees before him.

"Erin, please!"

"We're almost there!"

After countless minutes sprinting, the church never

seemed to get any closer, like the structure was an optical illusion; a matte painting, expertly rendered. Erin, for her part, never slowed, and John, as scared as he was, prayed for any kind of break, any kind of relief for his muscles which screamed out in pain. His heart thundered in his chest and his lungs burned.

Darkness permeated the woods, and he had to stop, had to rest. He gasped, huddled with his back against an oak. The noises had stopped, and the feeling of being chased had gone as suddenly as it had started.

"Erin!" he called out. She didn't reply.

John turned on the in-game flashlight, and looked through the screen. Erin's body lay before him on the forest floor.

"Erin!"

Her body was gone.

"Jesus, Jesus... Erin!"

Still no answer. He stood, and there, miraculously, only a few paces from him, was the church. Up close it looked even older, the stone weathered. The foundation was missing large pieces. Somehow it seemed... *taller* than it had from behind the library.

With cautious steps, John made his way toward the building, the soundtrack of the game uncharacteristically silent, his screen devoid of monsters and helpful icons alike.

He aimed the light at the front of the church. There was a massive, darkly stained wooden door carved with ornate images of... The more he looked, the more confusing the things carved on the door became. They were the same as the monsters in *Quiet Mountain*, except, well, *different*, in subtle ways. Ways that dug at the back of his mind with sharp talons. The Skinny Men, they were a lot taller, and the Snake Demons were very wide, and appeared to be floating off the ground. The carvings' details were incredible. This door was a real work of craftsmanship.

In the center of the door, a set of stairs, the carvings done in such a way as to appear to lead into the earth, flames crackling where the steps led. To a place John very much hoped was *not* real. He lifted the phone, and there was a fake pixelated lock on the door, the carvings completely gone. He lowered the phone, and the carvings had disappeared.

"The fuck—"

The door creaked open, and he expected to see Erin on the other side. Instead, there was only a massive, empty nave, complete with old, warped wooden pews forming a crooked center aisle. A pulpit stood on the stage. In the entirety of the enormous expanse, there wasn't a single window. Candles were set inside iron sconces fixed into the walls at five-foot intervals.

"Erin?"

The score to the game hadn't kicked back in. He looked on his phone, saw a shape scurry somewhere behind the pulpit. Quickly, he lowered the phone: there was nothing up there. He took a tentative step forward, unsure of what to expect, just desperate to find Erin, to get out of the church, out of Centralia. Hell, maybe even out of Pennsylvania; drive on through to the closest state and get a cheapy motel right off the highway.

He pressed on, despite every urge inside him to turn around and leave. Every nerve on fire to *get away*, yet, his body kept moving. Up to the pulpit. A book sat closed along its wide surface, red letters inset on an old leather-bound volume. Letters which spelled out **THE GOSPEL OF THE PIT.**

And it was strange, seeing this book—something about it made him relax a bit. Gradually, he felt his fear dissipate. How odd, there was no reason why a book—especially one with such an ominous title—should calm him so. And yet, he felt the anxiety loosen its stranglehold, and slowly felt better about the room, the church.

A small birch stick poked out from within the book, marking a section. John opened to the page, and saw a bold chapter heading:

## BUILDING THE CONGREGATION

*And they will come. Come to seek The Pit, though they know not of their desire. And the servants of The Pit will welcome them. Give them knowledge of which they had never dreamed. And they will revel in their baser natures, and venture forth to help build the congregation.*

Something banged against one of the pews behind him, but when he looked, nothing. Silence, the quiet of the sepulcher. He continued.

*They will bring new travelers to The Quiet Mountain, and to the blessed Pit below, where The First Ones dwell. Embrace the Ones, those who scratch and bite, for they are the truest, most attuned to the natural world, and their hunger is imbued in Everything.*

A warmth flowed through him, a peace he didn't understand. He should have been terrified, but he felt *so*

*relaxed* as he read the book. He sighed, content, blissful…
and read on.

*Chaos will rule, and the deceitful, the wicked, shall inherit all. Be
one with the terrible, the hateful, the damned.*
     *Blessed be the hungry. Blessed be the violent.*
     *May we all be swallowed whole.*

"May we all be swallowed whole," he said.

"It's so warm there, John," Erin said.

He turned, and any remaining fear was gone. John knew
pure, unfettered bliss.

"Erin, where did you go?"

"Where we all go," she said, and pointed her index finger
to the ground.

He smiled and grabbed Erin's hand. All of his fears
floated away.

For the first time in a long time, he felt like he was a part
of something. Wonder soaked him in kerosene, and he
longed for the spark.

"It's so beautiful there," the little boy said.

John lifted the phone to look to the floor. Letters of blood
spelled out:

*he who searches, finds*

"I can't wait to see," he said.

John grabbed the boy's hand, and with Erin beside him,
they descended the stairs behind the pulpit.

## AUTHOR'S NOTE

Funny enough, while I've watched my sister play *Silent Hill 2*, and went to see both of the films (even that wretched second one), I have yet to play a full *Silent Hill* through in its entirety. I have visited Centralia, Pennsylvania however, and I remember seeing a church on a hill on the drive in, and thinking how creepy it looked.

I made the visit with my significant other and we did in fact show up late, and we had very little daylight in which to explore.

I'd be remiss if I didn't mention the work of John Langan, Brian Evenson, and Laird Barron, whose work helped shape certain aspects of the story.

# SAIRENS

## BY JULIE K. GODARD

### FROM CO TO FLO

It's been hot like summer-in-Florida hot, because that's where we live, now. We had to move here because my dad got a job out here "and that's that." No discussion, no nothing. That was Mom's forte—discussion. She wanted to discuss everything, and my dad didn't. So that's how my childhood went, silence and yelling, yelling and silence; it wasn't bad, just typical. She's gone, now, dead at 32 and not much to show for it except me and my sister. She died two months and 14 days ago, and the doctors still don't know why—some kind of electrolyte disorder, hypermagna-something. Whatever it was, it killed her.

My little sister Delaney found her on the floor in the laundry room after school one day. Mom was a drinker and didn't eat very well—it was me and Dad pushing for vegetables at dinner or fruit for breakfast. "Freya, it just isn't on my list of things to do," she liked to say when I asked her why we didn't eat healthy. Well, it should've been, because now we have no mom. Just Dad, and he's kind of a mess right now. To tell you the truth, it's been nice to be in a different state, where people don't judge us except as the new people on the block, and don't have that hint of tears in their eyes whenever they look at me. But it's also kind of lonely. Nobody stops by with food or just to check in and see if we're okay.

Since we moved here, I've been playing video games on a pawn shop PS2—it's old, but it works. The console came with two games: *Grand Theft Auto* (which Dad ixnayed when he saw the half-naked women in it) and *Sairens*, a Japanese horror game that I just started yesterday—it stopped working five minutes in, and I need another copy, now.

Delaney's been quiet since Mom died—she's seven, and used to be the charming, friendly girl in the family. Now she stays in her room, drawing pictures she won't let me see. One day I looked when she was at school. All the pictures were of Mom: in the kitchen in her favorite green "mermaid" dress, in the backyard, or leaning out the back door to tell us it's time to come in for dinner. Not one picture of the rest of us. I think it's kind of weird, but at least she's able to get her feelings out. My psychologist, Dr. Linda, says I use the video games to get out my anger over Mom's death.

The weekend after we got here, Dad tried to put the house in order, meaning he pushed all the boxes labeled with our names into our rooms, and put away enough of the kitchen and bathroom stuff for us to function and cook meals. If we want something else we do without, then find it by accident while looking for something else.

Dad's a call center guy, which means he is a pro at answering phones. He doesn't want to talk when he gets home—says he's "all talked out." This Saturday, we're all eating cereal and sitting on the couch together, watching TV.

"Where are the Saturday morning cartoons?" Dad asks.

"Dad, they have entire cartoon channels now," I say. "And most of the kiddie cartoons they show on Sunday morning."

"Why?" he asks, not really expecting an answer. Delaney finishes her cereal and sets the bowl surreptitiously on the floor where one of us is likely to trip over it.

"Delaney," I say, channeling Mom, "pick that up and take it into the kitchen." Delaney does as she is told. Dad just keeps eating his cereal. My sister comes back and sits down as far from me as she can. She doesn't like me telling her what to do, but someone has to. Dad is lost in his own fog most of the time, and only seems really *here* on the rare occasions when we all laugh about something. Delaney flicks listlessly through the channels.

I finish my cereal and take it into the kitchen, grabbing Dad's empty bowl on my way. I put them on the counter on a dishtowel after I've washed them—we still have no dish drainer. *It's not on Dad's list of things to do.* I gaze out the kitchen window at the oppressive greenery; it's May and the weather has begun to get too hot and humid. I want another copy of that video game, so I tell my cell phone: "Find used video games near me." A map pulls up with 4 dots on it, one of them in downtown Del Mar.

"Hey Delaney, want to go on an adventure?" I say, walking into the family room. She doesn't look up from the TV, but nods. I get a pang thinking how bubbly and cheerful she used to be; it used to bug the crap out of me, but now I miss it. Then I start thinking about Mom, so I say:

"Dad, can we bike into town? I want another copy of that video game that crapped out on me." He shakes his head, sighs, and stands up. In a gesture of affection all too rare since my mom's death, he pulls me to him and hugs me, tight, tighter. Then he lets me go, pushes me gently away, and says:

"Sure. Why don't you two explore a little bit. That will give me time to put some of this stuff away." He waves his hand grandly around the room at the stacks of boxes and looks down at me. I nod, taking the remote from Delaney's hand and turning the TV off.

"Are we really going?" Delaney says, looking up at me in her Elsa and Anna pajamas.

"As soon as you get some non-Disney clothes on," I answer.

## THE VIDEO GAME STORE

In Florida, the smells in the air and on people are more intense. I'm not just talking about body odor and sweat; the heavier, more humid air here carries scents straight to my nose, a mixed-up jumble of fragrant jasmine blossoms, salt air, and spices. Everything seems stronger here, somehow—not as dissipated as in the thin, dry air of Colorado. The slight breeze created by biking takes the edge off the humidity. Dad has given us money for helping unpack the house, and we lock up our bikes outside the video game store. The store is in a strip mall and lit by overpowering fluorescent lighting—a hot, sweaty boy is playing a console in the center of the floor. I head for the empty front counter while Delaney wanders off to look at games.

I can't get *Sairens* out of my head; I *need* to find another copy. I flip my sweaty hair up and feel the snaky caress of air conditioning on the back of my neck. I close my eyes for a second, and when I open them a tiny Asian woman is standing there, staring at me with black eyes.

"Uh, hi. I'm looking for a PS2 game, *Sairens?*"

She frowns slightly, turns to her computer, taps some keys, and turns back to me.

"We don't have that title anymore," she says, clasping her hands behind her back.

"Can you call around to other stores to see if they have a copy?" I say, noticing that her nametag says Hisako. She studies her computer screen, whips a candy-colored smartphone from an invisible pocket, taps the screen, and brings the phone to one delicate ear. She speaks rapidly in Japanese, looking at me with that slight frown. Suddenly I see myself through her eyes—a bored white girl looking for an ancient video game with my crazy little sister in tow, and I'm an out-of-towner, too. I restlessly examine my pale Colorado skin. She talks for a long time, and never calls anyone else. I try to look uninterested, but I catch the words "shibito," and "*Sairens.*" The discussion gets heated, and for a moment Hisako is nearly screaming into the phone. The boy playing the video game looks up, and Delaney walks over, pushing into me in that way I hate.

Finally Hisako hangs up the phone, looking less composed, and says, "I have a copy of the second game, *Sairens 2,* in the back." She disappears into a tiny back room.

I had no idea there *was* another game, and worry I'll miss part of the plot—but what choice do I have?

Hisako comes back with a battered-looking copy of *Sairens 2* covered in Japanese characters. She puts it on the counter, smiling fixedly. *This must not have been released in the United States,* I think excitedly. *New digital territory.*

"How much?" I ask her. She points to the price tag on the back: $120, and then quickly says, "I can give you a discount." I pull my $60 out of my pocket. She glances at my sister, then back at me. "Fifty percent discount for new customers." I stare into her black eyes, not quite believing my luck. I hesitate for a moment, thinking how much Mom hated video games, but was proud that I could play better than most boys. I hand Hisako $60 and she stuffs the game into a brown paper bag and shoves it across the counter at me as if she wants it off her hands.

"Enjoy the game," she says, suddenly looking much older. I notice wrinkles around her eyes and mouth.

"No receipt?" I say.

"No returns, no refunds on imported PS2 games." I nod, and mumble thanks. She nods back, and rocks back on her heels a bit. We are the only ones left in the store. I take Delaney's hand, and as we walk out into the heat I hear the heavy, sharp clicking of the lock on the door behind us.

## THE CAFÉ

Delaney complains that a video game store is not an adventure, so we decide to get lunch at a café across the street. As we walk over, she asks me endless questions about Mom. I answer them in a bored voice to hide the fact that talking about Mom still isn't easy for me. I rattle off Mom's favorite color, her hometown, where she and Dad met, and tell her what it was like when Delaney was born and how much I didn't want a little sister.

"But you love me now, right?" she says. I nod. The door handle of the café is shaped like a mermaid. Inside we find a small Japanese woman behind the counter who looks as old as the restaurant. The décor is an ugly combination of sea shanty and '50s diner; fishing nets hang in the corners, and an old, silent juke box sits next to the counter.

"Please sit down," the woman says with a Japanese accent, and shuffles over to the table with worn, plastic-coated menus. It's the usual breakfast fare, except on the back of the menu there are other options in Japanese. She stands next to the table, patient as the ocean while we decide.

"I'll have the eggs and bacon, with rye toast," I say.

"Me, too," Delaney says, "but with wheat toast. And fruit."

"And orange juices," I add. The little woman nods, the wrinkles creasing her face lifting in a smile. She scribbles on her pad and then regards us for a moment. Her eyes are that same odd, piercing black.

"You are sisters." It's not a question.

"Yep," I say cheerfully, smiling my best sisterly smile. I kick Delaney under the table, who is staring down at the Japanese characters on the back of her menu like she can read them.

"What? Oh, yeah, we're sisters." The woman nods and clears her throat.

"And how old are you, dear?" she says quietly, creepily, to my sister.

"I'm seven," she says, not smiling. Her foot touches mine fearfully under the table, and she looks toward the door. The woman nods again, laughing softly and says,

"Good, good. I'll get your food started." She shuffles off through the doors into the kitchen and I hear pots and pans clanking and rapid Japanese conversation punctuated by laughter with the hidden cook.

"She's creepy, Freya," Delaney says when the woman is gone. "Let's eat somewhere else."

"She's just an old lady—old ladies like little girls. Besides, we already ordered." To change the subject, I point out a painting on the wall above our table. It's of a beach, with several tide pools stretching out to the horizon in an orange sunset.

The painting scares me for some reason. I brush the thought away, and stroke Delaney's quivering hand. "Let's just eat," I say. We're really hungry, so we gobble down the breakfasts when the woman brings them out, then ask for the bill. As we are leaving, I glance back at the swinging kitchen door, and see two sets of dark, black eyes peering out at us from the round, plastic window.

"Goodbye now!" the old woman crows. "See you later!" Both of them begin laughing delightedly, as if this is the funniest thing they've heard all year.

## MESSES

On the ride home, rain starts coming down in sheets and we throw down our bikes in the yard to run in the front door. I trip over a cardboard box full of books and scrape open my shin.

"Ow!" I shriek, holding it while the blood slides down to my flip-flop and pools on the cream-colored tile.

"I'm in here, girls," Dad calls from the bathroom, and I head to the kitchen for a bandage. I hear Delaney close the door against the pounding rain and flop down on the couch in her wet clothes. I rummage around in the "bathroom box" for a mangled box of Band-Aids, pull one out, and glance around. The house is a disaster, boxes and their contents spilling everywhere.

*How on earth is he working?*

"Don't worry about the mess, Dad, I'll take care of it tomorrow," I call down the hallway. He doesn't respond, so I pop the game in and sit down on the couch next to Delaney. She is looking at something on my phone. Haunting, full orchestra music fills the house, low strings and human voices chanting and sticks clicking together in a strange, plodding rhythm.

"This game scares me." Delaney sets down my phone and bangs out the back door into the sweltering heat where the rain has eased up to a fine mist. There's a little garden shed out there she's always messing around in, and I'm glad she's found something to occupy her time so I can play my game. As the haunting music swells, I hear Dad close the door to his bedroom. He's taking his Saturday nap, which means I should be uninterrupted until Delaney needs dinner. I pause the game, close the wooden blinds, and settle into the dimness, glad to let the worries of the real world fade away for a while.

## THE GAME

The game world—an old school on a haunted island—is designed in black and white, with some sepia tone added in to make it extra creepy. When I find the first interactive item (an old black and white film reel from just before the town's demise), I put it on an old projector in a classroom and hit X to play it. It shows a family watching television when an emergency weather report comes on. The film is a documentary-style survey of weather damage to the town, caused by what looks like an earthquake. When the film stops I leave it on the projector and venture further into the school.

At the back of the deserted and shaken building is a locked door; as I get closer, the scary voices swell to a crescendo. In the first game, sometimes you had to revisit previous areas after you triggered certain events. I race back through the maze of the school to the sound of the creepy soundtrack, my character's bare feet slapping on the concrete floor and skidding around corners. Sure enough, I find a key lying in the grass outside the school. It's shaped roughly humanoid, with a woman's top half set into a curved fish's tail—a mermaid. I race back to open the door. It takes me a moment to figure out how to open it, but I select the key in the inventory screen and hit X. I hear a distinct, soft click and the door swings open.

Behind the door, the world is in vivid, shocking, dark color in contrast to the muted blacks and whites I've seen so far. Standing just beyond the door is a slim, young girl—naked, blood streaking down her body and intertwined with her long, dark hair. Blood drips from a mouth full of razor-sharp teeth, and in her hand she holds a bucket with human intestines draped over the sides and what appears to be a human hand. Her eyes lock onto mine—looking at *me*, not at my avatar—and my heartbeat elevates sharply. She looks just like Delaney. The door slams closed, and my heart knocks against my chest. I throw the controller down, suddenly frightened for my sister.

*Where is she? What is she doing out there? Is she okay?*

I leave the game running and slam out the back door of the lanai and race through the long crab-grass covered yard to the garden shed, calling her name. I don't feel like playing anymore.

## THE BEACH

"Delaney!"

I pull open the splintered shed door, but she's not there. On the walls hang rusty garden tools, and on a wooden tool bench are the shadow-outlines of what might be an old, rusty bucket and a three-pronged hand tiller. I back out of the tiny shed, wiping spider webs from my hair. On a whim, I round the corner of the shed and find a hole in the rusty chain-link fence leading out behind the houses.

I can't squeeze through, so I climb over the five-foot fence. Dropping to the other side, I follow a downward sloping path through the trees.

Walking as quickly as I can, I brush away vines and try not to trip over snaking tree roots that sprout out of the sandy earth. The sound of gentle surf reaches my ears, and then I come out of the trees onto a little hidden beach, with tide pools stretching across the rocks.

*A beach? This far inland?*

I know our house is nowhere near the beach, but I push away the confusion and scan for signs of Delaney. I see her sneaker washing back and forth in the surf, but I still don't see her. I run toward the shoe, the haunting voices of the video game echoing in my head.

Then I see her. She is sitting naked on the edge of a small tide pool on a rock, her long hair draped over her shoulder and trailing down to the surface of the water. Her hand is wrist-deep in the water, and she is so fixated on whatever she's looking at that she doesn't hear me yelling her name. When I am close enough, I grab her and jerk her up to standing, shaking her hard.

"Delaney!" I shriek, hearing the horror in my voice, "What are you doing down here?" She stares at me blankly and my eyes scan the trees behind us for signs of another person. I turn her around, checking for wounds and blood.

*Has someone…?*

She is still staring at me as if she doesn't know who I am. I turn her around to get a better look at her face, and hear a splash behind us. I let her go, spin around, and see the tail of a very large fish disappearing into the depthless black of the tidepool. There's a rusty bucket and trowel lying in the sand by the rocks. To my relief, there are no bloody intestines in it.

"Where are we?" Delaney asks, life returning to her eyes. "I thought you said there wasn't a beach by the house." This she says in a petulant tone, as if I'd lied to her about it.

"Delaney, put your clothes on." *We have to get out of here.* I keep scanning the tree line for any sign of someone else—I almost *wish* I see someone, because at least that would explain what the hell is happening to my sister.

I help her back into her clothes as fast as I can, not even bothering with her shoes. Chanting voices—the music from *Sairens 2*—fills my head, and all I want to do is get back to the house and lock the doors.

Once Delaney is dressed, she starts weeping.

"I miss Mom," she whimpers. We trudge quickly back up the path toward the house.

Just as I'm beginning to wonder if we'll ever come out of the vines and trees, the chain-link fence appears. Delaney stops and looks at it as if she doesn't know how to get through. I help her climb over the top and drop down on the other side, not wanting her to slither through the hole again. I climb over and glance back down the dark path, the shapes in the trees forming into human bodies in the dusk. I turn and push Delaney roughly toward the house, wishing I could be kinder but frustrated that *I* have to keep her safe while Dad just sleeps the day away.

In the house, the game's haunting music is still playing. On-screen, the bloody girl is gone, and the door is closed again. I turn the television off.

"Go change your clothes, Delaney," I say. I walk back to Dad's room, and he's passed out on the bed, glasses in one hand while his laptop casts strange images across his face in the half-light of the receding rainstorm. I gently close the door, thinking I shouldn't tell him about Delaney just yet. Not until I'm sure what's going on.

I've lost interest in playing *Sairens 2*; I eject the disc and put it back in its beat-up case, then place it in an empty cardboard box and push the box to the back of the top shelf in my bedroom closet.

## THE ANTIQUE SHOP

"This town is weird," Delaney says, brushing her long hair back behind her shoulder, and twisting it up to keep it from sticking to the back of her neck. I get a sudden flash of the bloody girl in the video game, but push the image out of my mind.

No rain today, just punishing humidity. We lock up our bikes in the same place, and I notice the streets are deserted even though it's ten o'clock in the morning; a lot of people probably commute to Miami.

We walk down to the area where the bookstore and the antique store are nestled next to each other like starfish in a tidepool. They both look closed, but there are "OPEN" signs hanging on chains in both windows. A bell rattles as we push into the antique store, and an old man behind the counter looks up at us through crusty glasses.

"Ah, I was wondering when you would come to my store," he says, and I'm not sure how to take that. "Del Mar is a small town," he says, reading my face, and I nod.

"I'm Izanagi," he says, stepping around the small, wooden register stand to shake my hand. "Welcome to Del Mar. Have you been to the beach, yet?"

I am startled at the mention of the beach, and before I can stop myself, I ask,

"How is there a beach this far inland?"

He chuckles gently.

"It's our *secret* beach," he says, "and it's the only one like it in the world." He pauses, concern passing over his face as he looks at Delaney. "Did your sister go to the beach?"

"Y-yes," I say, regretting coming inside, regretting talking to this old man who seems to know us. He smiles, but it's not reassuring.

"Good, good. She must go back, when she has the time. There is something there for her."

"Okay," is all I can think to say. I spin my sister around and we walk out of the shop, but not before I see that the dingy front window is filled with mermaid figurines of every shape and size, some of them with razor-sharp teeth jutting out over delicate, sculpted lips.

*Why didn't I notice that before?*

And:

*Why did we go inside in the first place?*

## THE BOOKSTORE

I wonder if we should even go in the bookstore, but I figure, in a lot of video games, like *Resident Evil,* any room with books on shelves is usually a safe room. I examine the front window display this time, and I'm not surprised to see books about the ocean—and yes, mermaids—displayed. As we pass through the front door, I glance up at the weathered, driftwood-carved sign. A smiling mermaid, of course.

Inside is the comforting smell of old books and spicy black tea. The woman behind the counter is not Japanese. Maybe American Indian.

*Seminole,* I think, having read something somewhere about American Indians in Florida. She has the same depthless black eyes as Hisako, but they are warm and welcoming.

"Hello," she says, and her voice sounds like Mom's. It's deep and comforting and for some reason I want to run to her for a hug.

"Hello," I say instead. "Do you have any books about the history of Del Mar?" Delaney wanders around the stacks, pulling books out here and there.

"Funny you should ask," she says, extending her hand to me across a marble counter that's home to an old, antique register.

"I'm Mahaia," she says, and I shake her hand. It is as warm and welcoming as her voice. She holds my hand for a moment, and looks searchingly into my eyes.

"Have you met the *este lane*?"

"The who?" I say, pulling my hand slowly out of hers. Her presence doesn't make my skin crawl like the other shop owner, but I still have no idea who she is.

"The woman in the restaurant, the man in the antique shop, the woman in the video game store," she says. I'm so startled I don't answer, and suddenly she crosses to the front door and snaps the lock closed.

"Del Mar can be a dangerous town," she says. "But I have something to help keep you safe." She walks toward the back of the store where Delaney is sitting on the ground with an old book perched on her knees. She looks content and happy, reading there in a little corner, hemmed in by old books on every side. The woman walks around Delaney, and stands next to a bookshelf lining the back wall. She looks at the middle shelf for a moment, then pulls a book. She runs her fingertips across the words on the front, mumbling to herself.

"This one," she says. "This book you must have today. Read it carefully, it will keep you safe." A shadow passes in front of the store, outside on the sidewalk, and we look up. Whoever it was is gone now.

"You must go. Take the book; my gift to you. It will keep you safe." With these words, she yanks my sister to her feet, and pushes us both gently toward the door. She glances both ways down the street through the window, then unlocks the door and pushes us out.

"That was weird," Delaney says as we walk back to our bikes. All the stores we pass are closed now, including the antique shop and the restaurant. I put the book into my backpack. We ride home.

## THE BOOK

Delaney goes into her room as soon as we get back. I glance at the PS2. I haven't played *Sairens 2* since that first time, and with what happened to Delaney, I haven't felt the desire to play again. I get a juice from the kitchen and sit down in the blessed air-conditioning to read the book the woman gave me.

It's called *Seminole Myths*, and as I flip through the pages I see a chapter about mermaids, with the page corner folded down. The chapter title has been circled in black marker. Beneath the title there are two mermaids, long, spiraling tales entwined together in a black and white sketch. They look like sisters. I flip back and check the date of publication: 1939.

I begin to read, barely noticing as my sister comes out of her room and heads into the kitchen. The myth is about two sisters who ventured too far out into the ocean and were turned into "snakemaids," forced to live in the water forever. I flip to the next chapter and see the page is folded down as well. This chapter is called "Animal Protector Spirits." I feel a swath of warm, humid air wash over me and hear the back kitchen door slam shut as I read about the Seminole totems, or protectors. There are pictures of the Florida black panther, an otter, birds, a wolf, a snake, and an alligator. The chapter is short, but I read it slowly, taking in the words and illustrations. When I reach the end, I want to check on Delaney.

I lean out the door into the humid heat of the day, a dull worry in my stomach.

The backyard is empty.

## BACK TO THE BEACH

I vault the fence, scraping my inner thigh on a jagged piece of metal, and I race down the path, not caring if I sprain an ankle or miss my footing.

*I have to get to the beach*. When I reach it, Delaney is lying on the sand, next to the same tidepool. This all feels so familiar.

"Delaney!" I run toward her and see her hair splayed out against the sand. She is being dragged back into the brackish tide pool, most of one arm and hand already beneath the black water.

"Delaney!" I scream again, scrambling to get across the few feet of shifting sand to grab her other arm. I hold tighter to her than I've ever held onto anything in my life, and as I start to pull her slowly back out of the water, she screams, one piercing, shuddering scream—and her arm rips off at the shoulder, spouting blood out too fast to mix with the oily water in the pool.

"I have you, Delaney, I have you! Don't let go!" I scream, pulling her to me and ripping my shirt off to try and staunch the blood. It's coming fast, too fast, and her face goes ashy as she instantly descends into shock, curling up against me like we're watching a movie on the couch.

"Freya..." she manages. The thing in the water finally shows itself. As we sit together on the beach, Delaney's arm bleeding out and soaking the sand like black oil, a creature rises out of the tide pool. It is tall, much taller than Dad, about the size of a large dolphin, and with a human head. I say *human* because the facial structure is that of a woman's face stretched over a fish's skull, thick lips over a wide mouth, large gills flexing at the base of her jaw. Its eyes are on the front of the face, glaring and distended and shiny.

*"Give me the girl!"* it hisses. *"They said I could have a sister."* Then it rasps and bubbles, as if its mouth is filled with water and sand, and hacks some blackened seaweed up onto the beach. It smiles the most terrifying smile I've ever seen, an amalgamation of sharp, blackened, sea-glass teeth splayed wildly out of its wide mouth, algae and sea slime dripping black water down its chin to pool on the rocks below.

I'm paralyzed, trying to think as the thing begins to pull itself over the rocky edge of the tide pool and across the sand toward us. Finally I scramble us up to standing, tying my shirt haphazardly across Delaney's exposed shoulder socket. The sand gives under my feet and works against us while the vile thing approaches. Now that it is closer, I can see the flesh of its fish tail, entangled with hooks, lines, and sea trash, its greyish-brown scales sloughing off as if it's got a disease—or as if it's dead. I think of the *shibito*, the undead people in the first *Sairens* video game, as I hold Delaney tight and head as fast as I can back to the treeline. My heart beats at the verge of my collarbone, banging steadily as I half-push, half-pull Delaney up the treacherous path from the beach.

*At least it's slow*, I think, not daring to turn around and see if the mer-thing is still behind us. The time back to the house is interminable, but when the chain-link fence comes into view I help Delaney over again then push her roughly toward the house.

In the house, I lay Delaney down on the couch as gently as I can. Behind me I hear the PlayStation 2 motor whir as the television flickers to life. It's *Sairens 2*—despite the fact I had shoved it away in the closet—and the door on-screen has opened again. The bloody girl—Delaney, of course it's really Delaney—stands there in polygonal horror, 32-bit blood running down her body as glass teeth jut from her mouth. Her eyes are black and dead.

I turn the television off and yank the power cord from the wall. I return to the back door and lock the deadbolt, but when I get back to the living room, the front door is open and the light is going out of Delaney's eyes.

*She told it we were here*, I think, *through the video game. When it showed me Delaney, that's when it all started.* I suddenly remember that Dad should be home from work by now, and run back to his bedroom. The door is ajar, and I push it gently open, already knowing what I'll find. The rusty bucket and the trowel lie on the floor beside his bed, draped with intestines—and one of his hands.

He's already dead, his laptop casting strange images across his distorted and gnawed face in the half-light of the receding rainstorm. I race back down the slippery, tiled hall to the living room where I left Delaney. *Left Delaney*, my mind thinks, *and now look what happened!*

My mother's laughing, living face pops into my head unbidden as I round the corner into the living room, but my imagination can't match the horror of what I see now.

The mer-thing is hunched over Delaney, face-down near her belly. I sink to my knees. The thing stops eating for a moment, its claws entangled in my sister's intestines, and stares up at me. The rotting mermaid tail has trailed slime across the tiles, mingling with my sister's blood. The book the Seminole woman gave me has been ripped to shreds and its pages are scattered across the floor in the dying light, useless to me now. I sob, then stagger to my feet. I know I should flee—that I should run, screaming, from the creature.

But I don't. I can't. It—they—have taken everything from me. Dad. Delaney.

The mermaid stares at me from across the room, breathing, licking at the blood around its mouth.

*"Would you...?"* it hisses, then coughs, its gills struggling to breathe our air. She raises a clawed appendage to gesture, waving me closer. "Sister..." it coughs. "Sister*sss*," it says, smiling those glass teeth, then drops down to Delaney's waist, where it resumes tearing away her flesh.

*"Ssissstersssss,"* she says between bites, her claws furiously working to tear at Delany—to tear off her legs.

Her *human* legs.

"No," I say, not sure I know what she is saying. Not wanting to know what she is offering.

"Sisters," a voice says behind me. Three figures loom in the darkness of the hallway. Rain has begun to splash in the hall from the open front door.

The woman who sold me the game.

The old man.

The kindly woman.

It's her that steps forward.

"Sisters," she says, tears in her eyes, as she takes my hand. I hear Mom in her voice. I want to run. But I don't want to disappoint her. I don't want to leave Delaney.

"You'll never have to," she says, smiling, a single tear curling down her dark cheek. "Okay?"

I nod, unable to speak.

"Okay." She looks up and her eyes follow the old man and the other woman as they come around to either side of me. Their knives are sharp and curved and crooked and the blades are like the waves of the ocean.

As they set about their work, the light returns to Delaney's eyes. *Black* eyes.

She smiles, and stretches her bloody hand out to mine.

"*Sissters*," she hisses, and there's something like love in that word.

## AUTHOR'S NOTE

With this story, there were so many things I wanted to explore—particularly how the unexpected loss of a parent feels to girls who are becoming women, and the shifting of responsibility from parents who are unable to cope onto children who are forced to learn how. In this story, the horror of loss is combined with true horror, and it's not clear which is more overwhelming for the main character. There are other themes running through this work, like the bond between sisters, and the little, daily ways in which they comfort each other. I've come to realize that siblings live in a separate world from their parents, and this world persists throughout childhood, adolescence, and adulthood in most cases. It is a world that parents don't know about and can't ever completely understand.

Finally, I wanted to pursue the ocean environment, the heat and humidity that weighs heavy on the soul even in a beautiful, tropical place, and the danger that the dark water and everything that dwells within it symbolizes.

The story is based on a Japanese video game I played for about two days once—it was so frightening to me that I couldn't play it anymore. The ambiance and the heavy threat of danger hanging over me as I played reminded me of a summer thunderstorm in Florida that lasted days. I often think of the video game, and was excited to have a chance to pursue and examine the fear and ominous nature of it in this anthology.

# DR. COAGULANT'S SPLATTER LAB
## BY JONATHAN RAAB

**T**he air is stale and thick with dust, its taste on my swollen and desiccated tongue that of graveyard dirt, freshly dug and re-filled. By the look of that mote-ridden air, and by the crooked shafts of cool blue moonlight reaching my shallow grave through cracks of the splintered cap of the ancient black coffin—I know that I have been given another chance.

I live again.

I try to groan, but a low wheezing sound is the only thing my re-animated lungs can manage. Do they scab over, I wonder, each time they are run through, whether by slime-dripping claw, twisted metal teeth, or whirring blade? Are my deaths cumulative in effect, those hundreds of wounds and snapped and reformed muscles and tendons diminishing, one shattered molecule, one rent limb, one crack in hardened bone at a time?

Or does Chain-Saw heal my body to what it was before the violence, restoring me to what I was?

No, not what I was—because what I *was* was something lesser than what I am now.

Before Dr. Coagulant. Before Chain-Saw. Before those blue monstrosities took Callie from me, their bulbous eyes staring dumb and unblinking along rubbery stalks, their lobster-like claws perched around her throat in warning that I should not approach as they made their escape. No, what I *was* was something weaker, something more fragile.

Something more human.

I will my lungs to fill with the air of my perennial tomb, my brain firing cracked neurons and sparking green, otherworldly energy along semi-necrotic neural pathways. My arms and legs shudder as the channeled energy of the void ripples across my flesh and overgrown muscles.

I catch my breath—my thick hands and fingers upon the lid of this casket made of splintered, dark obsidian wood—and as my eyes alight through the cap and squint past the shallow layer of dirt to the moon high, high above, I pause. My tired throat and heavy tongue manage a moan, a sigh, exhaustion where my will for revenge should be.

My mind flashes images of the battle I lost that brought me back here. One of the blue creatures with unblinking eyes on stalks, a body like melted crayons held together by razor wire, claws like industrial blades dropped down from the rafters behind me, when my attention was on the glistening ovoids spread across the high school gym's basketball court, my fists slamming like bricks of concrete and making them burst and pop in splashes of acid that stung my skin. Chain-Saw hung from my belt and spurred me on into an ever-widening gyre of violence, faster, *faster, they'll hatch soon, then we'll really be fucked*, his words wisps of gasoline smoke in my mind, then him begging me to let him fly, let him *loose*, but I could only use him so long before he needed to be refueled and I wasn't sure there was enough blood to be had before the next guardian, when I would need his whirring blades of teeth and bloodlust the most.

One of the ovoids beneath the shattered backboard began to crack, waves of green light spilling out and illuminating the low mist that hung a foot above the floor. Tendrils of blackened, root-like flesh crisscrossed the glossy wood panels, sending them up in uneven humps or weighing them down in depressions. But my massive legs pumped and my feet forward, my fists swinging to smash what eggs I could as I raced against time, hoping I could destroy the creatures in their leathery shells before they could free themselves from the embryonic muck.

Just as the cracks spread wide to reveal that laser-bright light within, I leapt, both fists raised high above me, and came crashing down into the egg as it tore itself open in slime-ridden petals. My hands found the horror within and brought to it death, all screams and cracking bones and cold, gelatinous sludge flowing over my shaking fingers like jelly.

*Caleb, behind us!* A moment too late.

My pursuer lunged forward, both claws closed but their outer edges slicing into my left arm and then carrying up my shoulder into what my transformation had left me for a face. I shrieked in pain; it crowed in victory.

But I wasn't finished, not by a Denver-high mile, and I wheeled around and landed my right fist against the chitinous skull that held those eye stalks, feeling the wall that housed its predator's brain give. My left arm was useless, so I lunged forward and brought my forehead down against those eyes, on trajectory with where I hoped the base of its head would be. My face smashed through the sinewy eye stalks, and the creature offered a liquid-curdling scream as my forehead met the front side of its partially collapsed skull, cracking it open further. With my good hand I brought down blow after blow after blow, my bicep and shoulder burning with the effort.

The creature became a mass of quivering limbs attached to a concaved pool of gore where its head had been. I caught my breath, breathing in the acrid scent of its blood and the skunky vegetative smell of the eggs spread around the gym. As I felt Chain-Saw's necrotic magic begin to re-seal my wounds after the kill, I heard that sound that signaled that which I had worked so hard to prevent—and failed.

The skittering of human fingernails across a lacquered floor. Dozens at a time, attached to spindly, finger-like legs, joined to mounds of flesh dripping with the natal slime of an unnatural genesis. One of them was on me before I could turn, whisking itself through the air like a cannonball made of claws and teeth and hate. Its angled teeth made ground beef of my still-injured arm, undoing the healing work of Chain-Saw's magic. I plunged my fingers into the hatchling and *pulled* the horror away from my wounds, which spurted flat streams of blood anew. Its teeth snapped and held on to strands of muscle. Searing, hot pain rippled up and down my ruined limb. I threw it toward the extended bleachers with all the force I could muster. It splattered against the old wooden risers, its meager purple brains liquefying out to dribble down the rows covered in black magic marker graffiti of high school gossip and lovers' hearts.

Another one slammed onto and then latched into my

right shoulder.

Another went for my left thigh.

Still another was upon my neck, burrowing through skin and muscle and finally my exposed spinal cord.

I remember slumping forward, my face slamming into the ground and the gooey remains of one of the eggs. But I do remember Chain-Saw's mocking voice, echoing across the endless void, that darkness beyond darkness, layered upon itself over and over again, rippling waves of unfathomable depths of deepest night.

*Is that the best you got? You weren't fast enough, Caleb. Not by a long shot. You'll never save her.*

I will save her, I insisted.

*Oh yeah?*

Yeah.

*Then get up and whoop some monster ass.*

There's too many of them — can't get them all before they hatch. And that mutoid got the drop on me —

*You're right. You're not fast enough. But I am.*

And now, that voice doesn't come across to me from the void. It comes to me from above, through a thin layer of dirt and a rotting coffin lid.

*Get your ass up, Caleb! We got work to do! Or were you just pulling my leg back there?*

As tired as I am, as much as I don't want to face the horrors that wait for me (*they wait for us, Caleb. We're a team now, remember?*) in the gymnasium of some slime- and tentacle-infested school, I know it's the only way. The only way to find her, to save her.

I ball my fists and push back and then launch them forward and up, sending the coffin lid flying. It disappears into the low-hanging clouds—clouds *too* low-hanging, too deep a purple, with sputtering green energy like St. Elmo's fire dancing along their ridges. I wrap my hands around the edges of the coffin and shove myself up into the air, landing clear of the shallow grave. The tattered blue rags—all that remains of my shirt after my muscles tripled and my bones snapped and popped with unholy growth—flutter in the soft air blowing in from over the mountains and meeting the swirling void-storm above. The moist, freshly cut cemetery grass kisses my fingers and I enjoy the scent, allowing it to pull me back into another memory or memories—of summer days and summer nights, before I lived in the city and let life grind away. Before Dr. Coagulant's monsters came and took Callie away from me.

*Let's get back in the game, Caleb.*

Nearby, Chain-Saw sits in front of a shattered gravestone. His blade is easily four feet long, home to a blood-oiled chain of razor-sharp, inhuman teeth. The grip and crossbar are wrapped in white medical tape, stained red long ago.

*Not so long ago, Caleb. Why, it was just this morning. How long do you think we've been at this? Get a grip, pal.*

The purple chassis' right side held his face, molded recesses for wide, glowing, reptilian yellow eyes within, a Cheshire Cat's grin of distended teeth curved below. Those eyes never blinked, but the irises and deep pupils followed me as I stood up to move toward him. That mouth barely ever moved, his words reverberating around my head rather than through the wet air of the storm. But that smile *did* grow wider as I approached.

*That's right, Caleb. Only way we're gonna get through that*

*gym is if you cut me loose. Don't worry about the blood. I'll be
ready when you need me. I'll always be ready.*

My hand finds the crossbar and I lift. I'm strong now,
stronger than I've ever been or have any right to be, but even
I can tell Chain-Saw is heavy. I heft him up and hold the
blade out before me like a knight's sword, my right hand
finding the grip, then the handle of the pull cord.

*Behold the butcher! Two peas in a pod, you and me. Wielder
and weapon, Yin-and-fucking-Yang, brother. Ooooh, lordee, I can't
wait to show Doc Coagulant who's boss!*

Thunder rumbles overhead. The graveyard stretches on
around us, the earth pockmarked with fresh earth, toppled
graves, the stone doors of tombs shaken loose and hanging
from ancient hinges. Dr. Coagulant's apocalypse is in full
swing.

The school isn't far away. I want to ask Chain-Saw why we're
cutting our way through here, why don't we just go around.
There's no way Coagulant and Callie are still here—but I
know his answer already.

*There's monsters here,* he'd say. *There's monsters, and we kill
monsters, don't we?*

*Fuck yeah, we do.*

The school is only half a dozen blocks from the museum,
where all this started. Well, where it all started for me,
anyway. I realize that I've been fighting, inch by inch,
building by building, block by block, and I'm still in the
heart of the city. I hope that I'm in the thickest of it, here, that

the infection, or the invasion, or the—whatever the hell it is that's happening—is concentrated here. That's why I'm having such a hard time cutting my way out. But a part of me says that I should know better. That this is the *easy* part, the beginning. There are probably worse horrors waiting.

I push those thoughts out of my head as I smash through the glass doors, shoulder first, and into the main hallway of the squat brick school.

I'm ready for the mutoids that emerge from the offices on either side of the hallway. I've done this part before. I snap Chain-Saw into the holster along my left leg hanging from my belt, and catch the first of the blue bastards with stringy arms and claws as they pour out of the side rooms. My fists send them flying back into each other and beyond into the glass case of sports trophies at the end of the hall, shattering the altar to athletic glories long past. The lights flicker overhead and the sound of their growling fury overwhelms my senses, but I know the rhythm now. I can fight through this part with my eyes closed.

When I'm finished—punching, stepping back to dodge their claw swipes, leaping, moving forward, killing—there's six of them splattered across the linoleum floor or exploded against the red brick walls, their purple blood running rivers and their burst viscera hanging like Christmas garland decking the hall. I pop my neck and grab Chain-Saw from my belt, holding him out before me. I go right (left leads to the school nurse's office, where the corpses of a few of the teachers lay violated and chewed-over—I don't need to see *that* shit again—and take the first left to find the blue double doors with fogged-over windows waiting for me. That green laser light and purple mist illuminates their frames.

Chain-Saw doesn't even have to say anything. I know what he wants. I know what I need to do to clear this part.

I pull the cord and his motor rumbles to life. The chain spins and those teeth-blades spit sparks as I pull the trigger. I lead in with my right shoulder. The doors part and we're inside, greeted by the humidity and the skunky vegetable-smell.

I rush at the nearest egg-pod and slice through it, sending sizzling blood flying in a wide aerial arc. I'm onto the next one, and the next, spilling placentae and half-formed finger-crab-creatures onto the ruined floor of the gym. The air turns acrid as their acid-blood begins to chew through the remains of the court's floorboards.

I'm faster this time. With Chain-Saw engorged in gore and that acid-blood, his whirring blade a song in my heart, my legs pump faster and my arms swing my sentient weapon wider. We're a killing machine, like this, together, hacking through the egg-pods one, two, even three in single swing.

*Remember the one that drops down.*

I remember.

*Really? Did you remember last time?*

Last time was the first time we were in here.

*Oh, ha-ha-ha. That's rich. You really believe that?*

It had to be. I don't remember—

*Heads up, high-speed!*

Chain-Saw himself leads the swing to bring him to bear behind us. We whirl around together to meet the mutoid that got the drop on me last time. The tip of the blade passes through the front of its neck, indistinct folds of flesh tearing loose, sparks flying where the enamel of Chain-Saw's teeth meet coiled wire buried in the creature's throat. I lunge forward, leading with the tip of the blade, and clip both of its eye stalks off with a subtle right-to-left movement. Black liquid squirts from those wounds. It screeches, reeling backwards. I turn to leave it to die, worried that maybe I'd missed an ovoid egg-pod.

*No!* Chain-Saw cries out, my skull shaking with his voice. *Give it to me! Bury me in that fucker's body!*

Revolted, but knowing that his power will be diminished if he doesn't refuel, I feed his whirring blade into the groin of the creature and lift up, completely burying Chain-Saw in the creature from loins to neck. He spins faster than before, chewing through the quivering mutant with blinding speed, mushy handfuls of chitin and internal organs and blood spattering my face and arms and chest and legs. I grimace and turn my face away, but as the body disintegrates under Chain-Saw's frenzy, I feel his power restored. My arms and legs shake with raw energy, ready to do more violence, my blood carrying a hot desire to my hands to rip and tear.

Chain-Saw spins to a halt, and what remains of the mutoid sloughs off to the gymnasium floor. Chain-Saw is pure black now, covered in sticky ichor.

*Whew, baby! That was good! Was it good for you, too? Your dick move a little? Admit it!*

I try to talk, to tell him to shut up, to focus, where the hell are we supposed to go next, but I can't. Instead, I just say:

"Yeah. It was good." My voice shakes a little.

I holster Chain-Saw at my side, sparks of green energy popping as I break my grip. As I stomp off toward the red door in the corner, the soft yellow and red light from the EXIT sign above my beacon, I survey the field of gore around me. My feet squish over writhing growths and through the muck of what remains of the aborted finger-crab-creatures, cool and not unpleasant against my skin.

*You're starting to enjoy this, Caleb.*

"I just want to save Callie."

*Sure, sure. Once we save Callie, it'll be allllll over. You'll just put me back in that mummy where you found me, and you can go back to life as usual. Think the museum will take you back once this is all over, hmm? Think you can just go back to your nine-to-five, paying bills and watching Netflix, drinking with the guys on Thursday nights, calling Mom and Dad once a month, playing Playstation and eating pizza?*

"That's the idea, yeah."

*You're dumber than you look. There's no going back, buddy. Not after this. Life will be a shadow. A pale reflection in polluted water. This—this killing, this glorious violence—you'll never forget it. You'll never forget what it was like to fight alongside me, to be a god.*

As I put my hands on the receding bar that opens the door, something doesn't feel right. The floor is rumbling—slow at first, almost imperceptible. But after Chain-Saw's feeding, I'm more aware of everything—my heartbeat, my skin stretched over bulging muscles, the taste and smell of the air, the movement of the earth below.

*Oh, shit. You're not gonna like this part.*

The rumbling grows louder, accompanied by the sound of splintering wood, of cracking earth. The nearest backboard shatters, raining glass down into the gore-muck we've left behind. In that soup, something is moving. The tendrils. I'd assumed they'd be growing along the floor, feeding the ovoid pods.

They are growing *out* of the floor.

They converge at half court, pulled toward that dark spot, dragging floorboards and finger-crab-corpses along with them. The wreckage disappears into a growing black pit as it opens, pulling everything down like quicksand. The tendrils disappear into that darkness, leaving only ruin in their wake.

The rumbling stops. The air is still.

*Caleb...*

"A guardian?"

*Yeah. Good thing you fueled me up.*

The pit moans in answer. Cords of ringed, black flesh, impossibly dexterous, flutter up from the dark to the surface, then feel their way to the edges of the pit. They're almost beautiful in the way the dozens upon dozens of feelers or fingers or whatever-the-hell-they-are move like smoke, almost shimmering, indistinct.

*Fire me up, buddy.*

"Maybe I can wear it down first. Save some of your energy for the end."

*It don't work like that. Not with this one.*

"Oh," I manage, feeling fear — real *worry* — snake into my mind for the first time in... hours? Days?

Details like time lose all meaning after you die and come back to life.

*Hey, hero. Let's get with the program, yeah?*

"Yeah," I say, snapping him out of his holster. He's rumbling and sparking that green energy before the cord's even pulled back all the way. When I look back to the pit, those anemone-feelers are gone. With both hands on Chain-Saw I hold him out before me, and I notice that green, sparkling fire hasn't dissipated.

"What's happening to you?"

*Max-level, buddy. Real good stuff. You're gonna like it.*

"I don't like this."

*Sure you do! Just keep your distance from this thing. And swing me like the Savage Sword of Conan. I'll take care of the rest. You don't even gotta go near it.*

"I do like that."

*Yeah, well, the trick is gonna be—*

The earth shits out the guardian. A long, ever-growing tube of brown-and-red threads of flesh, bound together in a massive, writhing cylinder segmented by pallid rings of bone or cartilage. From its sides hang the desiccated tendrils that once birthed the finger-crab creeps, the ruins of ovoids bleeding that green acid.

And its head, oh, boy. Its head. A spear-like protrusion, the same raw-muscle-and-marbled-fat-meat consistency of the rest of its body. It aims that spearpoint at me and segments scale back, revealing those tendrils that first crept to the surface. Their tips alight with a glowing amber, and it takes the shaking of the ground beneath my feet to snap me out of my amazement.

My first instinct is to leap forward to its head, but its size and the distance—and the likelihood that those flaps would recede further to reveal teeth or more feelers or something much, much worse—gives me pause. Instead, I drop my head and shoulders like a linebacker and begin to churn gymnasium floor toward the segment bobbing in the pit. I mean to slice the worm right in half, end it fast.

I should know better. Nothing's this easy, not this far along.

*Caleb, no, leap back!*

Its head collides with my body as I'm mid-stride, sending me spinning through the air toward the bleachers. I'm wondering how in the holy hell it managed to swing itself down and at me so fast when the pain of the impact registers. Then I'm smashing into the upper rows of the old wood platforms and planks of the bleachers, metal supports ripping at my flesh and failing to break my fall. I open my eyes to the darkness, my mouth heaving to suck in fog-ridden humidity down to my lungs.

*Over here!*

The words are like diesel smoke in my eyes, burning. I'm starting to think that means he's angry. Or worried.

I try to sit up, but my broken ribs have other plans. I let out a low moan and my hands move around in the dark, grasping for Chain-Saw. He can't heal me if he's not nearby. I've figured that much out already. My right hand finds the blood staining through the blue rags that hang off of my shoulders, and I wonder: what happens if I die without him at my side?

*HURRY-MOVE-GET-UP YOU DON'T WANT TO FIND OUT, KID!*

Smoke in my eyes, again. He means it.

Rows of wood splinter and columns of metal bend and pop and *twang* under immense pressure. The worm guardian has slammed itself down against the bleachers, mercifully, stupidly far away from where I landed. It releases a shriek that echoes and reverberates, a Foley-sound animal cry chiptuned with the reverb cranked up to max level. Then it's down again, more rent steel superstructure and splintering and split panels. So close that I instinctively cover my warped face with my hands. Then that smoky burn again, and I'm flipping myself over onto my chest through sheer force of will, my shattered body a cry of fire.

I know I'm not going to make it if I crawl forward, no matter how fast I move. The worm guardian is already extricating itself from the wreckage, preparing to raise its head back up once more before ending my life in a rain of underfunded high-school shrapnel.

So I do the only thing that makes sense. I grip floorboards. My fingers crease into the smooth, sealed wood of the gym floor, and shove myself with all of my strength *backwards*, toward the guardian's waiting head. My skin sputters and tears along the floor, my exposed toenails send up sparks, my blood trails my path, and my chest is a heaving, tangled mess of pain. I expect my feet to find the creature's head, or to go legs-first into its waiting jaws, to be pulled apart by its glowing tendrils. Instead, the creature lifts its head and segmented neck-body into the air, oblivious to my maneuver. I fly through the wreckage of the bleachers and land feet-first against the far wall of the gymnasium, hidden beneath the far-side bleachers that are as yet undisturbed by the guardian's assault. Then he's swinging down again, smashing through the remainder of the bleachers on that half of the gym. There it lingers, shooting out its feelers and releasing that ragged, reverberating moan once more.

You missed me, you bastard.

*Clever move, high-speed! I'm over* here.

I ignore the pain of my ribs and the smoke in my eyes and nose. Through the slats of the bleachers I see Chain-Saw, laying on his side, useless without me, me without him, near half court.

I want to stand up, but the pain is too great. The worm is still distracted, confused, searching for me. There's only one thing to do.

I brace my legs as I execute a push-up, form-perfect like my brother showed me that summer he came home after Basic, before he went to the desert and the only time I saw his face again was on an airbrushed photograph above my parents' mantle. I think of *that* pain instead of the pain of my shattered chest, and it powers me through the bleachers and through the air, my arc near-perfect, landing directly astride Chain-Saw's toppled form. This should hurt, but being this close to him, his magic already at work in my body, righting my wounds.

*I knew you had it in ya, kid. Ready for try numero two?*

My hand finds the crossbar and I lift, my ribs mending together one dark particle at a time. I have Chain-Saw held out before me now, his rumbling chassis and blade aglow with green light, and the pain in my chest is a dull roar. Ahead of us, the worm is pulling its body from the ruins of the bleachers, screeching in its confusion.

*Now don't try to rush it this time. That ain't gonna work. Even together, we ain't fast enough.*

"So what then?"

*Swing, pal. And don't forget the throttle while you're at it.*

I lift him high over my left shoulder and hesitate, for just a moment. That's enough time for the worm to catch sight of me. More of its body spills up and out of the hole at half-court. It slithers through the air, pointed head aimed directly at me.

My finger depresses the throttle and Chain-Saw's words

become some sort of moan—an overloaded telepathic signal that nearly blinds me and sends my teeth a-rattling and the liquid on my eyes evaporates in little puffs.

Those flaps around the worm's mouth begin to peel back and I bring Chain-Saw down across and in front of my body in a wide swing. The air rushes toward me, filling now-empty space, and the *boom* of the energy release sends me skidding back a few feet. A brilliant green arc crackles and flies toward the worm, its feelers out but then receding rapidly back into its maw the moment it senses the energy approaching. There's ozone in the air and I'm struggling to catch my next breath, and within that eternal moment my weapon cries out to me.

*AGAIN*

And so I balance on my right foot and step forward with my left, raising Chain-Saw above my right shoulder. I squeeze the throttle and his moan doesn't quite liquefy my eyeballs, but it's close.

The first arc is too slow; the worm lifts itself back and up toward the rafters, and the semi-circle of energy floats harmlessly through the worm's spinning and flowing coils.

But we unleash a second blast, and the worm has spent its considerable length at expense of space. The more of it that flows out of the earth, the less room it has to maneuver. The energy flies forward, but the worm knows what to expect.

How many times have we fought this battle? I wonder. Do the monsters get second chances?

*Only when you fuck-up,* Chain-Saw's voice comes to me, less overclocked and more like his usual self. Whatever power we gained from refueling is diminishing with each strike.

*Look at you, figuring it out without having me* explain *every god-damned thing to you. I got one blast left in me.*

All of this happens in the second and a half it takes me to lift him once more. Instead of slashing across my chest, I strike forward like a spearman. The energy releases and the green sparks around Chain-Saw dissipate. One final half-ring flies forward.

The worm contorts and its head ducks to the side, and the third and final shot floats on harmlessly by. In that split second of realization, a weight in my gut drops out, and my arms feel weak. The worm's growling raises a few notes. It senses victory. Its head floats a few meters closer, preparing to launch itself at me.

But then:

*Dodge!*

I leap pre-emptively, knowing the creature is too fast for me to respond and hoping I get the timing just right. It sees me moving and overcommits too early.

Just as the first ring hits the edge of the gym. And bounces *back*.

Then the second. Then the third.

The worm's colliding with the floor of the gym at the edge of the three-point line where I've just been standing, sending floorboards snapping and flying. I'm landing, then I'm rushing toward center court, toward the hole, and finally the limits of its body pass up into the air.

The fucker's *floating* mid-air.

I rev up Chain-Saw—I know he's only got a few seconds of energy left in him—and leap toward the tumor-like growths along the base of its tail. The creature's lunging toward me now, having to navigate through the maze of its own body flowing forward, its lower segments suddenly a noose for its own head. Chain-Saw's whirling teeth barely miss the end of the bulbous growth as it pulls higher into the air.

But the worm cries out. The arcs are coming toward us, slicing through segmented muscle-fat-flesh at three different angles.

If atoms are mostly empty space, and matter exponentially more so, then how can three four-foot-wide arcs of unholy destruction magic ever hope to collide with and cut through the hardened skin of an entity that shouldn't exist in our material plane?

*They just do, kid. Sit back and watch the show.*

The guardian's body closes around its own neck, holding its head in place. What should be an earth-shattering cry comes out as a pathetic whimper as the creature constricts its own throat in a binding of its own making. Great rushes of green blood spatter and rain down across this half of the court. Segments of worm stop flowing and rotating mid-air and collapse to the ruined ground below. Now we dodge the inevitability of gravity and buzzsaw-like occult energy applied to monsterflesh. It's a good dance, a moment of fun. Chain-Saw is *heehee, hoo-hoo*-ing as I let him swing out to my side, me holding on tight with my left hand.

As the arcs fade out in a brilliant pixelated static-burst, one after another, the worm-guardian's many segments lie spurting green blood and rocking back and forth, logs separated by smoking, cauterized flesh. Its head is the last to fall, disgorging a rush of those anemone-feelers and jet-black bile in a loud burp.

Me and Chain-Saw are both panting, but we're whole.

*Alright kid... You can... Guess what's next...*

"The pit, right?"

*That'll take us to Doc Coagulant's lab.*

I holster Chain-Saw at my side, then leap ahead, not even bothering to look down into the tunnel created by the bore worm. I'm sure I'll find a landing. I'm sure Chain-Saw's right about it being where we need to go.

On this kind of high, I'm sure about a lot of things.

In the dark, you lose track of time. With only the light of the glowing eyes of your sentient chainsaw to light your way, it's easy to lose track of where you're going, how long you've been walking. Whether you're awake, or whether this is some twisted dream, a come-back hello from your hallucinogen-experimental-phase. Maybe you're back in the coffin again. Maybe this time, you can't punch your way out.

The blood-red light ahead puts to bed those thoughts.

We emerge into an overgrown thicket. I punch the brambles and displaced tree roots into splinters, and step out of what I realize is a metal run-off tube. Before us is a stagnant, forgotten pool filled with junkies' needles and floating plastic flavored-vodka shooters. Beyond the tangled mess of toxic vegetation is an abandoned asylum, two wings visible to its sides and stretching toward us like the feet of some great modernist Sphnix, its central concrete-and-shattered-glass hub rising four stories high. It's dark inside, but I know—*we* know—he's in there. Waiting.

Lightning crashes across the swirling sky. Purple, wide. In a single break in the cloud above, the moon floats, closer than before, blood-red now. Changing. Different. Corrupted.

I leap over the pool and pull myself through the mud, hands resting on the trees that are gnarled and ruddy, twisted by the influence of the corruption spilling from the epicenter of this apocalypse. The earth smells sour, and the storm clouds swirl at some central point just beyond the rise of the asylum.

This is where his apocalypse began.

*This is where we're gonna end it.*

I cross the courtyard, which is overgrown with weeds, its driveway crumbling and barely visible under too-thick tendrils of vegetation. The growth here is more unnatural with each step, the influence of corruption spilling forward, inch by rotten inch. There's a fountain here, wide and at the center of the drive, in which stands a decapitated cherub, thick brown water spurting in uneven, gurgling bursts from its throat of clipped bronze. I turn my gaze to the main entrance ahead, and yet I feel the statue's missing eyes on me.

At the top of the wide concrete steps wait the asylum's massive double doors, stretching several feet above even my unnaturally extended height. They are made of old wood held by rows of blackened pig iron, somber angels' faces marking each bolt. I place my hand on the wrought iron ring and pull the door open. It's not even locked.

A wide atrium greets us, with a front desk and nurse's station, empty and abandoned, papers fluttering. A "SECURITY OFFICE" to the right with shattered glass window and door hanging off its hinge. Overturned common room chairs and table. Mildew or mold is thick on the air. I can taste it, even without opening my mouth. Light filters in through the shattered, central skylight above. Ahead the atrium stretches on to elevators, offices. To my right and left are hallways of closed, darkened doors, and right-angle turns forward and back leading to their respective wings. I step forward, fists raised.

An old, bulky television hangs from the wall behind me. It flickers to life in a burst of tube-pressure and static. I turn to see a face forming in the blizzard—half pattern recognition, half ghost in the signal.

His chin is sharp and angular, his cheeks pallid and recessed. His eyes are ringed in shadow, his shock-white hair slicked back. A pair of small-framed, circular glasses rests on his nose. He looks up, as if noticing me for the first time and I'm interrupting his work.

"I'm disappointed you're still alive. But not surprised." His words and face are static-ridden, riding twisting waves of signal that bend and twist. Above the entrance and to the right of the blocky hanging television is a single camera, aimed directly at me, its red light blinking.

"Where is she?" I demand, stepping forward and raising my fist. "If you give me Callie, I might not smash your face in."

"To the point, I see. I prefer some formality, some manners. I suppose that's the problem with your generation. Instant gratification, instant fulfillment. That is why you're all miserable. Why you're poor. Sometimes, I wonder if my efforts on your behalf are worth it. If our successors are unworthy, why bother to leave them a world of value?"

*We should keep moving, Caleb. He's trying to distract you.*

"You're destroying the world!" I shout, knowing I'm being baited, knowing he's delaying. But my anger—*our* anger—is making me shake. I want this confrontation.

"I'm doing no such thing," he says, one eyebrow arched. "I, Dr. Reginald Coagulant, am not this world's destroyer. I'm its savior."

"I don't care about what you *think* you're doing," I say. "I just want Callie back."

"I know you believe that. But you won't stop—it won't *let* you stop—until I'm destroyed and my work is undone. I can't allow that."

I heave the chair through the air, and it collides with the television. A shower of sparks and glass rains down to the grime-ridden linoleum floor. I walk over to the camera above the door and leap up, yanking it from the wall, snapping cords and crushing the lens in my bare hands. Shards of glass scatter like sand in my blood-encrusted palms.

"Humanity is like a sponge, Caleb," he says, his voice drifting to me from somewhere down the hallway to the right of the main atrium. I follow his words, my feet treading over the cold floor carefully. Each step forward is a risk. Another trap, another horror, may spring out at me with each step.

There's less light in the hallway, and even less as it forks off to the left. The lights are out here, but blood-red moonlight sneaks in through cracks in doors or through holes splintered open by inhuman hands or disrepair. Another closed circuit television is set at its far end. It's brighter than it should be. Coagulant's face hovers in the mist of static and signal noise.

"A sponge, but a sponge that transmits. Picture our minds as radio towers, and our thoughts as signals. Powerful signals. Sometimes, those signals bounce around, or even bounce back, warped and twisted in on themselves by their journey through the cosmic psychosphere. That's what ghosts are, did you know that? Lost signals, come back to haunt us. One of the many things I've discovered in my work."

I progress slowly, Dr. Coagulant's floating screen-head growing closer with each moment. I'm not scared, not exactly, but wound tight. Encountering a monster would be a relief; *finally*, the waiting would be over, and I could explode into a comfortable frenzy of violence.

"But it's not all empty space out there, Caleb. Not at all. There are things in the void. Things that listen. And hunger. Hunger for what our minds are, what they are capable of. We transmit, but we can also receive. Absorb. Our minds are pliable, Caleb. As is our flesh. You are living proof of that. That *thing* at your side has twisted you, used you. It's consuming you. Even now, it nibbles on your memories, on your sanity. You feed my servants to it. You trade their blood for dopamine. But the longer you allow that parasite to wield your body as a weapon, the sooner you'll be consumed and discarded."

*He's lying.*

We're at the turn in the hall, the television hanging above. Another set is further down the hall, a beacon of static-light in the shadows. I realize smashing them isn't going to do me any good. We keep moving.

"I had no quarrel with you. It wasn't until you joined

with that entity that you became my enemy."

"You took Callie from me."

"My servants recognized you had an attachment to her, and I needed to lure you into the fight, to battle you on *my* terms. I believed that the guardians would have disposed of you by now. I see that was a miscalculation."

The four doors in this wing of the hall are all closed. No light spills from the cracks. As the pink slime dribbles out from beneath them, I realize why.

"You attacked the museum, you son of a bitch. Your monsters killed those people. If I hadn't been there, you would have killed them all."

"*Noooo*," Dr. Coagulant hisses. "Yes, some lost their lives to the claws of my mutoids. I admit that, at first, I couldn't control them as well, as perfectly. But my abilities have grown, Caleb. I am truly master over them. And to be perfectly rational, a few dozen dead are a small price to pay for security."

The currents of slime flow forth in spilling, vibrating waves. Collecting at the center of the hall, all four currents. Massing. Becoming solid.

"I had to destroy that thing that now possesses you. It is one of *them*, Caleb. One of the greater ones, those who would bend humanity to their purposes. To feed upon and consume us."

*Bullshit.*

"These—and the ones you've faced—are nearly mindless, they are animals, constructs and mutants, the results of my synthesis of void-creature and our material plane. They are warriors conscripted in the cause of humanity's defense. But the others—the creature at your side is a herald of our doom. If it's not destroyed, it will destroy *us*."

As the slime grows and rises into vaguely humanoid, transparent forms, I think of the attack on the museum. The screaming and the bloodshed—we fled into the nearest exhibit, looking for a place to hide. I had seen Dr. Coagulant's stalk-eyed mutoids dismember the security officer, then the desk attendant. Their progress slowed only when they paused to feed on a family of five.

Chain-Saw—before he was Chain-Saw—called out to me from the mummy's case. Barely large enough to hold the remains of a child, it was covered in runes and pictoglyphs, large, black, dead eyes painted on in astonishing and vivid detail, especially considering its age. The archaeologists assumed it was pre-Ute, but the markings and ceremonial nature were unlike anything that any of the American Indians of Colorado pre-history were known to possess in their culture—to say nothing of the painted figure's inhuman, bulbous head, its wide eyes, its slit of a mouth, hands depicted over its golden chest, fingers slim and long. Too long.

Something crashed in the hallway, and a scream was cut short. Then a sound like slicing through iceberg lettuce.

He said, *We can end this. We can work together. I know who is responsible.*

A golden light emanated from the case, growing to reveal the creases in its sides. It seemed that one moment I was staring at it from behind the velvet ropes, then the next I was reaching my fingers into that glowing crevice, pulling the bristling material apart.

Inside, a beating heart. With too many chambers.

Beating. Spraying geysers of green blood into the air. A glowing, yellow mist swirling around it, the air burning my eyes and lungs.

*We can keep her safe.*

I remember grabbing the heart. I remember pressing it to my chest. I remember the sound of my ribs splitting open to accept it, whip-lash tentacles striking out from the thing as it pulled itself into me, forcing itself into my veins and my blood.

The transformation wasn't painful behind those first few moments. But when it was over, when I was taller, more muscular, my face twisted into a grim, skull-like mask of bone and fury, I saw Callie. She backed away from me, eyes wide, a whine escaping her lips. She was afraid of me.

That's when the mutoids grabbed her.

*After* I had transformed.

*They would have killed both of you.*

"You were incidental. Not part of the equation." Dr. Coagulant waves a slim hand before his face. "Had you simply stepped aside, my servants would have seized the case. I would have destroyed the entity here, and your journey would have been unnecessary. But now you've brought it to me. Wasted effort, wasted resources. My army diminished. A shame. But I will rebuild."

His face splits into quadrants, pulled in opposite directions as the signal breaks.

Four slime-men drift toward me, dripping arms outstretched, eyes and mouths simple ovals with bars of sludge stretching across them.

I charge into them, fists swinging. They break under my blows, spattering against the ceiling, the floor, the walls.

First my fists, then my elbows. I swing harder as I feel them shiver and shake, absorbing some of the force of my strikes. In seconds I am coated with slime—and in moments, those drops and spatters leap from my skin, collecting in pools in the center of the floor. The stains on the walls and ceiling follow suit, drifting down to join together.

*We don't have time for this,* Chain-Saw says. *We're so close. I can smell him.*

So we round the next corner. Ahead is a set of wide, double doors. The time for caution has passed. I'm ready for this to be over. One way or another.

We are through the doors and into Dr. Coagulant's lab. On each side of the wide, open space, stand giant glass chambers, vats full of glistening, bubbling liquid of all colors and consistencies. Shapes and forms float within—some resembling human bodies, others chunks of meat, collections of bones, pulsing flesh. The air tastes of antiseptic overlaid a thick, rotten-blood smell. Metal operating tables, medical gurneys. Discarded needles, blood-soaked bandages, scraps of clothing cut by surgical scissors. At the far side of the room, adjacent to rows of computers and what I guess is radiology equipment, sits a figure, slumped forward, a stained-through white sheet covering its forearms and lower half. It's twice my size in height and girth, easily. Its muscle tissue along its massive arms and legs is exposed to the air, skinless, glistening with the slop of bile or blood. Its head is long and distended, a horse's skull wrapped in a thin layer of pink, hairy flesh. There are no eyes in its sockets and yet, as it stirs to life and points its nose at me, I *know* that it can see me.

I waste no time worrying whether Chain-Saw is ready or

not. He's in my hands and revved up in a flash. He's just as eager as I am.

The guardian stands up and the sheet falls away. I was wrong—it's at least three times my height. Wrapped around its waist is another hospital sheet, torn into a loincloth. Its thick arms are held together before its body—wrists and hands joined and locked into a shaft of dark, rusted-out metal. The base of a weapon.

A chainsaw. Pure, shining chrome, with three-inch high sharp blades spaced out along its cutting chain, the chain itself dripping with fresh oil.

Dr. Coagulant's voice calls to me from crackling speakers hidden in the recesses of the lab.

"You face your death now," he's saying. I'm already rushing toward the horse-headed horror. It's stomping toward me, the ground shaking with each step of its massive legs and hooves.

Coagulant is saying something else now—some grand monologue on the future of mankind, as determined by him, of course. It doesn't matter. Chain-Saw locks mid-spin with the guardian's weapon. Its strength is immense, and I feel my arms beginning to give. The power of both of its arms— locked together into the base of its weapon—is focused on this downward push, and I realize I'm in the worst position possible. I relent on the pressure and roll to the side. Its whirring blade barely catches my shoulder but buries itself into the floor, sending chunks of tile and dust into the air. I'm on my feet again and charging in. Chain-Saw takes a bite out of the creature's arm. It responds by lifting its leg and smashing its hoof into my chest, breaking my right arm and sending my head snapping back. We crash into a rolling metal cart, spilling a tray of scalpels and bone-breaking instruments around us.

*That wasn't the right move,* Chain-Saw says. His energies are dancing around my wounds, but the guardian is stomping toward us. *Let's try something else next time.*

I grab for his crossbar, but the guardian's whirring chainsaw eats through the top of my skull, climbs down my neck, and splits my chest cavity in two.

It happens so fast, it doesn't even hurt.

Much.

Inside the coffin, it's dark. Much darker than before. The last couple (few? many?) times I woke up inside, there were splintered boards, graveyard dirt pouring through, the moonlight spilling in through the cracks.

The coffin cover is whole. I don't linger. I press my hands against the lid.

Nothing.

I grunt with effort, and nails pop and wood begins to break. Claustrophobia-panic sets in, and I'm pumping, shouting, smashing my way out. The cover disintegrates and grave dirt pours in, flooding my mutated nose and mouth, choking me. With a scream of fear more than fury, I am shoveling my way through the fresh dirt and clambering out to the surface. The graveyard grass smells sweeter than before, the cold flecks of rain splashing against my face the kisses of freedom.

*Let's go, Caleb. We ain't got time to dawdle.*

"WHAT'S HAPPENING," I choke out, struggling to control my breathing.

*What, you afraid of the dark now? Just a little incentive. To keep you moving. To keep us moving. You think it don't cost me nothing to keep bringing your stupid ass back from the dead? You think I'm just a limitless font of life? You got the wrong god for that one, pal. That's some other guy's schtick. You're gonna have to meet me halfway. We're so close, pal. So god-damn close. But you can't keep fucking up. We gotta take down that next guardian pron-to. Then we'll get our hands on Coagulant.*

"What happens then?" I wheeze, standing up.

*No spoilers, pal.*

We're in the same graveyard—but it's closer to the asylum, somehow. Directly adjacent, in fact, just to the west. I cross through a thicket of twisted trees and out onto the asylum grounds. There's a side entrance to the wing here. I smash through the door and find myself in a side room, which leads to the hallway of the slime-men. Dr. Coagulant's face appears on the television monitors here. I've broken the sequence a bit, changed when he shows his face and where. But the words are the same.

"I'm disappointed you're still alive. But not surprised."

I don't bother with the twenty questions. I've heard it before. Our brains are transmitters/receivers, dark entities, my role in humanity's destruction, he's the *real* hero.

I'm through the double doors. Chain-Saw's powered back up to full strength after our little dirt nap. Not shooting-waves-of-energy powered up, but ready to rock nonetheless. Coagulant's voice echoes across the lab as I'm halfway to the guardian. He starts moving as soon as Coagulant begins to speak.

"You face your death now."

I bring Chain-Saw down across the creature's head, the blade shooting sparks as it makes contact with its exposed skull. Chain-Saw bounces back, and I ride that momentum to spin around and go in for another strike, this time against the creature's left arm. It's on its feet (hooves) now, and pulling back its blade. Chain-Saw digs in and climbs up the beast's arm, stunning it. I follow that momentum through and leap up onto the platform behind it—some kind of altar, complete with burning candles that are very-fucking-likely made from human fat—and turn to face the nightmare. I swing Chain-Saw forward, blade-a-spinning, his voice a growl of rage and effort in my mind. He chews through the creature's right shoulder flesh, sending blood and hunks of greasy meat up in a spray—but glances off its shoulder blade, his spinning chain grinding to a halt.

*God-damn it this isn't working we gotta try something else.*

The guardian is howling in rage, lifting its joined arms and weapon overhead and turning, slowly, ready to bring down another killing blow. I have just enough time to strike again, and hope I do enough damage to stagger or wound it.

Or, I can try something else.

"—grisly manifestations, Caleb, and you'll see the futility in this game, and even come to see me as a visionary of sorts—"

I step forward. I fall to the ground, crouching. I lift Chain-Saw up by the crossbar and handle, and depress the throttle.

The guardian roars again as Chain-Saw chews through the meat of its groin. It brings its bound arms down, crashing the blade against the altar behind me, splitting it in two. Chain-Saw's blade grinds to a halt again.

*FUCK.*

I'm not waiting around. I scramble forward. Before the guardian can turn around, I swipe Chain-Saw—once, twice—above each of the creature's hooves, hoping like hell there's something like an Achilles tendon in its anatomy.

Dr. Coagulant drops his supervillain monologue bit.

The creature crashes forward, landing on its knees with a thick *boom*. Howling, howling all the while.

Chain-Saw can't seem to penetrate its skeleton… but he can sure as hell shave off the creature's flesh.

We work together with surgical precision. We're attuned to one another now, operating as a single unit, a single force. Cutting, slicing, tearing tendon and cartilage, finding resistance in the creature's skeleton and then trying again someplace else. And always, always, blood.

Its howls become screeching pleas for mercy. Its own chainsaw blade still spins—I suspect it's operated directly by some sort of internal nerve tether—but we've cut the strength right out of it.

I'm growing impatient. I want to finish this. So I start working Chain-Saw around the guardian's neck. Chain-Saw's spinning faster and faster now, that green energy cracking and popping along his form again, smoke pouring from his eyes and frozen mouth.

Our persistence pays off. We hack, and hack, and *pull* bone-shredding teeth through the guardian's spine, sending its horseskull head tumbling forward into its own spinning chainsaw blade. Its head is reduced to a slurry of jagged bone bits and chewed-through fleshy matter, something grey like brain liquefying into a showering arc of muck.

*NOW WE FINISH THIS.*

"Enough!"

Dr. Coagulant's voice isn't coming through the speakers anymore.

He's behind us. He's wearing a velvet-red surgeon's gown, with form-fitting black gloves held out before him—holding Callie.

She whimpers and yips, seeing me, terrified of me—but perhaps recognizing who I am, under this mass of muscle and blood.

"Give me back my dog," I growl. There's murder in my words. Coagulant takes a step back, then produces an oversized, silver syringe, its glass chamber filled with a glowing purple liquid. The heavy gauge needlepoint floats inches away from Callie's brown fur-covered neck. A single point of glistening purple glow hangs from its tip.

"Don't come any closer!" Coagulant shouts, his voice cracking. He's shaking, now, his eyes wide and wild. This is not what I expected—where is the final speech, the vainglorious appeal to the glory of science and progress? The villain on the precipice of victory, overconfident in his monologue, before he reveals his final monstrosity to seal his inevitable victory?

He's just a scared old man.

I holster Chain-Saw and hold up my hands.

*KILL HIM LET'S KILL HIM.*

"I don't want to do this anymore!" I say, shaking my head. "I really don't care about any of this!"

Coagulant's eyes squint and his left eyebrow arches up.

"No tricks, Caleb! This void-serum and stem cell cocktail will turn your beloved dog into a monster that even you can't slay!"

"I don't want that!"

*KILL HIM WHAT THE HELL ARE YOU WAITING FOR LET'S KILL.*

"You've brought that entity here, to my lab! Why should I believe you? You're a servant of one of the enemies of mankind!" The needle drifts closer to Callie's neck. He's holding her too tight. She squeaks in pain.

"Wait!" I pause, then shake my head. Déjà vu. "Wait, wait. Have... have we done this before?"

"What?"

"In my head, when we're talking like this..." There's a flash of something—light and sound, the smoke of Chain-Saw's fury. The needle plowing into her flesh, the liquid plunging inside... Callie's changing, legs growing, mouth filling with teeth, her mass expanding and expanding... she's a hound of hell itself, breathing fire and bearing down on me... I'm forced to fight her...

The coffin. Punching my way out. Harder than before. Always harder than the last time.

"No."

*CALEB NO WHAT THE HELL ARE YOU DOING DON'T DO THIS WE CAN SAVE HER.*

I rip Chain-Saw away from my leg, and send him flying into a row of containment tanks, cracking the glass and sending a stream of green goo spilling out onto the floor.

Dr. Coagulant looks from my discarded weapon to me, then back again.

*Big mistake, Buck-o. Big god-damned mistake. You've given me enough, you dumb sumbitch, and I don't NEED you anymore—*

Smoke is rising from where he landed; the green goo is spilling out onto his blade, which is spinning and grinding. The liquid in the vats along the row begin to boil, sending up waves of stinking humidity across the lab.

A vein- and slime-ridden stalk emerges from Chain-Saw's frozen mouth. Then another from each of its eyes. The stalks take sharp downturns toward the floor, segmenting themselves. More stalks emerge from Chain-Saw's rumbling casing.

"Coagulant! Give me my dog back!"

"What?" he says, staring at Chain-Saw as it stands on its new legs and points its blade toward the mad doctor.

I waste no time. I leap across the lab and wrench the needle away from him, crushing his hand. The needle falls to the floor, but Callie leaps into the crook of my right arm and we're running toward the doors, back into the hallway.

Behind us, Coagulant is favoring his broken hand— before recovering the needle and plunging it into his own neck. Chain-Saw is moving toward him, moving on glistening, goo-dripping spider's legs, a mist floating above, something in that noxious cloud like the face of Hell itself, ram's horns and a mouth full of jagged teeth.

Dr. Coagulant's skin is bubbling and tearing, re-forming itself into new, weaponized horrors. Finger-bones shoot out from warping flesh, angular and sharp.

The doors swing close behind us, and they fight their climactic battle without anyone to watch.

Running through streets. Eyes staring out at me from darkened homes and buildings. Some are human. Most are not.

Something feels off. Different. I'm growing weaker, more tired, the further I get from Chain-Saw. The blue rags hanging from my shoulders seem larger, and I'm aware now that my feet are bare. I take my time to avoid the wreckage of cars and overturned city buses rather than just leaping over them.

Callie is curled up against me, her pink-and-black nose wet and buried in the crook of my arm. The storm still swirls overhead, and green light arcs across the clouds, but its center and fury is miles behind us now, a whirling vortex over Dr. Coagulant's splatter lab, where the fate of this world is supposedly being decided.

I don't care about any of that. I'm just glad I have my puppy back.

Lights ahead—artificial, bright. Humvees and soldiers with guns, standing in silhouette before floodlights pointed toward the terrors of the city. As we draw closer I'm stepping over the bullet-shredded remains of mutoids and the burned-up sludge of slime-men. I skirt around the burst carcass of a frog-like creature the size of a delivery truck, its death the smell of formaldehyde and brimstone.

This is the line. They've been holding the contamination out of the suburbs on this side of the metro, while I've been heading in, deeper and deeper into the heart of mutation and chaos.

Callie offers a sharp yip. The clacking of metal and the shouting of orders reaches me. I raise a hand up to shield my eyes from the lights. My arm is thin, weak. I'm just me again. I wonder if my face has returned, too.

I need them to see a human being seeking refuge from a supernatural holocaust. I need them to take a risk. To decide not to shoot.

Callie lifts her head, whining like she does when she sees people and wants to make a new friend. I walk forward, into the lights. The soldiers are pointing their guns at me, yelling to be heard.

Whatever they decide to do next in the eternity of our present moment, I hope—more than I hope that we might live through this—that I won't wake up with graveyard dirt on my lips, my eyes searching for light, looking for cracks in a black coffin lid above.

## AUTHOR'S NOTE

Sometimes, style over substance works. The *Splatterhouse* series, for example, features simple gameplay—walk forward, dodge the enemy attacks, make sure yours land—but they are fondly remembered (and are collector's items) because of their presentation. Gleeful horror-synth music, murky but atmospheric sound effects, colorful enemies, spookhouse-painting backgrounds, and over-the-top gore and slime effects. Hit a mutant with a 2x4? Watch it splatter against the background. Fighting giant bloody aborted fetuses? Here's a chainsaw. It's the atmosphere, art direction, and a sense that the developers want you to have exploitative-horror-movie *fun* that draw you in and keep you playing.

Likewise, *Blood* (1997) for the PC achieves the same effect through the use of spooky settings like mausoleums, a crematorium, a runaway train, and haunted houses while throwing foes like cultists, gargoyles, hounds of hell, and of course re-animating zombies (set them on fire or blow off their heads to be sure they stay down) at the player. Your starting weapon is a pitchfork of all things, and you begin the game by emerging from your grave.

These games—along with the original *Alone in the Dark*, *Doom*, and *Resident Evil*—really capture the carnival ride *fun* that horror is capable of. You get the sense that you're breaking the rules, that you're seeing what's not meant to be seen. This story is my tribute to those titles.

# A LUMP AND HIS BOY

## BY RICHARD WOLLEY

Andrew Drexler caught me on the playground again, and fighting back didn't help.

Instead of only feeling his warm spit, which he dangled above my face, I also got to taste my own blood. It ran down slowly from my nose. I tried to squirm free from being pinned under him. That just ended in him pushing his bony knee into my chest and punching me in the nose. My eyes teared up with the one quick jab and I never saw when the wad of saliva hit my cheek.

I ran to the mountains near my house after that and hid in the sage brush until it was safe.

When the coast was clear I walked home. The neighbors didn't see me, or avoided making eye contact as the blood crusted on my face.

When I got home, I detached the safety-pinned key from my pocket and opened the door. My fingers fumbled to turn on the lights as I made my way to the partially finished basement bathroom. All of the bodily fluids washed off and away down the drain. But not the shame.

I caught my own gaze in the mirror on the way out. It reminded me how everyone stared and did nothing. I broke eye contact with my disappointed reflection, and I imagined it shook its head as I left it in the basement.

When I got upstairs, a brief note was left on the bare kitchen counter.

*Got asked to do a double tonight don't wait up. Love you Ethan, Mom XOXO*

The first thing I did to cheer myself up was to play The Clash's *London Calling* on my cassette player. "The Right Profile" was just running into "Lost in The Supermarket." Thankfully, the music filled up the empty spaces of the house.

I had traded my cousin four shiny Marvel flair trading cards and a purple-clothed Granny Gross Ghost action figure from the *Real Ghostbusters* cartoon for the cassette, but I wasn't sure if it was a fair trade, so I stole a *Spawn* and *Spider-Man* from him, just to be sure.

I poked holes in a Mexican TV dinner and popped it into the microwave. I danced around to "Death or Glory" as I waited to peel back the plastic on one of my favorite meals. The whirring spin of the microwave ended with a ding, and I rushed over to my meal. I passed the plastic tray between my fingers to keep them from burning. The plastic film came off and I felt the warmth of the steam on my face. I bounced around, waiting for the two tamales, enchilada, Spanish rice, and refried beans to cool. Then I sucked them down right at the counter.

I had lost my lunch tickets earlier in the week and had

gone without lunch at school since. I didn't want Mom to be mad or have to worry that I had misplaced them again.

I let the cassette roll to a finish. When it did, I needed to fill the silence again before it got to me.

I spread out the green-and-white-lined paper Mom had gotten from a temp job across the coffee table. I put a copy of *Predator*, recorded from cable, in the VHS player. I copied images from a *Nintendo Power* onto the lined paper, and drew level designs for a platform game while the choppers started and the monster began his hunt in the background.

I really wished I had a video game system to play. I begged Mom but she just said they were too expensive. I used to play whenever I went over to my cousins', but we hadn't been over to my uncle's house for a while for some reason. I missed them. They were my only friends.

Instead of actually playing, I dreamed of the games as I put them down on paper.

The hours passed and I paused my drawing to watch Dutch face the beast. When it ended I was filled with dissatisfaction. I wanted the creature to take his skull this time. Just once. I wish I had those claws next time I saw Andrew Drexler. I'd gut him.

I went back to my drawings before the alien's self-destruct bomb went off, and tried to draw my own version of that creature from the jungles. I could picture in my head how I wanted it to come out, but it never worked that way. It mostly came out looking like some kind of cartoony blob with sharp claws. Kind of like if Kirby had mated with the Predator, then was covered in wax, hiding its best features. But the eyes were evil and pointy. I liked that.

The VHS rolled from *Predator* into various cartoons and

then the Ewok movie. I stopped drawing and watched.

My eyes grew heavy.

When I woke up, I was in my own bed.

I got out of the covers and snuck to the door of Mom's room. She had passed out in her work clothes on top of the blankets. She must have carried me into bed. I woke because I needed to pee. I almost wet the bed again, but this time made it to the bathroom, and since I was up a little more cartoons couldn't hurt. Maybe, if I was lucky, there would be scrambled bits of naked ladies on the channels we didn't quite get. So I snuck into the family room and turned the volume knob of the TV all the way to nothing. The glowing images bounced off the walls as I put on more cartoons. I turned the volume up ever so slightly. Mom would get way too mad if she caught me again.

The glare intensified, until I realized it wasn't coming from the television. My gaze darted over to the window. A green glow emanated through the curtains.

I snuck out to investigate.

I inched the door carefully shut, so I didn't wake Mom. I had already snuck in to watch cartoons, and I knew sneaking outside was much worse. When the door was finally closed, I turned my focus back to the green light glowing just above the driveway.

It was too bright to look at directly, but somehow didn't light up the whole neighborhood. It only shined one direction—toward me. I squinted, still trying to see what it was. Its brightness forced my eyes back shut, but continued to burn into my closed eyelids. The little I could make out, it was almost like there was a rip in the dark sky. It made a gargling noise, and sounded as if something was throwing up. I thought I saw teeth surrounding the opening like a great mouth, but I just couldn't quite make it out.

Then it was gone.

Cautiously, I crept out onto the lawn. The cold morning dew swept across my bare feet, until they hit something warm and rubbery. I squinted to see what was in the tall grass that needed to be mowed. Something was there—pale, white.

Moving.

While I stood over it, a piece of it raised and lowered in rapid succession. The movement seemed to omit almost a whimper. I couldn't tell you why, considering it was just a blob of goo, but something about it seemed wounded. Helpless. Like I'd stumbled upon a baby kitten too young to be away from its mother. I couldn't just leave it defenseless.

I reached down slowly to the smooth and featureless form to see if it would respond to being pet.

It scurried backwards, just beyond my reach.

"Don't worry. I'm a friend." I bent down and it inched closer. "Come on." It came closer, then rolled or crawled or whatever it was doing into my hands. It hadn't hurt me, so I lifted it up. What could it be? It was no bigger than a mostly deflated basketball.

Whatever it was, it needed some help.

I stepped into the garage, quicker than I should have, and the side door slammed behind me.

Mom would probably hear that. I looked around, but couldn't see a good place to hide the lump.

I whispered to it, "Trust me," because it had seemed to respond to words before and shoved it down the back of my pants. Right on cue, Mom was fuming in the doorway.

"Ethan, what're you doing out here?" Her voice was scratchy with sleep.

"I thought I heard a cat out here," I said.

"Buddy, really? It's four a.m. Get inside! I need to get a good night's sleep for work tomorrow."

"Sorry. I'll come inside shortly." I said.

"Now!" She pointed to the door behind her. I knew to not press it and waddled past her, through the front door, and back to my room. She followed and watched me lay down in bed, then shut the door behind her as she stomped off to her room.

The lump moved up the small of my back, out from my pants, and crawled under the covers. I tensed up as it moved towards my face.

It nuzzled beneath my chin, then continued to move up. I noticed it could change its shape as it wormed its way around my jawbone. It snuggled against the side of my face—it was like having a hot pad that thought it was a puppy on my skin. I nuzzled back into it.

"Maybe we can be friends," I whispered to the small lump. Its warm touch and slight vibrations—was it breathing?—lulled me to sleep.

When I woke up it was Saturday. Mom had picked up another shift, a double, and was already gone. That meant I had the whole day to myself to play with the lump, and I wouldn't have to deal with anyone.

It wasn't in the bed, so I checked underneath.

I searched the closet, the dresser, under the sink, and even in the toilet. Nothing. After an hour of looking, I just about lost hope and plopped down on the couch.

That's when I saw it, hunkered down behind the entertainment center, back in the corner.

"What're you doing back there?" I said, and approached it. Its shiny pale skin had a slightly blue hue, and its top bubbled up unevenly. "Oh no, are you sick, what's wrong?"

It sat there in the shadows, shifting back and forth, the blue color spreading and receding along its surface.

"Are you… hungry?"

I grabbed the first thing I could find to feed it, which was some candy from a jar on a side table. I had no idea if it even *ate*, but it was worth a try.

First, I tried feeding it one of the fruit punch-flavored hard candies, because they were my favorite. I held out the candy, then gently pressed it into his surface. Lump's smooth body absorbed it, and it disappeared. Nothing happened. Then, I tried a black licorice-flavored piece because it was my least favorite. The lump still didn't react. So, I just dumped the whole jar on him.

When all the candy was gone, his skin began to… boil, or ripple, or something. Several pore-like orifices opened, and he spit out a thick, chunky substance. That seemed to drain him more.

"Gross! You got it all over." The goo-pile spread across the carpet toward my knees. "Mom's going to be so pissed!" It smelled like a mixture of the sewage plant south of town, and the time a tenant had left a dead cat in one of my uncle's rental properties for who-knows-how-long.

The lump quivered and turned a darker shade of blue.

The movement of its body almost made a whimpering noise. It slithered over to me, I bent down to it, and went to pet it. This time, a slimy appendage shot out toward my finger, drawing blood.

"Ow!" I pulled back, and looked at the small amount of blood that ran down my finger. "I get it. You need *real* food."

I rushed to the kitchen, and brought back bread. Lump only turned a darker shade of blue the more it absorbed. It started to whimper, and I grew desperate. I dug through the freezer and decided to microwave some chicken nuggets. After I fed him the first piece, the blue color began to fade. As I fed him the rest, his pale color returned, and he didn't try and bite me again.

Meat! Of course. So, I heated up six more and it ate that batch.

Lump's mood was much better. It bounced up and down around me, stretching and jumping, then bouncing off the carpet like a rubber ball. It made a noise—I'm pretty sure it was a happy noise—like a dog barking into a shredded plastic bag larynx.

"I get it, I get it! You want more."

So, I moved onto the fish sticks. After that, when I pulled out the bag of all the raw chicken breasts. Lump leapt up and ripped the bag, spilling the frozen chicken to the floor. It rolled over them, one by one, and gobbled up the uncooked pieces. I fed it hamburger, pork chops, deli meat, and broke eggs over its body. Lump absorbed everything.

I didn't notice in my frenzy, but it stood about two and half feet tall when I ran out of meat.

"You look like you're doing better, Lump. You're bigger. That's neat-o!" Lump rubbed up against my leg in appreciation. I felt like I had made a new buddy. "What do you want to do now?" I led it in to the family room. "Do you want to see my drawing?" I held the doodle of the Predator up.

Lump began to vibrate and contort. It shrunk down... and started to become what I had drawn. It bubbled and its surface rotated hues, but soon, unmistakably, it became the lumpy, goofy creature I had drawn. Even the cartoony, uneven limbs had been replicated. It mostly looked silly, and flopped unevenly as it stalked around on its stumpy legs.

I smiled and wrapped my arms around Lump. It leaned back in to me as I hugged it. It really did understand me. Too bad I couldn't draw better.

"What now buddy? Should we watch some cartoons? You know what, I bet you'd love *Predator*." It either didn't understand or it ignored me, because it slithered out of my arms down to the floor, then began to walk towards the door. It seemed as if it were looking for something. "Well, I am really not supposed to go outside, but Mom won't be home for hours. Just remind me, I need to clean up your vomit when we get back."

I opened the door and stepped out. Lump followed just behind my legs. We walked down the sidewalk. Lump kept bumping into the back of my legs, staying close. When we turned the block, Mrs. Peters was watering her plants.

"Hi Ethan. Sure is a nice day." She was our only nice neighbor. I waved hello and smiled. "Your little... friend sure looks... strange." She squinted. Good thing she wasn't wearing her glasses.

"Sure does!" I said. "Bye, Mrs. Peters." I rushed off, so she couldn't get a better look.

*I better head up towards the mountains* I thought. *Less people to see my strange friend.*

We turned the corner and walked fast, up the half block to the hills to where the pavement ended and the brush began.

"Let's go!" I pushed through the prickly bushes growing over the rail-thin dirt trail between the sage brush, and Lump followed.

I could taste the dust in the air as we moved quickly through the underbrush. We came to the juniper trees that sat at the base of the foothills that rose up to join the mountains beyond. Just a few steps into the line of junipers, I stopped in my tracks. A white tail deer stood not more than ten feet away.

While it wasn't uncommon to see deer in these parts, it was still neat to see them so up close. They were normally very skittish. It took quiet steps slowly across the path. I stopped completely and sat down slowly so as not to spook it. I turned back to make sure Lump understood, but he was gone. I turned back towards the deer. It lifted its head, and looked right at me with its alert black eyes.

Its head snapped to the left, but was too late to react.

Lump shot out from the bushes, then propelled through the deer's rib cage, its insides and bones bursting in an instant.

I stood back up and watched in frozen shock, mouth agape, shaking whenever I heard a grinding snap of bones or a high-pitched squeal. The deer tottered to the ground while Lump roiled around inside. The animal's body began to pull into itself as Lump absorbed it from the inside.

The deer appeared to thrash, but that was just Lump

furiously devouring it from within. Soon Lump's white-grey mass overtook the creature, absorbing every piece of it—the hindquarters, the neck, the head. The front hooves were the last to disappear.

Lump was much, much larger now. It was far bulkier than I was, but still moved and gliding across the ground as if it weighed nothing. He rolled forward, raising up, looming over me.

"Woah!" I said, finally breaking the silence, "I guess you're still hungry, huh buddy?" I reached to pat its head—or, rather, the top of its body—but held back, worrying for a second that I would get sucked inside if I made contact. But Lump lowered itself to me, letting me pass my hand over its smooth surface.

It began to re-shape itself back into the Predator, growing arms and legs, a torso, a well-defined, monstrous head and face. But all of its features were sharper now, with greater detail, becoming less what my drawing looked like, and more what the creature was meant to be. Lump looked meaner now, as if built for hunting, and its legs were even and muscular, losing their awkward fumbling. Its eyes were still like my drawing, however—sharp and angular. Lump was taller than me now, but not quite as tall as the movie Predator. It turned and stalked off into the brush.

"Where you going?" I stepped forward to follow him. He had already disappeared into forest.

"Where do you think *you're* going, you little turd?"

I was just three steps heading into the brush after my not-so-little friend, when I turned to see Andrew Drexler standing at the edge of the bend on the path we had taken into the foothills.

"I think I remember you trying to fight back yesterday. Too bad you're too scrawny to do much." He cocked his head to the side, and looked me over. Sizing me up.

He took a step forward.

"Yeah, so?" I tried to sound tough, but I knew it didn't work.

He took another step forward.

"When did little wussy Ethan suddenly get a spine?" Drexler grinned.

He took one more step.

"When I realized you aren't *shit*." I swallowed down what was in my throat. Something else bubbled up in me that I hadn't been able to muster before—I couldn't feel the shame I had felt the other day, or every day. Not again. To prove that to myself, I decided to seal the deal.

"I know your mom left your loser dad."

With his next step forward, I could feel his breath on my face.

"You better shut up," he growled

"It's not his fault she left, it was yours." This came out of my mouth without hesitation, but also before I properly formed it in my head. I knew it was mean, too mean. I braced myself, but not soon enough. His fist connected with my nose, sending me sprawling back. Pain spread though the bridge of my nose, back through my eyes, and left me momentarily stunned. I stumbled back but caught myself, then tried to shake the pain from my face and get my eyes open.

"Is that it?" I shouted, faking tough. I could taste the blood on my lips and running down the back of my throat. "Nobody cares about you." He grabbed me, and threw me down into the dirt.

When I hit, I felt the impact, but no pain. I tensed up. Nothing.

I opened my eyes.

Drexler stood above me, wide-eyed, looking over my head.

I half stood up, and immediately felt woozy. Something warm and wet poured down the back of my neck. I put my hand up to it when I felt it start to run down my face. I saw the red on my fingers and still couldn't figure out what was wrong.

My vision quickly was surrounded by black, and everything was gone. It wasn't like when you go to sleep. It was as if my consciousness had been completely deleted. Removed from existence.

I don't know how long I was gone. A couple of seconds, a couple of hours—it didn't make a difference. I was nothing.

But then—pain. I came back with a jolt. I jumped up, becoming aware of my own body again. Rubbery tendrils of liquid filled my mouth, nose, and my throat. Then they withdrew, and the air rushed back to my lungs. I gasped as they started pumping oxygen once again.

I struggled to open my eyes. The forest, the foothills, the mountains beyond. A rock was behind me, where my head must have fallen, had bits of hair, blood, small fragments of bone, as well as something pink and chunky across it. I reached back and ran my fingers across my head. No wounds—just some missing hair. And… scar tissue.

Ahead of me, more blood. But it wasn't mine.

The dirt path was now a crimson mud hole. Intestines hung in the juniper trees like garland strung on a Christmas tree. The smell was overpowering—metallic, but with a hint of sewage. The same smell of Lump's vomit on the living room carpet when I tried to feed him the candy.

Lump stood at the center of the muddy recess, crouched low over Andrew's mangled body. He wasn't absorbing anymore... he was feeding, with a mouth, with teeth.

"Did you... did you save me? Did you... kill him?"

Lump shifted colors and form, no longer like the Predator—just the humanoid outline of it, but hunched now, closer to the ground, its legs snapped back like a dog's—or a velociraptor's, like in *Jurassic Park*. But its arms were still muscular, its fingers claws grasping at Andrew's remains. The alien's face and head had given way to something more like a crocodile, his mouth full of teeth that stood in that sliced and snapped through flesh and bone alike. Lump was becoming more its own creation. One of its own choosing.

It turned its long snout toward me, and Andrew's meaty leg. It nudged me forward, then pushed past me, further up the trail. Lump seemed to know where he was going. He wanted me to follow.

We climbed over the ridge, then followed a gulley back down the other side of the hill. At the bottom, we walked along a chain link fence that ran along the abandoned train yard, until we came to the large drain pipe that ran under the tracks.

"Are we going on a sewer adventure!?" I tried to lighten the mood, but Lump didn't slow down. It kept heading to the large drain tunnel with a singular purpose. The tunnel led into the sewers. All the kids dared each other to go inside and explore, only ever making it so far until we lost our nerve and would end up running back out.

At first, I didn't see anything. I smelled it. It smelled like urine and boxed wine. It was the movement I noticed. He almost blended in with the walls of the sewer because he was all hair and shabby clothes, greying and falling apart. It was a hobo.

Lump had sensed him, and didn't hesitate. Before the bum could react, he ripped open his rib cage in one swift crack with its long, outstretched arms, like it was the lid to leftovers. The bum couldn't even scream—Lump slurped up his insides like day-old spaghetti. It was dark in the tunnel, but I wanted to see the old man's eyes. I watched the life go out of them.

When he died, it was like he wasn't even a real person anymore.

Lump sucked in anything alive we came across. Rats, cats, and anything else I didn't have time a good look at. I did notice Lump would pick and choose. Some things, he would devour completely, chomp-chomp-chomp. Others, he would shred and eat certain parts. It was like he was looking for something specific.

Most things didn't have time to scream.

Sure, it was gross, but it was kind of neat, too. With each one it had gotten easier. It helped if I got to see their eyes.

Plus, it was for Lump. I didn't know why he was doing what he was doing, but I didn't need to. I'm sure he had a good reason. I would do anything for my buddy.

After a while, I started to get worried. It had been several hours since we had started, and it was getting late. We'd spent hours combing through the forest together, coming upon squirrels mostly, a few deer. Joggers, bikers. People I didn't recognize, which made it easier.

As the sun began to set, we came down through the foothills and took the last bend to home. My legs were tired from trying to keep up with Lump. He was fast—faster than anything that tried to run, anyway. But he always made sure to let me keep pace when he wasn't moving in for the kill.

As we returned to the sidewalk and headed towards home, Lump veered from our direct course, and made a beeline for Mrs. Peters' open garage.

"Where are you going?"

Lump paused and lowered his body as if he was about to pounce on some unsuspecting prey. I rushed over, and grabbed its slippery mass. "You can't do this! That's Mrs. Peters. She isn't like the others."

An appendage grew out of its back, grabbing my shirt and throwing me head over feet into the shadow-filled garage ahead. Then he positioned himself over my chest, his gaping maw hanging open over me, growling his disapproval. It reminded me of one of the times my uncle was angry and drunk. He pinned me against the refrigerator of a rental property once. It hurt my arm then. I told Mom I'd fallen. She found out the truth eventually, or figured it out. Maybe that's why we stopped visiting.

"Ow." He started to press one of his arms down across my chest, until I squealed in pain.

"What's going on?" Mrs. Peters stood in the door to the garage, the light from the house outlining her form. "Ethan? Are you all right, honey? Who's with you there?" She found the light switch and the shadows fled.

Lump was on her in a flash of teeth and blood. He reached an arm out to grab her by the throat. Blood poured from her wrist, as her hand dangled by a thin strand of flesh. She gasped a frightened noise that failed to become a scream.

Lump carried her back through the door. Geyers of blood erupted across her immaculately clean kitchen and shot back out the doorway.

Mrs. Peters was a *person*. She was not a bum, or rotten Andrew Drexler, or strangers on the trail. This felt very different.

Bad, almost. But… maybe not so bad.

When it was over, Lump trailed through her sticky remnants and out of the house. I sat back up, and followed. He probably had his reasons, just like my uncle had.

I followed Lump back out through her yard, down to the sidewalk. He stomped off ahead, leading me back home.

He pointed his snout to the door, then waved me forward with one of his clawed-hands.

I opened the door, and he slid inside, quiet as can be.

Mom isn't home yet. Maybe I hope she never comes back. I think she is what Lump is waiting for.

But what can I do?

He's my only friend.

## AUTHOR'S NOTE

"Friendship is magic," was all I was going to write, but then I decided, what the heck.

The story idea came from *A Boy and His Blob: Adventures in Blobolonia*, and tonally has a lot in common with those creature-feature friendship movies of the eighties (e.g. *Gremlins, ET, Munchie, Batteries Not Included*, etc.). Except their sweet friendship is based on serial killers who kill in pairs (e.g. Henry Lee Lucas and Ottis Toole, Lake and Ng, Bittaker and Norris, etc.)

Anyway, Ethan is supposed to be the beta partner of the two, so desperate for connection. I based the day-to-day stuff vaguely on how I grew up with a single mom, then added more on top to make Ethan his own character. Forming a bond with someone is a basic human desire, and normally a good one. It's macabrely fascinating when it isn't though.

# I'M A GOOD PERSON, I MEAN WELL, AND I DESERVE BETTER
## BY J.R. HAMANTASCHEN

**R**obin looked nice tonight. She was dressed in an effervescent dress that, while not tight-fitting, at least acknowledged the appeal of her petite form and hearty bust. She had applied a little bit of makeup and eyeshadow, too.

Bryce preferred the *au naturale* look, but the eyeshadow gave her a hint of an edge, a little sass. She had pretty eyes, and the eyeshadow feminized her, tilted the appeal of her androgynous vulpine beauty back firmly to the feminine side of things. Her hair was done the usual way, pinned-up in the back, which he liked. He liked the crook in her nose, the nose that most girls (her included) probably grew up feeling ashamed and insecure about. An asshole could say it looked a bit like there was an extra bone there in place of where the cartilage should be. But everything about her was decisively cute, and her nose was that kind of charming imperfection that, in their brief foray into dating, he'd firmly identified her with and maybe even fetishized a little bit.

She wore rouge lipstick, noticeable but understated. Red was the color of lust, he'd read in an article, and that bode well of her interest, he thought. That, and that she agreed to a fourth date with him, this time an unabashed date, a full meal and everything.

But he tried not to get too ahead of himself. That was emotionally dangerous. His mind was always analyzing the odds. Rouge and a dinner date. Good signs. But this was an unusually early dinner, 6:15 p.m., more befitting of the senior citizen early birds than a couple in their mid-thirties. And they were the earliest of the early birds—there were literally no other guests, and they'd arrived at the weird liminal phase where the wait staff were still setting up a bit and were resentful that you cut down their time to prepare. But maybe he shouldn't read too much into the time, maybe she just liked eating early—hell, he liked eating early—but his mind refused to turn off, always the dating thresher, churning in input and spitting out conclusions.

He met her there, which was always a smart bet. Don't want to waste needed conversation talking points on the pre-dinner repartee. That's time you can't control—imagine having to wait for a table for an hour and spending all that awkward, uncomfortable, impatient time together.

So he was already there when she arrived, sitting at the table. When she arrived, he bounded up and pulled her chair back for her. It was simultaneously genuine yet ironic, which was a fairly good description of how they both had separately represented themselves on their *Kettle of Fish* pages.

"Ahhh, what a gentleman," she said with a smile, ironic

in her use of "gentleman" and what a hoary cliché pulling out a lady's chair was, but genuine in appreciating his interest and his effort, at least, to impress. "Pulling out all the stops, are we? Watch out!"

"Ha, you know it."

They made small talk for a bit and he pointed out the drinks menu. She perused it and he didn't say much. Let her read it, he thought, but that was displacement. He just didn't know what to say. That was one of his bigger fears: not saying enough. He felt he was an interesting person, but too often all that interesting stuff was buzzing around in his mind and he didn't let it out. Dating and sharing and intimacy didn't come naturally to him; he didn't feel comfortable with it until he knew he wasn't being judged, that he was loved and appreciated. In a sense, he put the cart before the horse: he needed the adulation, and then he felt comfortable with sharing intimacy; that women expected sharing, intimacy, and the connection before the adulation was a fatal expectation of his emotional sequencing.

"Did you know"—oh boy, goddamn the man who begins a conversation with "Did you know?" or "Know what's interesting?"—"that the word 'Jeep' comes from the abbreviation used in the Army for the General Purpose vehicle, G.P." She worked as an analyst for a car company. "Yup, you can take that fact into the boardroom."

"Promotion, here I come!"

"Ha, yep. Thank the internet and a slow day of work."

He had to be careful. Dead air tended to turn him into an Interesting Fact Generator. Could be good for a cocktail party, but no girl wanted to fuck the human embodiment of Wikipedia.

"Well," she drawled. "Let me one-up you."

"Okay, okay, I'm game, let's hear it."

"So, you know what the 'Q' in Q-tip stands for?"

"Nope."

"Quality," she said, throwing up her hands like a rap baller.

"Well, look at that."

The drinks came and—this was pivotal—after she went in for her first sip and they cheers-ed, she smiled from her drink at him in a way that froze his insides and made his heart stop. Inadvertently—it apparently not being enough that she agreed to a fourth date—he'd subconsciously been dedicating mental processing power to monitor all the signs she was into him. Hair teasing, forthcoming laughter, steady eye contact: running the metrics behind his eyes like an undercover economist. But he needn't worry. That look sealed the deal. It was a look of joy, of the pure sensual pleasure of enjoying another's company and being open to the electricity of good companionship. It relieved him and unnerved him. He wished he could change his reductive thinking—she was a human being, a *great* human being, for God's sake, he should stop with these objectifying comparisons—but all he could think about was that he was a dog who finally catches the car and doesn't know what to do with it.

He wanted to tell her that he really liked her, and that he wanted to save this moment in time in case something went wrong later in the date, so he could backtrack to this moment and start again. Like the beginning of a stage in a videogame and he'd stocked up infinite lives. Of course, if he said that, he'd fuck everything up, and, accepting the logic of his own premise, would have to jump back in time to right before he said those words.

He sipped his cocktail—gin and bitters and lime and sugar and a fancy name that added $5 to the price—and he liked it, but that didn't even register because he was acting like drinking was something that just got in the way of talking.

"Know what else is interesting?" he said, kicking himself mentally for it—he hadn't even swallowed fully before he started.

"No, tell me," she said, and he detected a less-enthusiastic reception than before.

"Well, I don't want to just spout out interesting facts, but bear with me, this one is interesting."

"Raising the stakes. You better deliver." She leaned in in such a way that the menu pressed against her dress to make a steeple of cleavage. He never averted his gaze from her eyes. It was just a lovely detail he noticed in his periphery.

"Well, do you know that they never toast in Hungary?"

"No."

"Well, and I don't know if this is true, but it's what I've been told—"

"Duly noted. 'Told,' you mean on the streets?"

"Yes, of course, the streets, the streets are always talking about Hungary." He was performing that weird obligation to generate witty repartee, and he found it a little bit annoying and disruptive when she joined in. This was a solo act. He was doing his best to even remember the factoid, which was hazy and half-remembered. Was it that they only didn't toast over beer? Eh.

"Well, after the Hungarian revolution against the

Hapsburg Empire in like, the 1850s, the Austrian army leaders executed the Hungarian generals, and they celebrated it with a toast. So, from then on, Hungarians never toast when they drink beer."

"Interesting, interesting." She made a face that registered her appreciation, like she was storing the information. "What was the Hapsburg Revolution?"

He sipped and shrugged. "I don't know. If they want me to know, they need to tie it in with some beer or food-related fact or something."

"Obviously," she smiled.

The performance ritual of repartee was draining his mental battery. It's interesting, how things are considered mildly unpleasant, and then something comes along to drop the end out from under you and make things so much worse. Here he was, juggling being charming with a mild headache; his mild self-hatred of his dating game-playing and his wavering about whether dating as an activity was even worth the effort; his desire just to declare his affections for her and move onto the next steps; and all the other tests to his endurance, when... the bottom fell out.

The mysteries of the human body. There's a nesting fullness you feel when you need to move your bowels, but that's usually the key—fullness. A fullness, like a shifting tractor trailer. There's weight there. Not this. This was a water hammer in a sewer pipe. This was a 7th grade Earth Science lecture on potential kinetic energy. This was his asshole puckering up with flop sweat in the midst of turning into a swamp. This was the type of shit you fooled yourself into thinking you could control with the proper positions you assumed and the seasoned contortions of your asshole, but in reality you knew it was going to come out hot and burning and for a second you'd think, *Jesus, what have I been doing with my life?*

His stomach gurgled. He kicked himself for his early-, mid-, and late-morning coffees, for those unneeded shots of vanilla-hazelnut-flavored chemicals he'd added to them. The sour sludge inside him turned his hunger off like a light switch. There's that pyramid of needs. Hunger, water—those are on there at the bottom, the base of the pyramid. Young guys will act like sex is there as well. Look lower down, in the footnotes section. There's a caveat:

"The need to shit rules out all other needs."

He yearned to return to the gentle patter of conversation he'd established. Like an old man on his death bed, how foolish he was for not realizing how good he'd had it not so long ago.

He was a strategic man by nature. Especially where something important was concerned—a job, school, a significant other—he had the tendency to break down every action into a play-by-play like a coked-out John Madden, until it was usually just him alone and a trusted friend hashing out and debating what exactly happened, long after the opportunity came, went, or passed and everyone else had moved on.

One of his long-standing life hacks: never go to the restroom before you order food. This didn't just apply to dates. It's inefficient, and the other party will be impatiently waiting for you to return and be doubly attentive to the passage of time.

He resumed saying something, under the quixotic delusion that he could flag down a waiter and put in a food order before he had to take the bathroom out of commission.

Nope, there'd be none of that.

"I'll be right back," a line which, if their relationship survived some length of time, was destined to become an inside-joke euphemism.

He retired to the restroom before they even had gotten dinner menus. *Before they had even gotten dinner menus!* He thought of that word, *retired*, and it seemed apt, because after this he'd have to take a nap and perhaps retire from ever showing his face in public again.

He navigated his way to the restroom, a couple members of the staff intuiting the urgency just beneath the placid mask of his face and pointing him in the right direction

*Le Latrines*, the sign on the door read, complying with that unwritten rule that every restaurant above a sufficient level of hipness was required to have some whimsical name for the place where people pissed, shat, farted, ralphed, put on makeup, and maybe did coke.

He twisted the knob on the door and it didn't turn. Oh god. Oh god. Occupied. And it's only one stall.

One stall, for every man, woman, and child. Providing one unisex stall should be a crime against restaurant design. Under almost all circumstances, he wouldn't have the guts to shit in a unisex stall, only allowing himself to pee and maybe later squeak out silent farts at the dinner table if the pressure got too bad. He could just never bring himself to defecate where there's only one unisex stall; the pressure was just too much for him. He'd immediately imagine a line of innocent, angelic American Apparel models lining up right outside.

He remembered his own traumatic experience at a

Barnes & Noble many years ago. Barnes & Noble must have known that every customer secretly resented it for some reason or another, and tried to appease them by providing a separate bathroom for men and women. But not the Barnes & Noble he'd ventured into. No, not *that* Barnes & Noble. This must have been a closing Barnes & Noble, where management said "Fuck it, we'll show these ingrates, make it a unisex bathroom."

He'd never forget the look on that beautiful woman's face after he came out of that bathroom—her pixie-ish short dirty blonde hair, her button nose, her button-up shirt that looks so cute on girls of her type, her angular cheeks, flush with blush; the one stud of a nose ring, that little indication that in other circumstances she'd be cool and understanding and open-minded—and that unconscious twitching of her nose, that look of dread and embarrassment and shame that registered knowing that this filthy creature in front of her had just befouled the space she was entering, a creature of honeyed charms and fairy dust entering a labyrinth of emanations bespeaking pestilence and contamination.

He twisted the knob before him, again, and... it opened, albeit slowly, with another person opening the door on the other side. She was trying to twist the door open from the other side at the same time and they'd been working at cross purposes.

"Sorry about that," he nodded and slid past her.

"My bad." She wore flannel and had deep black hair. Other than that, he couldn't see much of her, but she seemed nice and big-hearted.

He made his way in, and, lo and behold, he was wrong in his estimation. There were actually two bathroom stalls!

One with a ... what the fuck is this? There was this trend in restaurants to convey the crucial information of MAN or WOMAN through quirky signage. That may have made sense at certain themed bars; if you see a male pirate or a mermaid on the bathrooms at a seafood restaurant, well, that's pretty intuitive.

But here. One room labeled Mars, with the Mars symbol—a circle with an arrow pointing northeast in red—and another door labeled Venus, with the Venus symbol—a circle with a cross below it—in light blue.

God, he had to be a fucking astrologist here. Which was which? What other purpose is there of signage than to be clear and direct? Literally, the point is to convey a message clearly. That's why a STOP sign reads "STOP," instead of representing a cleverly illustrated parable of a before, present, and after situation.

Venus rhymes with penis? Could that be it? No, he felt that the jutting arrow was a proxy for the penis, and even if that was wrong, society still felt comfortable gendering colors, and light blue usually denoted the feminine.

He tried Mars, and it opened.

His asshole almost gasped in release upon entry. There was an undeniable rush, a dampening of the back of his underwear. Why? Did his body just think that when the button comes undone and the pants come out, it can just spray shit everywhere like a fire hydrant? Mind over matter, mind over matter. His bowels protested with each second, and in the anticipation of impending release was an unspoken euphoria and satisfaction that society dare not name.

Alexander, he decided. He would call himself Alexander. It made him feel smart and cultured, and tales of conquest and adventure were the only things he ever enjoyed about high school. Alexander the Great had conquered, like, the entire known world at the time. Just went on in and rolled all over people. That would be his inspiration.

He took long, reflective pauses as he walked the several miles to the Deer & Fox, as befitting a conqueror debating his options. He put his fingers to his chin, softly stroking a beard that was not there, just staring off into the distance. One second, five seconds, or thirty seconds: it made no difference, he wasn't actually thinking anything. Just assuming the position.

He crested the hill overlooking his destination. Alexander, formerly Steven Acevedo—the unloved, overworked, and underappreciated former line cook at the Deer & Fox—prepared to stride into battle. Let the history books forget how he arrived this day, the undignified means of last resort: literally walking several miles along the shoulder of Route 6. Let the royal decrees leave that out: Steven's broke ass seeking his revenge on foot, all those cars full of spoiled housewives giving him dirty looks because walking in suburbia is for poor people and because God forbid this town have a working bus system.

Steven's car had been out of commission for over two months now. His car troubles were a source of inexhaustible amusement to the rest of the staff.

"Is his car back on the road yet?" someone in the kitchen

would ask, as if he wasn't right there.

"Close," someone would reply. "It's in the driveway." Even the people who didn't speak English would join in. It was a joke to everyone, from the manager—who is supposed to be fair and impartial, who is supposed to be putting a stop to that sort of harassment; and maybe if you fucking paid me a little more I'd have the car on the road and be able to make it on time—to the pretty hostesses, to the others in the kitchen who were supposed to be his family.

He'd laugh off the jokes at first and tease back, but he wasn't good at it; he was too transparent, it was obvious how much it burned him up. He'd liked working as a cook, he read books about the industry; there was supposed to be a sense of camaraderie between all the staff. And he'd been there longer than most (granted: there was a high turnover), but there didn't seem to be enough deference; a couple of people teased him and all the new guys thought it became the thing to do, the bypass for bonding.

And then, to think, all the people he'd bum rides from quit or leave town in a matter of weeks, and he has no way to get to work on time other than the impossible, terrible bus system, and he's late enough times and he's fired, just like that. All those motherfuckers still talking about him, no doubt. He doesn't have anything: no education, no family, no nothing, except that job. And where were they? They were supposed to be family, right? They sweat together, hustled together, bled and burned their skins together.

And he was good at it, goddammit. As much as everything about it sucked, he loved that place.

He looked down at hands outstretched before him and watched the forms take shape. He had what appeared to be an undulating baseball poking out just beneath his skin, cresting and falling like a lapping wave. He pivoted and flexed his sore right thumb. Black mist sprayed out with each flex. It reminded him of a cartoon choo-choo train belching smoke. It even made a faintly audible gusting sound, like a stuffed nose on a winter's day. He didn't know if he chose to make that noise, willed it, or if whatever was allowing him to do this had access to some remote memory of a cartoon choo-choo train and fashioned this to amuse him. He didn't care, really.

He'd woken up one day having already come to terms with it.

He'd been fired ten days ago, on a Friday. He'd spent the weekend getting drunk and feeling sorry for himself, cursing himself, cursing this place. Monday, he found himself instinctively waking up for his morning shift, as if he needed to be somewhere.

He looked in the mirror and saw one of those composite posters looking back at him. There are those posters, he didn't know how they were made or how to describe them, but those posters where one larger identifiable image was made up of several smaller images of the same person in different poses. Half the time, the subject of the poster was Bob Marley, for some reason. He didn't know why.

Well, that had been him one morning. Except the smaller images weren't him, but a shoulder comprised of egg-shaped black balls, beady eyes of succulent blueberries, a tornado of angular, writhing shapes for a torso. He had opened his mouth in surprise, convinced this was a dream but still playing along, and his tongue was an oversized squamous brick that somehow still fit fine in his mouth.

Tendrils of thick grain—cookie dough, he thought—pushed their way out from under his nails, flapping a bit like Spanish moss in a breeze. They extended down to the grubby floor of his basement apartment. When they reached the floor, they flowed back upward, unseen, through his fingers, burning a bit like fluid through an IV, traversing through canals in his arms he never knew he had, or never had before.

That morning, he'd made five strands of finger-dough rise up and vibrate like slithering snakes. The egg-shaped black balls underneath his shoulders bore no faces but he knew they were directing their attention to him. His nails painlessly burst open with appendages the color of cobalt, the shape of carrots, the texture of glass. Then they retracted and his old nails were there again.

The constituent parts of his new body had explained everything to him. They'd done that trick with his nails because they knew he'd think it was cool. It'd made him feel like Wolverine, bitches. *Snikt!*

Sometimes, dreams do come true.

He stared at the restaurant. Kind of pathetic, he thought, all this power for such an unworthy target. In movies, to show a character is good, mature, and above-it-all, the character will have the opportunity to take revenge and get his justice and then, nah, pass. Like, saying, you're beneath me.

Like anyone would do that. That's why those are movies, and this is real life.

Two pillars of crooked bone protruded up out of his shoulders, tapped three times—*click, click, click*—crossed each other like whirling scimitars, and popped back into place. That was cool, like he was a super soldier or something, a samurai.

He wanted an adjustment to his face, something to scare the shit out of people right before he killed them—wanted his mouth to spread out like the wings of a manta ray, little suckers and teeth embedded into his checks. But he couldn't will that, for some reason.

He went down on his knees like this was the culmination of a life-long quest, like he was nothing but a modest servant fulfilling the calling of a higher power, seeking to set order to a universe gone wrong.

His elbows shook and clicked and chattered like they were filled with rattling dice.

This was going to be great.

He forced himself to complete the task as quickly as possible. There wasn't even that dreadful couple of seconds of anticipation, when the bathroom door closes and the other occupants enjoy their last seconds of calm before the embarrassing multi-tonal timbre of horrific noises. Between the time he closed the stall and the time he started, someone listening in from outside could be excused for wondering if he'd even had time to take his pants off before the wholesale slaughter began.

There was a cacophony of embarrassing bathroom noses, which he always associated with the older men at work. These were bad enough that he wanted to ask his father about problems in the family. It sounded like an old man coughing up his soup.

Oh god, what relief.

He didn't even look in the toilet afterward. That was a first. Maybe that signaled something, growing up, step one into overcoming his weird phobia and this obsession of his. The movement had gone on for so long and with such intensity that he half-expected the contents to ascend vertically and carry him straight up to the ceiling, like Scrooge McDuck astride his overflowing lucre.

With his bowels released, he felt a dormant gurgle of hunger pangs, as if the body stored pre- and post-digested food in the same area. Pro tip to remember: whatever you do, do not, under any circumstances, come out of the bathroom and mention that you have just become hungry.

He made sure he was as clean as possible, which accounted for his excessive flushing. There were certain tips and tricks he lived by. One of them was a commitment to being a devoted over-flusher. He flushed so much whenever he used the bathroom that he worried that one day some environmentalist would overhear him and accuse him of wasting water ("Fuck off, go after someone who uses a humidifier," he would say, his riposte already prepared). Better to be safe than sorry: the only thing worse than having to be occupied in a toilet stall on a date is to be identified as the person responsible for clogging the toilet. He always flushed post-movement, and then after every 4-5 toilet paper deposits. He figured that should be common practice, though more often than not someone sharing the bathroom with him when he was washing his hands at the sink would give him a sideways glance, borne of curiosity, of this unassuming man who deemed it appropriate to flush 3-4 times. What horrors had taken place behind those closed doors, he imagined them thinking.

He could nod in agreement with his Green friends and "like" articles online about the need for conservation, but a small plot of virgin Amazonian rain forest was torn asunder for the exclusive use of his asshole.

*Oh my god.*

He felt the expected stimulus one expects while wiping. But there was a sensation that should not be. While parting his matted posterior hair, there was, enmeshed within and between, the tactile sensation of plowing through a nugget of hot mud.

*No, no it can't be.*

The human body could not allow this, no matter how hairy or overgrown he should be back there. Millions of years of human evolution should provide for, at the very least, the human body not providing its own hair hammock for feces.

*Oh my god.*

This date was over. It just had to be. How could he recover from this? And no matter how diligently he worked at cleaning himself, could he ever be sure? Any time she wrinkled her nose or smelled her entree, could he rest assured that she was not aware of the rancidity wafting between them? How many times would he need to check his feet to make sure no feces-encrusted toilet paper dangled from his shoes? Or—God—worse, that there were no smelly remnants on his clothing?

It wasn't fair. They were so aligned. It couldn't be, it's just not fair, that this was to befall him on this day, on this date, with this woman, who otherwise should be so perfect for him. He was a good person who tried; he was good-looking, 6'3", broad-shouldered, and well-groomed.

But this was unrecoverable. This was a dumpster fire. This was shitting the bed.

No, worse—shitting yourself.

Hoodie up over his head like a cloak, arms outstretched in the middle of the dining area. Alexander stood between tables; a server he didn't recognize leaned to the right carrying a jug of ice water. He intuited that she rolled her eyes as she made her away around him, made a vowel-less expression and a face reading "Some fucking people," that insta-face expression that servers made whenever they were briefly interrupted in their duties, that immediately dissipated as they continued their mad scramble dash that was the dinner-time rush.

"Sorry," he said meekly, instinctively cowered, and immediately regretted it.

"Everybody!" he bellowed. "Everybody," he called out again, this time pointing down at himself while he spoke, as if it wasn't clear where the focus of the attention should be. "Everybody. In our life and times, there comes a time when enough is enough. Where there's only so much you can take..."

"Ohmygod, ohmygod." He scrubbed at himself, that hopeless scrubbing you do when you get a fresh stain on a new white button-down and you know it won't work but just hope it does, this time. He even ran out and dotted toilet paper with sink water. He was, quite literally, rinsing his ass while out on a date.

The restaurant-goers looked at Alexander blankly. Some checked in for the beginning of his spiel, concluded it was something they wanted no part of, shook their heads and went back to their meals. *Crazy panhandlers in restaurants now?* Others kept their gaze, curious but hesitant. Other tables chatted excitedly about the upcoming, unexpected show.

"Only so much you can take. This place, this restaurant, it's treated me so badly. So, so... unjustly."

"Save it for Yelp!" a girl's voice rang out from the back.

Laughter.

"Quick, someone get that guy a refill," someone else shouted from the same vicinity. He continued.

"How much injustice, how much embarrassment, how much wrongness, is one person expected to take?"

"So what he's asking is—'who's coming with me?'" More laughter. He heard competing laughter and interpretations from the audience, some people repeating the line in a Jim Brewer space-cadet haze, others adopting the original version's pathetic, intense neediness.

"What justice is—"

He felt overheated and small—pathetic even in his moment of glory.

Bryce continued to clean himself off. He disentangled some small pebbles, shards of sharp crustified shit that reminded him of cleaning out specks of glass from a broken light bulb. Had there been times when he felt discomfort while sitting, thinking maybe he was sitting on his keys, when in reality it was the gravel-like friction of accumulated shit debris? Could such a thing be possible? Could it be possible that he was someone who showered every day, made reasonable efforts to live up to basic standards of hygiene, yet found himself in such a situation?

Come to think of it, anal hygiene and cleanliness is something no one ever taught him or talked to him about. He remembers being a little boy and complaining about being itchy back there, and his mother explaining how you need to make sure you're clean back there, otherwise the "stuff" (as she called it) back there will make you itch. Were there other life lessons he didn't know about? Should he be clipping himself back there, much the way some men clip their pubes? Should he get a dedicated razor?

No one laughed, no one catcalled anymore, not after he covered his face with his hands, gnawed on his fingers, and spit and flung wildly as much liquid outpourings as he could.

The response started as laughter and coursed swiftly into horror.

"Jesus Fucking Christ," someone said.

"Manager, manager, someone get the manager. This isn't funny, I'm having a pleasant meal, this isn't the time for... this performance art," someone stammered.

The restaurant had windows that allowed some of the remaining natural light to stream in. On the upper corner, where the ceiling met the wall, hovered a red, humanoid creature. It made its entrance without fanfare, without acknowledgment. Someone spotted it and pointed it out to someone else, who pointed it out to someone else, until the restaurant was abuzz with excited chatter and cackles, but of the kind that is obviously tense. A loud scream or shriek would put people over the edge.

"Ahhh, ladies and gentlemen and assorted assholes of all types, our first guest!" Alexander stretched out his hands like a celebrity television host. "For my first trick, a blast from the past, a special guest from *Ghouls and Ghosts*. I'm sure some of you stupid hipsters remember that, right?"

The creature floated as if treading water, but in the air. It stood maybe four feet tall, but that was hard to tell as it was not standing upright. It had deep red, rough skin, with light blue bracelets on both ankles and on both wrists, and oversized grey bat wings whose breadth probably matched the creature's height. The color coordination was odd and unexpected and was the subject of a couple quick observations and jokes. What also caught everyone's eye was its nudity—other than those bracelets, it was entirely naked, yet it had no discernable genitalia, but only a rounded nub, like a Ken doll.

It moved inorganically, in a pattern. Its short, hooked arms and legs kicked in and out, its wings flapped rhythmically, but there was absolutely no variation in the pumping of either its limbs or wings. And it just hung there in space, with no whooshing of air or sound produced by its flapping. Its face was rough, its mouth a perplexing rictus somewhere between a grimace and a smile, and its nose was bulbous and uncomfortably hooked. It just stayed up there, pumping its limbs, pumping its wings.

Someone clapped and hooted.

"Yeah!" a crowd of guys yelled.

"Do Mario next!" a girl who knew nothing about video games yelled at another table, the equivalent of yelling "Free Bird."

"Bowser!"

"Bowser!" in a pitch and intensity that was all wrong for jocularity. "What else do you retards want?"

Somehow, more than the grisly display and unexplainable creature flying overhead, the use of the politically incorrect term 'retard' did the most to signal to the crowd that something was dangerously off-course.

"So if you remembered, when the knight in *Ghouls and Ghosts* got hit, his armor would fly off! And when he got hit without armor, he turned into bones. Let's see what happens if one of you morons gets hit. Will your American Apparel protect you?"

The red demon assumed a sitting position and floated in the air, moving horizontally toward the center of the restaurant, still well above all the diners. This was too much now, and a huge exhalation went out from the crowd. Several *oh my God*s could be heard and loved ones clutched each other tighter to reveal that they were scared, and that this was no longer fun or funny.

The creature's expression never changed. It moved its arms in a robotic, almost jaunty fashion, and swooped down in an arc like a pendulum.

People shouted and shrieked. Some were stunned and confused at how, despite being closer, they could not make out much more detail about this unwanted guest. It hovered close to the ground in a straight, uninterrupted line, as if it was taking off on a runway. Then its direction arced, as if it was taking off to the ceiling again.

It made its way toward a table of three, and it collided with the unfortunate, smartly under-dressed hipstery kid in the middle. Most instinctually averted their gaze from what they suspected would be the undignified, chaotic crunch and tumbling of bones and bodies. The creature didn't even register the collision, the arc of its flight completely unaffected.

The poor kidult, though, registered the blow, toppled backwards off his chair, and quite literally exploded into chunky fragments. Tables overturned; the red sauce in the pasta appetizer got a new thickener, the drinks new bloody garnishes.

"AND SO IT BEGINS!"

Alexander worked himself into a frenzy. He contorted his back and his joints, head-banging, a man in perpetual spasm. He gnawed and raged, tore and ripped. A substance the shape of bologna and the consistency of caviar extended out from his breast. He tore it out and threw it to the horrified onlookers, where it somehow splattered, shattered, and rolled into four separate pieces, their momentum never stopping, picking up speed, the velocity of their movement the same whether they rolled or used their powerful lunging legs.

*Four pieces of sentient, Spam-like meat,* Krystal thought, the only one of her party able to process what was happening before her. But those thoughts were gone when one of the creatures was upon her, squishy and suffocating, unbearable pain followed by the upper half of her torso separating and skidding along the greased floor. She recognized her separated lower half across the room by the tight Theory jeans she'd just bought yesterday.

A star-faced mole jumped atop the sentient strips of meat and hissed at them. It dipped the prongs of its face into her bloodied wound and, contented, it scampered off to further its feasting.

More and more minions assembled, borne from the growths he tossed about the room. An army. *An Army of One,* he thought, and that seemed right, since they originated from within him, from the pieces he tore off himself, from the sheer determination of his iron will. A floating pineapple of eyeballs. The star-faced mole. A McDonaldland Grimace in a Viking helmet. Head crabs.

Bodies ascending and descending and dividing into uneven quarters. The chaos and abandon was too much and too unplanned—he wanted to hold some of the chaos in abeyance, understand exactly what he was working with, try and plan certain punishments for certain people. Truth was, he just acted; he had no idea what he would be conjuring up. Hell, he didn't even plan for any of the customers to get hurt, it just happened; a sentiment he'd accepted as he stared at the fresh corpse of a hipster beardo—eyes bugged out, a white gelatinous square the texture of tripe wrapped tightly around his mouth.

Why did he feel bad, of all things? He should move beyond that. Morality was for other people.

Out of the corner of his eye he recognized Manny, the head chef, bolting straight out from the kitchen and toward the front doors.

He extended an open hand toward his closest minions—dark brown, round creatures the size and shape of bowling balls, covered in cross-cutting, viciously sharp quills. They even rolled like bowling balls. Three of them were rapaciously chewing on what, at some point, had been a face. One cleanly chomped off several fingers from a disembodied hand, made an awkward face following the crunch of what must have been a wedding ring; constricted its face as it made a hearty swallow, and revealed what may have been a smile.

"Critters," he called them, unthinkingly. "Attack!" And he pointed at a fleeing Manny. Manny turned back for the briefest of moments, saw the finger directed toward him, and resumed bolting, emitting something like a guttural yelp.

The creatures continued their feast.

"Attack!" he shouted again. The creatures continued unabated and undisturbed.

Even among the ruckus, Alexander heard a loud smack and knew it was Manny, falling hard. His vision was obscured by booths and tables, but he distinctly heard Manny yell, a yell that lessoned in intensity and volume until you'd conclude it was coming somewhere more remote, maybe underwater. Alexander adjusted his position to see what had happened, to find a hazy outline of Manny, visible through the translucent sheen of whatever Jellyfish-like creature he'd disappeared into. The creature sat in the repose of a giant Toad, even as protesting hands pushed tiny stalagmite-like ripples through the base of its head. A few seconds later, some adjustment, and ambiguous motions later, the movement stopped, the mass of what was Manny subtracted, like sand from an hourglass.

Luck smiled upon him. How could he be in the wrong, when everything was now so right, when fate convened to give him these powers and make sure his harassers got their just rewards? He'd commend that creature, promote it somehow, even though he knew not what that meant and feared they cared not a whit for or about him.

He saw a tall blonde girl outside the restaurant, looking in, pounding on the glass, sheer terror and desperation on her face. She pounded and lost resolve, descending for a moment into a crescendo of tears as her friends were slaughtered before her.

"Get her!" he yelled as a general command.

If there was any discernable change in the arrangement of the battlefield, he was unaware.

"Get her. Make sure she does not escape!" Somehow, the woman outside clued into what he was saying or directing, and ran.

She escaped out of sight.

"Get her! You let her escape!" He pondered how many other people had simply fled, and concluded it must have been many. This was chaos, and he and his minions appeared to be on different wavelengths. He wanted swift, organized justice. They seemed content just being fed.

"More food. Food. In the kitchen. Plenty of food. Live food."

He hadn't taken a tally on how many of his minions had been wreaking havoc in the diner, but he suspected plenty had left the restaurant already to satisfy themselves. There was certainly less commotion than when he started. He looked for the star-faced mole—that was his favorite, the one he was most impressed with—and couldn't find it. There were panes of broken glass and open doors. As to make the abandonment all the more obvious and embarrassing, there was a green, viscous trail way of slime leading straight from the center of the dining room straight out of the front entrance.

The Critters were still here—one was face-deep, or perhaps body-deep, since the entire creature seemed to consist solely of a face—its Sonic-like quills cresting out of the inner cavity of a corpse. Another sat on its haunches, its stubby legs sticking out, not a care in the world, perhaps even vibrating with pleasure as it burped through its meal.

He walked closer to the Critters—they for some reason becoming his lodestar—a feeling of oppressive ineffectuality gathering in his chest. He accidentally kicked the soft frame of an over-sized slug. Its delineated head raised and twisted 360 degrees; its head was that of a horrifyingly real, too-scaly and too-green Hypnotoad. Its head lowered down and it ignored him, though a weird ambient slushing noise emanating from its midsection became temporarily louder.

He feared it would strike him. He tried to look casual and avoided eye contact.

*What have we here?*

Wedged in the corner underneath a table, where the booth met the wall. A quivering, shivering young lady. He reached underneath, felt the firm, impressive outline of her lower body, and began dragging her out. She screamed and kicked, jamming one of his fingers. It took him longer to pull her out than it should have. He wrapped both his arms around her ankles and pulled, but she was stronger than she appeared and held onto the edge of the booth. His minions heard the tussling and turned in his direction (with the exception of the floating pufferfish, which continued staring vacantly ahead, drifting listlessly).

He tugged hard enough, her hands gave way, and she slid on her back out from under the booth. She assumed a sit-up pose and rained punches on the bridge of his nose. He fell back, hard, on his ass, like an obese woman crashing through a lawn chair. Christ, he landed so hard, he half-expected this was a comedy bit and he'd just landed in a pie or dog shit or something.

She bolted up and ran right past him. She shrieked, turned and surveyed the confusing, intimidating landscapes. Overcome with nausea, sensory overload — soft round organs, bright streaky blood, violent, puncturing angles — and ran to the first unguarded path of escape. The kitchen.

"Follow her!" he shouted, hoping the creatures might listen. "She ran into the kitchen. There is more back there. Food.

"But not her. I want her for myself."

Bryce looked into the mirror and sighed with a heavy heart. He checked his phone. Twenty-three minutes. He had been in the bathroom twenty-three minutes. What would overcome her, he wondered, her hunger from waiting, or her repulsion about wondering what could possibly take him twenty-three minutes in the toilet. Maybe her revulsion canceled her hunger out? Wishful thinking. He half-expected to find out that she left. Maybe she thought he bailed. God, can you imagine that? Shitting for such an inhumanly long length of time that your date can rationally, plausibly conclude that it's more likely that you abandoned her than you were just fulfilling an unfortunate human need.

Maybe it'd be better if she did leave. Less embarrassing, perhaps, than going out there and seeing her face and coming up with some small talk to deflect the 500-pound floating piece of shit in the punch bowl.

He adjusted himself in the mirror and again liked what he saw. He looked good. This sweater fit him well. His skin was largely blemish-free, his recently shorn hair respectably stylish. He fake-smiled, sighed again, washed his hands like he was about to perform an appendectomy, and made his way out.

He left the Men's room (or whatever room he had turned into the Men's room), turned right, and pushed open the sliding door that connected the bathroom area to the dining room. He pushed it partway open until it moved no further. He pushed harder, and it made a little bit of headway.

*Okay, be cool,* he thought. The odds of being stuck in the

bathroom are pretty slight. God, can you imagine that? As if a twenty minute sojourn into shitting was conspicuous enough, he announces his return by being publicly stuck in the bathroom?

He retained his composure and tried again, simultaneously pushing the door and trying to wedge himself through the opening. The door snapped back a little when he transitioned his energy from pushing to wedging, and the door socked him in the lip, as if throwing a quick jab. His nose and lip burned with that angry, unpleasant energy of an unexpected jolt, like when you smash your funny bone or... well, get hit in the face with a door.

*God, can you imagine if I'm bleeding now? Imagine that? Gone in the bathroom for twenty-plus minutes and return BLEEDING.* It literally made him laugh. Maybe that'd be for the best, maybe he could say he was mugged in there or something. *Can you imagine launching a police investigation to save face?* He laughed despite himself.

He kept his head down and made a beeline for where he knew his table to be. He didn't see her sitting where she should be sitting, and he looked down and his stomach burned and sank. *God, could it be possible that she actually did leave?* The burning in his stomach became a stabbing, sinking feeling of despair.

That idea didn't seem so funny anymore.

He slipped on a pool of liquid and went bow-legged, then slipped forward and went down, hard. He landed on his left shoulder, splayed out on his left side, and closed his eyes. He was in some kind of liquid: water, he assumed. But it smelled bad, almost copper-like. Toilet water. Imagine that. *Imagine I shit myself, spent twenty minutes in the bathroom, bloodied my nose on the door, and then fell in fucking smelly water in front of an entire restaurant. Kill me.* He closed his eyes. *Just let me fucking die here. Let me close my eyes and never wake up.*

No one rushed to help him up, but he didn't hear any exhalation of energy from the restaurant-goers, no "whoops" or "ohhhs" or anything. Perhaps they were all in stunned silence, mortified on his behalf.

He turned to his side into what, not long before, may have formed the base of a perfectly acceptable face. Plucked from its roots, it was now a garish lopsided curlicue of bone, teeth and sinew. He jolted and shot out a hand and *my god, the texture of the thing,* it was emulsified, the base of it stayed put and sunk into itself. He screamed, stood up—

...and saw all that was before him.

Somewhere in the back of his mind, in the smarter part of his subconscious, he recalled a quote. *One death is a tragedy, a million is a statistic.* All this, laid before him, all deathly silent but there, all *there,* all these people and their derivative parts. The thick wire-framed glasses of a guy that had been sitting next to them. Several such glasses, actually; Clark Kent-styled glasses had obviously been popular at this hipstery-eatery, there were so many varieties: broken ones, bloodied ones, some still dangling from faces. He registered the gallows humor but didn't laugh. He just turned back around. He wanted to slowly walk into the bathroom and blow his brains out, but he didn't have a gun and he couldn't move.

He looked back over his shoulder. A green, hulking creature with the gait of a gorilla—all strong shoulders and long arms—dragged the fresh corpse of what appeared to be a teenaged boy. With three-foot arms outstretched, it launched the body up over the banister to the top floor of the restaurant. There wasn't the loud thud you'd expect, but rather a soft bristling of vegetation, like the body had landed in a nest.

The creature lumbered across the room, in no rush, to do the same with another body.

"Robin," he called out. "Robin! Robin! Robin, are you here!?" If he'd thought about it rationally, he wouldn't have done it. There was no doubt this creature was already aware of his presence, but it dumbly continued its task. It had a simple, unamused, simian look.

"Robin!" he yelled again, this time pivoting in place to yell it across the entire dining hall. "Robin, are you here!?" He heard a loud cracking pop from outside, the sound that Hollywood-experience told him was a handgun.

Jesus. Somehow, the sound of something so concrete and familiar—Thank you Hollywood, and God Bless America—brought him back to reality. He scanned the bottom floor and saw no sign of Robin or her clothes or anything else. His search became so frantic that, instead of regarding the oval slug possessing the face of a monstrous toad with a sense of wonder, he thought of it as nothing more than a fat, wasteful impediment, an inconvenience to his visual search.

*Maybe she ran away, maybe she got away.* He walked toward the closest door, which opened to the hallway leading to the kitchen.

"Did you ever see the movie *Critters*? Well, did you?"

She nodded, the nod of a trapped victim buying time with a terrorist. She was pinned in the corner, surrounded by this bubbling facsimile of a man, supported by his flanking fan of four vicious-looking, squat creatures. They *did* look like the creatures from the movie *Critters*. That was the first thing she thought of, too.

"'Crites,' they were called in the movie. They look just like them." Alexander pointed this out to his captive audience. The creatures chattered and stood there, their small limbs and tiny hands folded, their large mouths, row-after-row of sharp and grinding teeth, their cherry-red cat-like eyes.

"Are you a Crite?" he turned and spoke to the nearest creature. "Are you a Crite? Is that where you came from, is that what you are called? I loved that movie as a kid. That has to be what you are."

None of them seemed to respond, maintaining their deathless, voracious gaze. The only difference among them was one of them breathed with a heavy wheeze.

"Someone call the prop department," he joked to no one.

He turned back to face her

"So, what do you think of all this?"

She shook her head, unsure of how to answer, but knowing that she had to keep the conversation going. The more he viewed her as someone to talk to, the less likely he was to kill her. It was hard to look at him; the area around his lips looked like bubble wrap fashioned out of pastrami.

"I'm trying to identify all the... monsters, I guess, that are here. I think I saw one of those plants from *Super Mario Brothers* before, you know, those red-and-white plants that come out of the green pipes? That was cool." He smiled, and it was horrible, a mass of bleeding caviar rearranging itself into a human expression. "I feel my face changing, and I'm happy about it. I wanted to change my face, and I feel like it's happening. I'm getting stronger, it must be.

"I don't understand why it's so gross, though. I don't like that. Why does it always have to be gross? Why can't it be something beautiful? I can't even see it, but I can just tell it's gross, the way it feels."

He looked down at his hands. They were wider and broader than human hands should be, and it was harder to demarcate the separate fingers. There was a hazy filament of hair catching the light.

"What should we do, guys?" he asked the four Crites standing behind him. Funny, they looked like cheesy props, flat and unreal, like projections on a screen. They didn't seem fully textured, like there were important details missing, like how they breathed or how they smelled—that's right, come to think of it, they didn't seem to have any discernable smell at all.

"Even when my fantasies come true, I'm not in control, I guess." His face had changed so much that his expressions weren't readily classifiable. "So, what should we do? To be honest, I don't really want to kill you. I only wanted to get revenge on the people who worked here, and not really, I don't know. I think I just wanted to scare them. I wanted to scare the manager but I didn't even see him today. I don't really know what to do, to be honest."

She nodded slowly, as if she was his confidant and was really objectively weighing the questions.

"Can... can you let me go? I won't tell anyone, I promise. No one would believe me, anyway."

"No, I'm sorry, I can't do that. I mean, I understand what you are saying, I do, and no one would believe you, but I imagine the police are already on their way, and they'll believe what they see with their own eyes."

"You... can't... yes, you can do that. Just let me leave."

"No, I'm sorry," he said, but slowly, with the gravity of a henpecked father deciding whether to let his kid borrow his car, like he was asking for forgiveness as the subtext of his refusal.

"Then… what are you doing with me here?"

"I, I don't know. I like you being here, I guess."

He took a step closer to her. He was perhaps a foot away now. "I don't know, I don't plan on, like, I don't know. I like your company though. Do you think maybe you could take your shirt off, actually? I don't know, it might cheer me up or help me think."

She swallowed hard. "Wh-at? I. I. If I do, do you promise to let me go?"

Her attention turned to the entryway and she almost shouted with excitement. There stood Bryce. He just stood there, in plain sight, as if he came to a threshold after entering the doorway and couldn't come any further. He was surveying everything he could—this horror show before him, and the layout of the kitchen.

Bryce was bad at estimates, but he was maybe six feet away from them, and he felt the heat of steam coming off boiling water, from active pots and pans. Underneath rows of torn vegetables, he saw metal shapes. Hopefully, those were knives.

It took an additional beat for the bubbling mass that was Alexander to turn and face him. He looked disappointed and the air was tense with something other than murder, as if Alexander was an ex-boyfriend trying to keep his composure, sizing up her new lover.

From another entry-way—this one leading from the cold storage room—came another form, making its entrance known with a sound approximating wet towels dropped on to the floor. Its entire aura was imbued with stagnant water—even when it wasn't moving and stood there, staring, there was the sound and scent of tepid water, of slipperiness. It stood about five and a half feet—not particularly imposing—on two webbed legs, with its webbed hands extended slightly horizontally, as if planning to give someone an exaggerated hug. Its body shone a sickly form of green, slick and long, almost like a seal. The face was vaguely humanoid, full of lumpen masses that might have been tentacles, but too indistinct to make out. There didn't seem to be any mouth.

Alexander pointed at the new visitor. "'*Zombies Ate My Neighbors.*' It has to be, right?" He wished he'd actually seen *Creature from the Black Lagoon*, because he knew the fish monster from *Zombies Ate My Neighbors* was inspired by that movie. This was a poor, low-budget facsimile. "Man, I haven't played that game forever, but it has to be."

Bryce seized the opportunity. He grabbed the nearest pot by the handle and lifted it high over his head, ready to bring it down like a hammer. It was heavier than he expected, and the lid fell off with a heavy clunk and narrowly missed his foot. As he arched the pot over his head, he realized why it was so heavy: it was half-filled with boiled water. Miraculously, he lifted the pot fast enough and tilted it just so the water emptied our harmlessly behind his head, although he felt steaming water residue on the bottom of his jeans. Still moving on impulse, he swung the pot down as hard as he could on top of Alexander's head.

The impact wasn't as dramatic as he expected—there was the forcible collision with bone, but also something softer, bone wrapped in marshmallow. Alexander went straight down on his back.

The Critters retained their look of voracious detachment, their mouths still open, their cat-eyes still frighteningly red yet immobile. Then—*thunk*—Bryce felt a reverberation through the pot. A cruel-looking quill was vibrating, half-deep, into the metal. If he hadn't been holding the pot at around face-level, that quill would have gone straight through his windpipe.

One of the Crites changed its position and was back on its hind legs. So that was the fucking bastard culprit.

"Fuck you," Bryce screamed, this time swinging the pot like a golf club at the big wide target that was this Crite's face. Now *that* was satisfying—the impact literally lifted the round fat ball of quills and teeth off the ground and arced it toward the stovetop.

The other three Crites hissed and growled and made high-pitched noises.

*Womp.* One swing from the fish creature was enough to take out another Crite. It followed up with three identical swooping strikes on the now clearly dead Critter. It looked at another one, but its facial expressions didn't change, and its movement was rote and almost mechanical. It swung its arm back again to make another horizontal strike, and as insane as this all was, Bryce could not help but realize that this strike looked identical to the previous strikes, as if this creature had only a certain range of programmable actions and was doomed to a life of infinite repeats.

A quill flew into the mid-section of the fish creature. It flinched and flashed white for a brief moment, and continued moving forward. It was struck with two more quills and it flopped down and died a surprisingly efficient and unlabored death. One second it was marching forward, then it was down on its back in a heap, and then it was simply gone.

But that was enough time. When the firing Crite turned around, Robin was already upon it with a sharpened kitchen knife. She sunk the knife into its fleshy stomach. Again, and again, and again she plunged her knife, and the screaming was almost intolerable, so reminiscent of a pleading, wounded dog or tortured cat. Bryce felt almost sick to his stomach, as if they'd just done something unrepentantly inhumane.

She stopped stabbing it only when it rolled onto its back like a cartoon tortoise.

The last Crite launched itself at Bryce. It made no gestures that indicated it was about to leap. It was just suddenly in the air.

It bit hard into whatever its teeth came in contact with. Unfortunately for it, that *whatever* was Bryce's trusty hammer-pot. The Crites looked almost like giant brown Koosh balls, and this one played the part as it soared through the air. It landed with aplomb against the industrial-strength refrigerator door, which was slightly ajar.

The creature took a moment to regain itself, then shook itself into convalescence. It bit at the air.

Robin ran beside the struggling creature, kicked it with

her foot toward the refrigerator door, and slammed the creature between the door, again and again and again, to the point where she was actually able to close the door fully while the top part of the creature thrashed and chomped futilely, emitting the same disturbing, dog-like shriek of its stabbed brethren. It spasmed a couple of times, and when the door opened back up, there was a pool of green blood and a distorted mass of gore between its stubby legs and the rest of its body.

Bryce ran over to Robin and pulled her back from the refrigerator. She relaxed in his arms for a moment, then grabbed the pot—now substantially dented—and ran over to the Crite that had first shot the quill at them and which Bryce had subsequently punted across the room. It lay prostrate on its side—from viewing just the fuzzy back of it, it was almost cute, like an innocent wooly brown bush—but that didn't cause her any mind: she smashed it. She smashed it until she was sure it was dead.

"Robin, I'm so glad you're alive." Bryce ran toward her and noticed that—that green creature, it had been here before, right? Where could it have gone? It was gone, just disappeared.

"There—there was fish-like creature-thing there before, right?"

"Right, you're not crazy." She spoke slowly and deeply, catching her breath. Her tone was too brusque, not as warm and relieved as he'd like.

He held onto her back, coaxing and comforting her.

"Wait—there's still him..." she signaled toward the increasingly-humanoid shape of the deformed monster. His forehead and the area between his eyes were deeply bruised and a lightning bolt scar ran its way down between his eyebrows. *Harry Potter*, Bryce thought randomly. Under the bruises, the monster's face had reverted, becoming unremarkably human.

"We need to make sure he's dead, we can't take any chances. He caused all of this out there. He's a monster, a *literal* monster."

"Agreed," Bryce nodded. He took the pot by the handle, hesitated, gave it back to her, and took up a butcher knife. From the way he held it, you could tell he didn't have a lot of experience cooking chops for himself. He choked up on the handle, holding it tight. Resolute.

"Ok," he said, and moved in closer to the recumbent body. Alexander was splayed on his back, arms spread on an invisible crucifix.

Bryce prodded the shape in the left side of the rib cage. The shape groaned but did nothing else. This would be a lot easier if the guy shocked back to life or something, and he could get this over with in the heat of the moment.

"I think, I think he's out cold." Bryce knew that sounded stupid, if he were watching this on a movie screen he'd be screaming "Fucking c'mon, man, do it!" and then complaining loudly that the witless character was asking for it when things inevitably went awry.

"No. We can't allow him to escape. He needs to die. You saw what he did. He killed all those people. He was going to kill me. He was going to rape me, even. He caused all these… all these things… It's a fucking massacre out there." She stopped herself from breaking down completely but exhaustion was overpowering her composure.

"I know." He went down on his knees and straddled the

body, chopping knife at the ready.

He didn't know how to bring the knife down. A hard *thwack* into the skull, as if it were a watermelon?

"Can you give me like, a cutting knife?"

She brought him a sharpened blade. *Used for fine cuts*, he thought, which took on a sinister connotation.

He put the blade to the bastard's throat. It helped to think of him like that, a bastard, a murderer, he killed all those people.

"You fucking bastard. You fucking, piece-of-shit murderer." No response. "You, you fucking killer, how could you?" He was speaking unnecessarily loud. Can't this guy wake up or move or something, so he could kill him and pass it off to himself as self-defense? He wished he had a gun, although he'd never shot a gun before in his life and wouldn't even know what to do with one.

"Do it!"

Bryce gracelessly pushed the blade into where the man's Adam's apple should be. He envisioned a tactile slice, one quick slash, a controlled seepage of blood, and that's it.

Misfire. He put only a quarter of the blade in and found resistance, grimaced—he was committing the throat-slitting equivalent of slowly tearing off a Band-Aid—course corrected and overcompensated, plugging the knife at an awkward angle. Blood sprayed wildly. The knife was partially buried and obscured, like he'd dropped the blade into a cooling cake.

"Aww God. He's dead, he's dead: he has to be dead." He stood up, covered in warm, coppery blood, the opening of the wound actively gurgling.

They stood there, both panting. Several wordless

moments passed between them. It was over, he felt. This was a natural concluding point, the curtain to fall, the credits to appear. The weight of the whole day made itself evident, a feeling of nausea and frazzled disconnection came over him, and he fell to the floor. She bent down at first to maybe help him back up, but collapsed upon him in what became an affectionate embrace.

Police and emergency officers assisted them, swarming about—more than he'd ever seen before. The conflict wasn't over, exactly, and he was oddly grateful for that. He half-expected everything to just disappear, and for the authorities to find just this hideously slaughtered disfigured body in the kitchen, the placid presence of undisturbed restaurant-goers undercutting his entire cockamamie story. That was selfish, he thought. It would be better if this was a dream, an unreality. Then there wouldn't be all these bodies.

There was a shoot-out that took place out of sight, and one shooting directly in front of them that was particularly shocking for being so abrupt. That gorilla creature moseyed out from somewhere, spotted the officers, and grunted. It picked up and threw a nearby body part at them, apathetically, as if following a set pre-program.

It went wide, wide enough that no one needed to dodge. One of the officers fired. The beast clutched its left shoulder with its right hand, pivoted, groaned, and slowly walked toward the officers.

Another officer fired, this shot low, around the groin. The

creature repeated the movement as before: clutching its left shoulder with its right hand and groaning. Several more shots. The same movement, the same animation, and then the creature practically hopped backward to land on its back, where it outstretched its arms and its tongue and just stopped moving.

Not a minute later, the beast was gone.

There was one other lasting memory that stood out to him: A burly, mustachioed officer was speaking animatedly with this hands, giving directions to his cadre. He moved his hands in a chopping movement while he talked, like he was doing the Braves Cheer. Something like a moray eel—or a red-and-white spotted plant—about one foot long shot out of an unremarkable but out-of-place wide, green pipe that sprouted out of the wall, and soundlessly chomped into the officer's hand, before just as suddenly disappearing—bloody fingers and all—back into the pipe, which likewise popped back to non-existence.

They were pushed and ferried out amidst the commotion, and they never stepped into the Deer & Fox ever again.

Robin's breasts heaved with her breathing. They showed nicely through what appeared to be a form-fitting, stylish white blouse. No, something more threadbare than that—he could clearly make out the contrast of the maroon bra she wore underneath.

The disfigured man reached out toward her. His face was

orange, puffy and indistinct.

The man pulled Robin forward. Her breasts pitched upward from the force and jiggled vigorously as she stopped short in his grasp. He grabbed around her, trying to dominate her, to get leverage on her shoulders. The man squeezed one of her breasts painfully. She pushed him away, and his fingers were crumpled up within her shirt, so when she pushed her shirt extended, exposing her deep décolletage.

Bryce's erection flooded full and sharp, pressing hot against his pants. It was his first glimpse of her perky breasts, but also not, because underneath the dream he registered that he already knew what her breasts really looked like, but there was something powerful and erotic about this sight, the thrill of a slip, the power and control of the image.

He charged and knocked out the disfigured man with one straight blow—

Bryce woke up next to Robin. Actually, next to her was not fully accurate—she was already half-up and getting ready for work. He only saw her back. His stomach sank and that was enough to know the vitality that radiated off her was limited to the dream world. The only thing that carried over from the dream world was his erection.

He laid awake in bed while she prepared for the day. He felt her staring at him impatiently to get up—they often tried to leave for work at the same time—but there was something satisfying in staying in bed for a bit, the slightest form of obstinacy he could muster without overtly riling her. The covers were still over him, and he rested his hand on his privates, the erotic elements of the dream still in mind.

He looked up at her brushing her hair. She looked back at him, looked away, looked back at him, and gave him a slightly annoyed look to show that she didn't see the point in breaking and maintaining eye contact. She wasn't going to give him a goofy or warm smile just because. She wasn't his cheerleader.

He groaned and got out of bed and let his half-erection jut out from his boxers. She didn't acknowledge it. He let it hang, untouched and unremarked-upon. He felt he was making a statement of some sort.

It had been almost a year since that defining date at the Deer & Fox. They'd lived together for the last six months, and they hadn't been physical with each other for the last two.

"I'm going to shower," he told her.

"Ok."

"What time is it?"

She looked at her phone, and said, in a phlegmy, impatient way: "8:30, no, 8:35." They normally wanted to be out the door by 9 a.m. so they could get in sometime between 9:30 and 10:00 a.m. They were running late.

"You don't have to wait for me, I guess."

"Yeah, I figured. I wish you would have told me earlier, I wouldn't have waited."

"I figured. Sorry. I can get in later than you though."

She made a testy sound. "I know."

She was already half-way dressed.

"I left two wheat bars out for you if you want to bring them to work. I brought some, 'cause I don't have time to make breakfast."

He offered a sarcastic woe-is-me, okey-dokey head nod.

She maintained her frigid distance, zipped something up, and left the room.

He didn't want them to go to work like this, to leave and start the day on bad terms.

"Hey," he offered, as she came back in the room. Her chest jiggled a little when she stopped abruptly, and, absurdly, it made him feel bad about himself and what was becoming of their relationship. He hadn't seen her chest bounce of her own accord (or his) for quite some time now.

"Hey, what's going on with you?" That didn't come out right, at all, and it was dreadfully obvious.

No response. She left the room. He heard the refrigerator door close. "Nothing is going on with me," she huffed when she came back. She was eating Fage Greek yogurt, the one where you mix the honey and yogurt. He could see the clump of honey on the spoon as she mixed it in.

"C'mon, something's up."

She positioned her shoulders defensively and sucked the honey off the spoon in a desperate, rushed way. Funny, he didn't know there could be so much emotion conveyed through yogurt-eating.

"C'mon, I don't have time for this shit. I need to go to work. Can we not talk about this now?" She usually didn't curse in reference to their relationship.

"Well, I'd normally let it go, but this has been going on for a while. You just called our relationship 'shit,' for one thing."

"Just... don't. Let's just not talk about it now, okay?"

"Okay."

She put the half-eaten yogurt down in the kitchen and walked to the closet to resume looking for a top.

He felt an intense, burning sense of aggrievement that manifested in his chest and shoulders.

"Look, I do want to talk about this. We always not talk about things when you say so. We always go by what you say. You are important to me, this relationship is important to me, and I don't want to spend the whole day worrying about what's going on with us, I want to talk about it now."

"Look—" she started, her arms up as if she was literally stuck between a rock and a hard place and needed to wedge herself out. "I have a lot to do today, you know my boss has been a major bitch recently and I have a lot on my plate, and you can't stress me out this morning, and you can't make me late! Don't you understand that? Don't you get that? If you cared about me, you would not fuck up my work or make things so difficult for me!"

Oh no, here she was, getting worked up. She had a subtle way of shifting blame—now he was morally responsible for her inability to control her emotions and what effect that may have on her work day. And why was it that she could call her boss a bitch, but god forbid he say that she was acting bitchy?

"...and you always make me late, I make breakfast for you and wait for you to leave with me, but no more. I can't do that anymore, you need to wake up earlier, or let me wake up earlier and leave without you."

"Okay, okay," he said, extending his fingers out in a soothing, deescalating way. She was right about that, at least—he had made her late a couple of times, but he couldn't stand it in when she made him feel totally responsible for everything.

She was fully dressed now. He knew this was fucked up,

but he had felt more sympathetic to her when she was half-dressed.

She turned back to him, last bite of yogurt in her mouth. Her expression wasn't good—it was largely frustration with a sprinkling of the heavy sorrow inherent in carrying out a dreadful but inevitable task, like taking the cancer-ridden dog to the vet for the Big Sleep.

"I can't do this anymore. I can't. I can't. I can't do this anymore."

"Baby, don't be silly."

This was going nuclear. He'd thought about it ending, too, and there was excitement and freedom there, he knew, but no, he didn't want it to end, not like this, not now.

She shook her head, her eyes were closed and there was a streak of wetness along her cheek. "I'm sorry, I'm sorry, I just, I can't. I can't do this anymore. I'm sorry. I'm sorry. I just, I don't, I just don't feel like this is going to work."

"Baby, c'mon, let's just go to work and we can talk about this later."

"No. I'm sorry. I... I just don't feel like I'm in love with you anymore."

"*Baby!* You're just stressed, I'm sorry for bringing this up before work, it's my fault. It's my fault, you did nothing wrong, I'm sorry." Usually, taking the blame and appearing plaintive was enough to escape long enough for her to calm down so he could live to fight another day.

"No." She shook her head, eyes still closed. "I'm serious. I've been looking into getting another apartment. I have one picked out already. I'm sorry, I'm sorry. I should have told you before. I'm sorry, but I'm serious. I'm just not in love with you anymore. I've fought it, I've pretended otherwise,

I kept telling myself I loved you. You are a good person, and I appreciate what you did for me—"

"What I did for you? You mean, saving your life? As in, I *literally* saved your life."

"Yes, I know."

"Look honey, let's just talk about this later, okay?"

"Bryce. Look, I'm sorry, but this has to be done. I'm sorry that this is the wrong time. But, it's not working out. I'm sorry, it's not working out. I need to go to work now, I'm sorry, but it's not working out."

"Baby, c'mon, you don't mean that."

"I know what I mean. I know what I am saying."

"You can't possibly. We love each other. I'm your hero. You say it all the time, why, you said it even, like, just last week, when I fixed that cabinet for you."

"Bryce... I shouldn't have said that. I like to make you happy, I'm sorry I... have been leading you on for some time, I suppose."

"I quite literally saved your life. I quite literally am your hero. There were magazine articles written about us. I'm a fucking hero. I literally did everything I could to—"

"I know, Bryce, I know. I appreciate everything you did for me, and—"

"Everything I did for you—you mean preventing you from being raped and brutally killed. That's what you mean, right, when you say that?"

"Bryce!"

He didn't know what angered him worse—her breaking up with him, or her pat formality in doing it. She was like an executive getting through a difficult but predetermined business decision.

"You have to... we have to be able to work this out."

"I'm sorry, Bryce. I'm... I'm sorry."

"I literally saved your life. I fucking saved your life."

"I know. I know, I feel terrible about this, but... I'm sorry. I, just don't feel... think I'm in love with you. I mean, I know I'm not in love with you. I'm sorry, I just, I just know I'm not in love with you—"

"You can't do this, after all I've done, after all we've been through—"

"It's not—it's not a judgment on you. I can't, I can't weigh the pros and cons of what you do or don't deserve based on what you did for me. This isn't a formula. I'm telling you, I'm telling you, I'm sorry, I have love for you, I so greatly appreciate everything you did for me—"

"Saving your life. Let's be clear about what I did. I literally killed a maniac for you, literally killed monsters— can you believe this, literally killing fucking monsters, risking my life to kill monsters to literally fucking rescue you, and this is how I'm repaid for it."

"Repaid? My love for you isn't a gift that you earn by achieving something for me—"

*Of course it fucking is, of course it all is,* his mind screamed in protest.

"—you don't win me. I'm not the prize—"

"You said you'd never be able to repay me. Do you remember that? You said you would never be able to repay me, and that you would always be there for me. So I'm asking you, please—please—don't leave me. Let us work this out."

She breathed deeply, as if quibbling with someone pointing in vain to a contract technicality. And in a sense, he was, and he knew it.

"For everything I've done for you, for everything we've been through together, please, we have to work this out. I'm a good person. I'm a good person and I'm sorry, I try, you know I try to be good." He was crying, unmistakably and unabashedly.

"You said it—you promised me—that you'd be eternally grateful to me. That you loved me, that you'd never be able to repay me. So please, do this for me, repay me this way: don't leave me."

She didn't respond, not verbally at least, but she ploddingly shook her head.

"I'm sorry. It's not a thing I can work out. You are nice, you are a nice person. You will find someone else to be nice to, someone else to love. I feel like I could be anyone. You just want to be loved so badly, I feel it has nothing to do with me. You just want me to cheer you on, to hug you and treat you—almost treat you like a dog or something, like you are my son or something and I'm your biggest booster, your biggest fan. I just... I just can't. It's not... "

"I can't fucking believe you—"

"Don't! I can't do this now. I'm late for work, we can talk later."

"I can't fucking believe this is how you... how you treat me. How you repay me—"

"Fucking repay you!?" He made a strategic mistake, he knew. Whatever welling of sympathy he'd evinced within her was gone. The course was now irrevocable. "Again, I'm not your princess that you rescued from the castle. You don't own me. You didn't win me, so just stop it! Just stop it and act like an adult. And if you want to get all technical with me, and bring up every fact and detail from the past instead of focusing on how I've fallen out of love with you, then if I never met you, I'd never have even been in that restaurant to begin with."

"Okay, whatever," he turned around to head back into the bedroom. "Whatever, I can't believe you, I can't fucking believe you." He plopped back into the bed, the vertigo of sadness and uncertainty overwhelming him, seeping into the cracks of his rage. It felt better when these emotions were converted into rage, into indignation.

"I'm a fucking hero, you know that. I literally saved your life, from god knows what, from getting eaten, from getting raped, from who knows. You had a different tune back then, let me tell you. You'd have been begging for me back then, and now, look at you." His conflation of pity and anger was mismanaged and received poorly, he could tell, and while he talked, she hedged, torn between consoling him and just storming out. She finally made a face of hands-in-the-air disavowal, packed up her work things, and said she was leaving and they could talk tonight. He noted with some inner sadistic glee that she dotted her eyes a bit as she left.

He didn't want to move out or have her move out. Things weren't perfect, far from it, but he liked the life he had with her, liked the feeling her had with her. He looked at her and saw the best of himself.

"I'm a fucking hero," he told himself again, this time into the pillow, in a sulking way he'd perfected throughout this life, in a type of self-pitying performance art. It felt good to repeat that, and what he had done for her was undeniable, it could never be taken away. It was an assurance into Heaven, into sainthood. He had always stayed faithful to her, even when the hero-narrative went full blast following the media blitz.

It felt good to be indignant and full of hate. People forget that. There was something soporific about it, anesthetizing. Bad feelings sunk inward and were expelled outward, leaving him cleansed.

"I'm a fucking hero," he consoled himself again, burning up into the pillow. "I'm a good person and I deserve better than this. I deserve to be loved and treated better. I deserve to be with someone who appreciates me.

"This isn't how things are supposed to end."

## EDITOR'S NOTE

This story originally appeared in *With A Voice that is Often Still Confused but is Becoming Ever Louder and Clearer*, a collection that is absolutely worth your time. Here J.R. captures what happens when Mario saves the Princess. Are they destined to be together? How can a relationship like that function if you're not on even footing? I suppose it's possible, but our hero certainly doesn't succeed, not when it really counts.

Maybe that's why the Princess keeps getting captured by Bowser. It keeps the romance alive.

# RESET
## BY WILLIAM TEA

**H**e'd been here before.

Such knowledge offered him little comfort. If anything, it made the situation even more alarming.

When he awoke, he found himself in a grim, grey chamber. The stone wall felt cold and damp against his back. The air was musty and still. It smelled ancient. Decayed. Darkness filled much of the place, so dense in spots it almost seemed tangible. The gloom was broken only by a ghostly spear of moonglow, streaming in through a window to his left. Its light split into thirds, courtesy of the iron bars soldered into the frame.

From somewhere above, ice-cold droplets of water needled his body with short, sharp shocks. An aching rhythm throbbed in his ribs and shoulder blades. He kicked his legs but found only air beneath. At some point while he'd been unconscious, someone had bound his hands in chains over his head. The entirety of his bulk dangled now from manacles around his wrists. His own weight pulled his arms taut so that the steel cut into the flesh of his thumbs, his elbows bent at unnatural angles, and his shoulders swung loose, slipped from their sockets.

The ache was enough to occupy his mind at first, but then he became aware of something else.

He was not alone.

Shapes moved in the shadows, barely perceptible undulations in the inky black. From that darkness came faint sounds. He strained to hear but could make out nothing more than ragged breathing and sad little moans.

He tried to calm his mind. Tried to think. He'd been here before. He knew that much. But how did he know that? He couldn't remember anything before the moment he woke up. He tried to think back, tried to remember anything from before his waking. Who he was. Where he came from. Something. Anything.

Murk swallowed his mind, the darkness within proving just as impenetrable as that of the room. Every time he thought he'd gotten hold of some memory, it fluttered out of his grasp, leaving him with no more than what he'd started with: a nagging, gnawing certainty that, yes, he had been here before.

That, and a growing dread. A fear that felt familiar. Something bad was going to happen. Something that had happened before. Something that some lost part of him had once known intimately.

His vision started to adjust. He could almost make out some details in the shifting shapes around him. Then there came a rumble of thunder, and a flash of lightning flooded in through the window, illuminating the room for just a second. It was a second that felt like an hour. All at once, he wished he could go back to not knowing what hid in the dark.

There were others like him, bound in chains.

A woman stood against the wall, bulky belts of metal clamped around her torso, designed to do more than just hold her in place. They clutched her so tightly that her skin bunched up around the rusty bands, purple and angry. A gash under her breasts leaked a slow trickle of blood, as did another on her thigh. Shimmering tears streaked the woman's face, but she seemed to have no breath left with which to sob.

To her left was a man. On the right, another woman.

The man was hunched over, his back bruised and torn open from the lashes of a whip. His head laid sideways on a thick plank of wood attached to a table. A similar plank pushed down on the other side of his face from above, squeezing his cheeks so hard his tongue stuck out, fat and swollen between his lips. Atop the upper plank, a huge wooden pillar was wrapped in spiraling notches like a giant screw. Or a vice.

The man's hands were not tied, but nailed to the legs of the table. His feet, to the floor. Though he struggled to pull himself loose, thrashing wildly at the device that held him, he managed only to aggravate his wounds. Blood oozed up around the nails that pierced him.

The second woman, meanwhile, sat on the ground. Her legs were spread apart and her head was pushed down between them so that her spine curved, vertebrae jutting up through the skin of her back. Her wrists and neck were clamped between a pair of boards. For a moment, he thought she was simply pilloried. Then he noticed the poles that rose up on either side of the stocks, and the gleaming blade that hung between them. Unlike her male counterpart, she was frozen in place, eyes wide and glassy, afraid to move for fear of engaging the guillotine.

A butcher's block stood in the center of the room, a cleaver embedded in it. Streaks of pink stained its surface. Along the walls, numerous axes and knives had been mounted. A cat o' nine tails, too.

Then, *it began.*

Something was there with them. It eluded sight, but the effects of its presence were plain as day. It tightened the metal belts that held the first woman. Her flesh bulged as she gasped for air. Her screams were high and thin, not much more than whistled whines. Bubbles of skin bulged above and below the constricting bands, then popped, spewing ichor. Some invisible force grabbed at the limp flaps of burst flesh and pulled. It peeled them back from the muscle, slowly, methodically. She was being unwrapped like a birthday present. Glistening slivers of bone peeked out from her slimy, shredded meat. When the last scraps of skin had been removed from her torso and face, her breathless shrieks at last fell silent.

The unseen presence next turned its attention to the hunched man. Seemingly of its own volition, the vice that held him began to turn, the top board pressing down on his head. The man's thrashing became more frantic. Wet, throaty screams turned to gurgles, muffled by his own swollen tongue. His face turned a deep burgundy as sickening cracking sounds rang out from his skull. Thin, rust-colored rivulets trickled from his nose, his ears, even his eyes.

The screw kept turning. The man's chubby circle of a face thinned and lengthened into a slender oval. His tongue flopped forward from between his lips, cut loose by smashed, clenching teeth. The screw turned one last time. His eyeballs slithered from their sockets. His thrashing finally stopped.

The woman in the guillotine was lucky. Her death was the fastest. The guillotine blade fell and sliced through her like a razor through tissue paper. Her head and hands both fell to the floor. The stumps were clean, smooth. It took a few seconds before they started to bleed. Round and red, with small circles of bone peeking from their centers, they were like bloodshot eyes staring out with strange white pupils.

There was only one person left in the chamber.

It was his turn now.

One of the wall-mounted knives floated in mid-air. Then it flew at him, embedding itself in his kneecap. He howled, heaved, and gagged, but all that came up was bile. His suffering had no time to recede when another torment found him. He looked down and found the cleaver he'd seen before, apparently with a mind of its own, hacking at his shin.

The pain erased thought itself from his mind. He lost his sense of time, of space, of self. All that existed was the wretched, stabbing hurt that surged through his synapses, and a panicked animal need to get away from that hurt. He whipped his head from side to side and tugged at the manacles above, to no avail. He cursed and hollered and begged his unseen assailant to have mercy. But the only response he got was more hurt.

A thin cut drew itself onto his chest, and something

slipped inside. He felt invisible fingers grabbing clumsily at the edges of the wound, stretching it wider. It soon expanded, a huge gaping mouth coughing up carnage. He could see his own ribcage. The previously cold air seemed scorching now as it rushed to fill hidden crevices in his body.

*Pain* became a meaningless word. It didn't even begin to summarize what he felt. His brain cells crackled, overloading with sensory information. His body finally started to go numb, replacing the all-consuming hurt with a deep, immersive cold.

The world turned crimson.

Then, he was gone.

She licked a splash of red off her finger.

Almost out of ketchup. Damn.

She dabbed up the last smears with the remnants of a half-eaten chicken finger and watched the boys huddled around the *Phobetor* machine. She didn't much like that one. Of all the games in Neon City, it was the only one that made her feel uneasy.

Like many of the arcade's offerings, the title sounded like little more than vaguely futuristic nonsense. *Robotron*, *Zaxxon*, *Sinistar*, *Polybius*; they were all full of spaceships and race cars, fire-breathing dragons and barrel-throwing monkeys. Sure, they were all about shooting things, crushing things, blowing things up. But they were like *Looney Tunes*. The colorful characters and whimsical fantasy worlds diminished the effect of their digitized explosions and electronic screams.

*Phobetor* was different, though. Sandwiched between a neglected *BurgerTime* machine and an out-of-order *Marble Madness*, it stood out with its garish green and purple cabinet plastered with Halloween iconography—dark castles, fanged vampire bats, grinning white skulls. There was no mission or goal in the game itself, no monsters to fight or obstacles to overcome. It was just a horror show.

Players progressed from one grotesque scene to the next, each screen populated by crude simulations of what appeared to be innocent human beings. Human beings in elaborate death traps and cruel torture devices. Human beings you were supposed to maim and murder in graphic, barbaric ways. For fun.

Not even that *Death Race* game they used to have—the one where players ran over pedestrians for extra points—had been as heinous. The graphics had been laughable, for one. But this...

Scarlet lights flickered on the monitor. Blocky geysers of blood spouted from the man onscreen as the pixelated flesh flayed from his pixelated bones. The visuals weren't necessarily disturbing. They would even be absurd, if not for the sadistic ideas they symbolized.

The insistent chirp of her wristwatch alarm jolted her from her thoughts. Break time was over. She gobbled up the last of her meal as the calculus textbook on the tabletop mocked her. It remained open on the exact same page she'd turned to when she first sat down. She'd been trying to study, but this place was hardly conducive to concentration. The strobing rainbow lights. The high-pitched beeps and blips. Laughter. Shrieks. Too much noise. Too much chaos.

She wished she had more time between school and work, time to stay home and really focus on her education. But money was a more pressing concern right now. The food stamps helped, but they just barely got her and her mother through the month. And even with that help, the money the two of them brought home together was only just enough to cover the rent. And with the way mom had started drinking...

Now was not the time to dwell on such things. If the boss came by and found her sitting at the arcade's snack bar, even just a few minutes past the end of her break, he'd blow a gasket.

She put her schoolbooks back in her knapsack and cleaned up her trash. As she made her way to the door marked Employees Only, she glanced back for a second.

Level 2. The kid at the controls of the *Phobetor* machine lowered a chained victim down into a river of gore. The laughter that came out of the boy and his friends as a cartoon crocodile rose up from the stream and closed its jaws around the man's legs was glittery and delicate like the music of a windchime. The smiles on their faces couldn't have shone more brightly if they had just come down the stairs on Christmas morning.

He'd been here before.

He was starting to remember.

He awoke, as always, into darkness. Into a musty, damp chamber with stone walls that stank of age and spilled blood. The others were there again, too, same as before. Same as they'd always been.

How many times? How many times had he done this? How many times had he hung from these chains, watched everyone around him slowly die, then felt his own body transform into a shuddering, red rag doll as his flesh tore away in fraying chunks from his limbs, his chest, his face? How many times had he felt life itself ebbing away? How many times had it all turned black and cold, only to reset, as if it had never happened at all?

These were not dreams. These were memories. Dreams did not carry with them the all-too-real sensations of physical trauma, which his nerve endings recalled with awful clarity.

Had there ever been anything other than this? Try as he might, he could not remember any other way of life. Nothing that had ever meant anything to him. Nothing that motivated him or gave him a sense of meaning or purpose. Nothing that indicated a life worth living. He had no recollections of family or friends. No childhood antics or teenage romances. Nothing before this room. He could hear rain and wind from outside its four walls, could see moonlight rushing in through the barred window. But he had no idea what else was out there.

Where was this place? In a city? On the edge of a forest? On top of a mountain? In the middle of the desert? Was there anything outside this room at all? Was this the totality of his reality?

He could remember nothing, except that he had been here before. And that was new. Before now, he could only remember *not* remembering. But that was changing.

Perhaps more would come to him in time. He hoped so. Hoped, but he did not believe. A terror rose in him, a terror separate from his knowledge that the time of sharp things and weeping wounds was almost at hand. It was the terror that this was indeed all there was to his life. That he remembered nothing that gave him a sense of purpose because this *was* his purpose. He existed only to suffer and die, again and again and again.

An ear-splitting peal of thunder roared from somewhere far away, followed by a wink of lightning. It would be starting again soon.

He got the distinct impression there were eyes on him. He was being watched by someone hidden. Whatever invisible force it was that unleashed such cruelties on him time and time again, he had to believe it was driven by a conscious mind. Where there was a hand, even one that went unseen, there was a face and a will behind it. Someone or something out there oversaw his torment. Someone or something took great delight in it. His life and his death were sources of entertainment.

Whoever, whatever it was, had all the power. He had nothing. Nothing but the terrible knowledge that he'd been here before and that he'd be here again, and of what was coming next. But there was something else. Something growing in him. Something new.

He was beginning to hate.

The *Q\*bert* machine was down.

The boss was going to have a cow. *Q*bert* was one of Neon City's best earners. Now, it was the fifth game to crap out on them this month, along with *Marble Madness, Missile Command, Gauntlet II,* and *Space Harrier.* Those last two were also big money-makers.

She taped an out-of-order sign across the game's screen, then returned to her early morning rounds. It was Saturday. The Karrasburg mall, which Neon City called home, had just opened. The only other person in the arcade, besides the new girl at the snack bar and the manager in the back, was a blond teenager, already glued to the *Bishop of Battle* machine as headphones blared punk rock in his ears. Soon, though, the place would be a hive of activity. Weekends were always busy. The kids would come to celebrate their liberty from schoolwork with a riot of color and sound, liquidating their carefully hoarded allowances into pocket change, which could be crammed, quarter after quarter, into the cabinets' hungry slots.

She finished checking the machines and made sure the coin dispensers were full. She looked at her watch and realized she had a few minutes to spare. She'd hardly had time to look herself over at home before she had to run to catch the bus. So, in the employee washroom, she studied herself in the mirror, hoping that the makeup was doing its job. She didn't want anyone asking her about the marks.

The bruises on her jawline weren't too bad this time, but the fingernail scratches on her neck stood out, still ragged and sore. If only she'd thought to bring her cosmetic bag with her, she could cover them better now. As it was, she did her best to push up the collar of her work shirt so that they remained obscured.

She was so focused on her reflection that she jumped when she felt the hand on her shoulder. It was the manager. There was a call for her in the office. Her mother.

The lines on her throat burned.

Hell, what now?

She took the call in the back room, where half-assembled arcade machines lay naked and awaiting repair. When she picked up, she could tell the old woman was already drunk. This early in the morning? It didn't make any sense. She was supposed to be at the shop now. Except...

Except she *had* gone to the shop. She'd gone in with liquor on her breath, slurring her words, and the boss had finally had enough. Mommy was out of a job. And if darling daughter felt like giving her any shit about it, she could find somewhere else to live.

She tried to console her mother, but it was no use when she was like this. It wasn't long before the woman's alcohol-roughened voice screeched curses at her through the receiver, retorts against imagined slights. Then the old woman hung up.

How much money did they have left between them? How long would it last them until mom could find more work? How would it look to an employer that the woman had lost three jobs in just as many months? If her mother was still like this when she got out of work today, what would happen when she came home?

There was always something new. One step forward, two steps back. She'd been raised to believe that everything happened for a reason, but lately it seemed life was just a parade of abuse that offered neither end nor reward. Some nights, when she went to bed, she fantasized about not waking up. It just seemed so much easier.

She turned her thoughts to the god she'd been taught to pray to, wondering: Would there ever be anything other than this? Try as she might, she could not imagine any other way of life. Nothing that motivated her or gave her a sense of meaning or purpose. Nothing that indicated a life worth living.

She put the phone back on the hook and sat down, among screws and circuits and hollowed-out game cabinets, to cry.

He'd been here before.

He'd be here again.

And again.

And again.

And again.

He didn't know why. But someone out there did. Someone far beyond the world he knew, this ugly little world of death and rebirth and death again. That someone had long thought itself his master, thought him nothing more than a marionette whose strings could be pulled to make him dance and die for its entertainment. And for a long, long time, that someone had been right.

Not for much longer, though.

He had power too, a power all his own. He just had to learn to tap into it, to focus it. He could teach himself. He had all the time in the world. The windows were brief, just moments really, the space of a few breaths between waking and dying. But he would use those breaths well. He would use them to study the unseen enemy that ravaged him, figure out how it projected its will here from someplace else, devise a way to access those channels and fill them with his own desires.

He pictured his enemy in his mind as best he could. Pictured a disgusting, arrogant grin. Let that picture become a shining beacon toward which he could funnel his energies. He projected his memories onto the image, countless memories of dread and demise, of rage and sorrow, of skin-rending violence and bloodied frenzy.

Previously, he'd thought his life devoid of purpose, at least any purpose other than pain. He'd been wrong. He *did* have a purpose. He'd found and forged it himself. And in that purpose, he discovered power. Power with which he could strike back at whatever predator it was that preyed on him. Power with which he could escape this cage. Power with which he himself could be the master instead of the puppet.

It was a power born of hatred.

It had grown very, very strong in him, his hate. It had long ago eclipsed his fear and now, at last, it eclipsed his agony. His was the hate, fear, and agony of infinite lifetimes. Condemned to suffer and die for the amusement of some invisible, idiot god.

With his hate and fear and agony, he would pierce the veil between worlds. And he would repay his suffering in kind.

The arcade was always loud, but this was different.

The explosion she heard was not an electronic sound effect. Kids ran back and forth, but not the way they usually did. Not with smiles on their faces.

She followed the source of the commotion. Something was wrong with the *Phobetor* machine. The monitor was shattered, a plume of smoke ribboning out from a hole in the center of the screen. A crowd had gathered around to stare. And on the floor…

A young boy—he couldn't have been more than 12 years old—lay unmoving in a pool of blood. Glinting shards of dark glass were embedded in his forehead, in his cheeks, in his eyes, in his neck. Someone started screaming as she rushed to the boy's side. She put her hands over his throat to stop the bleeding. He didn't seem to be breathing. Another voice from the crowd called for somebody, anybody to call 911.

Then, it began.

From the hole in the *Phobetor* machine came a hundred tendrils, each one a collection of a dozen wires braided around one another. They slithered out of the cabinet and hovered in the air. Another scream sliced through the crowd, a preview of many more to come, as the silver ropes lashed out. They wrapped themselves around arms and legs, around faces and torsos. The members of the mob couldn't get away. They were bundled too tightly together, the aisle of the arcade too cramped, hulking black game cabinets looming on every side.

She couldn't move. Not an inch. Her mind struggled to make sense of what she was seeing, the effort draining her brain of all its power, so much so that she couldn't even will herself to run.

Adults and children alike were yanked off their feet. They kicked and squirmed as they were pulled into the air, their limbs bound in loops of metallic tendons. The cords pulled their bodies taut, stretching arms and legs in opposite directions. A nauseating racket, like firecrackers going off, filled the arcade as people's bones dislocated and cracked. And still the wires pulled. One man's arm was wrenched clean from its socket. A wet knob of bone peeked out from the dripping jelly crater where his shoulder used to be. The man's shrieks did not stop until his head was liberated from his body.

A boy was torn almost perfectly in half. The split began along the side of his neck and quickly plunged downward, sketching a scarlet thunderbolt all the way down to his crotch. When his body finally gave way, skin and muscle and bone snapping apart, his innards fell to the floor, the grisly offerings of a human piñata. She couldn't name the organs, couldn't tell the bulbous globs from the curled tubes, but she knew his rectum must be among them, as the putrid reek of shit permeated the air. Above, the two gutted halves of the boy flopped lifelessly from gore-soaked cables.

All of a sudden, her brain didn't bother trying to make sense of anything anymore. One single thought completely overwrote her struggle to comprehend:

*Run!*

She tried to muscle her way through throngs of people also attempting to flee. More tendrils came slinking out of the broken *Phobetor* screen. They latched onto the neighboring machines, *BurgerTime* and the still unrepaired

*Marble Madness.* Some foul energy surged and sputtered along the lines. The air was thick with static electricity. The hairs on her skin stood on end.

The cabinets quaked, agitated by whatever power the *Phobetor* machine pumped into them. Their monitors glared too bright. Blinding. The heat of it almost enough to make her sweat. Hairline cracks spiderwebbed across the glass.

She put her hands over her eyes and dropped to the floor as the screens exploded, throwing white-hot shrapnel into the mob. When she finally forced herself to look again, she found the body of a teenage girl lying next to her. What was left of the girl's eyes stared through her, seeing nothing. Shards spiked her face, one cheek torn so savagely that it fell open, folds of butchered gristle dangling down.

Out of the ruins of *BurgerTime* and *Marble Madness* came more tendrils—twisted wires alive with crackling blue energy. They spread from machine to machine like a parasite's hooks.

*Rampage. Galaxian. Tempest.*

One after another they were invaded by the creeping electronic plague.

*Spy Hunter. Dragon's Lair. Space Paranoids.*

One after another their monitors exploded outward, filling the arcade's aisles with a crossfire of sparks and broken glass.

From each machine spilled forth more tendrils, but not all were concerned with colonizing other arcade cabinets. More people were pulled into the air to be brutalized. Some had their limbs ripped out or their bodies split apart. Others suffered fresher hells.

Some were fortunate. Some were simply strangled or

electrocuted. Many more had it far worse. Many more had their eyes gouged out and their tongues slashed to strips and their teeth pulled loose. Some were whipped to death by the heavy cords, each strike carving deep red canals into their flesh. Some had every orifice invaded by wires, filled quite literally to bursting. Some had their entire bodies twisted, the top halves in one direction, the bottoms in another, until their ribs splintered and poked out from the skin and their eyes rolled back into their heads.

When they were done, the snake-like things dropped whatever was left of the dead to the floor and slithered off in search of more victims. Victims whose heads were wrapped in layer after layer of metal until their skulls caved in. Victims whose torsos were slit opens so their guts could be pulled out piece by piece. Victims whose flesh was peeled back, flayed right from the muscle, until they were no more than glistening pink puppets with roadmaps of blue veins, raw and pulsing.

The stench of singed hair was everywhere, as well as that of spoiled meat.

Neon City was a necropolis.

She stayed low on the floor, hostage to the fear that shuddered through her, trying to hold her breath and control her shaking. Playing dead. Working up the courage to make a run for it.

She waited and watched. Then, in a brief moment when all the tendrils were occupied with other victims, she took her shot and bolted for the exit.

She never had a chance.

A cable shot out at her from the fanged maw of an *I, Robot* machine, catching her foot. She fell face-first into a pile of skinless bodies. Reeling back, she wept and swatted globs of yellow fat from her chin, then felt something metal brush her hair. A tendril coiled itself around her neck. She tried to pull it away, but it suddenly snapped tight, trapping her fingers there against her throat. With a violent jolt, it dragged her up to the ceiling. She wheezed, desperately drawing in what meager amount of air the anaconda's grip allowed. More serpents came to explore her flesh.

They wrapped around her wrists, her ankles, her waist. She recognized the taste of copper as glowing filaments crept into her mouth like slender insect legs.

Tiny currents of electricity prodded the wet tenderness of her tongue and mouth. The hot strands pushed deeper. They clawed and scratched at her throat from inside, shredding her esophagus as they sought even more forbidden depths. Something twitched in her stomach. Something sharp. Now, the copper taste in her mouth wasn't the wires. It was blood.

It was like she'd gulped down a gallon of acid. Every inch of her burned from the inside out. She felt sweaty and sick. Her body convulsed, urging her to vomit, but the cords lodged in her throat left her only to gag perpetually. Razorblades danced beneath the surface of her skin. She could feel her muscles being pulled apart, fiber by fiber. Could feel the hollow places within her flooding with the blood that spilled from severed arteries. Could feel metal scraping bone as the wires etched a secret language onto her skeleton.

*Pain* became a meaningless word. It didn't even begin to summarize what she felt. Her brain cells crackled, overloading with sensory information. Her body finally started to go numb, replacing the all-consuming hurt with a deep, immersive cold.

The world turned crimson.

Then, she was gone.

She'd been here before.

When she opened her eyes, it was like she was waking from a deep, bottomless sleep. She didn't remember nodding off, though. Certainly not here. Not in this place.

Candy-colored lights blinked against blackness. A hundred conversations mingled together with the short, playful tunes that squeaked and buzzed from the surrounding machines.

An open textbook and a paper plate with chicken fingers on it sat before her. Little by little, it came back to her. She was on her break. This place, this was where she worked. The arcade. Neon City, that's what it was called. Had she really dozed off while eating? Maybe she was pushing herself too hard. Between school and her job and everything going on at home, it made sense that she was exhausted.

Why, then, was there this other thing inside her? This growing dread. A fear that felt familiar. Something bad was going to happen. Something that had happened before. Something that some lost part of her had once known intimately.

No. That was ridiculous. Probably just nerves. The calculus midterm was tomorrow, and her grades this semester were already in rough shape.

## 201

She licked a splash of red off her finger.
Almost out of ketchup. Damn.

## AUTHOR'S NOTE

The theory that violent entertainment creates violent people has never held much weight with me. I grew up reading books by Clive Barker and Edward Lee and playing games like *Splatterhouse* and *Doom*, and I turned out just fine. More or less.

Still, I was intrigued upon learning that, in 1986, Exidy released an arcade game called *Chiller*. Little more than a constant barrage of senseless torture and death, *Chiller* was outright banned in parts of the world. Although critics have long unfairly lambasted video games as so-called "murder simulators," this one actually fits the bill.

My fictionalized version, *Phobetor*, takes its name from the Greek god of nightmares. The idea that "life is but a dream" isn't far removed from Simulation Hypothesis, which posits that the universe we inhabit is basically a computer program. Far-fetched as that may sound, is it really so different from the things a lot of us already believe? The phrase "intelligent design" could just as easily refer to a piece of software as it could the whole of creation.

Many people place their faith in a divine, benevolent creator figure. But think back to every video game you've ever played. How many times have you killed an NPC just to see if you could? How many times have you jumped your own character off a cliff for a laugh?

Simply put, how benevolent are you when you're the one in control?

# ONEIROVISION
## BY BRIAN O'CONNELL

T he exit was just around the bend. He was so close.
But they were waiting for him at the door.

"Shit, man," laughed Ace, grabbing Harry and pulling him over to the wall. "We almost missed you."

Harry looked around. There were just two others. If he could get free of Ace's grip, he could probably make a break for it.

"God, you're disgusting," muttered Ace. "If I had it my way, I'd—"

Harry kneed Ace in the balls and shoved him into his two goonies. He pushed open the door, the others shouting behind him.

It was a sunny day, a clear sky shining between New York's looming skyscrapers. Harry's father'd probably be in Central Park, playing crappy guitar music for a few soggy dollars to add to his measly salary.

To avoid any possible retribution from Ace, he looked for a quick route away. He darted across the traffic-clogged street, working around a construction crew on the road and entering a dark alleyway.

The cramped alley was long and dark, the sky just a sliver between two tottering concrete walls. He was, as far as he could see, alone. Puddles littered the place—though whether they were beer, piss, or vomit, Harry couldn't tell. A reeking dumpster squatted near the opening, piled high with bags of trash and half-finished food. Harry held his nose and ran past it.

He slowed to a leisurely pace once he was within a safe distance of the dumpster. The alley was abnormally claustrophobic. He could hear movement up in the higher echelons of the stained brick walls, as if birds nested there, although the sounds he heard sounded like they came from something much larger than mere pigeons.

As he scurried forward, he passed a single, solitary door—a dark metal color, with a single word scrawled on it in faded slashes of chalk:

*abattoir*

He didn't know what the word meant.

Underneath it was a cardboard sign. The same spidery handwriting marked out in dark black marker:

## JACK BAALS AMAZI G NEW VIRTUAL REALITY EXPERIENSE VOLUNNTEERS W NTED IMEDEATLY

*Virtual reality?* It was something he'd heard of—there had been a news report on it a while back—but he'd never imagined seeing it in person, especially not in his boring neighborhood.

He stared at the sign for a little longer, but realized his

dad was probably heading home by now, so he ran to the end of the alley—it seemed longer than he'd originally thought—and out onto the pavement. Above, the grey sky frowned down, cold winds blowing in from the east.

"Where the hell have you been?" his father shouted as he opened the apartment door.

"Huh?" Harry said, throwing his bag aside. He sank down into the couch, looking up at his father.

"You're an hour late," he snapped, his brow furrowed with frustration. "Was some sort of club going on?"

Harry looked around, stunned. He was sure he'd come straight home, except for the detour in the alley. He couldn't have imagined the walk taking more than fifteen minutes.

"I don't know what you're—"

"Cut the bullshit," his dad snapped, and sat down in the armchair. He leaned in, inhaled deeply, and looked him in the eye. "Harry. Is there a girl?"

"W-what? No," he said, surprised. "Dad, I—I took a slightly different way home, and I stopped to look at… to look at a shop. Then went straight home."

His dad stared at him for a long time. His stern eyes were set deep in a brow long creased with frustration, a heavy weariness draped over his whole frame.

He suddenly stood up and walked into the kitchen.

"Whatever. Lie to me."

He heard his father opening the door to the fridge, followed by the clink of a beer bottle. The first drink of the night.

Later, at dinner, whenever Harry tried to start a conversation—to say something, *anything*—his father just grumbled.

His father left the room as soon as he'd finished his meal, and as he shuffled on his coat he called "I'm going out. You know the drill." He slammed the door behind him.

Harry sighed and finished his dinner.

He was accustomed to his father's various "moods." He seemed to not care when something was important and overreact when something wasn't. When Harry'd first brought up Ace, his father had just said to take a different route; when he came been home unusually late, it was sex or drugs. That didn't even make sense: Harry was only just thirteen, and even *he* acknowledged that he didn't have a strong grasp on such ideas yet.

He watched some cartoons until eight o'clock. He knew from experience that his father wouldn't be back until ten at least, so he decided to go to bed early. As he settled into bed, his thoughts drifted away from his lost time and towards the sign, the promise of VR. That single word, scrawled in chalk.

*abattoir*.

His sleep was deep and dreamless.

With Ace being out sick, Harry's path out of school the next day was unobstructed. As he crossed the street, he got a nasty surprise: his father was parked across the street, waiting for him.

Honking loudly, he rolled down the window, shouting "Hey, Harry! Get over here!"

Some kids were staring, a few outright laughing. He felt the blood rushing to his cheeks.

He paced around to the back seat, sliding in and slamming the door.

"Easy," his father snapped.

"Dad, why are you here? I want to walk home—"

"Harry, calm down. I just thought I'd pick you up today…"

They argued the whole way home. As soon as they got to their apartment his dad went into the living room and played the guitar like there was no tomorrow. Harry sulkily did his homework on the kitchen table. They ate dinner in separate rooms.

The next few weeks were hell.

His father picked him up every day after school, always in the same place. Thankfully he didn't attract as much attention, but that didn't matter to Ace, who would routinely shove him around after school and taunt him for his overbearing father. This often caused him to be late to the car, which made his father angry, and when he tried to explain he was met with a simple "Christ, Harry, just kick his ass and be done with it."

One night, when his father was slouched in the armchair in the living room, flat beer in hand, Harry crept in and asked "Is something wrong?"

"Huh?"

"Is something wrong? Other than me disappearing for an hour."

His dad paused, breathing deeply.

"I think I'm going to lose my job."

Harry paused, stunned, and then felt anger well up inside of him. *That* was the problem? That he might lose his job? What gave him the right to take it out on his son?

He thought about saying something, but he figured he'd regret it, so he just walked out of the room.

After Ace beat the living daylights out of him the next day, he stumbled out onto the school's lawn and stopped when he saw his father's car. So he was *still* bothering him, even after he basically admitted that Harry's behavior wasn't the issue. Great. Why should he encourage his father's whining? His dad picking him up wasn't really that big of a deal, but walking home had given him some sense of maturity. His dad picking him up took away that sense of independence. He would walk home, then, and call his dad when he got back to the apartment. He'd have to take a slightly different route in order to avoid his father's field of view, but no matter. At worst he'd get grounded, at best he'd get his privileges back.

As he turned to cross the street he felt a twinge of guilt, but it faded when he thought of his father's own misdirected anger.

As he walked, something drew him down a familiar path, toward a certain dark alley. He stopped in front of a solitary metal door. The sign was still there:

## VIRTUAL REALITY EXPERIENSE VOLUNNTEERS W NTED IMEDEATLY

*I should go in.* The thought popped into his head unbidden, as if it wasn't his, a message from another mind.

It was a stupid idea. He didn't want to worry his father, and yet—

And yet, here he was.

*Virtual reality.*

His favorite thing in the world was to go to an arcade; he imagined VR would be even better.

*Come on. Just have a look around. They probably won't even let you in.*

He knocked.

The door swung open as if someone had been looming behind it, waiting for him. Standing in the frame was a man in his early-to-mid thirties, a boyish look about him, with combed brown hair and a brown-orange suit that looked like it belonged to a '60s real estate agent. His skin was as white as a sheaf of paper.

"Hello!" he said, and smiled warmly. "I'm Mr. Baal—you can call me Jack if you like. I run the place."

"Uh, hi," Harry stammered, taken aback. "I was, just, I noticed your sign, and…"

"I figured," Jack said, and chuckled musically. He removed the sign from the front and looked at it. "Yeah, our guy who wrote the sign, he isn't very good at spelling. I should really start doing these myself." He looked back at Harry. "Want to come and see?"

"O-okay," he stuttered.

Abattoir, on the inside, was a long corridor with steely metal walls and flickering fluorescent lights. Doors lined the corridor, each numbered in chalk, but oddly out of order, and underneath each numeral were bizarre little symbols he didn't recognize.

When he shut the door behind him, the air rushed by outside, as if they had stepped aboard an airplane.

"Follow me, young man," Jack said, and kept walking. "By the by, what's your name? I don't think I caught it."

"Harry," he replied, catching up.

"Harry. Good name," his host continued. "I had a friend named Harry, once."

They turned a corner. The hallway was almost exactly the same as the corridor he had just walked down. The monotony of the building's passageways gave him an uneasy feeling.

Another turn and still the same. Harry suddenly realized how fast he had been to jump into this, to follow a stranger without knowing anything about him—how isolated this alley was, and how labyrinthine the corridors—

"Here we are!" said Jack, and Harry jumped a little. Jack opened the door.

Jack ushered him into a sparsely furnished room, the walls still that aged metal, the concrete floor splotchy with irregular dark stains. The dim lights flickered above. For some reason there was a dirty mirror and a rusty sink that looked like it might not even work anymore, both placed near the door, and on the back of the door there was a blank whiteboard.

At the far end of the room there was what looked like a dentist's chair, and on the table next to it was a large black... *object* like a thick pair of goggles, with some cumbersome mechanisms attached to the end.

The word *"ONEIROVISION"* was printed in a slick red font across its front side. A pair of headphones and a set of wire-covered gloves were connected to the headset, and a long cord linked the set to a computer tower, a monitor nearby.

*"Wow,"* was all Harry could say.

"She's a beauty, isn't she?" his guide said, smiling. "You want to try her on?"

"Yes, please," was his breathless response, and before he knew it he was sitting down in the dentist's chair and Jack was fiddling with the headset.

"It's gonna feel a little awkward at first," Jack said, carefully picking up the contraption. "But we can tighten the straps a little."

Harry sank back into the chair's yellowed cushions. Jack came over with the headset, gloves, and headphones.

"Sit up, please."

The headset went on first. It was extremely uncomfortable, pressing into his eyes like swimming goggles when Jack tightened the straps. The darkness before him seemed infinite. Next came the headphones.

"So what'll I be seeing?" Harry asked—probably shouted, since his hearing was muted.

"Oh, it's, uh… it's a video game," Jack said, his voice softened by the headphones. "A kind of fantasy thing. Unless you'd rather one of the other scenarios…"

"No, that's fine!" he shouted again, and felt excitement well up within him. He was going to be playing a video game—except, like, *in* the video game. It was the most incredible thing he'd ever heard. He couldn't wait to start playing.

"It's also going to be a little scary, but you can handle that, right?"

"Yeah," he replied. His dad had shown him *Tales from the Darkside* a few months before, and he watched *Are You Afraid of the Dark?* and *Goosebumps* on Saturdays.

Jack's cold hands pulled the gloves (uncomfortable as well, slightly bumpy on the inside) over his hands.

"You're gonna hear some feedback on the headphones," shouted Jack. "And you might see these… flashy things that pop onscreen. They're just little glitches."

He gave Jack a thumbs-up, but it felt weird to move his fingers inside the gloves.

Jack walked over to the corner. Keys clacked on the monitor.

Something red flickered in the darkness, but it was gone in an instant. Then the word: "START" flashing in green, very far off. Jack hit a key, and the screen went dark again.

A floor made of black cobblestones faded into view. He lifted his hands and looked at them. They were strong, calloused, tan.

"Whoa!" he cried, and a grin involuntarily leapt to his face. "It's so real!"

He didn't hear Jack's answer because the audio was

coming in—a mournful orchestra, sighing in his ears. He looked up. Standing before him was a human caricature. Its naked, emaciated skin was dead white but shot through with dribbling grey-black shades; its arms were long and dragged behind it like ropes; its eyes stared out at him from pitch-black hollows; its flesh sagged over its angular bones; the back of its head curved back and down; it grinned a lipless grin; and its nose was a dull red.

It looked so *real*.

"Hero," it croaked, mouth out of sync with the words, *"are you ready to save the Princess?"*

He nodded, eagerly, but his mouth was still wide open from shock.

The sad song of the orchestra was still going, but it was underscored by noise: a fire-like crackling, and a subtler, whispering sound. He couldn't make out the words.

Doors he hadn't noticed opened out onto a red light.

*"The Princess is trapped in the Black Tower,"* it smiled. *"You must save her… or die trying."*

All of a sudden he was moving into the red light. As he did, something flickered across the screen, white and indiscernible.

The light cleared and he found himself gazing upon a blasted landscape. The cracked red earth was broken by pits of fire, while lightning-shadowed mountains loomed out in the distance. A strong wind blew the thin coating of red dust into his eyes—well, what *would've* been his eyes. Things flew across the sky, screeching. Against a golden sun, a far-off tower silhouetted itself, sagging from years of neglect.

"Oh my God!" he cried, half-laughing.

*"The Princess lies yonder,"* said the thing, and its long arm

pointed to the decaying tower. "*Now go, Hero, and save our world!*" it cackled, and the door clanked shut behind him. He was moving again, striding down steep steps. A sulfurous smell singed his nostrils—no, a trick of the mind.

He passed by a pit of fire when he heard a voice from the flame.

"Help!" it cried. "*I am imprisoned in the fire!*"

He reached his hand out (noticing how strong his arm had become) and stuck it into the flame. If there was another flash, he didn't notice it. His hand came out of the roaring conflagration grasping a golden sword coated in symbols and signs. It spoke, and glowed in sync with its words. "*I am that which you have rescued,*" it said. "*Thank you for rescuing me. In return, I shall be your Sword.*"

The VR set was more comfortable now, and he was growing less awed by the startling visuals of the game. When was he going to get to fight monsters? And was that whispery feedback ever going to stop?

Suddenly, something swooped down from above, laughing madly. He turned around and there loomed a winged creature, pig-headed and horrible.

"*A demon of the Black Castle!*" cried the Sword.

The thing lunged at him. Impulsively, he swung the Sword and slashed the blade across its soft pink face. Black blood spurted from the wound, smoking on its skin. It squealed.

"*Now's your chance!*" said the Sword. "*Kill it while you can!*"

The demon had recovered and swiped at him with its talons. He raised the Sword high and swung it down into the creature's face, cleaving it in two. It made one last choking screech before falling limp onto the ground, its acidic blood corroding the ground.

"*Incredible!*" the Sword said, its blade flashing at him in the sunlight. "*You truly are the greatest of heroes.*"

He grinned. He was, wasn't he? But he couldn't be proven so until he rescued the Princess. So onward he moved, the Sword praising him all the way.

After a couple more scrapes with monsters—an insectoid scavenger, a bloodthirsty ghoul—he finally approached the Black Castle. Its single dark turret leered at him from far above, its crooked, twisting body unlike any architecture he'd ever seen.

Running up to the gate, he shoved his way through the red door and dashed up the cobwebbed spiral staircase that he found within. It was pitch dark, and the whispering voices seemed louder, urging him to go on.

He reached the top of the staircase and faced a black door with some esoteric symbol scrawled on it in chalk. Without hesitation, he shoved it open, and burst into the room.

He found himself in a well-lit hall bedecked with rotting banners. The Princess—a beautiful young woman wearing a flowing pink robe—stood in a chalk circle filled with ominous symbols. Dark tendrils were wrapped around her legs, holding her prisoner.

At the far end of the hall was a gigantic black portal, and within its twisting shadows he could just make out a large, white figure. It reached out a pale, bony hand, a million times larger than that of the entity that had greeted him in this world.

It groaned a word he didn't understand.

"*Ohhhhh,*" the Sword moaned, and it lost its luster.

"*Oh! Flee this place, now!*" cried the Princess. "*Or you will surely be slain.*"

"*She is right,*" said the voice from the portal. "*You were only able to defeat my minions because of your magic Sword, who is currently... indisposed.*" A malevolent cackle rang throughout the hall.

"*Run!*" the Princess wept.

Rage boiled in his heart. This thing had kidnapped the Princess and killed his friend. He couldn't bear it.

He let out a great roar, and dashed towards the portal, blunt sword upheld. He leapt into the inky blackness of the Voice's domain, swiping at nothing.

"*Oh, fool,*" it said, "*let it be so.*"

A giant's hand swung at him from behind and clutched him in its grip, squeezing tight. "No!" he cried, and swung his sword down on the fingers, releasing smoky clouds of crimson. A horrible roar echoed across the void. He swung again, severing the fingers at their joints, and dropped out of the Voice's grip... just in time to see *another* hand, this one coming from above. His blade stabbed the palm.

Another scream. "*Murder!*" it cried. "*Treachery!*"

The hand withdrew into the blackness of the portal, but he followed. Beyond its limits, he found a pale, protruding stomach. He roared again, and slashed, sawing back and forth. A mutilated hand tried to grab him, but he dodged back before leaping forward to strike at the twisted belly once more. With one cut, he severed a thin layer of flesh and muscle and the thing was disemboweled, its organs tumbling out.

In one great flash the corpse-belly and the darkness of its domain vanished. He found himself once again in the hall. The dark tendrils holding the Princess were broken, and she wept with joy.

"*Oh, thank you, Hero!*" she cried.

"*Good job!*" said a familiar voice, and he lifted the Sword, now shining again. "*The wicked monster's spell on me is broken!*"

"*Would you like to go again?*" said another voice.

He turned and saw the creature he had first seen in this world: sagging flesh, red nose.

"What?" he muttered.

The world became dark around them, and he saw the Princess and the Sword disappear.

"*Would you like to go again?*" it repeated.

He thought it over and then smiled broadly. "Yes," he said. "I think I would."

The thing made no response, but he looked down and saw the familiar cobblestone floor.

"Hero," the creature croaked, "*are you ready to save the Princess?*"

The flying pig-thing lunged at him. Impulsively, he swung the Sword at it, and slashed the blade across its soft pink face. Black blood spurted from the wound, smoking on its skin. It squealed.

*"Now's your chance!"* said the Sword. *"Kill it while you can!"*

The demon had recovered and swiped at him with its talons. He raised the Sword high and—

The world went black.

He looked around, puzzled, but didn't see anything. What had happened?

He gradually became aware of a growing discomfort all over his body. He felt so sluggish and tired he didn't think he could move. He became disoriented, aware that he was wearing something on his hands, ears, and eyes.

He lifted his hands. So, *so* difficult. It felt as if his bones were rubber. He felt around his face. There was a bizarre device strapped onto his head. A word popped into his mind unbidden:

*Headset.*

Somehow he managed to pull it off, along with the devices on his ears. He squeezed his eyes shut against the painful light, then struggled to keep them open as they adjusted. He thought he knew this place. What was it? It was…

*Abattoir.* He had gone to Abattoir, for… for a VR tutorial. His name was—Henry? No, it was *Harry*. He was Harry, and he was thirteen and he lived in New York City with his father.

How many times had he played through the game? How had he so utterly lost himself in it?

He tried to lift his head, but the movement was so painful he immediately sank back into the chair. Gently tilting his head to the right, he saw something on the side of the chair.

It was an IV, filled with clear liquid and connected to a

tube. He followed its length, downwards, towards the bed… stuck into his own arm.

He froze. What was he being injected with? Why was he being given an injection in the first place? Furthermore, what was wrong with his arm? It was incredibly pale, and was distinctively chubbier than he remembered.

He didn't recognize his own body.

His stomach bulged from underneath his stained shirt, and he felt like his feet might burst out of his shoes. Every ounce of him was straining against its limits.

He reached toward the syringe in his arm and, shutting his eyes to the pain, he tugged it out. The pain shocked him, jolting his system.

He tried to scream, but all he could manage was a faint wheeze.

He began to pull himself up, but his bones were so weak they shook under the pressure. It hurt so badly. He gave another push.

He fell forward, nearly falling flat on the floor, but he managed to stand almost upright. He put one of his hands against the wall for support, and he began to walk forward awkwardly. He approached the mirror.

When he saw his reflection he screamed, or tried to.

He was, indeed, very obese, but that wasn't what worried him. He looked *older*. His hair fell around his ears, there was a smattering of drool on his chin, and he could see the beginnings of peachfuzz on his jawline. He could pass for an eighth grader if he tried!

He wiped the drool from his mouth and kept moving, horrified, along the wall of the room. The handwriting of an uneven, quivering hand stood out in sharp black against the whiteboard:

```
KIDNE (1)
GALL-BLADDUR
SPLEEN
```

A pit grew in his stomach. He lifted his shirt, and found a vertical scar along the side of his chest.

*Oh God, oh Jesus Christ.*

He pulled open the door and moved along it into the flickering hall, which was mercifully empty. But he didn't know in which direction to go, and the random numbers gave no indication.

He decided to try left; it was as good a direction as any. He crept along the wall, feeling like he could stumble at any time, his stomach knotting itself into a ball.

He saw a door with a symbol that for some reason looked familiar. On impulse he flung himself across the hall and pushed it open.

It took a second for his eyes to adjust to the darkness, but the smell of meat hit him full-force before anything else.

A set of wooden stairs led from the door downwards into a wide pit of black gravel. A gigantic thing crouched in the darkness, fetal. It looked exactly like the creature he had first seen in the game, but enormous, nearly house-sized. Objects were strewn about its legs, glistening wetly in the darkness, and with horror, he realized these were organs—perhaps human. As he watched, nauseated, the monster extended one of its long arms and daintily scooped up some of the entrails, nearly squishing them in the process. The beast reared its head back and unhinged its jaw, snake-like, dropping the viscera into its gaping maw.

He slammed the door shut and dry-heaved. Glancing back up at the door, Harry realized where he recognized the symbol. It was on the door to the turret of the Black Tower.

He stumbled blindly and painfully away from the door, turning any corner he found, hoping for some stroke of luck that would lead him to the exit. *Oh, God,* what was his father thinking? Did his father even care? Did he think he'd run away, or been murdered? Had he been looking for him?

He tripped over his bulging shoes and onto the ground. It hurt like nothing he'd ever felt before. He tried to scream again, but his voice failed him. Tears came to his eyes. He looked at the arm he no longer recognized and clawed at it desperately, watching the red scratch marks form on his flesh.

He heard footsteps coming. He pulled himself up with a titanic effort and dragged himself around a corner just as someone entered the hallway. A voice muttered something, and footsteps faded into the distant passages of another corridor.

Harry turned and felt a glimmer of hope. He thought he recognized that door. And three doors to his left, he recognized that one, too. Was this the way out?

As he turned another corner, he saw more and more doors that he recognized. He was on his way towards the exit, then; he would burst out through the door and claw his way into the street. It was going to be okay. Yes, yes, *yes,* he recognized all of this. The exit was just around the bend. He was so close.

But they were waiting for him at the door.

"Well, shit," laughed Jack, bursting out of a door just before the exit. Two human-sized versions of the thing that had greeted him in the game followed, grinning listlessly at his side.

Jack pulled a gun out of his suit and fired. The flash and the pain happened in the same moment.

Harry collapsed, whining like a wounded animal, trying desperately to scream. Warm blood ran down his leg, and sharp pain radiated from where the bullet remained lodged in his flesh.

"They say mental torture works a lot better than physical torture," mused Jack, "but I call bullshit on that. If you stab an animal in the leg, it's going to scream like it never has before."

The two abominations lifted Harry up with their grotesquely large hands. He wriggled weakly in their grip. There was another jolt of pain in his leg and he winced, his eyes watering.

"Humans are basically animals anyway," Jack said, placing the gun in his jacket. "They're stupid, easily distracted, and only useful for their meat. Of course, you have to make them complacent for their cooperation. That's what OneiroVision is for."

They carried him away from the door, the exit—his only hope—receding with each painful shuffle back. He feebly raised his swollen hand towards the door, but it was gone, now. They'd turned a corner.

"When we lived in the forests and mountains and lakes, people said we wanted their souls," Jack said. "As if we'd ever settle for anything so intangible!"

They turned another corner. The fluorescent lights moved in a dull row above him. He thought of his father.

They were back in the room. His room, another room—

it didn't matter. Back in the dentist's chair. He tried to get up again, but thick straps held his wrists in place.

"We've got a few others like you in here, and when you're running an operation like ours, this kind of stuff can happen from time to time," said Jack, washing his hands in the sink. "But we're working out the bugs."

One of the creatures picked up the headset and turned back toward Harry.

*No*, he thought, *no no no. Shoot me instead. Please.* He turned to Jack, shaking his head, looking for even a hint of mercy.

Jack only laughed.

The IV needled into his vein and he winced. On came the gloves.

*No!*

The headphones and the headset drowned out the world.

There the thing stood, the computer analogue of a real monster, grinning at him. *"Hero,"* it smiled. *"Are you ready to save the Princess?"*

He drifted into the red light, and, as it flashed, he thought he could make out words. But he couldn't see what they were.

The flashes just kept coming, but they bothered him less and less as time went on. He stopped thinking about Abattoir, and his father, and his life. The game was so immersive. He *liked* being the barbarian warrior. In fact, after saving the Princess from the clutches of the Voice an innumerable amount of times, he wasn't sure that he had ever been anyone else at all.

## AUTHOR'S NOTE

Virtual reality is where I see video games going. It's already becoming a household thing, with highly affordable technology like Google Cardboard, and games have only gotten more and more immersive over the years… so I don't think it's that much of a stretch to say that one day VR will be the norm and not the exception.

I wondered if it could be used for the wrong reasons by the wrong people (as technology always is). And in the mid-'90s, when "OneiroVision" is set, the promise of using it would've been tantalizing to anyone, especially children. I got a nice high strange vibe from that idea.

That was basically the genesis of this story. Little bits and pieces (paintings by Alan Brown and Francisco Goya, some Clark Ashton Smith, the Steve Skeates-Richard Corben comic "The Hero Within," Stephen Gammell's cover to *Scary Stories to Tell in the Dark*, a love for body horror, etc.) started falling into place. A recent reading of *Providence* by Alan Moore and Jacen Burrows also inspired the idea of throwing subtle hints at Abattoir's true nature early in the story. Looking at it now, though, the main influence is probably R.L. Stine's *Goosebumps* series, which I read a lot when I was younger.

While I do occasionally play video games, it's rather infrequent, so I needed some help. Thanks to Christopher Bo, Thierry Martineau, Thomas Sterns, and my younger brother Brendan for helping in that regard (sometimes only by example, but still). Thanks also to the fantastic Jonathan Raab, who made this story the best it could be.

This was not the first Abattoir story written (although it's the first published), and it certainly won't be the last, as I plan to revisit its corridors sometime soon. Abattoir has a thousand rooms, and there's something nasty going on in every one of them.

# LEEDS 2600

## BY MATTHEW M. BARTLETT

**H**hen the familiar raspy call of the bicycle bell rang out, I rose from among the pile of unwrapped gifts and ran to the kitchen window to see my cousin Kendrick's old green Schwinn leaning against the side of the garage. My first thought was that something was wrong. Why else would he show up alone at our house on Christmas morning? He lived three towns away, and it was cold out, bitterly cold, and the wind was kicking up great clouds of snow from the rooftops.

Kendrick practically burst through the kitchen door, shivering and sighing, a crust of ice gilding the edge of his knit cap. Mom and Dad greeted him with surprise and possibly feigned exclamations of joy.

"Just visiting," he said, "just coming by to say Merry Christmas!" Dad offered him a cup of cocoa, then pulled out a chair at the kitchen table. He followed Mom as she went to call her sister to see if everything was okay at home.

Kendrick looked up at me, his hands gripping the mug,

knuckles flecked with dry skin like ash, cheeks red with cloud-like splotches. Little tawny rocks of sleep crowded the corners of his eyes. I wanted more than anything to pick at them. Kendrick looked left and then right, as if checking the kitchen for spies, then he pulled from the inside pocket of his coat a small black cartridge.

"For your Atari," he said, and handed it to me. It wasn't wrapped, and it had no label, just the remnants of the one he'd torn off—traces of adhesive like clumps of snow left after a cold winter. Scrawled in thick black lines—I caught a whiff of that pungent permanent marker smell—was **LEEDS 2600**.

"I made this," he said, eyes serious. "Now that the protection spell can't hold you anymore, it should be of some efficacy. It's important, Loretta, that you know about Leeds before Leeds knows about you."

I already knew a little from my classmates about the myths surrounding the town. Ghosts of long-dead occultists and grave robbers. Disappearances, dangerous derelicts and their tent cities in the trees, all of it somehow connected to some creepy radio station down at the low end of the dial. It was just rumors, I thought then, just the stuff conjured up by the bored residents of a town on the wrong end of the state, so far from Boston, to try to make the city seem more interesting. Besides, I never spun the dial any further down than 96 WTIC FM, whose signal carried the Top 40 hits all the way up from Hartford.

Kendrick lowered his voice and leaned in. "And while I'm at it, look, I'm a little high, so maybe I shouldn't be saying all this, but... Loretta, when you get your first car, I want you to have the dealership take the radio out, okay? And never go into the woods, not past the point you can still see the road, or a house. No matter who tries to get you to."

Somehow, coming from him, it bore more weight than the babble from the other kids. He looked so serious when he said it, so worried. I would do as he asked.

I always had a little crush on Kendrick. He was tall—gawky, even—with long dirty-blonde hair that fell around his shoulders in curls. His thick glasses sat atop a bent beak of a nose, framing lively, alert blue eyes. He had a receding double chin, cheeks ravaged by acne, and full, puffy lips occasionally bisected by the yellowed edges of his buck teeth. His flannel shirts were always too big for him, his jeans frayed and stringy at the seams. He called me Kid and Sweet Girl and Lovely Loretta, and was the only one of the adults—hardly, he was sixteen or so, but he was the most mature of all the cousins—who would indulge a twelve-year old girl with pimples and braces and a book always at hand.

It's been a long time since Kendrick disappeared. I never thought he had come to harm and I refuse to believe that he's dead. His was simply too restless a mind to stay in any one place for too long, and I think his family did the worst thing they could do to him short of neglect or abuse: they bored him.

*I* didn't bore him. That has always been a point of pride for me.

He was the kind of kid to take everything apart to see how it worked. I think it was only a very basic sense of right and wrong that prevented him from becoming a serial killer. I remember him holding a stray cat in his lap, prying open its mouth gently but firmly with his fingers and looking down its throat. The cat protested and Kendrick released it, but there was a deep disappointment in his eyes, and a fervent, obsessed look. It worried me. Maybe electronics and computers were a distraction. Maybe they saved him.

But maybe — and I don't like to consider this — maybe he disappeared in order to fulfill that forbidden desire: to separate people into their component parts and study them.

I know he'll come back to me one day and tell me all about where he's been and what he's been doing. I can't wait. I hope they let me see him — they're very cautious about my having visitors.

*Nurse Angel sails into the room, tapping with the tips of her fingernails on the open door as she passes, not to request entrance, but to avoid startling me. I admit, I do startle easily. Still, I dislike rudeness, and entering without asking permission is terribly rude. Only Kendrick could get away with it. Kendrick and, I suppose, Nurse Angel.*

*-Good morning, Loretta. What are you writing today?*

*-Another diary entry, Nurse Angel.*

*-Can I see?*

*-No.*

*-Come on now, Loretta. It's part of your therapy. We have a* Full Disclosure *policy, my dear, and you know this.*

-Zero Tolerance. Full Disclosure. Open Door. *All your*

*policies are two words, Nurse Angel. Did you ever notice that?*
*-I never did, Loretta. Thank you for enlightening me.*
*-Don't condescend.*
*I chuckle.*
*-That's my two-word policy, Nurse Angel.* Don't Condescend.

See, Kendrick was always very solicitous towards me. When I was little, maybe eight, our family was over to his house for a barbecue. After we ate, his Dungeons & Dragons buddies came by. While the parents drank and told stories and roared with laughter outside on the patio, the kids all hung out in the basement. I was sitting cross-legged in the blue beanbag chair, my teddy bear Rochester curled up in my lap, listening to the strange and unfamiliar language of the Big Kids, when all went silent. I looked up, and everyone was staring at me.

Kendrick laughed and said, "I was talking to you, Loretta." He asked if they could do a "protection ritual" on me. At the time I had a very limited understanding of what the ritual was supposed to protect me *from*… but it sounded good on general principle. I had to be unclothed, but my cousin let me change on my own behind the water boiler and wrap myself many times over in a king-sized bedsheet, and when Jimmy Goodrich looked at me funny, Kendrick smacked the glasses off his face, and then confiscated them. No pervert stuff happened, by the way, no matter the accusations of my parents and the innuendo of the staff here, lurid garbage that says more about their own twisted imaginations than it says about Kendrick and his friends.

The ritual consisted mostly of the boys chanting, and me repeating strange syllables they were throwing at me. At one point Kendrick rubbed some kind of brown dust behind my ears—the aroma of charcoal and clover and something vaguely flowery. Then he gave me a necklace with a small purple-blue stone.

"That will hold you," my cousin said, "until puberty." I had no idea what puberty was, but it sounded like something far away.

Whatever the aromatic dust had consisted of, whatever the chanting had meant, I really did feel protected. The bullies at school retreated from me—some still taunted me, but from a safe distance. They never shoved me anymore, never kicked me in the butt or swung me into the lockers by my backpack. I imagined a force field around me, a kind of agreeably fragrant aura shimmering in the air. I could reach out, I imagined, and feel its outer edge. I never slept better than I did in the four years before I turned 12.

That necklace is long gone, but I still have the stone. I kept it with me wherever I went. I have it with me still. Kendrick gave me a lot of gifts through the years: books, musical instruments, puzzles, and brain-teaser games. I kept all his gifts in a trunk at the foot of my bed, and all but ignored everything given to me by Mom and Dad. *LEEDS 2600* was the best thing he ever got me, not least because he designed and built it himself, but because it probably saved my life, just as it probably put me in this gentle prison with its seasonally decorated cork-boards and its two-word policies and its sweet but no-nonsense nurses with long needles in syringes full of primary-color liquids.

*Mid-mornings are quiet in the ward. The morning medications have all been dispensed, the patients mollified, sedated, or else knocked out cold. Televisions mutter in the other rooms. The* Quiet Television *policy, one policy with which I happen to agree, dictates that the volume must never go up above a 3. So the overlapping of voices and music is not altogether unpleasant. Birds twitter outside. Faux fingernails tap at computer keyboards. The phones purr.*

*I've become quite adept at detecting unfamiliar foot-falls. The nurses walk with an officious gait, they go clunk-clunk-clunk. The doctors too, but the sound is softer, somehow more self-important. The patients shuffle, of course, or step lively, recovering some semblance of youth in their demented thralls.*

*But the steps I hear now quicken my heart, for they are noticeably different: they are measured, patient. They slow—it's barely perceptible, but they do—as they pass open doorways. Somebody is searching for someone. Searching, possibly, for me.*

*I wish for that protection spell to reassert itself. I wish for those searching steps to come from Kendrick's always-untied sneakers, not the hooves of some horrible, ghoulish goat-man.* Wishes are like dishes, they never get done, *Mom used to say. She was constantly inventing little phrases like that, phrases that crumbled under the merest scrutiny. Honoring Mom's words, I stop wishing and ring for a nurse.*

The night after Christmas, Sunday, a school night. Mom and Dad had gone to bed. I waited until I heard Dad's rasping snores and I crept from my bed, retrieved the cartridge from my trunk, and inserted it into the Atari. I turned on the television. The screen went black. I don't think I'd ever seen such a deep, untainted black on that old Samsung. It looked like you could reach in and pull back a hand soaked in ink.

**COHARK PRODUCTIONS LTD** appeared in white on the screen in a blocky font. Against all that blackness the words were a ray of light beamed into the dark of my bedroom.

The music began. You know that old *bleep-bloop* Atari music. Something like a simplified, synthesized mix of "Tubular Bells." The words disappeared, leaving a ghostly afterimage that ultimately faded. Then a small white square, not much bigger than a deer tick, appeared in the middle of the screen. More dots clustered around the center like rapidly metastasizing cancer cells as the music sped up... and then the colors filled in, turning the cluster of squares into the pixelated image of a girl, maybe the heroine of the game.

I hopped up and clasped my hands over my mouth. Though it was just a stack of pixels atop a couple of outward-facing L's for legs, I recognized myself right away. Red hair in a pony-tail. My favorite blue-and-white checkered dress. A little line of brown dots that somehow expertly mimicked my eyes, which always looked a little squinty. My little legs rotated and my avatar strode purposefully to the right, off-screen. The black deepened and the music segued into something more like Brahms.

A row of trees, evenly spaced, grew up from the bottom of the screen, then a dense grey line bisected by yellow lines lifted them up to the middle. A road. Under the road, that thick and inky black. Above, a dark blue sky in which little square stars twinkled. My little avatar came in from the left side of the screen and stopped. It turned to face me and a little red explosion of pixels appeared on its face. It expanded and contracted, that little mouth. *Bleep, bloopbloop,* it said. *Bleeleeeleeloooleeloop.* I laughed out loud, because it sounded like a robot talking underwater. I felt just on the edge of being able to make out words. The other me stopped and stared. I ejected the game and popped it back in, watched the opening sequence again.

*Bleep, bloopbloop. Bleeleeeleeloooleeloop.*

*Bleep, bloopbloop. Bleeleeeleeloooleeloop.*

I woke up when Dad turned on the light. I was sitting Indian-style, leaning forward, face almost touching the screen. The night had gone by as I sat there. I was so late for school that he didn't have time to yell at me.

I didn't concentrate that day. I just wanted to get back to the game, to that strange and inky street, to hear my avatar speak her impenetrable patois, and to start the girl's journey. When I closed my eyes, the colors behind them took on the shapes and aspects of the game, clustering themselves into pixels that formed and re-formed as buildings, trees, people, blinking as they changed color and shape.

I closed my eyes a lot that day. My teachers didn't seem to notice.

*Nurse Carol pokes her head into the room.*

*"What is it, dearie?" she says.*

*"Nurse, can we go outside?"*

*She helps me from the bed, slides slippers onto my feet. Walking down the hall, past the nurse's station, past vacant gurneys and medical waste repositories and doctors in blue conferring in intimate clusters, I listen for the footfalls. The searching steps... I hear them... we're approaching them. My grip on Nurse Carol's arm tightens.*

I'll steer her down the long hall by the courtyard, *I think. And then I see him. It's just a flash as he traverses the corridor left to right, beyond the doorway at the far wall. He is hunched, covered mostly by a tattered, fly-blown black blanket gone charcoal-grey with age and time. His shoulders skim the ceiling tiles. His neck protrudes from his chest, his horrible horn-topped head covered up by the blanket, only his raw, scraped, blood-matted snout visible. His hooves discolor the floor tiles. One buckles like wet cardboard. The lights flicker above him. People pass him, consulting clipboards or staring at the floor. I am the only one who can see him, it seems. That doesn't make me feel any less unsafe.*

*When we reach the end of the corridor, we turn left toward the exit. I don't dare look behind us. My heart is beating so fast and so hard I fear my ribs might crack. I hunch, draw inward. Nurse Carol strokes my back, whispers words I cannot make out. We step out into sunlight. I tug her arm and we head for the far end of the lot. I want to feel safe, but I fear that even in the birdsong-filled brightness of a late spring afternoon, that abomination might burst from the building, stride across the lot, sweep Nurse Carol aside and bring me into the woods, where terrible things dwell, things that can take you apart and put you back together... wrong somehow... things that make you into a monster.*

*I close my eyes and listen to the birds and the whispering treetops. Somewhere in the sky a plane groans its long and weary groan. I think of Kendrick, and again I start to wish—to wish he was at my side, holding my arm, watching for trouble. I know, I know. Wish in one hand, put a joystick in the other.*

I went right to my room when I got home. I spread out my homework on the bed and switched on the TV. I laid down on my stomach and pushed in the cartridge, then turned on the Atari.

My avatar, who I had decided to name Lottie, did not try to talk to me this time. Instead she danced on the screen to the electronic music, her little stick-legs pumping. I tilted the joystick and she began to walk. The trees moved behind her, as on a platform. Ones and zeroes, wires and circuits and signals, console and cartridge interlocking invisible fingers somewhere behind their molded plastic facades. Processors, chips. Colors: green trunks, green treetops, black background. Thin black vertical lines to counterfeit the texture of bark. Zig-zag lines to indicate leaves. Somewhere in the machine all the little parts were doing calculations, responding to the movements of the joystick, the pressure of my thumb on the circular red button. The impulses of her brain moving her hand. Calculations in the neurons, thrumming with echoes of Kendrick's work—he is in the machine, in a way, his will and his thoughts enmeshed in the circuitry.

The noise of her feet, little baritone squelches. There were more trees now, or little Lottie was moving past them faster. Another noise, something new. I stopped Lottie in her tracks, leaned forward, and turned my head so that my right ear was closer to the television's speaker. A quiet squelching, growing steadily louder. Something approaching.

My heart started to beat faster, and the faraway squelching did, too. I grabbed for the joystick, fumbled with it, and then sent little Lottie running, the stick pushed all the way to the right. The trees slid by. Faint colors flashed between them, suggesting eyes, as though there was someone—or a lot of someones—watching in the middle distance.

Little Lottie ran and ran. Then it appeared before her... a hole in the ground, underneath it a ladder. The squelching sound of footsteps shook the walls of my room. I sent her down the ladder.

She walked now below ground. Above, the footsteps faded. The roof rose until the surface of the ground disappeared beyond the upper boundary of the screen. Carnival music now. And onto the screen rolled an enormous Ferris wheel, little carts dotting its circumference. Behind it rolled a cart with a podium at which stood some sort of pale grey figure. At the center of the wheel where the spokes met was an image of the visage of what looked like Jesus—a bearded face with swollen eyes, a drooping mouth, and a crown of thorns. It stayed right-side up even as the Ferris wheel turned. I tried to pilot Lottie past the wheel, but one of the carts scooped her up and she rose into the black sky.

Then the crown of thorns began to separate, break off. Each piece became a brown spider with black eyes on the end of wriggling antennae. They crawled up the spokes toward my cart. The one in the lead, the largest, reached the cart just as it reached the apex. I hit the button and Lottie leapt to the next cart, all the spiders changing direction to follow her. She jumped to the next, and to the next, and then down to the ground. I sent her running.

From the right now came a bouncing skull. I hit the button and Lottie jumped it. Then something I couldn't identify, something rolled up and grey, like a fetus, bounced toward her. I jumped that. Then a torrent of them, skull and fetuses, heads and curled up spiders. I couldn't save her from them all. Some hit her head on, flattening her. She'd rise and re-form with a little popping sound, then a skull would bounce off her head and she'd fall to the ground again. My head started to sweat. I wanted to scream. I wrestled with the joystick, moving her forward, sending her jumping.

Then it was over. Lottie was harder to move now, bent a little at the waist. I felt exhaustion too, and the beginning of a terrific headache. A ladder appeared on the screen and I sent her up. The below-ground part sank and Lottie was on the surface again. Before her stood an angled wall of simple brick, bisected by a black gate. She approached. The gate opened for her and she disappeared as she passed through.

The woods, the wall, and the gate were replaced, from top to bottom, by the number ONE. The music was low, bouncing, foreboding...

The door to my room slammed open, and I heard my father's voice calling my name. He sounded distressed, full of fear. I didn't like hearing him like that. It made me feel unsafe. I tried to speak, to calm him. I'm fine, I just fell asleep. But nothing came out. I pushed myself up into consciousness.

"Oh, Loretta," my dad said. I felt warmth down below and realized I'd wet myself. The television roared static. Mom appeared and shut it off. They hustled me out of my room and out of my clothes to the tub. Dad ran the water and Mom asked me if I felt sick, if I needed to go to the hospital. "I'm fine," I told her.

*I feel very much alive, energized. All I want to do is get back to the game.* I didn't tell her that.

I missed school that day, no great loss. They took me to Doctor Moyer, who couldn't account for my having passed out. In his little room that smelled like tongue depressors and rubbing alcohol he had me follow his finger with my eyes. He peered inside my ears with his little light. He pressed his cold little stethoscope onto my back, had me breathe, listened to my heart, pressed down on my stomach with his surprisingly warm hands, asking if I felt any pain. I felt no pain.

"She's fine," he said. "Nothing to worry about."

*We sit, Nurse Carol and I, on the curved cement bench facing the fountain, a big-bellied angel vomiting dirty water from between pursed lips, sinking in it, up to her knees now, her eyes, without pupils, begging the sky to call her home. I keep a careful eye on the doors and windows of the institution. The nurse drones on and on*

*about her life, her grown children, their jobs, their struggles, their kids. I'm not listening, not really, but the sound of her voice is so soothing. I consider the idea that she might be my protector, that Kendrick's spirit, or soul, or whatever, is in there somewhere, calling out to me from behind the wall of Nurse Carol's monologue. I can almost make myself believe it. Such is the nature of faith: it is merely a pretty mask made of wishes, swathed in finery, bejeweled in baubles, covering a face contorted—made ugly—by fear.*

*"Let's go in—it's getting chilly," says Nurse Carol.*

*Button up, buttercup. I'm not sure it's safe yet.*

*"Let's stay a little longer. It's not that cold."*

*"Piss and ginger," Nurse Carol says, shaking her head. "Ginger and piss. What are we going to do with you?"*

Friday night I dreamed about little electronic Lottie striding down real sidewalks, past denuded trees and ramshackle houses, past boarded-up schools and churches with ruptured, sunken steeples, past overgrown lawns and parking lots bracketed by slumping chain-link fences. I'd wake and she would be behind my eyes, trying to talk to me, making little electronic sounds of frustration.

Then I'd slide back into dreams. In one, Lottie approached the surface of the television, becoming more and more blurred the closer she got. When her body filled the screen, it split down the middle, and a sickly looking avatar emerged. He wore a tall hat and his skin was as grey as his clothing. His face pushed from the screen and his mouth opened to blackness… until a pile of squirming pink neon worms poured out into the room. Quickly they covered the surface of the floor and began to pile up toward the ceiling. Dream-me tried to swim up through them. I could feel them slithering into my nostrils, my ears, and my mouth, the nauseating rot-smell making me gag.

One of the worms wore the face of mother.

"Too many worms devalue the currency," she said. "Ain't got no hogs no more, remember?"

At some point everything faded and I plummeted into a deep and dreamless void.

I opened my eyes to a bright and cloudless Saturday morning, the whole day before me. My parents headed to Boston for lunch. They asked me if I wanted to go, I said no. I'm old enough to stay home.

"I guess," Dad said. "But I don't want you in front of that television all day. Get your homework done early so you're not scrambling tomorrow night. Or read a book, kid. We've got shelves chock full of them."

"I will."

"Sure."

I pushed the curtain aside and watched their car back out into the road and speed off.

Back to the game.

I closed the curtains, like I was concealing a forthcoming misdeed.

I switched on the television and the Atari.

Little Lottie danced, she called to me, and then, again, she walked.

In the road before her glowed a set of blue headphones. She touched them and they went to the top of the screen. The words "**YOUR WEAPONS AND DEFENSE CACHE**" appeared above the headphones icon.

We walked on.

The trees changed color, brown to grey, and the leaves fell to the ground and vanished. The stripped branches flickered and disappeared, the treetops narrowing and bending at right angles, a yellow cluster of pixels forming at their terminus. They had become streetlights, and featureless buildings grew up behind them from the horizon. Lottie continued through this new cityscape, passing streetlight after streetlight, greys and yellows. The music faded out and the only sound was the squelching of her feet.

*Ok*, I thought, *time to stop the game. There's nothing happening here, and I have homework to do, and reading.*

*But...*

*Just a little further.*

On and on. Nothing but streetlights and a cityscape in grey. The blue background deepened, went to dusk, then to dark, then to black. The yellow from the street light bulbs colored the room.

I slept, my thumb pressing the joystick, while Lottie walked. I don't know for how long. Void, again. Blackness, deep and inky and all-encompassing. What woke me up was static, insistent and fierce, pouring from the little speaker like smoke. Cold rode the wings of the static, pulled up the bumps on my skin, numbed my toes and my fingers. When

# 243

I looked up at the screen, fear shot through my body in spasms and shudders.

Lottie was surrounded by tall trees—green, squared-off treetops along the slightly curved top edge of the screen. Grey faces with **X**s for eyes shot around the treetops and something large and tattered moved behind the thick bars of the trunks. Lottie had gained another weapon while I slept in that trance-like state. Next to the headphones floated a sharp wooden spear.

I summoned them down to her without even touching the controller.

The headphones shot down over Lottie's ears and the spear flew into her hand. One of the grey faces zig-zagged down with alarming rapidity. I pressed the red button and Lottie caught the thing on the tip of her spear. It slid down the shaft slowly, leaking red pixels. The other faces screamed, their eyes tearing open, black mouths elongating their faces into distended ovals. They sprouted wings and became fat leeches. Another flew down and Lottie caught it on the spear. Red pixels shot out in all directions from the thing, filled the screen until it was all red. I backed away from the screen, which was giving off an intense heat. The door and windows of my room shuddered in their frames. The ceiling glowed red and bubbled. I reached out and shut off the television, pulling back a singed finger.

When Mom and Dad got home, I was sitting in the corner of the couch downstairs in the living room, swaddled in blankets, an ice-pack in my hand.

"I burnt myself," I said, holding up the ice-pack. "On the stove." They came around cooing and inspecting my reddened hand and ruffling my hair. They ordered a pepperoni pizza, my favorite, and we sat down for dinner as a family for the last time.

*I'd kept Nurse Carol occupied with pointless anecdotes and meandering stories until I felt it was safe to go back into the building. When we get back to the room, I am still shaken, anxious. I don't want to be alone. I ask her to stay, and so she grabs her book and sits in the cushiony chair next to my bed. She reads to me, some bit of fluff, a historical romance with a conflicted soldier who has fallen for a cute little maid with a rebellious streak and a facility with weaponry. It is not a compelling story, and she drifts off amusingly quickly. Now she snores, head thrown back, her thumb bookmarking the page.*

*The phone rings, a jarring trill, very loud in the room. All the other sounds fade into the background. Nurse Carol snores no more, but a glance tells me she hasn't awakened; in fact, she's very still. The phone's call is insistent, shrill, it seems to grow in volume and resonance with each ring. No one is coming to pick it up. I rise from the bed and approach the phone, lift it from its cradle, hold it up to my ear, then pull it away with a hiss. The speaker is crowded with the cries of desperation, thousands of people clamoring to be heard. Somewhere in there is my cousin's voice. My hand goes to my mouth. I strain to hear. I catch only fragments.*

I'm so sorry... Lottie... got into... goddamned circuitry... never would have... Anne... Inter... my fault... never wanted...

*The other voices begin to crowd his out, to grow in volume, shrieking, babbling, howling. I call to him.*

Are you alive? Are you alive? Please, tell me if you're alive!

*Somewhere in the cacophony, another voice begins to rise to the surface, a goatish, grotesque sound, full of wormy, blood-saturated mud and desecration and dripping caverns far beneath the graveyard earth. I slam the phone down. I'm still calling out to Kendrick. The room echoes with the shrieks and screams. I cover my ears.*

*Nurse Carol wakes up. Her eyes are rolled to the whites. Her mouth opens.*

Snow day. That jolt of joy when LEEDS appears in bold, unequivocal letters under the face of the geeky meteorologist (to whom Dad referred as the region's most accurate virgin, to Mom's endless delight). The happy confirmation that comes with looking out the window at the snow pouring from the sky, the pristine dunes and drifts and dips that result from a wind-swept Nor'easter.

Mom and Dad had an earnest discussion; they're both going to brave the weather because they are working on Important Projects. Mom cooked up some eggs and pumpernickel toast, an extra treat, for weekdays usually mean the unimaginative pairing of cereal and milk. I ate to the sound of Dad shoveling and grunting as he brushed off the cars. At 8, they headed out, calling to one another... be safe... love you... I wave at them, blow kisses.

I was afraid for them, I wanted to call them back, to spend the day among them as they sipped cocoa in their pajamas and read the paper and joked around.

But the game beckoned.

I wrapped myself in blankets and sat before the TV, plugged in the cartridge.

Where was Lottie? The screen was crowded with little figures on a field of black, milling about, little heads turning left, then right, little legs moving under them, the soundtrack a cacophony of blips and bleats. I moved my joystick around, but none of them followed the movement. I put it down, finally, and watched as the little people swarmed over the screen.

Then the sound cut out. The people stopped moving. Their little heads tilted upward. All was still. A beat. Two beats. I started to rise to shake the console, and then all the lights shut off in the house. The refrigerator's hum wound down until it was silent. Somehow the television stayed on, though, the game still on the screen. The digital people, looking up. Even made up of pixels, their faces projected tension, tension quickly giving way to terror.

It came from the top of the screen, the goat-man, huge, filling the television. The avatars crowded to the sides to give it room. Its hooves brown and blood-tipped. Its legs knobby like old walking sticks. Its torso draped in a brown tattered shawl. Its white horns curled back to its shoulders. Its eyes took in the scene below, horizontal eyeballs sweeping left, then right, then back again.

Then it shrunk down until it was only twice the size of the others. They began to crowd back in, tentatively, like they wanted to inspect this new creature, to sniff at it. It occurred to me, then, somewhere back in my brain, that night had fallen. The only light in my room was that of the game. Had the whole day gone by? Or… and I remember thinking this was a real possibility… had the sun cut out along with the electricity? Was the light from the television the only light left in the world?

A frantic, overlapping bleating tugged my attention back to the game. The goat-man's arms had elongated, snaking out like segmented centipedes across the screen. Its pincer hands snipped off the head of one figure, then another, then another. Their heads floated up and off-screen, turning grey as they went, their eyes changing to **✗**s. Then the goat-man whipped off its shawl. Whatever it was between the goat-man's legs, there were two things of which I was absolutely certain: the first was that it was not—could not have been— the work of Kendrick. The second was that this was something that I was not meant to see.

The goat-man's long arms pulled in three characters, little round black mouths, electronic screaming and babbling, and deposited them into his shawl. He dragged them off-screen to the right. Headless bodies lay strewn everywhere.

**WHERE IS LOTTIE** flashed on the screen, blinking rapidly. Where indeed. I felt my eyelids fluttering. Faster and faster it blinked. In my peripheral vision, something very large moved through my room, something that gave off a great, damp heat, an odor of clover and decay. I froze. The blinking text stopped and the screen went blinding white.

I stared at that white screen until my eyes hurt. When the screen went red, it felt like dagger tips piercing my corneas. I think I may have screamed. The screen went black quickly, and trees grew up from the ground, filled the left and right of the screen, leaving the center open. The goat-man appeared in the center, a half circle of robed, hooded figures behind him. Slate grey chins jutted from the hoods, red lines for mouths, little pink tongues moving back and forth along those red lines. The goat-man undid his shawl and the figures he had stolen rolled out, limp-limbed, their little low-res faces somehow registering shock. Then the hooded men came from around the great goat and set upon them.

Lottie appeared at the edge of the screen. I gasped. She was in profile, watching the proceedings.

Then she turned to face me.

She stuck out her arm, extended a tiny finger, pointing at the scene, where an expanding, oval puddle of red had begun to form under the huddled, hooded men.

*Bleep, bloopbloop. Bleeleeeleeloooleeloop,* she said. *Bleep, bloopbloop. Bleeleeeleeloooleeloop.*

*What are you saying, Lottie? And where did you go?*

*Help me understand! Kendrick! What is she saying?*

Up from the violent scrum of hooded men rose one **X**-eyed character, its mouth curved into a jagged grin. Its legs, longer than before, dangled and danced like the legs of a hanged man still alive. Its arms undulated. Its face was elongated, its hair grey, its mouth in a grimace. It sang a low, mournful note. Another rose behind it, deformed and hunched. The third rolled out into the blood puddle, dead, dappled with green, its head bent at the jaw.

The goat-man's centipede-arm shot out and grabbed Lottie, and the hooded men descended. She screamed a single, piercing, buzzing note. As I raised my hands to cover my ears, a great, gnarled hand encircled my body and lifted me right up off the floor.

My room was crowded with people. Outside my windows was a deep blackness, deeper than the screen the first time I turned on the game. On the screen, and in my room, the hooded men doffed their hoods. I swore I saw Dad's face among them, and Mom's. Their hands grabbed at my clothes and I couldn't find the border between what was real and what was not. My mind became unmoored. It sailed off, a crushed, unsalvageable ship launched into dark and dangerous waters whose expanse knew no boundaries.

Lottie!

*The voice that comes from Nurse Carol's mouth is not hers. It's small and scared, shouted from somewhere back in that long red corridor.* I'm coming! I'm coming to get you!

Kendrick! Ken! What were you trying to tell me?

*Now a terrible groan, not Kendrick, but Nurse Carol. All the air flees from her lungs. She stiffens and then lets go. I peace-sign my fingers and close her eyelids, like they do in the movies.*

Was *that Kendrick calling from Nurse Carol's dying throat? His voice sounded too much like it did in my childhood for me to trust it fully.*

*Footsteps now, loud. Floor tiles crack and buckle, ceiling tiles go to dust. Framed pictures are pushed from the walls, glass shattering. I run to the door and lock it. It shakes in its frame.*

Lottie, *my cousin's voice calls, cracked and mud-caked and foul.* Lottie!

*I pull from my pocket the small, purple-blue stone. The doorknob rattles. Something smashes into it, hard. I close my eyes and wish I was Lottie. I wish for a spear. I wish I could fight. I wish I could understood what she said.*

*It could be Kendrick on the other side of the door. It could. Couldn't it?*

# AUTHOR'S NOTE

Confession time: I'm not a big videogame guy. Somewhere in my apartment might be a boxed-up Wii with which I had a brief flirtation a few years back. In the misty years of the early 2000s I bought a PlayStation 2 to play *Silent Hill 2* after having seen a write-up in *Rue Morgue*. When I reached the end of the game (with considerable help from the internet to get me past some of the roadblocks), I sold the console and the game.

In college, my friend (and radio co-host) Kevin and I gorged on *Super Mario Bros. 2*. I played obsessively and with great fervor, but, compared to him, I was a piker. He started missing classes in order to play, even though the game could easily be paused. At some point he had to beg the administration to not send him packing. I wonder if he still sees that odd Super Mario landscape in his dreams, if the music gets stuck in his head.

Ah, but the Atari 2600. I lusted after it, and when my brother and I finally got one, I played constantly. *Combat, Asteroids, Space Invaders.* I played the hell out of *Frogger* and *Donkey Kong.* For a while my favorite game was *Keystone Kapers.* Because I was listening to The Who a lot at the time, I associate the song "Substitute" with that little blue-suited cop chasing little black-and-white striped criminals across several levels of unsightly green backgrounds.

My clearest memory, though, is of *Pitfall.* For many, many hours, in the upstairs den, I *was* Pitfall Harry, swinging on ropes over crocodile ponds, jumping logs, avoiding flickering-tongued rattlesnakes and parading scorpions. I remember the little blip sound when he leapt, the electronic

Tarzan cry when he jumped onto the rope, the hilarious fart sound when he wasn't sufficiently deft to avoid being creamed by a rolling log.

I picture "Leeds 2600" as *Pitfall* mixed with *Silent Hill 2*, conceived by a lunatic on a heady mix of hallucinogens. The game is created by our heroine Loretta's computer-nerd cousin, and functions as a warning to Loretta: avoid the dark corners of her hometown of Leeds, Massachusetts. But even a homemade, unofficial Atari cartridge can be subject to the machinations of occult-variety psychic hackers.

One of the pitfalls (sorry) of writing a story like this is that now I dearly want that game to exist. I want to sit in a darkened room in the glow of a television and spend sleepless days and nights exploring. I want to risk addiction to see the levels of Leeds I haven't yet encountered in my imagination.

If I did my job right, you'll want to play too.

# THE OWLS OF UNDERHILL

## BY AMBERLE L. HUSBANDS

Eighteen was a damned good year for me. I had surprised the entire town by finishing high school, had a house, only two roommates, had a decent job at the local tire factory... Heck, I even had a girlfriend. A drop-dead gorgeous Yankee girlfriend, in fact, who had hung out with rock stars and models and even once, she claimed, made out with Patti Smith at an after-party.

*Patti Smith.* At an *after-party*.

Marla...

Marla was an artist. Marla had been to Paris, Los Angeles, New York. She'd decided to lie low in the land of her grandmothers—south Georgia, near the Florida line—after someone, some friend of a lover or something, had overdosed in their communal van, and the "vibes got too heavy." For Marla, our little sprawling hick town on the edge of the swamp was an ashram retreat she didn't need to renew her passport for.

The Land of her Grandmothers.

My own grandmother washed collard greens in her guest bathtub, my mother had carted home a roadkilled whitetail about once a month, and for years my father had spent five nights a week at a house across town, blaming Mom and me whenever he did come home. When I was twelve, I found out whose house it was and put a cherry bomb in her mailbox. Then I salted her garden. Then I set her pump house on fire, and she moved to Texas. Sometimes all it takes is a book of matches.

Marla's ashram was my jungle, full of monsters. Alligators, coyotes, boars big enough to run your truck off the road. Horned things that glared at you from the roadside but dissolved in the headlights moments later. Will-o-the-wisps. Swamp gas. Bale fire.

But Marla...

I was so in love with Marla I could trace its level inside me from hour to hour like a tide. My skeleton will be stained the rest of my life. No matter how long the rest of my life is—I will forever bear her mark.

She was my swamp, my black waters. *She* was the Land of my Grandmothers.

She wasn't a gamer but, heck, no one's perfect. And I was tired of waiting for the perfect woman. I mean, c'mon, I didn't even know there were *words* for girls like me until I was sixteen.

*Your princess is in another castle?*

Fuckin' tell me about it.

Then Marla landed like a lightning bolt in our little town. No luggage, no pedigree. All we knew was that she had been staying with Tony West, the guy who ran the landfill. Then she showed up at our house party, mixed two drinks and marched me back to my own bedroom. In the blink of an eye, I had a beautiful, sophisticated live-in girlfriend in a little hick town that didn't even have words for such a creature.

Landfill Tony showed up at the house once, waving a shotgun until the cops rolled by. He hadn't been back. Of course, it might have been the landfill catching fire that kept him busy, but, either way, I wasn't complaining. After that, being the other woman almost stopped bothering me. After all, Tony had been the other man. Who knew how many others there were before us?

More than a few, it seemed. Before she'd been there a whole week, there were two women, one man, and a mystery voice that none of us could agree on, calling the house phone daily, leaving messages for Marla. She refused to waste time talking to or about them.

Once a woman called from the Piggly Wiggly, wanting directions to the house. She said she'd driven down from Atlanta. Chasing Marla.

I was tempted to drive to the Piggly Wiggly and meet her, ask her about Marla in Atlanta, ask had she gotten calls from New York. Something in her voice reminded me of my Dad's other woman, the house-across-town woman.

I hung up on her. That was a Sunday, and I was supposed to be burning off the household's trash, standing in the hot sun over the fire, beneath the old skeleton oak tree in the backyard. But, after the call from the Piggly Wiggly, I knew that once the fire was going, it would burn for hours. Sometimes it just got too hot, or too high, and my hands got too heavy to reach for the water hose to control it...

I stood for a long moment with one hand still on the phone, the book of matches weighing heavy in my jeans' pocket. I rocked on my heels, back and forth, humming softly. Fire danced behind my eyes, but slowly it dawned on me: I was humming the background music from *Underhill Soul*.

'*Soul* was an online, multiplayer, noir-mystery game that I'd been playing for years. You start off as a detective's assistant, investigating a legendary murder. Your boss had tossed you the case as a cheap favor. The case went cold thirty years before your time; every gumshoe and gumshoe's assistant had taken a crack at it.

*Who put Brunhilde in the Witch Elm?*

It was an unsolvable mystery, but it led your character through the first five levels, taking you into developing situations and setting the course so that, at level six when your boss suddenly retired, you were either a brutal assassin for the people you'd met during your investigation, or an honest sleuth just trying to keep your bank account in the green and put a few thugs in the hole—or some ambiguous mix of the two.

Underhill reminded me of home. It was a city full of monsters. Even if there were no gators, there was plenty of swamp gas in the air. There were mad dogs and overgrown puss worms walking around pretending to be men, and behind them all were the underworld's board of elders, The Owls, nameless shadow men who turned gears and fed social machines that insidiously touched every character in the game. Once in a great while the map changed, streets moved around at night, storefronts just up and disappeared, and the only explanation was that The Owls had been up late. I chose to develop my character into an honest ol' private eye, by the way... who occasionally took on a contract for some whore-mongering rat when she needed to stock the pantry.

I didn't start the fire that Sunday.

I went and played *Underhill Soul* until well past midnight.

"You ought to get her to sit in on D&D with us tonight." It was the same thing Peavey said I ought to do on a weekly basis. "She could be really cool, with that whole earth-goddess warrior-princess vibe going on. The party could use, like, a succubus or something. Or some righteous sex-vampire."

"That *is* a succubus, stupid," Terry put in.

"No, but, I mean, a righteous one, like a good-guy, sex-vampire, earth-goddess, warrior-princess."

"Tiana is our enchantress," Terry said, sounding more defensive than he probably wanted to.

"But Tiana is a shape-shifting dwarf," Peavey argued. "She can't exactly enchant in bear form, can she?"

"...She's a sexy bear, Peavey."

"There's no such thing."

"There are some *very* sexy bears out there—"

The three of us threw amazing, epic parties each weekend and the kids who showed up somehow overlooked the fact that we were the ones they'd poured milk on in middle school. We were the ones with our own house.

"Peavey, she's never gonna sit through one of your

rambling-ass dungeon campaigns." Terry could be a real bitch, when he wanted to. "She doesn't even do cool games..."

I ignored them both.

"Cool games" was Terry's jab at my obsession; they thought of online games as antisocial and escapist, like they had any room to talk...

In the semi-privacy of our room, Marla had hung black velvet up around the busted futon I slept on. Sometimes when I came in she would have a canvas already propped up against the wall, her fingertips splashed with paint.

"Here," she'd command, as if it weren't really my room at all. She'd shut the door behind me—she loved a shut door—and immediately her paint-stained hands would be turning me, peeling the clothes back from my shoulders and positioning me in front of the heavy black curtain. "Stand there—right, stand there. Can you just... right, good."

Naked and feeling heavier than ever, I stared at an invisible fold in the velvet as she scratched away with her pencils, pinning my ungainly outlines into her sketchbook without mercy. I never figured out if she really was inspired by me, or just wanted a mannequin to pose. None of the beautiful, glowing women in her finished paintings looked a thing like me.

Each one of them burned on the surface of my brain. They were mountains, brick houses, planets in a radiant solar system Marla had explored long before finding me. The women on her canvases were El Dorados, Denalis, towering Sphinxes. I was just a shiny pebble in the adventurer's pocket.

"Gonna bother you if I play some 'Soul when you're done

sketching?"

"Hold still," she commanded, scratching away.

I held still.

My computer was a hand-me-down from when my uncle had decided to become a work-from-home child support lawyer or something. The computer became mine after the meth bust. My peers had cell phones before I had a desktop computer. Some nerds are born nerds. Others inherit their seedy uncle's home office rig.

He had a cardboard box of old PC games, too; they struck a nerve in me, and as it turned out I wasn't alone. Once I was old enough to be trusted with an internet connection, there were chatrooms and bulletin boards and weekly cyberspace bazaars where memories, tips, and secrets were swapped. A whole subclass of nerds shared my little obsession. And when we had exhumed and waxed poetic over all the existing games we could find, people got creative and began unleashing their own monsters, MMORPGs that either mimicked or outright plagiarized the retro mechanics we were all addicted to.

And *Underhill Soul* was one of the best new-oldies, offering a persistent world that never failed to capture my imagination, while visually preserving the finest top-down games of my childhood.

"Keep your feet still," Marla dictated.

"So... do you mind?"

"What?"

"Do you mind if I play while you paint?"

"Whatever. I have what I need." She closed her sketchbook, setting me free from the velvet curtain. I wrapped up in a robe and coaxed my dinosaur back to life, the computer humming warmly as it booted up. Marla had taken the curtains off my bedroom windows; she wanted the natural light during the day and the blackness, the moon and the crickets, at night. I had never noticed how the dead oak in the backyard loomed over that side of the house, its skinned arms thrown up like a broken dreamcatcher around the sun. Playing *Underhill Soul* with its bony shadows dancing across the room was even creepier, more enthralling than ever.

I had convinced Terry and Peavey to create accounts on *'Soul* right after we moved in together, and they had each played for maybe a week before losing interest and going back to their tabletop fantasies. But I did get a decent kickback in coins as their sponsor when they signed up.

My character — I loved my character.

From female/male/unspecified, I chose female. At youth/adult/crone, I'd made her a child, gave her black hair, grey eyes, a black outfit. She looked a little like a feral Wednesday Addams. In my head, she was twelve years old.

Even though I had language to explain some of the strangeness inside myself now — even though I had Marla — there were still a thousand sensations and desires I had no cipher for. Like how I couldn't figure out if I hated or pitied my father more. And the fires. I didn't understand the fires. I didn't know if I wanted to. But at twelve, things had made sense. Twelve had been a good year for me.

I logged in. The background music started low but swelled persistently, a soft musicbox tinkling that sounded like remembering troubled dreams from kindergarten nap time. I turned the speakers off for Marla's sake. Wednesday's office was a coveted suite near the center of Underhill, with a view overlooking the elm at the city's heart. The tree rose and spread dark, shadow-laced branches over a square of antiqued brickwork. A few NPCs hung out there around the clock, to help guide new players through their first clue-finds.

One persistent bit of player-to-player lore held that the Brunhilde murder actually was solvable, but once a player confronted the killer their account dissolved, all progress irretrievable. No one ever claimed to have done it of course, but everyone's uncle who worked at Nintendo had written the code for it as a side gig.

I took Wednesday down to the witch elm, like I did every session, to talk to my favorite NPCs.

The Grey Lady—elderly, grey dress, grey hair, grey umbrella—turned in a pacing, hesitant circle beneath the monster tree's shadow. I engaged her, and she turned to Wednesday with the same nervous, bewildered dialogue as always.

"What time is it?... No, no that isn't right."

Always the same. A bit of filler text that spawned countless conspiracies amongst fans. Maybe Brunhilde had been her princess, always one more castle away, and now totally unreachable.

I went to the Stubbly Man sitting on the bench a few feet away. A newspaper occupied the seat next to him; his dialogue was a bit more involved.

"Read the news today?"     Y/N

"Yes."

"Well what do you think of that?"

"It's a shame." / "Hallelujah!" / "That rat bastard!"

I had tried every combination imaginable, and nothing

ever came of it. When you clicked the paper, a seemingly randomized headline would be produced. Nonsense, but sometimes amusing.

"Hitler Claims Innocence In Disneyland Reactor Meltdown" or "Bob Dylan Chants Curses For Alligator Molestation." I kept a notebook handy to jot down the most entertaining ones for forum discussion.

Wednesday walked up and read the paper.

"Trans-Siberian Pyramid Monster Takes Top Model Prize."

Eh. Not really a winner.

"Read the news today?"

"Yes."

"Well what do you think of that?"

"That rat bastard!"

Nine times out of ten, my response was "rat bastard." It never failed to make little Wednesday giggle inside me.

The Stubbly Man returned to his silence.

The Grey Lady resumed her pacing.

Little Wednesday checked her bank account.

Oh...

"Hey Marla, you should really try out this game. You just create an account and it only takes a few minutes to—"

"I don't play games," she said, distantly.

"Yeah, but I think you'd like this. There's, like, this moral thermometer thing, and you have to weigh it all out, like, ethics and stuff, because the game sets you on paths and you can't really get onto others based on decisions you've already made, but there are parallel patterns you won't even see until you're on them, and, like, you could be a bad guy and not even know it until—"

"I just down have time for that shit," Marla interrupted, mixing up some color that didn't exist anywhere on my body. "Hell, I don't have time for real life, let alone for an energy suck like that."

"Oh. Yeah, I know," I could feel my hand turning to lead on the mouse, my whole body becoming heavier and more naked beneath the old robe. "It's just, you know, stress relief..."

Marla didn't say anything.

I looked again at the single digit coinage, tried to remember how many times I'd let Wednesday take a contract from the baddies—those NPCs always hanging out in the wharf-side cafes. You couldn't see the "moral thermometer" that dictated what opportunities were presented to your character, but it was functioning ceaselessly in the background, keeping track. One day you logged on, killed the snitch that netted you ten times what a single solved crime would; the next, you simply saw fewer unsolved cases on your desk, more bad men in cafes waiting to offer you work.

"Hey, uhm... could I just use your email, then? It's just, if I sponsor people who join, I get this reward—"

"I don't believe in email. It's disenfranchising the postal system, disconnecting us from the geography of the globe."

"Oh..."

She went on painting, humming under her breath. Some song that I guess she thought belonged to the Land of her Grandmothers.

Wednesday stood beside the Stubbly Man like a little urchin expecting a handout. I was proud as hell of all the level grinding I'd done while keeping her *mostly* honest. I liked the look of her rosy room on the City Center, the hefty stack of unsolved cases on her desk... but those crimes would get solved faster if she had a little cash to slip the informants, to buy the talkers in bars a drink or two. She could also use new boots—maybe even a pair with a kung-fu stat bonus...

Logging out quickly, I opened up Gmail and clicked to create a new account. I had intended to set up a ghost account for Marla, but at the last minute I realized I could do better.

Moments later, Natasha Wrigley was born, turned twenty-two years old, and coincidentally had a phone number just one digit off from mine. She lived in Spokane, and her password was LeatherFac3Luv. I decided I didn't like Natasha very much. She was a little flaky, but that didn't matter. We didn't have to be friends for very long.

Back to Underhill. A new soul was moving to town. I made Natasha name herself Nighthawks after my favorite painting. Marla criticized its heavy-handed symbolism, but I didn't care. If I had a happy-place to retreat to, it'd be the bar from "Nighthawks." It'd probably be down by the wharf in Underhill City.

Nighthawks was female, adult, average level of curvature, trench-coated, heavy-booted. I gave her a razor-hacked halo of raven hair; Wednesday's older sister, a dangerous black sheep.

She scoffed behind the Grey Lady's back.

She didn't bother with the Stubbly Man's newspaper. She didn't have time for fools.

I logged out, logged back in as Wednesday and—boom—working capital for at least a few cases had already hit the bank account. Cha-ching.

"Hey nerd, come here." Marla was tugging at my ponytail. "Lose the robe."

"I thought you had what you needed—"

She had me naked and on the futon in about three heartbeats.

"Not yet, Love."

"It's up-down, up-down, left—"

"No, that's *Contra*. This was up-up, down-down, left-right, left-right, B, A, start."

"But start wasn't part of the code. It just, you know, started the game. And the *Contra* thing worked on *Mean Streets* too, and *Queen Rosella*, which is what I was—"

"Up-down-up-down was for, like, thirty lives. Up-up-down-down was for unlimited lives. Why the fuck would you get thirty limited lives instead of immortality? You're a dumb ass, is why."

"And select," I put in, reaching for a beer. "You had to press select for two players. It's kind of like you're saying you plan on being single your whole life."

"Shut up," Terry mumbled, pulling his beanie back down to cover the tattoo, a slightly crooked row of gamepad arrows and red-button letters on the back of his neck, just at the hairline. "You know, I'll add select when I meet Player Two."

"If you meet her before your limited number of lives run out?"

"Peavey, shut up." I was beginning to suspect that Terry's

Player Two was going to be a plumber instead of a Peach, and nobody was ever going to make that painless in our little hick town.

"That's going to get infected," Janine Holyoke said as the party crowd pushed her into the kitchen. "They'll have to cut your head off."

"That's me, dead up from the neck up." Terry killed his Schlitz and threw the can into the kitchen sink and we watched Janine head towards the back of the house, towards the bedrooms.

"Who invited the Queen of the Damned, anyway?" Terry asked.

I knew her from school. Everyone knew her. Out of our graduating class, the only kids who hadn't made out with Janine Holyoke, male or female, were the ones who weren't sure whether it was incest or not and the two or three girls she hadn't been able to con into it. I hadn't been one of those girls. All black nylon and "Midnight-Morticia" hair dye, she vanished completely in the dark hallway.

"Creepy bitch..." I chucked an empty can into the sink. "Who the hell did invite her?"

"How come we always end up hanging out in the kitchen at our own parties?" Peavey asked.

"Duh, 'cause all the coolest kids hang out in the kitchen," Marla said, coming out of the wall of bodies like a laser cutting through fog.

The room glowed. My grandparents had their first glimpses of color television, their first tactile encounters with plastic, their first ride in a jet plane... I had Marla.

"Hey, did you guys see a little vampire, about five foot tall, probably as wide, in fishnets and a corset come through here? Cute as a button, like a little black hole in hooker heels?"

"Janine?"

"Yeah, that one."

Peavey pointed.

"Awesome. Hey, did you know they're burning a door in your backyard?" And with that, Marla vanished again into the tidal wave of the party. The room lost a little bit of glow.

In fact, it was getting downright shady.

Peavey reluctantly set out on patrol, carrying a bottle of tequila raised in one fist and a fire extinguisher in the other. I fished another beer from the cooler, biting my lips. Terry nodded and I tossed him one too.

"So, what's your girlfriend want with My-Little-Poltergeist?"

"Your guess is as good as mine," I said bitterly. All of my guesses were crap.

My skin felt too tight, and the air in the house was swampy, thick against my face. I sat on the counter, head spinning, as the roar of music from the living room fought to be heard over the heartfelt chanting in the backyard. Glass shattered and people shrieked in the driveway and for one insane moment I hoped it was Landfill Tony with his shotgun.

Suddenly I was going to puke.

I flailed my way through the living room with the triumphant last verse of Bowie's "Rock 'n' Roll Suicide" crashing overhead. Someone's boot caught my ankle on the back steps and I fell—spinning sideways, ankles and knees giving up in whiskey-soaked despair—and ended up behind the camellias emptying my guts into the wet black loam.

Normally I could just lean over, open up the hatches and let the excess spill out. We were all professional drunks by then.

But there behind the overgrown, waxy shrubs, there was violence. My skin tried to crawl away and hide as my stomach lashed out, grabbing and squeezing and flinging everything it could lay a hand on. I choked and trembled, gagging on solids I couldn't remember having eaten.

When had I last ingested real food?

I could feel the flames at my back, and through squinted eyes I saw the shadow negatives of the oak tree waving its branches above the blaze. I had a drunken half-idea in my head about the moon throwing light at the tree from above, while the fire beneath blasted back with all the strength it had. I thought of the tree caught in the middle, its shadows hung up amid the branches with no relief from either side, and I wondered what else could exist in that limbo. I wondered how Brunhilde had looked when they found her there, and I wondered who had asked The Owls about it.

"Hey, you okay?"

"Yeah," I croaked, shading my eyes. Peavey's silhouette bobbed against a bonfire hovering just under control. "Yeah, just... too much beer."

"Want a shot?" He waved the tequila in the air, catching sparks of light and scattering them over the lawn.

"No, I'm good."

"Cool. Got anything that needs burning?"

Nothing that couldn't wait.

I turned and pulled myself back up the steps, wiping my lips. Music poured from the house like hot oil. Dreadlocked kids were yelling into one another's ears in the kitchen. In the back of the house, someone was toodling a trumpet. The band kids had arrived; we were no longer the least cool kids at our own party. I could feel it slipping over the edge, out of control, but I couldn't care.

Man, someone was really cranking on that volume—I could barely hear myself think—

The screech of some dead rock star's guitar was so loud it shook the bones of my skull. My heart was forced to assume the beat or stop all together. In the living room, people must have been liquefied.

"Turn it down!"

I knew Terry was screaming, but I didn't hear him so much as feel his words as puffs of air bashing against the tornado of noise.

"Turn! It! Down!"

In the back hallway, the music seemed to resent being constricted. It was painful, persistent. The bedroom door was trembling beneath my hand; I didn't know if it was the noise or my own nerves. Maybe it was only my vision shaking. I squeezed the door knob—

The lights went out.

In the silence and abrupt darkness, I thought I heard one thing—a choked giggle from the bedroom.

"Marla?" I opened the door, and more darkness greeted me. Not sure what I had expected. Hints of the fire outside ghosted across surfaces in the bedroom and shivered on, never still.

"Hey, you in here? Marla?" The girl in the horror movie, calling after her lost puppy moments before the monster strikes.

No... I knew damned well what I had expected. That didn't mean it left me any less sick inside. A lighter flared in the blackness before me. Marla's perfectly cool, perfectly beautiful face caught the glow as she lit two cigarettes, sucking on both for a breath before handing me one. Across the room, I saw fire against Janine's face as she lit her own.

"Hey Sugarpie," Marla said, her Yankee accent having a ball with our quaint, darlin' pet names. "What happened to the music?"

"You know, there's nothing sexy about a jealous girlfriend."

"So who's jealous?"

It had taken me and Peavey all of two minutes to get the circuit breakers figured out. Then we chain-smoked in the laundry room for another twenty to let everyone get gone before flipping the lights back on. After some debate, we left the fire in the yard to its own devices. It couldn't have much more energy left than we did.

I watched from my bed as Marla smeared her canvas — some crimson thing with the figure of a woman nearly unrecognizable, but not quite.

*Cutest little black hole in town.* Janine stood like a broken pillar in front of the black velvet, more naked than I ever thought a person could be.

I was terrified to face the monster in the room with us.

I was the monster.

But I was terrified.

"Any more beer out there?"

"Don't think so."

"Shit..."

I went to my computer, pulled up *Underhill Soul* but then stopped. I was already logged in, but it took me a minute to figure out why I wasn't seeing little Wednesday's office overlooking City Center.

I wasn't playing as Wednesday.

I was Nighthawks.

She stood at the end of the wharf over a map-ending expanse of water-blue pixels. A few dull NPCs hovered near the docks, looking as lost as I felt in that first moment.

"Hey, have you been playing this?"

"What?"

"Have you been playing this game?"

Marla barely looked up.

"I didn't touch your precious computer, nerd-girl. If you're mad—"

"I'm not mad..."

Paranoia hit hard for a second. Maybe they knew I'd set up multiple accounts... whomever *They* were, maybe they knew I'd cheated. Confused, I glanced at the bank account in the screen's corner and—whoa. That was... that was a whole lot of killing. I tried to pull up Nighthawks' history, her journal, but the screen wouldn't load.

Just up the street from the wharf was a café called Tom's Moroccan, the best place in Underhill to find baddies, and the best place to accept contracts. The more a baddie you were, the more populated the Moroccan became.

Nighthawks left the ocean to its own dark musings and strolled up the street. Every single table outside the Moroccan had someone sitting at it. A wide-eyed waitress twirled back and forth between tables like a cat with one claw stuck in the carpet.

"I get nervous, when it's this crowded," the girl said. "This isn't the best part of town..."

Filler.

I'd never seen every table full. But of course the bigger, better jobs would be with the bigger, badder baddies inside. I took Nighthawks up to the door of the Moroccan and through it—

And she was stepping out of Wednesday's office onto the street. I was so used to that view that it took me a minute to realize I wasn't seeing the inside of the Moroccan.

I tried to take her back through the office door... and came out of a building labeled "The Lab" that stood a block away, on the other side of City Center.

"What the hell?"

Were the servers glitching? I took Nighthawks down into City Center Square, into the shadow of the witch elm, and found the Grey Lady. She was spinning in her nervous circle, like always. I had Nighthawks greet her.

""What time is it?" she asked. "No, no... you're not the one."

"Huh?" I squinted at the words on the screen. That wasn't right... was it?

"Quit talking to yourself, love," Marla muttered, still rubbing and splashing at her painting. I heard Janine mutter something, and Marla snorted.

I engaged the Grey Lady again.

"No, no... you're not the one."

I was positive that wasn't her normal dialogue. Almost positive. Were the NPCs supposed to give different answers to less-than-ethical characters? I'd never seen any chatter to that effect in the forums. Maybe there was some special event going on.

The forum wouldn't load.

"It's got to be the servers."

Behind me, Marla sighed loudly and turned on the radio. She turned it up loud. Whatever. I took Nighthawks down to the Stubbly Man and made her check the headline on his newspaper.

"Child's body found in hollow tree—Owls deny all"

A shiver trolled down through my guts.

"Read the news today?"

"Yes."

"That rat bastard... it's a shame." I tried again, and got the same thing. The Stubbly Man was saying my lines, not giving me a chance to respond.

"That rat bastard..." It sounded a lot less funny when he said it.

I went and read the plaque at the foot of the sprawling, monstrous tree, where normally a new player was given the briefest description of how a body had been found in the hollow trunk thirty years prior, blah blah blah.

"There are strange ruins here."

"Huh?"

I clicked the plaque again. "There are strange ruins here."

I went to the City Center Memorial Gardens sign.

"There are strange ruins here."

"The servers are fucked," I said aloud, for the bitter satisfaction of hearing Marla turn the radio up. I reached up to turn the computer speakers on.

Nighthawks walked back to the Lab, and tried to read the sign outside. Normally, it was a place where you could bribe a nice man at the front desk to run forensic tests for you. Normally, the sign read simply, "The Lab."

"There are strange ruins here."

That's when I noticed the windows. The lab's facade was now a single door in a brick wall studded with darkened, broken window panes. I took Nighthawks up the steps and through the door, wondering if the weird displacement would happen again.

Nighthawks stepped into the laboratory lobby. The front desk was unmanned, and, in fact, the building that was usually full of lab-coated NPCs of varying usefulness was now totally empty, with dark stains on the tile floors and smoking computer monitors on the tables.

"This shit is weird."

I could barely hear Marla's exasperated sigh over the radio blaring. Nighthawks didn't pay it any mind either... There was a door at the back of the Lab, now. Had that always been there?

Regardless, I knew it hadn't always been standing open, with what looked like one lab-coated arm stretched out in a spreading pool of darkness...

"Hey Marla, could you—"

"What the hell—"

"Look, I said I'm not upset, would you just—"

"What's with this piece of crap?"

I left Nighthawks staring at the crime scene and turned to find Marla at the radio, black and red paint streaked across her forehead. Perfectly streaked. Radiantly streaked. What was left of the monster in my guts melted.

"Marla, I'm sorry. I'm not upset, just... Could you turn that down?"

"I'm trying! I've been trying!"

"What?"

"I've—been—trying!"

"Just unplug it!"

The radio's speakers buzzed like a wasp's nest. I could feel the noise in my teeth. The bedroom rattled on its studs, the door bucked against its frame.

Fire swam through my guts.

Marla covered her ears, teeth flashing as she ran from the room dragging Janine with her.

I made a lunge for the radio's cord, snatching it from the wall just as a resounding *pop* snaked through the house, darkness following swiftly and bringing blessed silence back with it. The cessation of sound was a glass of ice water in August.

Outside, the backyard blaze flickered peaceably, the only light in the world.

Marla had left the door open. Peavey cursed and stumbled into something on his way back to the laundry room. Standing in the dark with the radio's dead cord as an anchor point, it was a relief to hear my own breath, my own slowing heartbeat. I could feel the stillness of the whole house. The refrigerator was silent, the toilet tank slumbered, even the imperceptible hum of wires in the walls was gone.

I might have been the only thing breathing in the entire world.

Then something in the house beeped and, with a starving gasp, the toilet began running again. The wires hummed. The bedroom light popped on as if nothing had happened.

The room was empty.

Just me and the dead radio.

Except there *was* music, barely audible over the general electric shivering of the house. Impossibly soft musicbox tinkling, hauntingly familiar.

Nighthawks was standing at the end of the wharf, staring out over the edge of her world, as pixelated smoke boiled from the windows of the café up the street.

The woman at the number listed as Janine Holyoke's in the phone book wasn't the Queen of the Damned herself. Her mother, maybe? Her lover?

"Uhm... I'm looking for Marla Marafino?" I croaked, my voice tired and abused. "Is she there?"

"...You've got the wrong number."

I hung up, took a trash bag and stumbled back outside to assist in the clean-up effort. Sunlight burned through my skin to slurry the raw alcohol I'd replaced my own blood with. Terry's electrician dad was coming and we had until noon to hunt down every Solo cup and beer can on the property or risk going deaf in the next power surge, or whatever they were. The backyard was mostly blackened stubble.

Peavey looked up sympathetically from shoveling a pile of charred souvenirs into a five gallon bucket. "Still no luck?"

I shook my head.

"She probably just flaked out," Terry said, hiding behind

an opaque pair of Lou Reed sunglasses. Even his hair looked hungover. "People like her do that shit."

I shoved beer cans and empty cigarette packs into my bag. "She left all her stuff—"

"When she showed up here... did she have stuff?"

"I mean, she left all of her paintings and everything... Oh, I'll get behind the camellias, guys."

"Yeah you will."

"She'll show up," Peavey said. "I bet there's at least a dozen kids from last night camped out in the park up on Sherman Street. She'll show up."

"Keys," Terry called, tossing another set of keys out of the tall grass and onto the growing pile in the driveway. We had half a dozen cars to relocate.

"I don't know, man... Last night was damned weird." I knelt in the faded flower petals and wet mulch, dragging out crushed cans and empty Solo cups and trying not to feel the cool shadows of the oak tree scraping across the back of my neck.

"She's a flake, I'm telling you."

"What the heck is this?"

Peavey fished something misshapen, smutty, unrecognizable from the fire-pit.

"Dude, that looks like bone."

Peavey had already managed to smear soot across his face, somehow. He weighed the thing in his hand, then snapped it in two and weighed it again. Frowning, he bent to sniff it.

"Peavey, for fuck's sake..."

I had no more clue than anyone else. A lot of the rubble was unrecognizable. Strange things in the ashes.

## AUTHOR'S NOTE

I have never been able to divorce thoughts about technology from a certain brand of ingrained paranoia.

Are They watching us through our webcams? Of course They are. (But not Them, no. The other ones; the last ones you'd expect.) Has some hopefully-disinterested third party noted every time I've walked past my television naked? Wouldn't surprise me in the least. Does the refrigerator really need to make all those hisses and pops and gurgles just to keep my milk fresh?

For me, it goes all the way back to watching my father and uncle bloodying themselves over car and truck engines in overgrown backyards. I'd stand knee-deep in the grass and watch them plead and curse gods who had no names but smelled like diesel and wet rust, whose presence was announced by a spark or the lack of one. There were different entities for things with two wheels, different ones for boats, and a giant gangly old-world beast in charge of semis, but they were all cousins. On good days, they kept you from blowing up when the cherry of someone's cigarette fell in an open gas tank. On bad days, they let you motor twelve miles out to sea before laughing through acrid white smoke as you paddled back to shore.

And beyond the nameless iron gods, there were goblins.

I never for a moment doubted the existence of goblins. They hung out in workshops and sucked sustenance from leaky pipes and loose fittings. Nobody knew for sure, but it was mostly accepted as fact that we'd imported them from Japan, sometime in the forties.

Goblins have branched out, in recent years. They're not

as exclusive as the rust gods; wouldn't turn their noses up over VHS players or microwaves, and certainly won't over a delectable little smart phone or 3D printer.

There have always been ghosts in the machines, at every level. So it was a thrill to learn that this anthology was happening. What caught me off guard was how out of the loop with gaming society I'd become; one of the many drawbacks of the adult lifestyle I've fallen victim to. I am extremely grateful to the old and new friends who came to my rescue with tips, advice, and—most crucially—games.

Hours and hours of games.

Hours and hours and hours.

The goblins who now cohabitate with the spiders beneath my sofa join me in thanking those friends. The circuit-swaddled, blinking, power-hungry ghosts haunting my living room thank them. And I thank them, along with Muzzleland Press for allowing me to commune once more with the spirits within the wires.

# THREE DAYS AS MR. MCGREGOR
## BY JACK BURGOS

**Y**ou don't spook easy, do you?" Latisha asked, releasing Ethan's hand from her grip. Her hand was caked in the same oil and tar that was dripping from the metal gears lying behind her on her worktable. In its center, a metal mesh head stared at Ethan with empty brown eyes.

Ethan shook his head. The same question had come up with the manager of Peter's Party Pizzeria, Justin, when he'd interviewed Ethan a few minutes before. The last night guard had quit without telling anyone, and they needed someone who wouldn't be spooked by the cacophony of rattles and groans that plagues old mall plazas such as this. Ethan had lied then, as he was lying now. He *really* needed the work, and Peter's Party Pizzeria would hire him without asking to see his security license.

"Why?" he asked.

"Well, the last night guard —"

"Justin mentioned that he left. But why?"

"Well," Latisha said, turning around and petting the skeletal head tenderly, "every hour, Peter and Friends are set to move around and stretch their legs. The bots are old. Their old gears stick together if they're left still for too long. So until corporate sends new parts, this is the fix. Scares the shit out of you if you're walking into the Pizzeria in the early morning to see Mopsy here standing at the door."

"Has that happened?" Ethan asked, still looking around the room for something to wipe the oil from his hand.

"A few times. They wander."

"It sounds like you don't need a guard." Ethan laughed. He had to admit that a giant animatronic rabbit staring at him through the window would probably startle him, but he wasn't going to admit it to his new boss's lead engineer.

"We probably don't," Latisha said. "But corporate wants every location to have one, so here you are."

"You ready to see your post?" Justin said, poking his head into the workshop.

"Yeah." Ethan waved back. "Nice meeting you, Latisha."

"Be seeing you."

Ethan followed Justin up to the second floor, to the very back of the building, to a room flanked on both sides by hallways. The outside-facing wall was covered in old, faded promotional posters for Peter's Party Pizzeria. The opposite wall was covered with old grey-and-white television sets stacked on top of one another, each but one connected to a camera somewhere in the building. The last remaining monitor displayed static.

"I'm guessing this is me?" Ethan said, spinning the squeaky rolling chair in front of the screens.

"That's you. Quick rundown. The A cameras are all on the first floor. The B cameras are the second floor. There are six A cameras: one at the check-in counter at the front of the building, one in the dining area, one in the kids' play area, one in the storage room, and one in the engineers' workspace. The last A camera is above the stage, so you can always keep an eye on Peter and Friends."

"Okay."

"B is simpler. There are two stairs leading up, the south stairs and the north stairs. There's cameras over each of the hallways facing the stairs. The last camera is behind you and overlooks the back door into the alley. Can you remember that? You'll have to memorize the cameras and their locations."

"I think I got it. Or I will."

"Cool."

Ethan pointed at the screen with the static. "Where does this one go? Can I just shut it off?"

"Oh. Sure, if you want to. There used to be a camera in the upstairs storage room off the south hallway, but we pulled it out when we built the handicap restroom."

"Ah."

"Oh! And the officer's manual—" Justin pointed at a white two-inch-thick binder, "—is right here. I'm gonna go ahead and get out of here. Latisha'll close up, and Mark should be here in the morning to relieve you. Any questions? You can't leave the building, so did you bring a packed lunch?"

Ethan nodded. "It's in my car."

"Good. You might want to bring it in before Latisha leaves. Other than that, you have my number if you need anything." Justin extended his hand.

Ethan shook it.

"Looks like you still got some of Mopsy's gunk on you. Might wanna wash that. Bathroom's—"

"South hallway."

"Good job." Justin said. He hurried down the stairs, holding one finger pointed behind him like it was connected to an invisible tether keeping their conversation alive past its time. "I'll see you tomorrow mor—no, tomorrow evening. If anything goes wrong, you have the manual, and that's got all our numbers."

Ethan smiled and waved, eager to see Justin's head disappear past the first step. He looked at his watch. 11:04 p.m. He took a deep breath and watched Justin's trek through the building and out the front door through the monitors. Now it was just Latisha and Ethan, at least until Latisha was done coating Mopsy's parts in oil for the night.

Ethan alternately watched Latisha work, examined the old Peter and Friends posters behind him, and stared into the stained ceiling tiles. It was about time something good happened to him, he thought. This was going to be the easiest job of his life.

It was nearly midnight when Latisha went home. She set the building alarm and left out the back alley door. Ethan could see her on the last B monitor, checking the door to make sure it was locked before waving at the camera and walking down towards her pick-up truck. Ethan sighed when he felt that his leg was sore. He hadn't noticed when he had started shaking it—such is the way with tics—but there were times when his leg shook so much that he felt like he'd run a triathlon. The problem was people. Even if they were several rooms away, they were unpredictable. And so very fragile. This nighttime gig would let him get away from them—to revel in the peace and predictability of solitude—but only *after* everyone else had gone home.

Ethan counted ten minutes from the time after Latisha had driven away, just to make sure that she wasn't coming back. Then he stood up, took a flashlight and the building keys from a drawer, and went downstairs. This was the moment that he'd been waiting for.

In his old sedan, in the glove box, he'd hidden a little pinch hitter—a small black box with enough weed inside to relax his leg and help him make it through the long night. He'd have to smoke it outside to keep from being caught. He'd take a couple puffs, then do his nightly rounds.

Ethan reached the front door before he remembered that Latisha had armed the building alarm. Ethan opened the beige panel and stared at the backlit numbers for a moment before realizing he had no idea what the code was.

*It's probably in the manual,* he thought. He'd have to get the code before he could go out to his car. He turned around.

Cottontail was standing in the dining area, between the theater and the check-in counter. She was the tallest of the animatronics, with her floppy ears giving her a nearly seven-foot height. She stood with her arms in front of her as if she were holding an invisible instrument. Her clean, metal, white fur reflected the beam from Ethan's flashlight into his eyes. He winced and flicked off the light. The dark didn't bother him—what bothered him was knowing that the animatronics didn't just whir and spin, they walked around, too.

"Well, what are *you* doing out here, huh?" he asked, knowing full well that she couldn't answer. Cottontail's wide, blue eyes stared blankly at the prizes that hung like meat from hooks behind the counter. "Did you want to play?" he said, grinning to himself. "Well, those toys aren't for you."

The speakers in the dining area crackled and popped.

A chill struck Ethan like a gut punch, and his gaze shot immediately towards the counter. There were two microphones controlling the speakers—one behind the counter and one in Justin's office upstairs. And he had no desire to check either.

"Did you hear that?" he asked Cottontail. He turned to look at her and stumbled back.

Cottontail's head turned a full ninety degrees to look straight at him. She was now only a few steps away.

"Shit—fuck." Ethan retreated back upstairs, eyes over his shoulder at the animatronic creature. When he reached the camera room, he locked both doors.

He checked the monitors. Cottontail was perfectly still in the dining area, still watching the place where Ethan had been standing. An animatronic statue. Nothing more. Ethan tried to catch his breath from the sprint up the stairs. After twenty years of smoking, his lungs felt as if they had grown thicker, more difficult to expand and contract. He pulled in a rush of air, held it, and released it again. He did this again and again until he felt his breath return to him. Then he looked back at the dining area screen, fully expecting

Cottontail to have moved.

She hadn't.

"That's right, bitch," he told the monitor. "Stay."

Ethan found the manual by the south wall and searched it for Latisha's phone number. It was listed on page 3, underneath all of the managers' names. LATISHA BENJAMIN (24/7 ON-CALL).

*Thank God.* He glanced back at the monitors. Cottontail was watching the camera now. Ethan gasped and dropped the manual. It crashed on the old office carpet with the sound of papers splashing.

After a moment of fumbling through the pages, he found Page 3 again, lifted the handset from the north wall, and started dialing before he realized there was no dial tone. Ethan hung up and tried again. Not a sound.

Something new had appeared on the monitor showing the back alley. Peter Rabbit, his tan fur colorless on the old screen, was outside, standing by the open phone box, his brown felt arm reaching into the wiring.

Before Ethan could react, the screen turned to static.

Ethan turned the monitor off, then back on. When the black-and-white screen faded in, Peter was gone, and the phone box was closed.

*I'm not even high,* Ethan lamented. For the past last two years, he'd awoken almost every night in a cold sweat. He'd see shadows in the dark that weren't real. He knew they weren't real—he just had to remind himself that, sometimes, his mind played tricks on him. Especially when he was sober. He pulled out his smartphone and dialed Latisha's number.

"Hello?" answered Latisha.

"Hi. This is Ethan—the new night guard. I have a... problem." He didn't know what to say next. He thought about telling Latisha that one of the animatronics had gotten outside and shut off the landline to the building, but he hesitated. It was a crazy story. Worse—it could be a prank that Latisha, Justin, and the other staff played on the new night guard. He'd told Latisha that he didn't spook; and he wanted to make that true.

"Shoot," Latisha said.

"I... what do I do if one of the animatronics gets out?"

"Out of where?"

"The theater. I found Cottontail going for the entrance."

Latisha laughed. "Like I said, it's just her stretching her legs. Just leave her alone and I'll have Jesse check on her in the morning. You should be fine as long as you don't open any doors for them."

"I think the landline might be dead, too." He decided against bringing up Peter. At least not now. *They can't open doors*, he told himself.

"Old building, old wiring. That just happens. Sometimes I just give 'em a jiggle and the landline comes back. Just write all of this down and give it to Jesse. She's the morning engineer. She'll take care of it."

"OK. Thanks. Sorry to bother you."

"Don't worry about it. Glad you caught me before I hit the sack. I snore like a train and sleep like a rock."

"OK," Ethan said. "Thanks again. Bye." He hung up without waiting for a reply.

*Leave Cottontail alone*, he thought. *I can do that.*

Ethan glanced at the dining area. Cottontail was standing in the same spot, staring into the distance. Peter Rabbit was on stage, watching the dining area, his red guitar held stiff between his brown, felt-covered arms. Maybe Ethan had imagined what he'd seen in the alley. There's no way that Peter could have made it outside without setting off the building alarm. Peter hadn't moved, and Cottontail was just "stretching her legs."

He kept himself busy the remainder of the night by laying his smartphone on the table and allowing it to play podcasts, which drowned out the eerie hum of the air conditioner and the rattling and groaning of the building around him. He kept his eye on the dining area and the stage, but nothing moved.

Neither did Ethan.

Jesse smiled at Cottontail and pet her fluffy ears. The morning sun made Cottontail's fur—both the metal facsimile and the fabric overlaid in other spots—look brighter than ever.

"There you go." She pushed her long fingers through a hole in the robot's white felt skin. "Come on. Let's go this way, baby," she said, and Cottontail responded by whirring and choking and grinding her way back towards the theater stairs.

"You treat her like she's alive," Ethan said.

"Well, she is to the kids," Jesse said. "They all are. You get used to playing along."

"Should *I* do that if they get out?"

"Nah. You don't know where the switches are. You put

your finger in the wrong place, and you're liable to lose it."

"Got it. I'll just leave 'em wherever they wind up." He turned towards the exit.

"Oh!" Jesse called to him. "It's 0315. The alarm combination."

"What?"

"The building alarm? The system log says it went off last night. I figured you'd gone out for a smoke?"

Ethan nodded, but his mind conjured the image on the back alley monitor: Peter—or something—prying into the phone box. *Had* he gone out during the night and forgotten about it? He'd had his last cigarette the day he'd had his last drink—the same day he'd picked up smoking weed. Two steps forward, one step back.

"Bad habit."

"Right. No—I get it. You just don't want the alarm going off. I mean, it works about half the time, but if it *does* work, you'll regret it. That thing is loud as a trumpet on Judgment Day. I guess you're just lucky it didn't trigger this time." Jesse smiled. "Just remember it. March 2015. Oh-three-one-five."

*March 2015. Why March 2015?* It had to be a coincidence. He'd had his last drink in March 2015.

*Never again.*

"0315. Got it. Thanks." He paused, thinking about what he saw—or thought he saw—on the back alley monitor. "Can Peter open doors? I know the others can't."

Jesse shook her head. "I've been working here since Day One, and I ain't never seen Peter leave the theater at night. He's the newest animatronic we got, though. The rest came here secondhand. Peter was made specifically for this place."

"So he doesn't have to move as much to keep his gears from sticking or whatever? He's basically brand new?"

"Born March 2015." Jesse smiled.

Ethan's blood froze. The last time he'd had a drink, he'd blacked out. He'd blacked out a lot, but he'd never woken up covered in blood before.

Ethan forced a smile. "Thanks."

She nodded. "Yup. See ya tomorrow morning." She walked into the engineers' work area, and Ethan could hear her starting a one-way conversation with Mopsy as the *STAFF ONLY* door closed behind her.

On his second day, Ethan came in early. He wanted to be ready for anything—but wasn't sure *what* he'd be ready for. He only knew that he wouldn't be made a fool of tonight. He wouldn't be shaken by lumbering kids' toys.

Peter's Party Pizzeria had just closed, and the staff were cleaning up. Justin and Latisha were in the workshop in the back, laughing. Ethan was headed up the stairs when Justin opened the door and called out his name.

"Heard you had to call Latisha last night," Justin said, grinning.

"Yeah," Ethan said, the blood rushing to his ears. "Cottontail gave me a bit of a shock."

"They can do that. I won't lie—*I* wouldn't do your job. I'm fine with them dancing and singing in the theater. The moment they're out of that box, I'm gone."

"Why doesn't Latisha just have them move around in the same place? That way they're not... wandering."

"They're all repurposed. Latisha says it's better for their old joints. And it helps with pretending that they're real."

"*I* don't have to do that, right?"

Justin shook his head. "Just the day staff."

Ethan nodded. "Good. No offense." He wanted to ask about Peter again, but he couldn't bring himself to do it.

"None taken. My husband thinks it's weird too." Justin waved and pushed past the door into the dining area.

Ethan walked up the north stairs to his little camera room, shutting both doors and locking himself inside. Then he watched the cameras. He checked the underside of his arm. In pen, earlier that evening, he had retraced the faded outlines of the code Jesse had given him—0315. As if he'd forget.

He laid his smartphone and flashlight in front of him. Yup. Ready for anything.

Latisha left at 12:13 a.m. Ethan set a timer on his phone for fifteen minutes. He kept most of his focus on the stage and Latisha's workspace. Peter, Cottontail, and Flopsy stood in their regular spots, holding their instruments in their arms. Mopsy was *mostly* rebuilt—beige felt now coating her mechanical innards. Her head was still lying on the workbench like a grisly, unfinished art project. She probably wouldn't be going on any walks tonight.

The timer chimed and buzzed on Ethan's wrist. His heart

leapt into his throat, and he struggled to swallow it back down.

*Damn it.* He hated how fragile he could be when his nerves were raw.

He took the building keys and jogged down the stairs to the front entrance. He tapped Jesse's code on the alarm panel, and it beeped twice in approval. The Armed light blinked off, and the Ready light on, painting Ethan's face with a green hue.

In less than a minute he was beside his car, an orange, nylon poncho draped over his shoulders, smoking a pinch of weed in the dark, empty parking lot of Peter's Party Pizzeria. He closed his eyes as he held his breath, reminding himself that all this was his anxiety. That his jumpiness was *his* issue, and unrelated to his work or to the robots that wandered the halls at night. He glanced at the front doors of the building, considering for a second not going back inside.

*Don't be stupid.*

He threw the poncho into the back, hid the pinch hitter in his glove box, and nearly opened the doors to return to the building when he noticed the red light bathing the entryway.

Ethan frowned and opened the door. A shrieking whistle warned that the alarm was about to trip unless the correct code was entered. He ran to the panel and flipped it open. He pushed the pound button and tried to push in the alarm code. The 1 button would not respond. The claxon was making his ears ring. Ethan felt nauseated, and his head swam. He tried to make out the numbers on the countdown timer. Twenty-three seconds. He'd wasted too much time.

Ethan shook his head to clear his focus, then he tried the

code again, holding the 1 down until it beeped. When he reached 5, silence fell across the building, and Ethan crumbled to the floor.

"Who the *fuck* armed the alarm?!" he shouted, having finally gathered enough breath. "Was it you?!" he demanded, half-jokingly pointing at Peter and Friends on the stage across the dining area from him. The animatronics stayed silent, staring blankly at the invisible audience in front of them.

*Who else would have armed it?* He shook his head.

"Someone's fucking with me. I know you're here. Latisha? Justin? Jesse?"

No answer.

Ethan returned to the security room, collected his flashlight and his phone, and began his patrol of the first floor. The sounds of scraping and whirring gears emanated from the theater. He checked his watch. 1:03 a.m. Perhaps the animatronic characters activated every hour, on the hour.

Ethan checked the north hallway on the second floor. Justin's office and the staff lounge were both clear. He checked the south hallway on the second floor—the bathroom was clear. The old closet door-to-nowhere was locked.

Ethan used every key on his security ring. None worked on the closet door. He thought it was strange that he'd be given the keys to every room in a building but one, but he assumed that Justin wanted his privacy. Maybe there were franchise secrets inside. He imagined manila folders being tossed by a shadowy silhouette across a circular table to various employees of Peters' Party Pizzeria, each stamped with a red "MANAGERS' EYES ONLY" warning. He chuckled at the thought. He could already feel his anxiety waning.

When he returned to the security room and logged that he had completed his rounds, he took the manual from the wall and searched the table of contents for the section on the cameras. He followed the instructions, learning to manipulate the controls, and pulled the recording back to around 12:30 a.m., when he left the building. He saw himself on the monitor, disarming the alarm and closing the front door behind him. A few minutes passed, and nothing happened.

The stage camera lost its picture to static. When the image returned, Flopsy was no longer in the theater. She was standing in the open doorway of Latisha's workspace. She was gazing directly at Mopsy's head that sat on the center of the worktable. Her arms were slightly raised, her elbows turned inward so that it looked like she was touching her cheeks with the palm of her hands. Her face retained the wide-eyed grin that had been molded into it.

Ethan looked at his watch. 2:03 a.m.

"I figured you out," Ethan said, prodding the screen with his finger. "I know your secret."

At the 12:42 a.m. mark, the camera lost its picture to static. He fast-forwarded and came out of the static at 12:47. Ethan switched the controls from the entryway camera to the stage camera, and he set the recording to begin playing at 12:35. Peter, Cottontail, and Flopsy were all in the picture. At 12:41 the camera switched to static and back to the theater. Cottontail and Flopsy were still in place, but Peter was missing. At 12:48, the static returned. When the picture reappeared, so had Peter.

"OK, so not all of you move on minute three," he said to

himself. He wrote down the times. He *was* a night guard, after all—hired to observe and report. That's what this was.

Flopsy wasn't downstairs anymore. Ethan stood up and searched the monitors. *Where are you?* he thought.

He found her standing in the middle of the north hallway. She was facing the back wall. In Ethan's direction.

He turned on the flashlight and put his hand on the north doorknob out of the security room. If he unlocked it, Flopsy could get to him. Ethan interrupted that line of thought. Of course, it was absurd. She was an automaton. She couldn't hurt him. She couldn't even know he was there if he were standing right in front of her. He unlocked the security room door and stepped into the hall.

Ethan aimed the flashlight at Flopsy, whose brown eyes glared right back at him. His beam reflected off whatever her eyes were made of—glass, metal, probably plastic—making them appear to glow red.

"What are *you* doing up here, young lady?" he asked, trying to relax. He smiled and approached Flopsy with care. She was only a few inches shorter than Cottontail, with dark brown fur that hid her features in that shadowy hallway. One of her ears stood straight up, while the other flopped down on her right side. The opposite of Mopsy's.

"You looking for your sister? She's downstairs." He touched her soft, wooly arm, hoping to lead her back downstairs.

Flopsy's left arm swung up, and her metal fingers wrapped around his throat. Ethan dropped the flashlight. It clattered as Flopsy pulled Ethan down to her hip, and Ethan was able to slip out of her loose grasp. He coughed desperately, trying to catch his breath.

Flopsy lifted her right arm and strummed an imaginary guitar. She began to sway her hips and sing with a crackly, electronic voice, towering over Ethan as he gasped for air.

PETER RABBIT, DON'T YOU CRY
THE MOON IS GIBBOUS WAXING
THE GARDEN SHIMMERS BRIGHTEST IN THE DARK
YOUR SISTERS' TUMMIES RUMBLE
MOTHER'S STEW IS MOSTLY BROTH
MCGREGOR'S BITE IS WEAKER THAN HIS BARK
THE DIM REFRIGERATOR
MARKS THE OUTLINE OF A GUN
YOU'RE GOING TO DIE WRITHING ON A LARK

Ethan pushed himself onto his back and crawled away from her. He ran and locked himself in the security room. He made the mistake of glancing at the monitors. Mopsy was standing in front of her own head in Latisha's workspace. On stage, Peter was watching the camera. Cottontail stood in the south second-floor hallway, her ears brushing the ceiling tiles.

"Fuck you!" He shut his eyes. He struggled to control his breathing.

When he looked up at the cameras again, Peter and Friends were back in the stage. Peter, Flopsy, and Cottontail were posed with their instruments, observing their imaginary audience, right where they should be. Mopsy was standing against the wall in Latisha's workspace. Although Ethan's neck was raw where he'd been choked, he found himself wondering whether he'd imagined it all. Flopsy hadn't tried to kill him then sung him a song. That couldn't have been real. He realized he forgot to check the time when Flopsy and Cottontail had moved last. He looked at his watch. 5:04 a.m.

*What the fuck?* His shift was almost over. Had he blacked out? He tried to check the security footage outside of the security room, but the replay feature wouldn't respond.

He laughed, shaking his head, rubbing at his neck. Were the red marks from being choked, or from his own worried fingers?

He waited, the minutes passing like hours, until he saw Justin on the south hallway monitor. Ethan unlocked the door and met him as he approached.

"Good morning!" Justin said.

"I'm going home." Ethan nearly ran down the stairs and out of Peter's Party Pizzeria, eager for his night to be over.

Ethan checked his neck in the mirror at home. Two red friction burns stretched across both sides of his neck.

He considered bringing a gun to work, but the thought settled in his stomach and squeezed. He didn't own a gun anymore, in any case.

He arrived late to his shift. 11:22 p.m. Mopsy, Flopsy, and Cottontail were all on stage, but Peter was missing. He flashed Flopsy his middle finger before pushing past the *STAFF ONLY* door. He found Latisha in her workspace with Peter. Peter's shirt was pulled up, and the felt skin on his back was pulled apart at the middle by metal pincers, revealing his inner workings.

"We were taking bets on whether you were gonna show," Latisha said.

"What's wrong with Peter?" Ethan said.

"He was being stubborn." Latisha patted Peter on the arm. "Weren't ya, buddy?"

"Stubborn? Walking around too much or something?"

"No. Just... not performing. When the music came on, he'd just stare at the kids." Back to Peter. "You gotta sing and dance for that money, kid."

It bothered Ethan how people—himself included—kept talking to the animatronics. They were just machines. They couldn't understand any of the words that were told to them.

"There's a door upstairs," he said. "It's locked. I don't have the key."

"The door by the restroom? There's no key—it just stays locked unless it wants to open."

Ethan blinked. "Unless it what now?"

Latisha laughed. "I'm kidding! The handicap bathroom's on the other side. They sealed up the wall on one side and left the door. You wanna see what's there—just go around."

"Why leave the door?"

Latisha shrugged. "Cheaper, I guess? Who the hell knows? Don't worry about the door."

"OK. Thanks. I'll see ya."

Latisha waved and continued working on Peter while Ethan took his post in the security room. Latisha left at 11:49 p.m. Ethan set an alarm for 12:03, when he expected the animatronics to move for the first time. With Peter out of commission, he'd only have to worry about Mopsy, Flopsy, and Cottontail, who were stuck where they were until the third minute of each hour.

Ethan's alarm chimed. On stage, Peter's "friends" whirred to life. They swayed and silently played their instruments. Then the lights on the first floor came on. The entire glass front of the building was shining across the parking lot like Times Square.

Flopsy, Mopsy, and Cottontail began to sing, but the sound of their music came not through the speakers in their throats, but in the form of three little girls' whispers behind his ears:

```
PETER RABBIT, DON'T YOU CRY
THE MOON IS FULL AND HUNGRY
THE LIGHT, IT BURNS THE BRIGHTEST IN
THE DARK
   HIS SISTERS' TUMMIES RUMBLED
   PETER ROTTED IN THE WALL
   McGREGOR LEFT HIM THERE TO FEED THE
WORMS
```

Ethan instinctively looked behind him, seeing nothing but the old promotional posters. He looked back at the stage, and the picture had become static. It crackled for a moment before the picture returned. The three animatronic rabbits were looking straight into the camera, their unsettling grins wide and full of metal teeth. The lights went black again, throwing the first floor into darkness. He took his phone and keys and went downstairs. When he passed through the STAFF ONLY door, the theater was directly to his left. The animatronics were all looking straight up at the camera, ignoring him.

"You'd better stay right where you are."

They continued to ignore him, still as statues.

"That's right." He turned off the alarm and went outside to smoke. Swimming in his first high of the night, that song repeated in his head. He shuddered. He looked through the window before opening the door again. The alarm still glowed green, but the theater was empty. If it was hide-and-seek they wanted, they'd have to wait until he did his rounds—which he would only do *after* he had found them all on the cameras.

The cool air of Peter's Party Pizzeria choked Ethan with its silence. Ethan locked the front door, reset the alarm, and made his way, slowly and soundlessly, back towards the STAFF ONLY door. Ethan shone his flashlight into the stage as he passed. The animatronics had left their musical instruments strewn on the stage floor. Ethan walked past Latisha's workspace, where a limp Peter stood, his caramel-colored felt arms hanging from his shoulders like dead meat from a hook. Ethan looked up the north stairs. Cottontail stood at the second floor landing, staring down at him. The light behind her made her appear larger and more predatory than on his first day.

"Yeah... no way," he said, shining his flashlight over Cottontail's vacant grin.

He took the south stairs up and locked himself into the security room. He'd found Cottontail—now he only needed to find the others. Ethan searched the monitors. Flopsy was at the foot of the south stairs, looking up at the camera. Mopsy was missing.

Ethan narrowed his eyes. "What are you doing?" He checked the time. 2:07. Ethan shook his head. It couldn't have taken him two hours to go out to his car, smoke, and come back. The landline rang, and Ethan jumped. He threatened the phone with his finger before picking up the receiver.

"Hello?" Ethan said.

"Call my mommy, please," a small boy's voice whispered. "We won't tell nobody what you did."

Ethan dropped the receiver. His hands were shaking. He felt a pounding heat in his temples—the budding of a hangover, the onset of the very feeling that pushed him one step closer to quitting drinking. The light in the north hallway flickered. Ethan turned around and met Cottontail's plastic blue gaze through the now-open door. Ethan screamed and fell back against the opposite side of the room. Ethan backed against the wall and used it to pull himself back up to his feet. Slowly, he closed the door to the security room—separating him from Cottontail. The frame was broken, and the door wouldn't latch. He checked the time.

3:02 A.M.

"Shit." Where had the hour gone? They would move again any moment. Ethan had to hide. He opened the bathroom door and screamed when he found himself face to face with Mopsy's brown face and floppy left ear.

The alarm on Ethan's phone chimed, and the security room door began to open, revealing a felt white paw. Ethan pulled his body back as Mopsy's arms came forward to hug Ethan.

"No!" Ethan screamed.

Flopsy followed close behind, ambling forward, the speaker in her throat giggling madly.

The locked door in the south hallway swung open. Ethan saw it as his only escape. He lunged through the door and shut it behind him, holding the knob in place.

*They can't open doors. They can't open doors. They can't open doors.*

At the end of the dark room, a panel of monitors began to light up. Was he back in the security room? No, he was in the handicap restroom. Or he should be.

The monitors each showed images of different rooms inside of someone's home. His home. But the date was wrong. Very wrong.

March 17, 2015.

He'd been a heavy drinker then. Lots of blackouts.

A small boy entered the kitchen camera from offscreen. The time marker read 3:03 A.M. Ethan checked the time. It was 3:03 a.m. for him, too.

Through the monitor, Ethan could see himself sprawled on the living room floor by the couch where he'd fallen asleep. The recording had no sound, but he could hear the boy rummaging through the cabinets for food as if he was there with him.

"No. Don't wake up. Don't get the gun," he said to himself.

The Ethan on-camera jerked his head up. He stumbled to his feet and shuffled to a small drawer near the swinging door leading into the kitchen. He pulled a gun from the cabinet.

*How do I know—no.*

Two gunshots. The boy fell to the ground and bled. Ethan covered his eyes.

*I thought it was—I didn't know it was—*

A light turned on above him. Ethan turned around, and he saw tan fur. Peter.

"**SO HUNGRY**," Peter said in a small boy's voice, distorted and twisted into a monstrous growl. He brought his arm down over Ethan's head like a sledgehammer. Ethan felt a cold crack over his left ear. He fell to his knees and looked up, his sight interrupted by bright flashes of light surrounding Peter like an aura.

"I'm..." Ethan said weakly, "...so...sor—"

The machine's face was locked in a rictus grin. Its limbs swung down toward Ethan like hammers.

Latisha stood with her arms against her hips, her eyes surveying what remained of Ethan's head, much of which now coated the walls and secret monitors of the handicap restroom. Then she turned to face Peter, who stood limply over Ethan's corpse, his felt arms soaked in blood and grey matter.

"Great. Now we have to get *you* steamcleaned."

Justin shook his head. "This is worse than with Cottontail. We may need to just replace the felt."

"It's your dime," Latisha said.

They exited the bathroom. Flopsy, Mopsy, and Cottontail were gathered outside the bathroom, staring vacantly at the door.

"Let me know what position we're hiring for now," Justin said. "Just not another security guard. Ruined my door." He mumbled to himself as he crossed the security room to his office in the north hallway.

Latisha looked at Flopsy and Mopsy.

"All right. Who's next?"

# AUTHOR'S NOTE

I find myself fascinated by the simplicity and allure of a game like *Five Nights at Freddy's.* The game revolves around you sitting at a security desk, watching cameras for movement and occasionally closing two doors and turning on a light. The catch is that there are animatronics lurking in the dark, eager to pounce on you and end your playtime in a brutally surprising way. The atmosphere of the game alone was enough to keep me playing.

While theories abound on the internet for why the animatronics are doing what they're doing, I wanted to imagine my own scenario within a similar atmosphere. As a person of color, I've been deeply affected by the murders of young men and women by people who claim to be protecting themselves. I wanted to tell a similar story, where Ethan's decision to shoot a home intruder results in the death of a child, and how that event affected him. When the animatronics come for Ethan, it's ultimately the guilt that he's been escaping that kills him.

# ANGELS' ARMAGEDDON
## BY AMBER FALLON

**H**is obsession started with a YouTube video.
Eighty-four seconds with barely any audio, mostly
just background noise over a strange electronic
melody. Someone with their back to the camera was playing
a retro-looking video game while the cameraperson,
probably wielding a cell phone, recorded the gameplay. The
monitor was blurry at best, but he could make out the
blocky-looking white shapes swooping and diving across
the screen like the aliens from *Galaga*. Bright blue slashes of
light knocked them from the pixelated sky one by one for a
few moments before a brilliant flash of red dropped them all
to the ground. Eight-bit blood dripped down the screen as
the player stared, neck tilted sharply in an unnatural angle.
The video swings off-kilter, showing legs and sneaker-clad
feet, as the person recording it goes to check on their friend.

"Hey man," he says, barely audible over the electronic
song emanating from the screen, "You okay?" Suddenly the

player whirls with almost inhuman speed, face contorted in a mask of hate and rage, his eyeballs solid black. He leaps up, knocking over his chair, and the cell phone clatters to the floor. The video displays a white wall with a framed landscape hanging on it. Screams, grunting. Blood splashes the painting. The video cuts off.

The video's called "THIS GAME TURNS PEOPLE INSANE!!!!11!!!!" and Jason Keefe watched it dozens of times before it was taken down by YouTube's admins.

He had been searching through videos of vintage video games, trying to locate the ones he'd played in his youth; happy memories of a time when his family was still whole. Collecting those games had become a hobby for Jason lately. He enjoyed the escape from his shitty gas station job and his boring, awful life. When he stumbled on that particular video, something about it stuck in his brain like a bit of popcorn sticks in your teeth sometimes. Even when he wasn't watching it, it replayed over and over again in his head; especially the brief flash of the player's awful, distorted face.

Jason wished he had thought to record that video somehow, already desperate to see it again, to search it for some sort of clue as to what game it was, but he'd have to make due with a few stills. He had taken screenshots of the video at 0:24, when the white shapes were swooping around, 0:51, when the 8-bit blood began to cover the screen, and 1:12, which froze the player's hate-filled facial expression. In the static image, he looked almost demonic, with those creepy, all-black eyes. That had to be a trick of the light, an odd reflection or something. Or maybe those special effects contacts they sold at Halloween. Right?

WELCOME TO 4CHAN!
/vg/ - Video Game Generals
HELP WITH VIDEO GAME
JLord666 11/17/17(Fri) 01:19:12 No.181682219  Reply>
Hey Guyz,
Anyone kno0w  what game this is from?

He posted the screen caps—blurry and indistinct, but it was the best he had—then he waited. Jason watched the comment thread, unable to keep his twitching fingers from hitting F5 again and again to refresh the page. If anyone knew anything about the game, it would be one of his fellow 'channers.

Seconds stretched into minutes and then minutes became hours with no response. Eventually, Jason decided to duplicate the post on Reddit. He had more luck there, at least in terms of upvotes and comments bumping the thread, but none of them were useful. Several people asked where they were taken from or demanded links to the video. Others claimed that it was obviously fake. Someone gifted Jason a month of premium content for a reply to one of the many users doubting the authenticity of the video.

Jl0rd666: I don't know if its real or not man, but I will find out

footballbelle9: Why would you want to?

Jl0rd666: Cuz I wanna know if there really is a game that does that to people

footballbelle9: So what if there is? Are you going to play it?

Jason stared at the screen, not really sure how to answer. Would he play it, if he found it? If it really did exist, would he be willing to bet his sanity and the lives of anyone around him on whether or not it could really drive someone insane, maybe turn them into some kind of monster?

Something about it was familiar. Like he'd played it before. Had he, years ago, but just forgot? He needed to know.

Was the player in the video already suffering from mental illness and the game just set him off? Maybe it was a seizure or something, caused by the flashing lights? Or maybe the naysayers voting down his post were right, and the video itself was just a hoax created to get attention.

Unless and until he figured out what video game had been shown and where he could get a copy, it was pretty much irrelevant. Besides, he was sure of himself and his mental fortitude; after his abusive father was arrested for beating his mother to a bloody pulp in front of him and his little sister, after testifying at his father's trial and seeing him dragged off to jail, after the phone call late one night informing them that the old man had been killed in a "violent incident," after working shift after shift for low pay at a shitty gas station just to help make ends meet, having a gun stuck in his face over less than a hundred bucks, he was certain he could handle whatever a video game could throw at his psyche.

Jason went back to 4Chan and checked on his post. There was only one reply. Just two little words, but they made Jason's breath catch in his throat.

WELCOME TO 4CHAN!
/vg/ - Video Game Generals
HELP WITH VIDEO GAME
D3m0nzFren 11/17/17(Fri) 04:16:57 No.181682384
Reply>
Angels' Armageddon

That was it. It had to be. Jason opened a new browser window and searched for "Angels' Armageddon video game." There wasn't much there. Less than a dozen results, with the first two being ads for games with similar titles.

There was an article on a website called Gamer's Grotto titled "Angels' Armageddon: Fact or Fiction?" It was dated two years prior and mostly consisted of still screenshots from the video Jason had already seen. He saved the images he didn't already have and read the paragraphs with baited breath, hoping for something concrete, some clue as to the game's existence, or lack thereof. Sadly, he came up empty. The writer of the article had no more information on the game than Jason himself, just worthless conjecture and opinions. The only thing Jason had learned was that the video he'd seen was at least two years old and as far as new information went, that was pretty much useless. The article ended by saying that if there was any chance that the game existed and did, in fact, turn its players into homicidal maniacs that it was better that there was next to no information to be found on the internet. Jason disagreed.

Another article on a site called J.D.'s Funzone had scans of magazine ads for Angels' Armageddon from old issues of *GamePro* and *PC Gamer*. There were two of the ads; one was a large, full-page image featuring a television set with the

Angel's Armageddon title screen displayed. The television was dripping blood, which formed the words "**THE LAST GAME YOU'LL EVER WANT TO PLAY!**" and a release date: June 6, 1996. Below this information, in tiny white letters, was the name of the company that produced the game in question: Apollyon, Inc. A blond-haired little boy crouched behind the television set, his features twisted into a malevolent mask, his eyes nothing but blackness. The other ad featured a dark-skinned little boy holding the game box in his hands and wearing that same awful expression. His eyes, too, were solid black. Jason saved both images before he began Googling "Apollyon, Inc."

Bankruptcy filings. Articles from reputable sources like CNN and Forbes about the overnight disappearance of the company under mysterious circumstances. Copyright notices. Nothing useful, and nothing that mentioned *Angels' Armageddon*.

The fact that there was so little information out there probably meant that the game itself wasn't real. Maybe it had been, at one time. But maybe it was just some kind of joke, like an old form of viral marketing or something. After all, people were awful. Just look how many people retweeted or shared things like murders, rapes, and suicides. It would have grown, spreading like social media wildfire... but it hadn't. Why?

Because there was nothing but a video created by a couple of kids, based on a weird old video game that lost funding before it was ever released. Someone had probably reposted it recently because it wasn't getting any attention. That was all.

Jason went back to comb further through the search results.

The next even vaguely useful hit was a post from almost four years ago… another Redditor asking if the game was real. Jason poured through the replies, disheartened to realize that this thread pretty much mirrored his own. Most of the responses were people claiming that the video was fake, a few people were concerned, and one commenter, all the way down at the bottom, was curious about the boy holding the camera/phone.

P0mpous5pider: what about the camera dude? Did he die? Does anyone know?
footballbelle9: <link>

Jason, of course, clicked on the link. It was an obituary for a boy named Thomas Johnson Hastings.

*Thomas Johnson Hayes, 17, of Breville, died October 7, 2007 as a result of an accident that occurred at his best friend's house. He was born June 8, 1990 in Harpersville, the son of Robert and Megan (Torelli) Hayes. He attended Breville High School, where he was a member of the track and field team and the debate team.*

*Thomas was a beloved member of the community and an active volunteer at the local animal shelter, Helping Paws, as well as a member of the area Model Airplane Association.*

*Thomas, or Tommy as he was known to his friends and family, is survived by his parents Robert and Megan and his Uncle Peter Torelli of Cliffside. He also leaves his maternal grandparents, Joseph and Alice Torelli, also of Cliffside. He is also survived by his girlfriend, Mary Elizabeth Kramer and his best friend, Anthony*

*Fiestro, both of Breville.*

*Funeral Arrangements are being handled by Masters and Sons Funeral Home in Breville. Calling hours will be Tuesday from 2:00-4:00 PM and 7:00-9:00 PM. The funeral will be held on Wednesday at 10:00 AM at the funeral home and at 11:00 AM at Our Lady of Perpetual Light Church in Breville. In lieu of flowers, the family asks that you consider donations to Helping Paws. Envelopes will be available at the funeral home, and may also be mailed directly to the shelter or offered online.*

The article was accompanied by a picture of a smiling young boy with shaggy hair holding up a fish he'd presumably caught, along with what was obviously a school photo.

Jason stared at both, feeling a lump rise in his throat. That couldn't be the cameraman from the video, could it? You never saw his face or anything, so how had someone identified him? It just wasn't possible. Someone had just looked up an obituary for a kid about the right age and had posted it as a reply. That was all.

Still…

Jason Googled the name "Anthony Fiestro."

LOCAL BOY CHARGED WITH FRIEND'S MURDER

DA REQUESTS LOCAL TEEN TO BE TRIED AS AN ADULT

ANTHONY FIESTRO FOUND MENTALLY UNFIT TO STAND TRIAL

LOCAL TEEN COMMITTED TO IRON HEIGHTS
MENTAL INSTITUTION

ANTHONY FIESTRO COMMITS SUICIDE WHILE
COMMITTED TO IRON HEIGHTS

Jason's eyes went wide. He clicked on the first link.

*Anthony Fiestro, 16, of Breville has been arrested for the death of his best friend, Thomas Hayes. Hayes was taken to the emergency room following an October 6 incident at Fiestro's home. The boy later succumbed to a combination of blood loss and grievous injuries. Police Commissioner Alexander Duggins has stated that the case is being treated as a homicide.*

Jason swallowed hard. It couldn't be true, could it? No. No freakin' way. Why wouldn't Thomas' obituary mention this?

He read the next article, and the next one.

At some point, Jason nodded off. He woke up with a start, his heart hammering in his chest. A nightmare. That's all it was. Visions of kids with solid black eyes and evil snarls on their faces lingered behind his eyelids while that haunting electronic tone played in his head.

He checked his post on Reddit. Several replies had come in while he'd been following clues down the Google rabbit hole, but nothing very useful. Then he noticed that the little envelope icon in the corner was red, indicating he had a new message.

It was short, but once more Jason's breath caught in his throat.

You Have **1** New Message

"$500"
footballbelle9
Reply   Block   Report

*KNOCK KNOCK KNOCK!*
Jason nearly jumped out of his skin.
*"JAY!"* his sister, Molly, shrieked in her ear-piercing way, *"Mom says you have to take me to school today!"* Jason shook his head and looked around, noticing for the first time that the sun had begun to leak in through his window shades. He sighed, turned his monitor off, and hurriedly changed into his uniform. He'd drop Molly off on his way to his shift at the gas station. He didn't have time to take a shower. He'd have to use extra deodorant and hope for the best.

"Go get your stuff," Jason demanded as he pushed past Molly on the way to the bathroom. As her footfalls echoed in the hallway, Jason looked at himself in the mirror. For a moment, he could have sworn his eyes were pools of solid black. He stared at his reflection until Molly started pounding on the door. He forgot to brush his teeth.

He was going to be late, but that was the least of his concerns. If that message meant what he thought it meant, he could have a copy of *Angels' Armageddon* of his own for $500. But to him, $500 might as well be $500,000. That was about what he made in an entire month at the gas station, and he gave his mother almost all of it to help with the bills. There was no way he'd be able to go a month without giving his mother that money, if he could even wait that long. He couldn't pick up extra hours, because his boss was already doing everything he could to keep costs down. Another job was out of the question; his schedule at the gas station was all over the place. But he *had* to have that game. He needed it like he had some kind of terminal illness and *Angels' Armageddon* was the only cure.

All through the morning, his thoughts were on the money. He didn't really own anything of value, at least not enough to get the game.

Then a dark thought occurred to him.

He could steal it.

Taking money from the gas station would be stupid, Jason knew. There were four different cameras that would catch him in the act if he tried to pocket money from the till. He'd be arrested before he ever even played the game.

But he knew enough about how the gas station worked to rob it. He knew when the shift changed, he knew who would recognize him and who'd be too stoned to care, who banked the larger bills from the till in the locked safe beneath the counter regularly and who didn't... Yeah, that would work. He'd wait until Robin was on shift, rush in with one of Molly's Halloween masks over his face, and demand the money. He'd be in and out before Robin put down her joint. There was even a sleazy twenty-four-hour check cashing store a few blocks away where he could wire the money, no questions asked. Yeah, that just might work.

Once the idea came into Jason's head, it wouldn't leave

him alone. He ached to know whether or not the game was even real, and if it was what it would do to anyone who played it. Somehow the idea of such a magical, evil thing existing—and him proving it, or experiencing it for himself—somehow it made his bleak, mundane life seem more vibrant, more worthwhile.

Even though he was basically a good kid and had never been in any sort of real trouble before, he'd have to go through with his plan to rob his employer.

Jason was jumpy and jittery through the rest of his shift. He jokingly told anyone who commented on it that he'd had too much coffee. That seemed to appease the curious regulars who could tell that something about him was off.

When it was finally time to go home, he looked at the schedule hanging up in the manager's office. Robin was scheduled the next night. Thanks to the owner's penny-pinching ways, she'd be all by herself from 10:00 p.m. onward. If he was lucky, she might even think she hallucinated the whole thing.

As soon as Jason got home, he raced to his computer.

"Ok. How do you want the money?" Jl0rd666

The response came almost instantly with a bank account number. He scribbled it down on a piece of paper he tucked into his wallet and tried not to count the hours until he could put his plan into motion.

The next 24 hours were a blur of nerves, fruitless internet searches, panic, and very little in the way of sleep.

While Molly was at school, Jason snuck into her room and helped himself to a cheap plastic Wonder Woman Halloween mask. He wrapped it in a baggy black hoody that was two sizes too big for him, thanks to the local clothing bank, and pushed it under some brush out by the street. Still feeling panicked and halfway out of his mind with nerves, he cleaned his room and the kitchen for good measure. Finally, the little hand began approaching the faded black 10 on the old wall clock. Molly was sound asleep. His mother would be at work for another two hours. It was time to make his move.

As he'd hoped, Robin was high as a kite when he'd run in with his mask on. He demanded the money out of the register, which Robin had shoved across the counter at him, laughing and asking where Batman was the whole time.

As soon as he was safely away from the cameras in the parking lot and by the pumps, he ditched the mask and the hoody in a dumpster. Sure, Molly might be upset, but whatever. She was never the same thing for Halloween two years in a row anyway.

Wiring the money hadn't even been difficult, save for the moment when he was worried he might not have enough, having forgotten about the wire transfer fee, but in the end it had all worked out fine. He'd sent the money, gotten a receipt, and been back home all within the span of an hour.

That he could easily be connected both to the mask and the late-night cash transfer never occurred to him.

With shaking hands, he woke up his computer and refreshed the Reddit tab in his browser. Sure enough, he had a message. It contained only a link, which opened a download through some kind of weird, foreign file-sharing site. An animation of an inky black liquid rippled across the screen, gradually shifting into the deep red color of blood before dripping down to reveal the word **APOLLYON** in glowing letters. The letters faded before the download began.

Jason watched the progress bar tick slowly upwards, more impatient than ever. If he was going to be arrested for his crime, he at least wanted to taste the fruits of his labors first. The achingly slow internet connection didn't help, but it was the best they could afford and there wasn't anything he could do about it anyway, except wait.

*"Jason! Mom says you gotta take me to school again!"* Jason snapped awake with a start. He'd fallen asleep in his chair, waiting for the download to finish. Sunlight streamed through the blinds, casting striped shadows on his still-made bed.

The download had finished.

There was an odd icon on his desktop now; a pixelated angel hovered next to his Steam account shortcut. Jason clicked it and began the install. The process was slow. An awful lot of data for such an old game.

*Damn.* He'd have to wait until he got home that afternoon before he could play the game now, and it was his mother's day off, so she might have other plans for the family.

The combination of fear that his crime would be discovered and anticipation over playing the game made Jason even more neurotic than he had been the day before. He was sure someone would have called the police by now, that he'd approach the gas station to find it surrounded by squad cars with swirling red and blue lights, Robin outside and ready to point right at him when she saw him. Maybe the officers wouldn't bother trying to arrest him. Maybe they'd just shoot him on sight...

The thought was oddly comforting.

But nothing of the sort occurred. Jerry was on shift when Jason arrived and he said nothing at all about a robbery. Maybe his luck would hold and Robin hadn't bothered to report it. Eventually the owner would notice the money discrepancy and check the security tapes, but for now it looked like Jason just might be in the clear.

The minutes ticked by so slowly they almost seemed to be going backwards. Jason couldn't stop thinking about the game. Soon he'd see what it was all about. Just a few hours more and he'd know the truth. He almost hoped it *was* cursed. If it wasn't, if it was just some unfinished software from two decades ago, and there wasn't nothing special about it, then all his effort, all his longing...

Finally, his relief cashier arrived. Jason bolted for the door in an eerie parody of the previous night and sped home.

As expected, his mother's car was in the shabby dirt driveway when he pulled up. Jason took a deep breath before going inside, already preparing excuses about not feeling well to get out of watching a crappy kids' movie or another awful dinner at Peter's Party Pizzeria with those creepy singing robots. He coughed exaggeratedly as he threw open the door.

"Mom? Do you have any of that red cold stuff left?" he called, "I think I caught something at the gas station…"

There was no answer.

"Mom?" Jason asked, making his way down the hallway.

It was then that he noticed the music. Tinny, repetitive, and coming from his room. It was the same music he'd heard on the video.

With his heart in his throat, Jason threw open his door. Molly's blond hair and purple headband could just barely be seen over the back of his computer chair. On his monitor, the shapes of white 8-bit angels swooped and dove. Jason couldn't breathe. The walls closed in on him. Time stood still.

Molly launched his chair backwards and dove at him, her tiny face contorted in a mask of hate and rage far stronger than anything a nine-year-old should know.

The little girl he'd taken trick-or-treating and to the movies on weekends was gone.

Her eyes were solid black.

Jason went over hard, striking his head on the door frame. Molly was on him instantly, tiny teeth tearing and rending, her face already smeared with blood. As Jason's eyes rolled back in his head, he caught a glimpse of his mother's eyeless body sprawled across his bed.

That tinny, 8-bit music was the last thing he heard.

## AUTHOR'S NOTE

I have always loved video games. From playing *Adventure* and *Frogger* on my Atari 2600 to *The Last of Us* on my PS4, there's something about the medium that has always thrilled me. There's something unique about being able to take risks and get that feeling of heart-pounding terror without being in any sort of real danger that draws me like a moth to a flame.

But what if it *wasn't* so safe? What if video games could influence the real world? As cool as it would be to have a Tanooki Leaf from Mario, there could be some darker, scarier implications.

# TERROR FROM THE 50-YARD LINE
## BY THOMAS C. MAVROUDIS

The girl at the bar is starting on her third pitcher of beer when I return from the restroom. I call her a girl, but we're women, roughly the same age—late twenties. She has a different name every time I see her. Iris. Lilly. Rose. Violet. Violet is my name. Tonight, I heard her introduce herself as Dahlia, which is real cute, because I grew up on Dahlia.

She's not alone. She's never alone. Men and women come and go, listen to a few stories and rotate. I'm sitting in the corner booth with my second Laphroaig, watching, listening.

Dahlia is telling a woman about the shampoo she uses, the brand best for washing gore out of your hair, when a man joins them.

"Oh, Todd's here! Hey Dahlia, tell Todd about the pizza joint."

"You want to hear about the pizza joint, Todd? Okay. In

the beginning, when I took up the crusade lifestyle, I used to wear a quiver—it was an architect's tube, really—armed with stakes of wood fencing, all jagged. There were zombies and blobs everywhere, and I had heard a werewolf howl. It seemed likely vampires were real too, so I wanted to be prepared. I traveled for weeks from neighborhood to neighborhood before I came upon my first vampire. And I killed her with a golf tee to the eye—just blew up like a hand grenade in a bag of bone-in steaks.

"I ended up having to use the fence-stakes on a bunch of zombies that caught me on a bad day without any better weapons. I didn't need them anyway because I kept a handful of pencils in my jacket to be safe—golf tees are unreliable. Later, I switched to chopsticks—when I could find them—because the pencil tips kept breaking off in my pocket.

"Then one night, after I failed to save a dog, I hit my first low. It wasn't the first soul I disappointed. Yes, dogs have a soul. I saw it leave that poor Collie as it was strangled by a disembodied tentacle. I was done. Giving up. I hunkered down in a pizza joint in this strip mall. It was decimated the day before by spiders the size of a Bullmastiff. I wanted to drink myself stupid on boxed Chianti, but I passed out from crying instead. I woke to the sound of boots pacing across the broken barware I'd smashed between pulls from the plastic wine spigot. In the shadow, all I could see were the vampire's white eyes. I was out of my mind, so I tipped my head back, offered my neck. But on the wall above my head was a wreath made out of garlic bulbs. I said a bunch of cuss words like a prayer and banged my head against the wall, trying to knock the wreath down so I could toss it away. The vampire snickered, thinking I was trying to *save* myself. I staggered up, braced myself with a chair like a walker, and pushed away toward the bloodsucker.

"And then it happened, lightning fast. The chair snagged on something, tipped up on one leg, slipped and crashed, taking me with it in a pile of kindling and bones. The vampire lunged and impaled itself on a broken chair leg. I couldn't stop laughing and crying. That is, until I heard a baby screaming in the bathroom."

"So you saved a baby? After it all?" Todd places a hand on Dahlia's shoulder.

In return, she clutches his elbow. "I wasn't supposed to die that day. I still had one life to save."

"Can you believe it, Todd? She's got all kinds of stories like that."

What I think Todd can't believe is Dahlia's outfit: tight blue tank top, olive green Daisy Dukes and boots from the Army Surplus store. What a ridiculous getup. Nothing beats comfy jeans, hoodie, and a fresh pair of tennies. And I mean first-day-of-school fresh, so you feel quick and invincible. Caches of adrenaline and oxy help, too.

Todd moves into Dahlia so the space between them displaces the other woman. "You're pretty awesome," he tells her.

"I am," Dahlia says, right before she chugs her glass of beer.

We're having breakfast in a diner; me at one end of the

counter, Daisy at the other. It's been going on like this, drinks in a bar, breakfast in a diner, for a few weeks. It's a pattern Daisy has designed, more than a habit or ritual.

The kid at the counter pours coffee into Daisy's cup. He's not really a kid, just has a young face he's trying to age with a beard. He asks her, "You've really seen a werewolf?" This comment lures the cook to look away from his griddle of sizzling meats.

"Were*wolves*," Daisy replies. "There's never just one. Like, you could be entertaining out-of-town friends with barbeque, or at a neighborhood block party, and as soon as a full moon rises, half the crowd is devouring the other."

"So what do you do? Do you have silver bullets or something?"

"Yeah, I hoard silver that I *melt into bullets*. I'm just teasing, but no, that's not how it goes. Not how it goes, at all. I can't make bullets. Who can? Can you? I did know a guy who lashed a bunch of silver spoons to a baseball bat. That was a pretty good idea, as long as his spoons never came loose, which they did. Once.

"My weapon of choice is a sterling silver serving fork. It was my Gramma's. See, I don't mind getting in close—I like it. People who don't know, who are lucky enough not to know, think werewolves must smell like dogs, filthy, wet fur and shit. But they have a musky, piney smell, under the blood. They would actually be hot if they weren't pulling the skin off your face like hot cheese from a pizza. Or trying to.

"The point is, it's got to be silver. That part *is* true. Werewolves explode into fur and gore with a single stab. With a few more thrusts of a silver fork, mummies pop into clouds of dust."

"Mummies! What? Tell me about that." The cook allows someone's eggs get too hard, someone else's hamburger steak get too well done.

I'm waiting for the kid to refill my coffee cup. Even if Daisy wasn't distracting him, I suspect he's a pretty awful server. When he finally comes over—with my tab instead of more coffee—I want to offer a tidbit from my own well of experiences, I want to tell him that you can stab almost anything with a sharp fork enough times and kill it. A sharp fork, a big knife and an energy drink really do the trick. But he doesn't linger, the woman opposite me is too enchanting, as if I'm nearly invisible. Like a ghost.

Funny thing about ghosts compared to all the other horrors—they don't exist.

Spurred by one of the raunchy gifts, a smiley-faced "back massager" that looks like a veiny mushroom, Columbine has joined a bachelorette party in the corner of a strip club next to a stage that features male dancers on Friday and Saturday nights. She shared with the ladies the time she used a similar novelty item as a diversion in a hedge maze, the obnoxious hum and powerful vibrations a perfect decoy against giant ants.

"Oh, my god, you're so fearless!" The bride, in her plastic rhinestone tiara, cheers and gives Columbine a high-five.

*Fearless* is too much, too strong a descriptor for me. I'm not fearless. What I am is *desensitized*. So many people with my experiences are. So many more are cracked, broken, their cores shattered like glass and crumbled like drywall in an earthquake—an earthquake caused by giant worms bursting through their suburban, hardwood floors.

I have a handful of dollar bills so I can stay seated near her. I don't tip much because I don't want the dancers distracting me. They think I'm a poor thing anyway because of my hoodie, or because I'm not wearing makeup, or because my hair isn't styled. The dancers, of course, love Columbine, as much as the bride and her accomplices do.

"No way! You were a cheerleader?" The bride exclaims under the opening riff of "Welcome to the Jungle," which segues too quickly into an R&B track, pissing me off because I love Guns and Roses.

"All-State," Columbine says, raising her arms as though it's happening right now. "That's where it all began, right there on the 50-yard line."

"No way," another reveler ushers, goading Columbine into another story. Not goading, but opening the doors wide, blasting them off their hinges. I wonder if they would be surprised to learn I was an All-State cheerleader, too.

The dancer hones in on me, as I'm the only one left at the stage seemingly interested in his bucking and shaking. I stare at him like he's some magical creature, but I'm trying to concentrate on Columbine's story without being rude.

Columbine takes a sip from a bottle of Coors Light. "All-City Field, championship game, top of the fourth quarter. My boyfriend at the time, Dirk Darling, was returning a punt when the roar of the crowd was replaced by this loud groaning so deep, it gave me cramps."

"What was it?" asked the only older woman in the group. Mother of the bride, I presume.

"Flying saucers, ladies. Three flying saucers hovering over the field."

Their eyes get as big as flying saucers ready to fly out of their faces. I can tell that Wade, the dancer, wants to hear the story. He struggles between the lure of my three dollars and listening to the most interesting woman he'll encounter for the rest of his dancing career, or the rest of his life.

"The place was frozen with shock. Because, what the hell was happening? Before anybody could say a word or make a move, these beams of light started zapping from the bottom of the ships, disintegrating every person with male genitalia. Dirk was like, one of the first. Then the Martians— for lack of a better word, because you know very well they came from someplace a lot farther than Mars—appeared on the field. And they didn't look anything like they do in Hollywood. No faces, no legs. All tentacles, grappling these tubes. Then, *Pop!* This bubble, this pink, see-through mucus, flies out of the tube and engulfs Misty, our squad leader. *Pop!* Now Kennedy is gone. *Pop! Pop! Pop!* My whole team is getting trapped in these cells, and they're screaming in pain. And all over the field are these piles of charcoal that were the South High Rebels and the Cherry Creek Bruins. Same thing in the stands. Then out of nowhere, literally nowhere, there were these two kids—couldn't have been out of middle school—saving the day! I know, right? The girl was blasting the aliens with a thing of canned air and the boy was shaking up cans of Diet Coke and tossing them like hand grenades— it doesn't take a Whole Foods clerk preaching about how toxic artificial sweeter is to understand its power as a weapon. And those kids did it. They rescued Tiffany, Kylie and me, led us to shelter at the hot dog stand. Before they took off, the boy gave me this look and handed me a bottle of bleach, and the girl ordered me to "move it" like we were in *Saving Private Ryan,* or something. So I did."

The bachelorette party cheers and gives Columbine another round of high-fives. Even Wade high-fives her. I'm surprised she told the story that way; that she didn't show them the scars from the corrosion burns of the alien mucus. But then I'm not surprised. She knows her crowd, knows how to play to them.

I had those burns, too. I have the marks they've left behind. I've been stabbed, strangled, bludgeoned, cut, clawed, bitten, stung, pinched, and poisoned. In another time, my abundance of scars might make me sexy, unique, but scars are the new tattoos—everybody has way more than they need.

"Hell yes, it's a real pyramid," Foxglove says, flipping her ponytail off her shoulder.

The man is in a suit and tie, a rolling valet bag at his feet.

"An Egyptian pyramid in the middle of a wheat field in Denver County."

"Technically, it's a wheat field in unincorporated Adams County. But, yeah."

This is the closest we've come to being one-on-one. Except for the bartender, the three of us are alone in the hotel lounge. The man trying to buy Foxglove's drinks is handsome enough, but whatever his end goal, he doesn't have a chance. She won't invite him in. She won't even hug him goodbye or shake his hand. But she won't allow herself to be alone, either.

"Why don't you come on up while I put my bag away. Then, we can have dinner or…"

"Listen Chet, I'd like to have a fling, but it's not going to happen. Let me tell you about this solider, Brian, tough guy on the outside, beautiful bod and face. He was defending an amusement park during a zombie outbreak. By this time, zombies were as common as squirrels; kids were even feeding them through the fence. Brian told me he liked the smell of my sweat. I told him I liked the smell of his gun oil. There was a lot of heavy flirting like that. There always is, until things shit the bed. What got to Brian were the midway prizes. Not the prizes, but what came after. Without warning, a brigade of plush bears, rabbits and Bart Simpsons began terrorizing the boardwalk, all claws and knives and discordant voices. Brian mowed them down with his M-16 as if he were cheating a shooting gallery. He reminded me of some cigar smoking action hero. But when the imps possessing the toys retaliated, Brian lost it, like I've seen so many times. The imps, these insidious little effigies of hate, surrounded him in a circle of living fire. And he just snapped—eyes bulging, shivering like a dog in a thunder storm. And I can't sleep with that. I've tried and tried, and I can't cuddle one more naked, crying man begging for his mother."

Chet doesn't get mad. He laughs, his hands raised in forfeit, and orders himself another drink. Nobody ever gets angry with Foxglove, which is odd because she really isn't that charming, not deep down. Despite her good looks and titillating adventures, she's off-putting. To me, at least. Like the hint of something rank, the scent of milk on the verge of turning.

She's running out of cute names. This morning she's calling herself Fern. She's added an adjustable, black baseball cap to her ensemble. I suspect it's to hide something, to cover a blemish, a secret. Her audience is a full counter of truck drivers. They ogle her breasts which are, at the most, average. But they still listen to her heroic escapades. The truckers point to objects in the diner, asking Fern what she's killed with it.

"Okay, pretty lady, I bet I can stump you. What about that *difibulator* on the wall?"

"I love those things," Fern declares. "The AED? You mean the defibrillator?" The frisky jab arouses a chorus of *ooos* and chortles from the spectators. "Yeah. All the country club pools have them and a few of the public ones. All you have to do is jimmy a couple of bobby pins into the circuit board and let it fly like a Frisbee. You'd think the pins would short the mechanism, but they weren't manufactured to be opened and rigged, so what the pins do is not only delay the charge, but amplify it. It's literally shooting fish in a barrel. Or gill-men, in my case."

They laugh and clap. She's a star. Everywhere she goes, the people are smitten. It's almost like there aren't other people in the world doing the same thing, risking their lives to rescue others.

"My preferred weapon of choice is a garden fork—I'm on

my third. It's important to note that garden forks don't have names. Neither do weed whackers, electric carving knives, or the totally random cricket bat found in a middle school woodshop.

"Bottles of bleach and bottles of weed killer don't have names either, but I call mine Ross and Rachel because sometimes, when you're not killing monsters, you get bored. Every few mornings when I take inventory, I shake my bottle of bleach and say, *I need more Rachel*. Maybe after I clear a Burger Time drive-thru of fungoids, I'm twirling my bottle of weed killer around my finger, blow on the tip and declare: *All out of Ross*. I wear them on my belt like a gunfighter. But not in public. It makes people too nervous—more nervous than they already are. Or, they think I'm the janitor." Some of the truckers laugh. Maybe those that don't are a little offended. I'm a little offended, but not by the janitor comment. I hate *Friends*.

"You get so used to rescuing people, it's difficult resolving to kill one." Elm says this to me. Maybe I think it in my head first and she is repeating it, which is her manner. Naturally, I keep my distance. We're downtown in an alley behind a pool hall.

When I finally corner her, it's only because she wants to confront me. She comprehends I'm a threat, unaffected by her stories, immune to her charm; the pheromone she releases, or low frequency drone—however they've evolved, whatever their means of attracting prey—doesn't work on me.

Blobs of sentient gelatin, chainsaw-wielding maniacs, hell-lilies that spew sulfuric acid: it's not hunting if you happen to show up and start killing these things, yet hunting is exactly what I've been doing these past weeks. Killing Elm couldn't be as simple as cutting her head off with a lawnmower blade. She didn't make it that simple.

I'd only seen it once before. This is a story I've yet to hear Elm tell. I was cleaning out a southwestern suburb by the reservoir. The kid was hiding under an octagonal trampoline like a fort. The frame was rusted and the canvas had ripped off from most of the hooks. I had no idea what she was hiding from, there were no indicators I recognized: no smell of rot or blood, no howling, no buzz of chainsaws, no greasy puddles of dissolved flesh. I tried to coax her out, but she wouldn't move, just flinched every time I offered my hand.

I walked around to the front of the house and saw these huge purple mushrooms spilling from the garage, fruiting like bubbles blown in a glass of milk. I cleared a path into the house with hairspray and a grill lighter. Her parents were sprawled out on the living room floor, their throats torn out. No surprise there. When I turned to check the rest of the house, there was the kid. I should have known better. I grabbed her wrist and led her to the back door to avoid the fungus, but before we got out, she stuck a flathead screwdriver in my shoulder. I looked at her like what the shit, yanking the screwdriver free. Then I tossed her over my other shoulder and ran outside to the backyard, reassuring her she was safe, that I was a friend. That was when I heard the *real* kid scream, still in her hiding place. I didn't get it— not at first. My mind spat up the first explanation it could: I thought they were twins and the one over my shoulder was possessed, fully integrated, beyond saving, so I flung her down on the concrete patio and jammed my garden fork under her ribs. She crumbled into a pile of coarse, oily sand. The girl sprang from her shelter and hugged me. I told her I was sorry about her sister, but she said she didn't have one.

I haven't been fooled since. That was years ago.

At least, I thought I hadn't been fooled. It all makes so much sense now, so much sense that I'm almost embarrassed. The bachelorette party was the easiest to track down because of the announcements on social media. The entire church was wiped out, wedding guests and all. Good thing that purple fungus is flammable—nothing that a couple cans of bug spray and a charcoal lighter couldn't handle. I'm sure if I had the time, I could tie every subsequent infestation of purple fungus to Elm. Dahlia, Fern, Foxglove, Columbine, Daisy, Iris. Lilly. Rose. Violet.

Elm is a monster like that girl so long ago, but different, worse. I can't really be blamed, and although I let so many people die, maybe in saving myself, I will be vindicated and her prey avenged.

Elm tells me, "You're not even a person." I know this is my own thought, but she says it with her voice, which is my voice. And regardless of all the hours spent watching her, all the hours spent mere feet away from her, I'm distressed to meet her face-to-face, as her face is my face, exactly.

"You're sick," I tell her. She speaks the same words simultaneously as me. This is her weapon, to make me think *I* am the monster.

"You *are* the monster," Elm says, another stolen thought. I try not to think.

Elm takes off her hat. Nodes of flesh protrude from her head, fungal blooms. She says, "*Can* I kill you? Can I kill *myself?*" She smiles, displaying earth-stained teeth. She is not quite my doppelganger. "Am I not *you?*" she asks, and I'm scared, because that time, they are her own words.

My hand, by its own cognizance, yanks a fluorescent rod from a box beside the dumpster and tosses it at Elm's feet. It doesn't wait for a result of the flash, instead reaching for a bag of ice salt on the steps and hurling a handful at Elm's face. I can tell the salt worked—Elm howls, brushing salt and meat alike away from her face. I arm myself with a splintered pool cue plucked from the dumpster.

She takes off down the alley, running pretty good in her stupid boots. But I've laced into a pair of kicks so fresh I just *know* I can run faster in them. Or maybe that feeling is just my renewed confidence, my refreshed sense of purpose, my primal instincts of survival flaring up, white-hot.

Outside of the alley is a parking lot that leads to a footbridge over the canal. If she gets to the canal, the game is over. Chasing after, I call out Elm, then Birch, then Fern, and she's halfway across the lot. I yell Dahlia, Rose, Ivy, Iris, and she's on the bridge. But when I scream Violet, she stops and looks back at me. She looks less than human, her tendriled hands on the bridge railing, nodules pulsating on her shoulders in the white halogen trail light.

Before she leaps over the railing, she reminds me, "You may not be the monster, but you aren't *you* anymore."

I heft the jagged cue in my hand, test its weight and balance, and then hurl it straight into her chest where her heart would be if she had one.

"Maybe," I say. Or maybe not.

## AUTHOR'S NOTE

The first horror arcade game I remember was a pinball machine called *Haunted House*. Featuring what I considered Dracula's theme song (Bach's Toccata and Fugue in D minor) as a siren call, the machine's three playing fields were infested with ghosts, floating skulls, and other Gothic terrors. It is the only pinball game I recall from childhood having a narrative. Or maybe I added the narrative, imagining myself as the frantic pinball.

# SNOW RIVER
## BY ALEX SMITH

She noticed her breath first—shallow, wet in the throat. Then came the cold. It invaded her armor. The woolen tunic beneath wasn't enough to protect her. The skin on her chin and cheeks had fused to her helmet while she slept. With as much caution as she could, she tore away her chin strap. She let her cheeks remain joined with the faceplate.

The leaf-stricken trees curled toward her, their sighing branches beckoning her awake. Beyond the canopy was the white sky, pinked clouds shifting ever so slightly in the air. The river beside her purred beneath the ice, urging her forward. Her flesh tingled to the chimes of the chill, awaiting motion. Surrounding her was a wide circle of obsidian stones, each bearing a celestial carving. She was alive, again.

Something dinged off of her helmet and flitted into the river with a sickening *pop*.

She hummed against the cold, preparing to sit upright. She heard something squirming in the snow by the riverbank. There was another ding, this one on her shoulder plate. It arced in the air before her and landed in her lap. A dart, studded with spurs. It was calcified, like a long gall stone, and covered in a cloudy gel.

Most of the abomination was hidden behind a tree, though the dripping antennae leaning out into view betrayed its position. It slid out from its hiding place, a puddle of mucus rolling before its single, pulsing foot. It was the size of a Mastiff, spotted with patches of blue fur. Its shell was a swirl of indigo and white. The slits under its antennae were like eyes shut in blissful meditation. The way it cowered tentatively gave it a benign, innocent look.

But she'd read about these. As a youth she had rubbed her small fingers over the etchings on pages of leather-bound tomes covered in Behenian symbols. The plague had spread far and wide, strangled the valley, and claimed both human and beast alike.

A flock of darts sang through the air. The darts were firm enough to pierce leather, even mail. Once dissolved in the blood, temporary paralysis set in, readying the host—her—for impregnation. She raised an arm to shield the slits in her helmet and they dinged off her vambrace and gauntlet, one after the next. She sat up, steel tassels clinking against her waist. She was under an inch of snow. It sifted through the joints of the plate, created little mountains on the ground beneath her.

How long had she slept here? How long since the pale hands of the Blue Woman had pulled her soaking corpse from the river and hummed the Lion's song into her ear?

The mollusk rushed her, the soft flesh of its foot moving in rhythmic waves like gelatinous curtains. She fumbled at her sides until she found the long sword, scorched-black steel riddled with veins of cobalt blue. It was a bastard, forged from lesser blades and quenched in the oils and milk of the singing lichen. The blade was crudely balanced, unbreakable, and thirsty.

As the horror slithered closer, the smell of sweetness and ice and the gentle swooshing sound of its foot sent a thrumming, welcomed fear rising up into her gut.

Its antennae fawned at her almost politely, then slapped onto the plate on her elbow, nearly wrenching away her arm. It reared back and two triple-jointed appendages unfolded from its belly. Each of them was an arched phallus poised to strike.

The river roiled in delight, awaiting an offering.

She flailed out with the bastard. It clinked against the mollusk's shell. Not enough force to stagger it, she knew, but it gave her an inch of time.

She plunged her sword into the snow, stacked her hands on the pommel to steady herself, and stood. The creature swung its arms at her greaves with enormous speed, smacking into her armor. She pulled the sword back up, riposted, and swung forward, this time more deftly, slicing one of its appendages into the snow.

The creature's antennae-slits opened and issued a gurgling cry of surprise. It fell forward, shell huddling over its remaining arm, inching backward. She had the tempo now.

Should the surviving arm strike her naked skin, she would be no more than a husk after a few days—food for the wailing young growing inside of her. It went on lashing, then sent another dart whizzing at her head. The missile glanced off of her helmet, went flying in the direction of the river. So the Old Knight's armor did its work.

She grunted and heaved her leg up and out, delivering a kick to the shell, toppling the creature, and plunged her blade into the exposed, sinewy flesh beneath. She drew the sword up the length of the body, releasing steaming entrails into the snow. Puss ejected from the long wound, spraying back at her in protest. It gurgled again, arm reflexively whipping about, slicing wildly into the air—its final attempt to deposit its young in her flesh.

She wrapped her fingers around the grip and pulled the bastard back out of the mollusk. As she wrenched the blade free, the horror gasped. The muscles stopped twitching, the antennae curled inward, and it lay there, motionless.

Its corpse would make a passable offering to the Blue Woman.

She stood there beside the body, catching her breath. The occasional bird's cry joined in with the throaty strum of her panting. She craved warmth and the feeling of fire lapping at the air before her.

A distant memory crawled into her consciousness: a large-jowled man in bulging green armor the shape of an artichoke, his eyes a foreign gold-flecked brown, his moustaches greying along the ridges of his smiling lips. The flash of a serrated dagger stabbing into her. She felt the warmth of blood and urine running down her thighs as she drifted into unconsciousness.

Memories were washed over fragments—vague and deceitful—like flakes of snow disappearing into warm skin. Was this memory hers, or did it belong to the elderly knight who once wore the armor, his blood having siphoned into its rusting joints? Lately, she couldn't tell the difference. Not that it mattered. She'd come to know her mind as an abandoned archway, recollections whipping through like frozen drafts, only to disappear into the ether. It was all a cold dream. She forced herself to forget. She needed to press on, to continue her inquisition.

She sheathed the bastard. Icicles, so quickly formed from the mollusk's fluid, sheered from its edges as it slid into its home. She drew her dagger and knelt to the body.

At the base of the mollusk's remaining arm she made an incision. She removed her gauntlet and pressed her bare hand against the cool, slimy muscle, then pushed into the cut. She rooted around the wound until she found something that felt busy with life in her hand—firm, trembling marbles amid the viscera. There in her palm were a dozen translucent eggs. Within each was a tiny slug. They writhed violently against the walls of their cells, enraged at the cold they now felt.

She frowned at them contemptuously. If their mother had found purchase in her skin, they would have hatched in minutes, squirmed into her brain, and feasted. Stomachs gorged on her mind, they could conspire within her to drive her body back to the river bank. There they would emerge from her orifices and ride the river south, further empowering the diaspora.

She searched her waist for her leather satchel. It had frozen shut. With a few light strikes from the butt of her dagger it cracked open to reveal a nest of roots, a hunk of red clay, and the vial of milk she'd stolen from a pewter bowl near a seaweed-encrusted altar. She rifled through the items until she found a roll of cheesecloth, wrapped the clutch in the cloth, and let it sit in the snow. The movement of the slugs slowed as they drifted into a frozen slumber. She dropped the ball into her satchel.

Rolling the mollusk into the river was no easy task in her armor. It was not a light thing, and the slippery goo surrounding it brought her to her knees more than once. Finally, she rolled it in, watched as it melted through the ice and sank. The Blue Woman would care little for such an offering, but it was an offering nonetheless. It had to matter.

There, amid the carved stones surrounding her, was a path of footprints in the snow.

She followed the path for hours, moving between the frozen trees. A memory flitted through the tunnels of her ruined mind—a girl's feet in wet leather boots. They were hers. She stomped amidst the chill grey sky of the moors picking wildflowers. Her skirt, damp at the edges, bounced upon her already powerful legs. A sheep bleated in the distance. The smell of soaking heather. She remembered the dense air, the deafening wind.

The heavens opened above her. A column of blue light unraveled into the hillocks beyond. The brutal din of mammoth hoof beats knocked her into the mud. The Blue Woman.

The moors. When was she last there? How long had it been?

It was nothing like this frozen wood she walked now, where the chill robbed the air of any ambient noise save the occasional shifting of an icy branch, the crowing of a winter bird. This was her inquisition, and she regretted more than ever the taking of the Oath.

Just as the day began its decay into dusk, she saw the edge of the wood. Circling a trunk before her, the trees parted to reveal a vineyard. There, at the edge of the forest, she leaned against a tree to rest. Terraced lanes filled with sagging, grapeless vineyard trellises stepped down to a muddy black courtyard, where three stone structures stood facing the common.

The building at the head of the courtyard was a humble manor, two stories high. Years of neglect had set the roof to sinking, and even from where she stood she saw chunks of missing brickwork. A thin line of smoke rose from the manor's chimney. A stable stood at the western end of the commons. It was small, probably two stalls at the most, and again had seen years of disuse and neglect.

The last structure was a substantial stone basilica that stretched back into the northern limits of the vineyard. It loomed over all else, charred and burnt. Two large wine vats stood close by. This was where the vintners and all others from the village far in the distance had once come to listen for the voice of their creator. A modest black cross reached from the steeple into the waning daylight.

There were whispers that Balwg nested within the church ruins, tending to her young.

One crumbling stone path led away from the zigzagging terraces of the vineyard. This path would bring her away from the basilica and to the edge of the Bleached Canyon. The Ivory Cathedral lay at the center of the canyon, its crisp edges and black glass windows standing in protest of all the crudities clamoring beneath it.

She knew that one day she'd reach the cathedral, kneel at the transept before the glowering altar, and ask for absolution. But not today.

The smell of wine spoiling in the valley had reached her nostrils. The vineyard called out to her. The corrupt awaited her there. They would help grow her skills for the final push.

She found the footpath leading to the vineyard and trudged forward.

It wasn't until she'd lowered herself to the third terrace that she saw movement in the courtyard. A tall, lanky man hobbled slowly over to a row of picklers near the main wine vats. He swayed back and forth, a ring of silver ladles bobbing at his belt as he went. He wore leathern coveralls, stained through in purples and reds. Long strands of grey hair bounced on his back. He flipped the lid of one of the vats, craning in his head. He shifted his head back and forth, sniffing at the intoxicant. The smell of spoilt wine now burned in her nostrils. Nothing had grown on the grapevines for ages — what fruit had they to vint?

She crept between the trellises toward the courtyard, trying her best to avoid crunching the snow beneath her feet. The scent grew headier and more putrid as she approached the wine vats. The stink of it was dizzying. The armor was heavy. Each step was a deliberate, carefully moderated act, a negotiation with the heavy plate to maintain its silence. She sucked in a deep breath and attempted to steady herself against a growing drunken feeling.

She continued her approach, hands on the hilt of her sword. She passed around a cart buried in snow, and then broke across the open ground to one corner of the manor. When she was close enough to touch its outer wall, her feet kicked into gravel mixed with snow. The sound of tumbling pebbles echoed into the yard.

The lean man turned, snorting. She cursed herself, waited. She thumbed the base of her sword out of its sheath, keeping her breathing steady, muted.

Something bashed her head. It was hard, and though the helm did its best to shield the impact, the sheer force of it sent her careening forward.

She slung her leg forward to stop herself from falling over, widening her stance for combat. But the lanky man had crossed the courtyard. He whipped at her with his ladle, then struck her with the heel of his hand, sending her reeling backward.

The other—the one who had landed the first blow—was behind her, grabbing her by the arms. She couldn't pull away.

As she struggled against her captor, the tall man approached, pushing his face into hers. His complexion was alive with a colony of lavender boils, pulsing in the twilight. That they looked like grapes repulsed her.

"An inquisitor," he hissed. His puss-colored eyes and knitted brow gave her a hurt look. "Come to slay Cath Balwg, no doubt."

"But I'm not!" she said, exasperated.

"And a liar," her captor grumbled from behind. His breath reeked of spoilt wine and flesh.

The tall man sewed his fingers into the eyeslits of her helmet and yanked, tearing it off of her head along with a clump of flaxen hair. There was a searing pain where the helm had fused to her cheeks in the cold.

She struggled against the grip of her second accuser as

her helmet clunked to the ground. Without her faceplate there was new freedom to what she saw: the panorama of the valley and the glaciers rising in the distance, spackled by sprays of ashen light. There were swirls of mud and snow on the courtyard ground where her feet dug in to seek purchase. The tall man's arms, narrow and muscular, were covered in the same violent pocks as his face. Behind him was the ruined basilica. Charred planks of wood warped and cracked amid the scorched stone of the walls. Red writing was scrawled on the door.

He studied her scarred face, ran the back of his ring finger over her cheek.

"To the vats with her," he said.

"Wait!" She curled her fingers under her belt and began working her dagger toward her hip. "We need to… I have an offering for the cat!"

They seemed curious at this, but it was useless to delay: when she held the sheath in her hand it was empty of the blade. The discovery sent her heart sinking into her stomach.

She felt something sharp at her neck.

"This won't help you," the man behind her said. He brandished the dagger before her eyes.

"See? She was going to kill us. Steal the wine. Starve the beast!"

Her eyes darted to the vats. A pipe was attached at their bottom. It curled up a hastily devised scaffolding, entered the church at a broken stained-glass window. They were feeding it.

"She's plotting even now!" The lanky man took her cheeks in his gnarled fingers and pulled her face close to his, sniffing at her hair. She felt something dig into her shoulder, as if a dog was gnawing at her back.

"Inquisitor," the man behind her whispered.

The smell of iron pierced the air as the gnawing sharpened into an acute, singeing pain. Warm blood trickled down her back. The grip on her arms slackened, and the lanky man stepped aside to let her stumble to the ground.

She tried to grab at the dagger, but he had stuck it where she could not reach. Then, still on her knees, she drew her sword, swung out into the air around her as the two men laughed. The flail of her sword sent waves of pain into the nape of her neck. She reached over her collar, grabbing at her shoulder. She growled into the courtyard as she struggled in vain to stand.

She saw her captor now. He was naked despite the cold, face sewn with boils like his companion, head shaved to reveal a ruddy, bleeding scalp. The boils crawled down his neck to his chest, his paunch. There, at his bloated, hairy belly, the pocks seemed almost organized, as if in a moment they may coalesce into… a figure? A word?

The vintner laboriously crouched to her level and watched.

"Get her sword," he said.

The tall man did as he was told, circling her. If he completed his flank it would be over. Sucking in a gasp of air, she steeled herself and swung out, fighting the pain. He leapt back, but her reach overcame the distance.

The bastard ripped into the tall man's leather coveralls at the knee, sending a spray of blood and sinew onto the muddy courtyard.

He yelped, clutched at his knee. "She got me!"

"Back up, fool," the nude man said.

He tried to slink away, but wasn't fast enough. From her knees she swung against her pain a second time, sending the bastard singing in the air and slicing the crippled vintner's throat.

She saw movement behind her attacker. The front door to the manor burst open. A large man stepped into the courtyard. He turned, saw the fracas, and set to running toward them.

"Bloody fool," the nude man said. He groaned and arched his back, spreading his legs under himself and poking out his stomach.

There, among the curly black belly hair and wine stains, the boils began to move. They crept over his skin into bright lines. His belly swelled.

The smell of wine and metal throbbed in her mind. Entrails and bubbles of whitened fat shifted out of his navel, followed by a black, pointed beak.

The man behind them came full into her view. He was stout, wide and muscular. Silver hair parted down the center of his head, and thick moustaches in curlicues sat atop his lips. His bare feet kicked up mud and snow with each stride. He wore only rags, though he was armed: he dragged a large black morning star behind him.

The beak protruded further from its orifice, revealing sodden black feathers. Hundreds of onyx eyes ran up and down its head. It looked at her and shrieked, sending her mind into a twist of pain, drowning her thoughts, her will to fight. She curled over, shielding her ears, screaming out against the sound.

The man in rags drew back his morning star. As he reached the naked vintner he swung, crushing down on his baldpate. The force was so immense that she could feel the crack of the skull in her ears. A chunk of brain escaped the skull and bounced into the mud.

The warrior didn't spare a moment. As the vintner's body hunched over the shrieking black crow that was caught in its half-birth, the warrior swung again, shattering the beak and putting an end to its deafening wail.

He went on hammering at the belly, smashing until black gel and red blood followed the morning star in gooey arcs with every strike.

He stopped, panting, and looked up at her.

"Well, that's done," he said.

"That shriek," she said.

"Could scramble your brain if the thing was fully born." He spoke too loud and his moustaches dipped and quivered as he spoke.

"But how did you—?"

He grinned at her and pulled a shred of cloth from each ear. He dangled them before her, chuckling.

"Protection!"

She labored to get up. She couldn't help but wince at the pain in her shoulder.

"There's something stuck in you," he said. "Allow me."

Leaving his morning star standing in the muck, he approached her. She stepped back, arms at the ready.

"Afraid?" he asked, hesitating. "I just saved you."

She sheathed her sword and said, "I could have handled him."

He gave a snorting laugh. "Fine. I merely aided you. May I?"

He stepped over the body toward her. There was

something about the smell of him. Humanity, warmth, earth. So comforting that her throat felt tight. She dropped her hands to her side and let him step behind her.

"I see," he said. "They caught you in the seam. It is all the way in."

"Pull it out," she said.

"Not here."

She followed him to the manor. It was a narrow, unassuming home. They entered the foyer. Small, smooth stone walls climbed to the second floor. The first thing she felt when they entered was the touch of warmth wrapping around her like an old cloak. A frayed tapestry hung above the staircase featuring old vintners wrestling grey vines that bulged with sweating grapes. Another tapestry was draped over a hump in the center of the floor, too bloodstained to be understood.

"That one won't bother us," the man said. He wiped his bare feet on a nearby chair.

She followed him to the kitchen. It was unused, covered in a thick layer of dust, but there was life near the stove. He rested his morning star against the pantry. There was a glorious smell to the room. It was arresting—a comfort beyond the mild warmth of the manor itself.

A steaming stock pot sat over the range. The smell of boiling leeks, sweet onions, and spices came alive in her mind.

"Don't worry. There's enough for two. But first let's get that dagger out."

He unbuckled her breastplate and shoulder plates, and without warning yanked away the blade. She cried out in pain, then set her teeth on a knuckle, cringing away the rest.

"There," he said. "Not so bad, was it?"

The throbbing subsided, leaving a hot sting in her skin.

"The wound isn't angry. A good sign."

She went into her frozen pouch, pushed the ball of frozen, unborn mollusk-horrors to the side and used her fingers to tweeze a red root from the bottom. She wiped beads of perspiration from her brow.

"Rub this in, will you?"

When the work was done, she leaned back against the dusty wall.

He pulled a dishrag from a rack and sat on a nearby stool, wiping his bare feet.

"Something freeing about wearing nothing at all," he told her. "Just, you know, gallivanting in the semi-nude. One day I'll ditch the armor and go naked like that thing out there."

"Thank you," she said. "Are you… are you here for the cat?"

"I am. Though there is no hurry."

They sat across from each other in the kitchen, eating the stew. It was only that morning that she'd been pulled from the iced river onto the bank by the Blue Woman. She could sleep for a week.

She occasionally stole a glance at her savior, wondering about him, admiring him. There was something familiar about his gait, the way he pivoted against his belly. But the moustaches—they frightened her.

"Is something troubling you?"

"I'm trying to remember something," she said.

"Why bother?" He helped himself to another ladleful of stew, steaming vegetables plopping into the wooden bowl one at a time. She couldn't remember the last time she'd eaten so well. This place almost felt like a home. One could settle into their stool, sup in peace, pretend that the world wasn't what it was.

"You think too much," he said, breaking the silence with his thick, overloud voice. He tapped his temple with the end of his spoon. "I can tell. We go from this life onto the next. Kill, eat, pray, die. No matter your path. Purifier, corrupt? I've come to think that none of it matters. I have taken to eating my way through."

"If it doesn't matter," she said through a mouthful of broth, "then why are you here?"

He froze, ladle hanging near the pot. His whiskers curled into a smile.

"I honestly can't remember why I took the oath. Do you?"

"It's my duty," she said, faltering. She didn't want to find out if she had forgotten herself.

"Fair enough answer, albeit predictable." He let the ladle drop into the stew. "Well I do it now because I like it. I revel in the work. Cleansing." He spooned a leek into his mouth and slurped it down. "I like the look on their faces when they realize what's coming. A mix of pain and disbelief."

She smiled and nodded, letting her hair cover her face.

"I will cleanse the church first," she said. "I saw a pipe connecting the vats to the stained glass windows. They were feeding something in there. I'll set fire to it all."

"Yes," he said. "But they've attempted to burn it down

many times. The stone remains. Something big lives in there."

"Balwg."

"Right. The she-cat. The Blue Woman would have us be its next meal."

"So," she said, "how do we kill it?"

"Fucked if I know." He curled his moustache. "Fucked if I don't know, actually." He laughed.

"You find this funny?"

"Oh come on," he said.

Her cheeks felt hot.

"Okay, okay. They're all *baaaad*. Corrupt. I get it. And Cath Balwg. She's a biggie. Rending inquisitors in twain and such. And the villagers worship her! It's something in what they eat, I think. Driving them mad." A half-chewed carrot swished around his mouth as he spoke. "Don't worry," he said, "nothing like that is in the soup. At least I don't think. But has it occurred to you that this is how the valley will be, no matter whether the inquisition succeeds? And they're just… I don't know… they're the new animals."

She put down her spoon. "New animals that sing a song driving all of the children in a town mad? Animals with spit that melts human flesh?"

"Fine," he said.

He picked the filth from beneath his fingernails with a bone, the unsettling *clicks* occasionally halting the silence.

"You're right, you know," he said. "I admire your faith. And I'll join you if you'll help me with my armor."

They left their bowls in a stack by the range and ventured back into the foyer. The cold was there again. She tried to concentrate on the warm stew working its way through her core. On the stairs, a blood-stained cloak covered a large lump. Brushed steel gauntlets poked out from beneath, reflecting moonlight from the window.

"Here it is," he said, whipping away the cloak, revealing the bulbous form beneath. A breastplate, impressions of artichoke leaves reaching upward to its neck.

She remembered.

And it seemed that he'd caught her remembering. He looked at her looking at the artichoke breastplate—stared into her.

"Funny, isn't it? The smithy knows my tastes, I suppose. The filigree on your armor. It's so faint. You can barely see the cross anymore. I like my artichoke a lot better." He exhaled loudly as he knelt to pick up the piece. "Mom always said 'eat your vegetables.' Well, I also wear my vegetables." He chortled at this, waiting for her to help him.

She tried to laugh with him as she remembered what happened at the stable:

She was nearer the Ivory Cathedral than she'd ever been—so close that she could make out the three colossi that kneeled at the glacier ridge. The sun had been out. A faux spring warmth peaked in the noontime. Floods of sheered ice and white water tumbled down the river in a mind-numbing roar.

A light drizzle in the afternoon mist turned to sleet as darkness crept into the canyon. The invader cold came again. The sleet pelted down on her, soaked her thoroughly, and in a moment of weakness, she burned her last summoning sprig in search for another inquisitor to share her journey. No one came.

Hoping to find somewhere dry to rest, she'd put down at

an old stable. Just as she'd removed her last leg of armor, two men grabbed her arms, pinning her to the wall. She remembered the feeling of cold, wet wood against her tunic.

A soaked horse whinnied against the frost.

And then he approached her from between them, a hulking form leaning over the scene, filling her vision.

"Rules are rules," he'd said, whiffs of alcohol assaulting her with each word. "You burnt the violet sprig. You welcomed both help and harm. We take what we need. You go back to the river, try your luck with the Blue Bitch."

And then he plunged a dagger—her dagger—straight through her chest.

What good did the Old Knight's armor do? She couldn't wear it all the time. What good had any of it done? The soapstone necklace etched with the sign of the Wolf. The bloodsong she chanted that night by the fire while she burnt the gilded lavender. None of it mattered.

She felt the warmth of her intestines tumbling down her legs as he gutted her. She'd felt pathetic. The pilgrims would find her lying in a pool of her own insides and drag her to the river. That was a lifetime ago, lost in the windswept archways of her mind. Only the very old memories, and the very young, found life among the debris. This one had clawed its way back into her mind.

He'd probably forgotten by now. But she remembered.

"What?" the Artichoke Knight said, waiting by the stairs at the foyer, watching her. "Never seen a vegetable chestplate before?"

"No, not that." She held back the tears spurred on by waves of revulsion. "It's a strong... it's a statement. I like it."

"Well," he said, lifting the artichoke over his chest, "stop staring then and get on with it."

She came around behind him, climbing the stairs to position herself. He held it in place for her as she began buckling the back straps. Coarse salt and pepper shoulder hair teased against his ratty tunic.

"It's heavy, though," he went on. "I think of finding something light. More freedom of motion and that."

She found the dagger in her belt with her free hand.

"Easy, easy," he ordered. Powerful muscles shifted in his back. "A little room for the blood to pump would be alright."

"Sure," she said, drawing the dagger. "Here, let me give you a little more room."

She plunged the blade into his neck. She felt the fight of his steely tendons and gristle as she buried it as deeply as she could. Then the blade found his spine. Blood gushed from the wound, squirted into her face. It tingled in her nostrils and filled her eyes.

He gurgled out a scream. Then he found her hair and yanked her over him, flipping her to the ground before him. He could have snapped her neck as she struggled to free herself from his grip.

But his hand went loose. He stumbled down the stair, clutching at the dagger in his neck, as she scurried away. He pulled it free, releasing a spray of blood.

She'd found the artery.

He fell backward, then reached out to grasp at a nearby drape, only to pull it down with him. He grimaced at her. His questioning, frowning eyes met hers.

"I remember you," she said. She gulped back a sob hiding in her throat.

She sheathed her dagger and checked her armor—

preparing herself for the charred church—while he sucked in short gasps of air, eyes quivering in desperation, begging her. The smell of blood and dust exhaling into the cold hung in the air between them.

"There it is," she said. "That look. Pain and disbelief."

He sat there, leaning against the wall cupping his wound, never taking his eyes off of her. The fountain of blood waned to a trickle.

She said a prayer for him. If the pilgrims could find him they would carry him back to the river—the artery snaking through the valley toward the bleached canyon, drinking the blood of purification as it went. If the Blue Woman selected him he would rise again, continue his inquisition. She hoped he'd be passed over.

The hand at his throat went limp, rolled onto his lap. His breathing stopped soon after.

Outside, the edge had come off of the cold. Thick, wet snowflakes cascaded into the torchlight and rested in the courtyard. The bodies of the vintners lay in humps in the gravel and mud, slowly drowning in fresh snow. The Glass Mountains towered beyond the valley. Her helmet was nearby—a bowl collecting the flakes. She was relieved to be without the chinstrap digging into her flesh.

She relished the snowfall. It was cleansing. She crossed the courtyard to the church, wrapped her fingers around the long bronze door handle. She made her entrance.

The Artichoke Knight—his blood still sticky between her

fingers—sang to her from the windswept halls of faded memories. There was something about his moribund words that burrowed deep into her. He'd become cynical, murderous. Had he tasted of some truth that she was too weak to know?

If she could only talk to the Blue Woman, find out for herself if the cleansing really did bring a final purification, a holy light that would bathe the valley. The Blue Woman always whispered to her at the riverbank. She could never talk back.

The musty scent of disuse coupled with the stench of the blood wine filled the cramped church vestibule before her. The floors, the pews, even the walls themselves stank of the fetid mix. Stone flaked off into her hand as she leaned over to collect herself at the baptismal font.

She walked into the church's hall. The roof towered above her, supported by stone pillars rising on each side and joining into vaults high above. Three rows of pews led to the sanctuary, but before the stage and the altar, the rows of pillars curved outward to create a wide, circular seating area.

A red-stained sluice descended from one of the scorched windows at the side of the stage. The sluice led to a bronze feeding trough near the foot of the altar. The occasional *plop* of flesh created a wake of liquid that spilled over the lip of the trough and onto the floorboards.

She crept down the aisle and stopped at the transept to observe the blackened altar. A bed of candles burned at the foot of the slab, flames licking lazily at the air. The wax pooled together into a moon shape. Behind the feeding trough at the far end of the chancel was a nest filled with a clutch of large, black eggs. Another egg-layer, its young poised to thrive in the doomed valley.

A whispering voice reached her from the recesses of the church. She didn't know the language, but understood nonetheless. It sensed her. It knew she was an inquisitor. This was its home—its nest. She was unwelcome here. Its tone was seething.

A draft hit the flames and she drew her sword, readying herself. The flames flickered, then drowned in a shadow so black that she lost sight of the altar. The very fabric of her vision bent along with the quavering shadow, and the wisps of candle-smoke swirled into a pulsating spiral.

A limb stretched forth from the void. The skin appeared wet, irritated, covered in a flesh-colored fur. The fur was thick, coarse, waving as though submerged in water. The shadow grew beyond the altar, sucking away the light until the entirety of the church was all but a pool of darkness. Then the black door receded around a feline form.

She stepped to the side of the transept and hid behind one of the columns, letting herself steal a look.

Fully borne from the shadow, Balwg sat over the altar, her hulking cat-like form filling the chancel completely, head bowed down to fit itself into the space. Her tail lazily whipped back and forth on the church floor. Her head was nearly human in shape; her eyes a cool, ocean color. There were no pupils; only swelling waves of checked grey and gold, rolling in search of her, quivering in their sockets. Her mouth was agape. Large rows of stained teeth reached back into the void of her throat. Spittle dripped from her tongue onto the altar in giant gobs. It sniffed at its bronze trough, then its clutch of eggs. Satisfied with their safety, the cat-beast scraped behind an ear with its hind leg and yawned, sending a churning whine echoing down the hall.

Balwg must have known she was there—sensed her—but yet she neglected her. She was an insect, a worshipping villager and nothing more. This was an advantage. If she could sneak up to the beast, she could have the first strike. She prayed it was all she would need.

Staying behind the row of columns, she inched down the hall. A well-placed lunge under the ribs would open the organs, poison the blood. Panic would follow. The more movement there was, the more the wound would open. If she picked her hiding spots well she would never need to face it. She could collect her prize and burn the putrid church once and for all.

She was nearly upon it, having reached the curving row of columns where the great hall widened into a circle. She waited until the thing seemed to become interested in the wine sluice. The sound of gulping echoed into the charred church. It was an effort just to peel away from her hiding place and into the stench. She circled her column and found the creature leaning down, shoulder blades risen up like towers to the ceiling, muscles shifting under the long fur as it drank.

She moved more quickly now, risking the sounds of her clanking armor to make her final approach. There, standing by its tail, she realized that it wasn't fur that covered Balwg as she'd first thought, but human fingers in waving crops. This sent a flood of horror into her stomach, nearly freezing her where she stood.

She stepped over the tail and lifted up her sword. A single plunge would open its large intestine. She heard the leather straps on the handle of her blade whining—she'd wrung them too tightly in her anticipation.

The gulping stopped. The thing had heard the leather, too.

She stared up at Balwg's shoulders, waiting. As it twisted its giant head toward her, she took another loud, awkward step toward its flank and plunged the blade in as deeply as she could. The finger-fur stood erect in shock at the pain, curling around the hilt of the blade. A foul-smelling purple blood oozed over her armored fingers.

The thing cried out as she twisted the sword inside of it, fighting against the sinew in an effort to do as much damage as she could. She planted a foot on its hide to get into position to yank the blade away for another attack, but now Balwg was twisting around, pulling her along with it.

It stood, raising its backside, lifting her high into the rafters. The beast began to circle, gnashing at her, but she was attached to the hindquarters—just out of reach. She flailed like a rag doll, legs loose below her, swinging in the air. It was all she could do to hold fast to the pommel of the bastard. The foul blood from the wound she'd opened ran under her armor, soaking her. The finger-hairs curled themselves tight around the blade.

The creature stopped circling and began a long, methodic shake of its finger-coat. She held fast. She used the power of this bristling and shaking and her own weight to tear herself and the bastard free.

Once loose, she flew into a wall. As she dropped down, she saw the arm of the sluice for a flash, then fell into it. She tried to stop herself there, slapping her arms over the ridges and into the foul wine, desperately seeking purchase. But it was too slippery, and she was falling again. She landed clumsily on the lip of the bronze trough, sending it sidelong into the air. The blood wine splattered against her armor and stung her eyes, the taste like spoilt wine and marinated sweet meat. She spit it away, wiping at her mouth, while the sluice collapsed behind her, shards of stained glass raining onto her armor.

A blow sent her into the air yet again, this time careening into the rotten pews. She rolled to a stop as she smashed into the pulpit, the Old Knight's armor now covered in moth-eaten bible pages glued in place by the blood of the creature and the red of the wine. Nearly unconscious, eyes still stung by the pain of the blood wine, she tried to stand. She parted the blood-stained clumps of hair on her forehead in time to catch the beast stalking languidly toward her.

It would beat her around the church like a toy until she was a collection of shattered bones. Several crushed ribs groaning in her chest from the last blow told her as much.

The beast approached, massive tongue hanging over shining teeth, eyes two tranquil ponds shining amid the burned-out transept, taking her in.

It was whispering something at her—a charm, a seduction.

She noticed that blood still dripped from its rear—if she'd opened its intestine, she may have killed it before being killed herself. But it was a meager consolation. If she died before taking her prize, the Blue Woman wouldn't reward the effort.

She stood, the bastard at the ready, waiting for the monster to move in for the kill. It pounced, its backside snapping against rafters as it rose in the air, claws extended.

She raised the bastard above her and let the creature fall onto her. It was this tremendous weight that sent the bastard on its path through the thing's footpad, finger-fur standing erect in pain at the blow.

The blade pierced the paw, snapping tendons as it went. But as the beast landed the paw went further, bending her arms, her knees. The floorboards gave out beneath her, and she plummeted to the floor below.

She landed in a rain of ash and slivers of wood in the basement. Bones clattered around her. Skulls pooled around her neck, empty grey eye sockets peering at her. A catacomb. Rows of long-dead monks lined the walls, old trinkets disturbed after years of peaceful rotting.

Balwg was above her, eyes peering into the jagged hole to the catacomb below. Her arm and paw, however, were still stuck through with her bastard, and had followed her down into the basement, almost crushing her on landing. The matted nests of fingers still reached for her. Bawlg wrenched, nearly pulling the sword out of her hands, but she held fast and yanked it free. Balwg wanted to free herself, but her shoulder was stuck, lodged between the floorboards, so she stomped her trapped arm and paw down in vain.

The black claw caught her shoulder plate and tore itself free from the sword. She would be pounded to mash if she didn't move.

The beast slapped down at her again, but she was ready this time. She rolled to the side of the narrow aisle between the tombs on either side, bones splintering in the air around her. Balwg mewled in rage. The horrific scream filled her mind such that she could barely think. It would free itself eventually, reach in and scoop her up, or slash her to death.

The thought came to her, clear and sharp despite the mind-rending screams of the creature and the sounds of cracking wood.

The mollusks—the eggs wrapped in cheese cloth.

Balwg stomped again, muscled arm quivering, claws raking a pile of bones from their resting place. This time, the horror found one of her legs. She felt the bone bend and shatter beneath the paw. It was her turn to howl in pain and rage.

She sheathed the bastard and drew her dagger, stowing it between her teeth. She tore into her satchel, gloved fingers rooting around until she found the frozen ball. It had thawed some in the heat of the manor—she could see the worms lazily awaking and splashing in their eggs. She wrestled her way out of the pile of bones, throbbing pain in her leg crying out to her to lie still.

Balwg's claw poked tentatively into the catacomb in search of her, then raked back and forth over the skeletons and ragged corpses.

When it reached her she hooked her dagger into its tendon, opening a slit between the crops of fingers. Balwg cried out and drew up her claw.

She wrapped her arms around the leg, clinging to it as it traveled up to the church floorboards above. But before she could be shook free, she plunged the egg ball into the wound, burying it as deep into the muscle as she could.

At this the beast screamed again, only now with the hint of something human, like a young woman's cry.

She rolled away and off, armor chattering, broken leg pulsating in pain as she landed among the pews. She clenched her teeth and moaned through the pain as she struggled to sit upright.

Balwg approached her, the color in her eyes shifting to amber, and then red whirlpools of rage.

She drew the bastard and raised it high.

Balwg lunged, teeth bared, thick tongue tightly curled back in its mouth. She angled her bastard and the teeth clinked against it. The beast snapped again, catching the bastard and her hand at the pommel. It ripped away the sword and her gauntlet, scraping her wrist and forearm.

Balwg spit away the blade and looked to her, still enraged. But then her countenance changed. She had a look of anguish, of surprise.

Pained disbelief.

The monster stumbled, barely avoiding collapse with her clumsy, bleeding claws. She shook her head back and forth, bristled her coat and looked around the basilica in a daze. Balwg took a step forward, letting her jaws fall open, ready to bite, but she stumbled again, this time nearly collapsing. There was a growing sense of pitiful confusion on her face as her body revolted against her. Balwg's eyes shifted their color again and again. The beast was stunned, desperate.

The worms had worked quicker than she had expected.

Balwg collapsed before her, tongue rolling out of its mouth, nearly landing on her broken leg. The wind working through the cracks in the church quieted, leaving only the shallow breaths of the beast to be heard. Balwg began to convulse on the ground, legs sweeping out and destroying the pews around it in a fight for control against the worms, teeth gnashing and biting at the air.

There was no winning this battle.

The convulsions went on for some time.

She dragged herself toward her sword and unlocked it from the gauntlet. Balwg lay paralyzed on the floor, shallow pants and wrenching finger-fur the only sign of life.

Soon, the mollusk's spawn would have total control. They would stand their steed back up, lead it to a water source, and crawl to freedom. She pulled herself toward the beast. The finger-hair no longer waved in poetic synchrony. It shook and twisted, reaching out in different directions in a disorderly panic.

She lay her gauntleted hand on Balwg's neck.

Some of the fingers wrapped themselves into hers in a despairing embrace.

"I know," she told them.

She thrust the bastard through Balwg's neck, severing the spine. The fingers reached forward, scrambling and twisting in pain. Then they went still, releasing her hand. She felt the warmth of the great cat's blood as it pooled where she sat, then drained into the catacombs below.

The worms would die on the church floor. They had no working host, no vehicle.

She lay there holding those limp fingers for some time, looking through the cracked stained glass at the darkling sky beyond. Her leg was useless, but using the bastard as a cane, she limped around the head of the beast, leaned against its maw, and used her dagger to cut free one of its dull, now-colorless eyes. She took a length of twine from her satchel and stitched it into the eye, then slung it over her back. She could barely walk, but she would bring the eye back to the river and make her offering. The Blue Woman would relish in the death of such a culling.

But the words of the Artichoke Knight were wrapping their tendrils into her consciousness.

*Kill, eat, pray, die. Die, eat, kill, pray.*

Balwg's own young—a nest of eggs incubating near the upturned bronze trough by the altar—were motherless now, soon to be burned in the fire. She held one of them in her hand, letting her thumb run over the imperfections. Flecks of lavender and gold ran in circles over the ovum, the pattern resembling one of the Behenian runes she'd studied as a girl. She gently placed the egg in her satchel.

She used her makeshift cane to exit the church, then stopped to absorb the scene she was leaving in her wake. The worms would emerge only to die near their host. Soon it would all be ash.

Her latest victory pulled her thoughts to the pact. Should she drain enough corruption from the valley, she would serve under the Blue Woman at the heart of the Ivory Cathedral, its spires bathing in austral light. All of the rivers met there, under its buttresses. She'd never been all the way to the Cathedral—though she'd gotten close.

How many more times would her corpse be shoved back onto the river bank for the hunt before she could kneel at the great altar?

In the meager moonlight in the courtyard, she sucked in a breath. She shivered as snowflakes found their way down through her hair to tingle on her scalp. It was a good shiver.

She found a blackened torch near the church and

approached the stinking vats. She took the flint from her satchel and struck it at the torch again and again. She wondered if there was any of that stew left in the old manor. Finally, the sparks flickered into embers.

She held the torch to the bottom of the vats and waited. The flames went on licking at the vat, doing nothing. The wood was too damp to catch fire. She was chilled to the bone, soaked in the death of her kill, exhausted. Just as she'd given up, the flames began to rise. They spread up the pipes to the windows of the church walls. Soon the church was ablaze.

She found some dry wood near the stables, fashioned a crutch, and limped her way back toward the manor. She would bind her leg in the kitchen, finish the stew, and make her journey back to the forest.

Inside, with a full belly and the warmth of the fire to coax her to rest, she felt she could live in the kitchen forever. But soon she felt the river beckoning. She thought of the black egg in her satchel—the one she'd taken from the church. The knowledge of this would keep her warm on her trek home.

She left for the river at dawn.

She dropped in to the freezing water, armor, bastard, and all. Fully submerged, the Blue Woman caught her and cradled her weak, broken form. The celestial lullaby of never-dying reached her ears in globulous alien waves, draining her mind of its memories one by one. But as she drifted down to the riverbed, the Reckoning fully upon her, she held fast to Balwg's last black egg, its feline young beckoning her to never forget.

She would try with all of her might to remember.

## AUTHOR'S NOTE

When Jonathan Raab sent out the call for *Terror*, we got to talking about *Dark Souls*: swords, monsters, disturbing and confusing item-gets! Yeah! We also agreed that *Dark Souls* can be a lonely game. Your only companions are phantoms. Scattered visions abound of those who died before you. And the meaning of your journey is obscure at best. Stories hidden in the loot speak of a world cycling between darkness and flame. Your troubling role in it all gradually reveals itself, but perhaps too late for you to make an informed decision on the fate of the world. "Snow River" sprung from that chat.

As I wrote, I realized it wasn't just Miyazaki and his team lingering in the shadows egging me on, but a host of other designers and games that I love. While Balwg the Cat is at home in this *Souls*-like world, the battle between my fateful paladin and her quarry calls back to *Shadow of the Colossus*, Ueda's masterpiece. Also, some dozen pages into writing, it occurred to me that *Souls* was in a way a mature, brutal variation on *Castelvania*. I began calling "Snow River" a "Soulsbornevania" story. When revisions came along, I was trying to mix "Zelda" into the neologism. Because in the end, its Zelda all the way down, isn't it?

Zelda, medieval-horror-adventuring, and the eternal conflict between cosmic nihilism and humanity's journey to find the meaning in it all, that is.

# THE DRUNKARD'S DREAM

## BY ORRIN GREY

### STAGE 1
### LA TAVERNE

I t was the mosaic tile on the wall of the kitchenette that made me choose the apartment. It reminded me of our first place together, that long one-room loft where the kitchen walls had been tiled in slate, not mosaic, and there was an inexplicable bas-relief of a trout above the sink. Where we drew hearts in the fog that formed on the windows in winter and could walk down to the post office and the coffee shop and the Chinese buffet around the corner.

The mosaic tiles were each about the size of a postage stamp, mostly blues but streaked with gold and silver, like the art deco version of a Van Gogh painting of constellations. They hugged the wall of the kitchenette, breaking up at the edges like graphics just beginning to pixelate. Where the kitchen in our first apartment had occupied one whole end of the room, here it was just a corner, a sink and a microwave and a hot plate, with a window that provided a view of the alley and the rooftop of the building next door.

At the other end of the apartment, though, was a big bay window that looked out over Main Street and the tourist shops. How you would have loved that window, curled up there with a book and a purring cat, to watch the town fall asleep or wake up. That was where I set up my drawing table, and I reclined on the cushions in the window seats while I watched old black-and-white movies on my lunch breaks.

Between the kitchenette and the bay window was just a stretch of empty floor where I put the futon and the old TV on its rolling stand. Not much else was left. Next to the door I put a little shelf that I had salvaged from a dumpster, and on top of it an old cigar box with a picture of a devil on the lid. Every time I got a check, I cashed some of it into rolls of quarters and dropped them into the cigar box, pulling one or two out and sticking them in my pocket whenever I left the apartment.

I had visited Basin Springs once when I was a kid. Nothing more than a stopover on some trip my parents were dragging me along on, to visit relatives I didn't know in some place I didn't want to be. We had stayed only for part of one day, but I fell in love with the little town, nestled in its valley and bisected by two clear streams crossed by dozens of footbridges.

Basin Springs was full of strange stores that sold old bones and Native American trinkets, antique swords and armor, cheap plastic do-dads that were made in China but designed to look rustic. It was a town of meandering alleys and half-hidden shop fronts, of parks where ducks puddled around in the cool streams and trees hid sculptures in shaded grottos.

More than anything, though, my young affection had been won over by the old arcade. Not like the ones that we had in the malls back home, but an arcade in the original sense of the word, a roofed space open to the elements, with arched doorways leading into the shadowed interior.

The arcade was situated between two streets running north and south, and in the middle of the two streams running east and west. It made up the whole middle part of a building, like a hive that had been hollowed out and filled with amusements. The doorways all bore gates with wrought iron bars that could be closed over them, but in all the time I've spent here since getting the apartment, I've never seen them shut.

In order to reach the arcade, I have to walk only three blocks from the apartment and cross a footbridge over the stream. It's an easy walk, rain or shine, day or night. When I first visited it as a kid, the arcade had seemed infinite, insurmountable. The way that used bookstores always feel, like I could literally browse there forever and still find something new.

It was a working arcade, but it was also a museum. Older games were at one end, with the newest arcade cabinets— rhythm games and shooting games and race car games—at the other. Pinball machines lined one entire wall, their backs emblazoned with the pop culture icons of the moment in which they were manufactured, so that walking along in front of them was like walking through the history of Americana: Elvira and KISS, Indiana Jones and Freddy Krueger.

In the deepest, darkest recesses of the arcade, at the end farthest from the main street, were old penny arcade machines that still worked, and still only cost a penny. Not even games, as we think of them now, but simple automata and motorized dioramas. A sinister-looking clown who covered a ball with a cup only to have it appear again from his mouth, a recreation of the hanging of Dr. Crippen, mechanical fortune tellers and an animatronic devil holding a hand of playing cards.

Somewhere in-between, nearer the dark end of the arcade than the lighter, newer end, was a game that I had never heard of. Called *The Drunkard's Dream*, it seemed to have been inspired by one of the old coin-operated dioramas. Not one that was located in the Basin Springs arcade, but one that I had heard of, in the House on the Rock up in Wisconsin. At a glance, *The Drunkard's Dream* resembled *Ghosts 'n Goblins*, but when it came to the actual contents of the game, it was something else entirely.

I don't remember seeing it when I was here as a kid, but my memories of that trip are all golden-shaded blurs, like looking backward through one of those tubes that turns all the light and into an exploding kaleidoscope of color. Since coming back, though, it is the one game in the arcade that I've played the most.

What first drew me to it was probably the artwork on the cabinet. In shape it was like any other arcade cabinet, with a joystick and a couple of big colored buttons that pushed in with a satisfying, smooth click. The sides of the cabinet were partially obscured by the games next to it—*Tapper* on one side, *Dragon's Lair* on the other—but they seemed to boast a garishly-colored painting of a dungeon tableaux, one that I would eventually come to partly recognize from the later levels of the game, with the titular drunkard center stage, leaping over rolling barrels while skeletons reached out from nooks in the walls and chains were frozen in mid-clank. In the upper-right-hand corner a woman in a red dress has her face turned away from the scene, her hair falling in a golden cascade down her back.

Each time I played the game it asked me to enter my name, and every time I did I always gave it the same one. Not my real name, but the one you always called me. It seemed right, and I thought that maybe, if I managed a high enough score, then it would be left behind somewhere, at least. A memento, even if no one else would ever understand.

The opening scene is a fancy dress ball at an old-fashioned English manor house. The only sound is a glitchy midi track playing a waltz. No text scrolls beneath the picture to explain what is going on, only the graphics—still highly pixelated, but slightly better than what the actual gameplay will present, like a cutscene in *Ninja Gaiden*, though the art style here is more storybook in quality, the animation only every a frame or two that repeats, to lend the illusion of motion.

It opens with a bunch of people, frozen in tableaux, dancing in their glittering gowns, their coats-and-tails. In the foreground, our protagonist stands against the wall holding an empty glass, a whole bunch of others stacked on the table next to him. His gaze is directed out at the floor, his back to the player, so we can't see his face, only where he is looking. At a blonde woman in a red dress, dancing with a tall, dashing man.

In the next scene our protagonist is outside in the hall, kicking at the rug, his head down, his face still hidden. He grabs the helmet off an empty suit of armor and plunks it down over his head, and that's how he will appear for the rest of the game: a short little man in a tuxedo and bowtie with a knight's helmet stuck on top. He only opens the visor to pour in more booze, and even then, what lies beyond is always hidden in shadow (so that we, the player, can better empathize with him, one can only assume).

He is standing outside, the knight's helmet turned to look over his shoulder at the lights of the manor house where they are cast on the lawn. Beyond the windows, we can still see the shadows of the dancers twirling and twirling in a never-ending waltz of just two frames, repeated again and again. Our protagonist turns from the house and gradually, one frame at a time, the tavern down the road edges into view. Then the game truly begins.

As we transition from the opening scene to the actual first level, the graphics drop in resolution considerably. What was already a storybook aesthetic becomes the simple, two-dimensional layout of a *Ghosts 'n Goblins*-alike, with commensurate gameplay style and difficulty. The status bar stretched across the top of the screen tells us the name of the level in a florid banner held aloft by pixelated cherubim, and has a picture of the drunkard's helmet with an X beside it and, beside that, the number of additional lives that we currently have stored up. The maximum appears to be three.

The status bar has no indicator of our drunkard's health, which seems to be determined not by his amount of armor, as in *Ghosts 'n Goblins*, but by his level of intoxication. At full health he slumps a bit, and animated stars swirl round his head. As he sobers up, he straightens and his tuxedo becomes less rumpled. If he ever sobers up completely, there is an ominous tone, followed by a sinking, three-note tune that sounds almost like mocking laughter. The screen seems to melt and run, the pixels all falling down into one another, and then the screen goes dark, replaced with an image of a broken bottle and the drunkard's discarded helmet along with the simple words, "You lose."

Thematically enough, our hero attacks by hurling empty bottles at his foes.

The only power-ups in the game come in the form of bottles of hooch, marked with one, two, or three Xs to indicate their potency. Grabbing one can refill your "health," but they also have a negative effect. As the drunkard gets more and more inebriated, the levels become stranger and more difficult. Backgrounds begin to swim and change, and the controls grow ever more sluggish and unresponsive. So there comes a point, when our drunkard is at maximum health, where dodging bottles becomes just as important as dodging enemies.

The first level is pretty straightforward. A tavern about two screens wide, split into three tiers. The drunkard can stand on the floor, jump up onto the surface of the bar, or up even higher onto a sort of shelf that runs around the top of the screen. The bartender seems to want him to leave, or maybe to tell him that he's had enough, and he paces back and forth behind the bar throughout the level, making noises that are probably supposed to be shouting but that sound like laughter as interpreted by the adults from old Charlie Brown cartoons.

The drunkard can't hurt the bartender, but the bartender

is constantly hurling things at the drunkard. Sometimes power-up bottles, other times empty mugs and bar rags and things that might be pots and pans. Besides this detritus from the bartender, the main threats in the first level are little purple devils who fly in from off the sides of the screen carrying big spoons, possibly filled with liquor. The devils seem to be in opposition to the bartender, trying to convince our drunkard to drink ever more, and whenever one of them is destroyed it usually leaves behind a power-up bottle. Drink too many, and the walls of the tavern seem to run, the colors switching to garish purples and greens, the bartender taking on a more terrible aspect, his face pale and skeletal, his eyes glaring purple, a mouth in his stomach.

The level is easiest if our drunkard can get through it without grabbing too many bottles, but regardless of how much he drinks, the bartender ultimately takes on that same distorted form at the end of the level, when he leaps up onto the bar himself and becomes the first boss, pacing back and forth, kicking bottles and mugs at the drunkard and occasionally stopping to belch a cloud of green smoke from the mouth in his stomach. Chuck enough empty bottles at him and he tumbles from his perch and disappears behind the bar, leaving it unguarded and allowing our drunkard free reign to very literally crawl inside a bottle for level two.

## STAGE 2
## UNE BOUTEILLE

I sold the house after you were gone, along with most of our stuff. I was still working full time as a freelance illustrator, and without your income I couldn't pay the mortgage. Which was just as well. Had I stayed, I would have paced the rooms like a ghost, and I know it, and you know it.

I had always intended to take you to Basin Springs, you remember me talking about it. For our first anniversary, for our fifth. But we never got around to it. Maybe that's why I came back.

When I moved to the little one-room apartment with the mosaic tile kitchenette, I had one big client, the only one who had stuck with me through the bad months. I drew pretty much all the covers for Otranto Books' reissues of old Gothic romances, those books whose original covers always had some woman in her nightdress running away from a big, dark house. On a good day, I could turn out two or three in an eight hour period. It paid enough to cover my rent and for me to buy groceries once a week from the farmer's market and the grocery store out on the edge of town. If I had any cash left over, or if I caught another gig somewhere, I turned it into quarters for *The Drunkard's Dream* and other games, or bought food from the stands and food trucks that were set up all up and down the main drag.

If I opened the windows of the apartment, the smell of fair food was always carried on the air. Corn dogs and funnel cakes and pretzels and cotton candy. When the wind was right, I could even hear the noise of the arcade from my apartment. A susurrus of blips and bloops and the unmistakable ringing of pinball machines. In the evenings, the shadow of the mountain cast the tourist shops below in purple shadow.

In the center of the arcade was a booth where its only visible employee worked, an ancient matriarch named Janice who sat behind the partitioned glass in an old conductor's cap and changed dollar bills into quarters, or handed out cheap plastic novelty items in exchange for tickets won in the skee ball machines. Up near the newer end of the arcade there were soda machines and a little shop attached to the building that sold slices of pizza and deep-fried Twinkies out of a little window during the day.

For the first few weeks that I was in Basin Springs, I did other things besides play *The Drunkard's Dream*. I walked around town, tried going to the movies at the little two-screen Gem Theatre. I haunted the tourist shops, walked through the public library looking for books that I had drawn the covers for.

I even hiked part of the way up the side of the mountain, explored the grounds of the Castle Inn up there, an old stone house that was now a bed and breakfast that overlooked the rest of town. Its garden paths were lighted with pale yellow lamps designed to mimic gaslamps—all the way down to the flickering—and were full of quiet cul-de-sacs for lovers young or old to have their trysts. There was a time when I would have loved it, the romance and atmosphere of it. Now it served only to remind me of your absence, and I didn't stay long.

Within a month, I was going to the arcade every day. When I finished my work, I would grab a roll or two of quarters from the old cigar box and head down the stairs to the alley. From there I'd walk over onto River Street, past the park where two swans lived and to the footbridge that led to the arcade. Sometimes, I would finish work early in the afternoon and play until dinner, when I would go back to the apartment and eat SpaghettiOs or ramen that I cooked on the hot plate. Other times I wouldn't finish drawing until night had already fallen, and I would go to the arcade anyway and play til midnight or later, waking up when the dawn cut through the bay windows to go back to work.

I started with the penny arcades, the old moving dioramas. Some of them were stained with dust and age. Those I stayed away from, but I "played" a few of the ones that were in better repair, dropping in my penny and watching them act out their scenarios, like those old-fashioned clocks that you see in murder mystery movies from the 30s and 40s. I arm-wrestled a scary-looking mechanical clown, and tried out a love-tester machine that told me I was "naughty, but nice," which was just above "mild" but just below "wild." Maybe you would have agreed; certainly, "wild" was something I never could have been accused of, even at my wildest. At least I wasn't a "cold fish."

I paced the length and breadth of the arcade. I tried my hand at pinball, something I had never been very good at, and spent an entire afternoon and a whole roll of quarters playing *House of the Dead* until my trigger finger went numb. I sampled every title available in the multi-game Neo Geo cabinets. Most of my time was spent among the older machines, the *Joust*s and the *Galaga*s and the *Pac-Man*s.

I kept coming back to *The Drunkard's Dream*.

The games around it were never very popular with kids or out-of-town tourists, so there was never really anyone around to interrupt me. I played for hours, usually until I ran out of quarters.

The second level opens with our drunkard quite literally falling down inside the neck of a giant bottle. For the first part of the level he is in free fall, with the only real gameplay amounting to moving the joystick from side to side to dodge bubbles that rise up from below. Some of the bubbles contain power-up bottles, which our drunkard can get by attacking, while others have strange little round homunculi riding on top who poke at him with what look like giant dinner forks. (The demons who haunt our drunkard seem to have a penchant for cutlery.)

At the bottom, the drunkard drops onto what looks like a big cork floating in a sea of black liquid. The cork fortunately stays underneath him for the rest of the level regardless of what he does, and moves back and forth when I move the joystick, even when the drunkard is also jumping. Once he's on the cork, the level of the black liquid begins to slowly fall, revealing ledges in the sides of the bottle that sometimes hold power-ups and other times harbor skulls that spit blue fire.

Serpents rise up from out of the liquid, coming in two varieties. The purple ones have fins on their backs and one orange eye, and they pop up just long enough to breathe a chain of fire at the drunkard. The green ones are segmented and jump up and out of the liquid in an arc before splashing down again. Meanwhile, more of the same purple demons from the first level gradually descend from above, making the screen a madhouse of pattern-based danger.

Eventually, the liquid drains down to the bottom of the bottle, where creepy maggot-like worms with pincer mouths wriggle around. Once they're all dead, the boss shows up. I call the boss the Green Fairy—I'm guessing that this is a bottle of absinthe we've been in all this time, which really makes a kind of sense—though it looks more like a locust, with a fan of lacy wings that appear from its back each time it moves or attacks. It carries a staff or wand from which it shoots bubbles that can trap our drunkard, making him easy prey for it, or for more of the maggoty worms that it occasionally shake loose from the top of the screen.

When the Green Fairy is finally destroyed, the screen begins to blink and rumble as the bottle breaks apart and finally shatters, plunging our drunkard into an inky black void through which he falls until he finally tumbles into the third stage, a rainy cemetery.

## STAGE 3
## LE CIMETIERE

Movies had taught me that funerals were slow pans across black umbrellas in the rain. I wasn't prepared for yours to be on a sunny April day, without a black umbrella to be found. Tempting as it is to say that I can't remember much about that day, it isn't true, not really. I can remember so many things, in such vivid detail, but they're all out of order, all jumbled up. None of them are connected to anything else. They just float there behind my eyes, like snapshots scattered on a black pool.

It's like that whole day and all the months that followed are a bunch of Polaroids that I had spread out on a table, and my mind couldn't bear to look at them all at once—so it just scooped them up and dumped them into a box, with no regard for order or clarity. When I try to remember back, I just pick one from the box at random—one image, one moment, one fragment of speech—and hold it up for a while before dropping it back in.

The sheen of your casket—the one that your mother had insisted on, though you had wanted to be cremated; the one that I paid for half the price of, while she paid for the other.

The white butterfly that landed on your headstone midway through the service.

The sound of the crank turning as they lowered you into the ground, after most everyone had already left.

The way that even the light in the house seemed different afterward, as though you were a crystal through which it had refracted, and with you gone, it now fell lifelessly on everything it touched.

Hands touching my shoulders, arms wrapping around me. Tears on the faces of people who, it seemed to me, had no particular reason to cry, while my cheeks remained dry until everyone had gone and I cried in the dark until I felt sick, until eventually I slept.

Days of drifting in and out, forgetting to eat, forgetting to do anything else. At first my clients were understanding, but that lasted a few days, a few weeks, a few months. Only Otranto Books stuck with me the whole way through, being patient when I blew deadlines, handing me more work when I eventually came back up for air and realized how dire my situation had become.

I think your family was scandalized when I sold everything and moved. I know that mine was. They had wanted some of what you had, what *we* had, but I couldn't bear to parcel it out, to decide what went where, and to whom. I couldn't even bear to sell it myself; I hired a local woman who ran estate sales. Before the sale began, I walked through all the stuff, let my fingertips rest on the scarred surface of the old kitchen table, the first piece of furniture we bought together after we were married.

Everything that I kept could fit into two small boxes. I put them in the storage space of the new apartment in Basin Springs, a crawlspace in the wall next to the kitchenette. I take them out sometimes, when it is late at night and I can't sleep. Letters you wrote to me. A rock that you found on a walk once, with a perfect hole through it, that I had carried in my coat pocket during all the years that I still went into work as a graphic designer at a big office downtown. Your copy of *Demian*, your favorite book in college, where you had underlined all your favorite passages. *"The bird fights its way out of the egg. The egg is the world."*

I still wear my wedding ring. I probably always will.

Sometimes, when I'm in the arcade, I can feel it tap against the joystick in my left hand. A different feeling than the stick against my finger, the quietest little click. Sometimes it makes me feel better, sometimes it makes me feel worse. That's life, I guess. Like the power-up bottles in the game. Each new thing you grab always has a chance of making everything harder.

As the third level opens, the drunkard drops out of the black void and onto the loamy earth of a pixelated cemetery. Rain is falling in the background, and an occasional flash of lightning splits the sky, showing swollen clouds and distant, skeletal trees. Tombstones line the level, and other markers like leaning crosses and a skeletal statue are occasionally illuminated by the errant flashes of lightning.

Groping hands reach up from the dirt as he passes, and every now and then a coffin will burstout of the soil, the lid opening on its hinges to discharge a shambling corpse, more bone than flesh. Some have only one arm, which juts out ahead of them as they shuffle forward like Karloff in an old *Frankenstein* movie. Other times the coffins contain weird skeletal bat-like creatures—gargoyles, perhaps, or demons— that spread their bony wings and then fly up, spitting fireballs. Regular bats fly down from the stormy sky, dropping bombs and power-up bottles before flying off again.

At about the midway point there is a dead tree with a hangman's noose dangling from one limb. When the lightning flashes, a body is visible hanging from the noose. As the drunkard approaches, a bolt of lightning strikes the tree, splitting it down the middle. In its wake, the corpse that was previously hanging there remains visible, on the ground now and pacing back and forth with the branch dragging behind him, noose still tied round his neck. It takes several hits from empty bottles to destroy him, so call him a mid-boss, I suppose.

From there it's more tombstones, more groping hands, more bursting coffins. Strange cemetery weeds add themselves to the mix, sprouting vivid flowers that spit thorns at the drunkard, and near the end of the level the headstones themselves begin to attack, floating up from the ground and hovering in the air before smashing down at him and shattering on the earth when they miss.

Finally, the drunkard reaches a grave set apart from the others, past a gap in the iron fence that marks the border of the cemetery. A grave for a sinner, a witch, or a suicide, dug away from consecrated ground. The grave is fresh, open, and from its depths rises the boss of the level, which is, of course, Death.

He looks like a pretty classic Grim Reaper, skeletal and hooded, but He terminates at the ribcage, with only a few vertebrae and the tattered edges of His cloak hanging down any farther. Death flies around the screen, hurling His enormous scythe like a boomerang, and smaller versions of Himself appear from within the shadows of His cloak to spread out and attack on their own.

Perhaps fittingly enough, Death is maybe the most difficult boss in the entire game, and I get to that spot only to perish and run out of quarters time and time again. It isn't until I've done it easily a dozen times that I come back with *three* rolls of quarters and set myself the task of finally getting past Death. (Where else but in a video game could such an endeavor be accomplished at all?)

Once the drunkard has finally hurled enough empty bottles, Death's scythe disappears and He raises His bony arms up toward the moon—which is just appearing from behind the bank of clouds—and then slowly dissolves from the top down, the individual pixels that make him up breaking apart and sliding down the screen only to blink and then vanish. Were that it was so simple in real life.

## STAGE 4
## CATACOMBES

After Death is destroyed, there's a brief cinematic as the drunkard looks at the tombstone and sees the name that I entered when I started the game. The name that you always called me. It's an unwittingly chilling moment, maybe for just that reason, but it doesn't last long. In the open grave there are stairs leading down, because of course there are, and so the drunkard has to take them, because of course he does.

At the bottom, the drunkard finds himself in some sort of underground crypt or dungeon—the very one depicted on the side of the arcade cabinet itself. The walls are lined with skulls and bones, and here and there mummies have been jammed into narrow fissures. When the drunkard approaches, they tear themselves free and shuffle toward him, their arms bound to their sides, their feet pigeon-toed. Some of the skulls in the walls light up and spit balls of fire, while others tumble from their perches and roll along the ground.

Here and there throughout the level are huge blue ogres or maybe golems who roll barrels at the drunkard. The barrels seem an odd touch in the otherwise crypt-themed level, but they also show up in piles that our protagonist has to jump over.

I wonder if they are meant to be casks of wine or spirits. I've spent some time contemplating the themes of this game, by now. The drunkard's travel from jilted lover to, well, drunkard, to the depths of the bottle, to the grave, to this purgatorial tomb. Mayhap the barrels aren't so thematically off after all. They make me think of Poe and Amontillado and that's a very short run from the crypt, indeed.

This level is tough. Every so often the whole place rumbles, and skulls and bones fall from the ceiling. There are these creatures that show up from time to time—wheels of fire with lion-like faces in the center, and five horse legs that radiate out. I don't know what the hell they're supposed to be, what they mean. And I've got to keep the drunkard's health relatively low, because when he starts to get too inebriated, the level becomes damned near impossible. The ground shifts and breaks apart, jutting out at odd angles. The walls come to life more and more, the skulls lighting up to spit their little round orange pellets of fire, skeletal arms reaching out to grab at the drunkard as he passes by.

In the end, the drunkard reaches what I guess you would call a crypt. If the rest of the level has been an ossuary, this looks more like what I consider a tomb. In the center is a sarcophagus with a carven lid, the kind where they used to inter knights that came back from the Crusades, or didn't. I expect the lid to slide open, the boss to come out of there, maybe a ghostly knight in a suit of black armor, carrying his head in his hands. Instead the screen shakes again, and there's a crack that splits the sarcophagus.

Torches burst to life on the back wall of the room, illuminating two columns, and behind them the statue of a giant skull. Then the skull's eyes begin to glow, not as bright as the torches, but more fitfully, humming in and out of existence. The skull rolls forward into the room, and I realize that this is the boss the drunkard will be facing.

Initially, the skull just rolls back and forth across the floor of the crypt, which is bad enough. It's huge, taller than the drunkard can jump over, so he has to leap up onto one of the broken pieces of the sarcophagus to make it over the rolling skull. I also quickly learn that its eyes are its only weak point, and only then when they're glowing, which is sporadic, with no pattern that I can discern.

After rolling back and forth a few times, the skull suddenly takes another tack. What look to be legs sprout from its mouth—its bottom jaw is missing—and carry it up the wall and across the ceiling, where it then drops back to the crypt floor with a crash that shakes the screen and immobilizes the drunkard temporarily if he is unlucky enough to be standing on the ground at the time.

On closer examination, the things that looked like legs are actually mummified arms.

Throughout all of this, the skull occasionally discharges smaller skulls that roll around the room until the drunkard destroys them. It's pandemonium, and I don't know how many quarters I pump into the game before the skull finally gives up the ghost—quite literally, this time, the stone skull cracking open and a snake-like wisp of smoke with two pinprick eyes escaping up into the air and then dissipating in the shadows of the crypt.

After that, the torches go out and the screen plunges once more into darkness until, one by one, fires begin to sprout up around the drunkard, urging him on through a passage that has now appeared in the wall of the crypt.

I had never been a drinker myself, but I became one after you were gone. I became anything and everything that I needed to be in order to insulate myself, to keep myself numb. Like Arthur in *Ghosts 'n Goblins*, I put on suit after suit of armor to keep that pain at bay, because I knew that if it reached me it would skewer me, pierce right through me, burn me down, and there would be nothing left. And that wasn't even the part that scared me. It was the time it would take. How long could I endure that agony before it destroyed me? Maybe it was better if I just destroyed myself first.

I abused the drugs that the doctor gave me, mixed them with booze, which was a big no-no. For the first time in my life I slept deep, black, dreamless sleep. Like sackcloth. And I wondered, "Is this what death is like?"

And if it was, I longed for it.

How many nights did I sit on the edge of our bed, rolling that bottle back and forth in my hand, wondering if there were enough pills to do the job, if I downed them all with every drop of liquor that I had left.

What kept me from it? I think it was fear. Fear that what waited for me on the other side of that big GAME OVER screen wasn't sackcloth oblivion, but rather all that pain I had been pushing away, with no barriers left between me and it. Truly, that would have been hell.

And living wasn't far removed. What I could never explain to anyone was what I lost when you were gone. Not just you, not just your laugh and your touch and your advice and your companionship. Not just the way that I could always count on you, when I couldn't count on myself. I lost a part of myself. I know that everyone always says that, but maybe that's because it's always true.

We had been together so long that I no longer knew what parts of me were really me, and what parts were you. In your absence, I had to begin to sort those out, and I couldn't do that in the old house. It had become a dungeon, one in which I imprisoned myself, and to which only I had the key.

Did anyone understand that? Does it matter if they did? I had to sell it, though, at the same time, I regret it every day. But it was killing me, and some part of me welcomed that. The slow rituals that I went through every day, doing, each time, what I would have done had you been there. Did I expect that you would suddenly appear? No, not even once. The cold knife of grief, even held back by drugs and drink, was still lodged too deeply to allow me even that false hope. No, I just did them because they were what I had always done, and what else could I do?

I became a ghost, clanking about the house in chains that I had forged, not in life, but instantaneously in the white-hot moment of your death. Every day they weighed on me more and more heavily, and every day I knew that I must succumb to them eventually, or make a change. That sooner or later the pain I was feeling would become greater than my fear of the pain that might wait for me on the other side, and I would go to that bottle of pills, or something else.

When I remembered to drive to the store, every tree along the side of the road was a siren, calling to me. Saying that if I just steered a little to the right, then there would be a loud crash and silence and darkness and I would no longer have to feel anything at all. Not even this muted pain, bracketed by pills and booze.

That's why I left, why I kept so little of the life we had built. You have to believe me. I had wanted to stay, to rebuild something in the ruin that you left behind. But that place was contaminated now with the knowledge of what I could never have again, and every surface was radioactive, not with memories, but with the memories that would never be made.

Did I run away to Basin Springs? Maybe, but I prefer to think that I did something else. That I brought your memory with me here, since I never got around to bringing you while you were alive. I had an unhappy childhood, filled, you always told me, with more worry and pain than was my lot. This was a place where I had been happy, for just an afternoon. Happy the way that I always was when you came home to me, when I kissed the back of your neck while you were making spaghetti, when you fell asleep against my chest and I could feel your heartbeat, your breath. I wanted to bring what was left of you here, to share it with you, and to share you with it. And I had to do it while there was something left of me.

At least, that's what I like to think.

## STAGE 5
## L'ENFER

You killed yourself. There, I said it.

You had struggled with it before, when you were younger. Pallid scars on your thighs from cutting, on your wrists from a previous attempt, when you had held ice cubes to the spot to numb the pain. By the time I met you there was medication, and you were better.

You still thought about it sometimes, talked about it, but we were getting by. And then insurance changed, and one medication was suddenly no longer covered, so you were on a different one and it was supposed to work the same way, and yet one day I came home to poppy-bright drops of blood on the kitchen floor.

Not that there weren't warning signs. We knew you were getting worse; I even took you to the emergency room one night. Ten hours of you huddled under a blanket on a bench in the corner of a sterile white room, me sitting on the floor beside you, holding your hand.

They took away the bags that we had brought in with us, locked them in a cabinet there in the room, wouldn't let us have anything out of them. For hours we sat there alone. From time to time a nurse came in, asked questions, took vitals, drew blood. Eventually a social worker arrived, asked some more questions, gave you some platitudes. Then they just let you go.

It isn't that they didn't care. Help was on its way. We had the number of people to call, we had discontinued the bad medicine, were trying to refill a script of the stuff that had worked before. But these things take time, and sometimes time runs out. Sometimes you're just running along through a level, running and running and running, and then suddenly the little clock in the upper right-hand corner hits zero and then everything freezes and drops out from under you and you're just gone.

Your therapist said that it wasn't anything I had done, that it wasn't anything you had wanted. You didn't want to die because you were miserable, unhappy, hurting. It was just the medications, an unfortunate interaction that exacerbated a condition that had always been there. An imp in your brain, just waiting for the opportunity to whisper in your ear when your defenses were down. A stark reminder that our minds are controlled, not by us, but by chemicals that we desperately try to balance, like ancient alchemists attempting to strain base metals into gold.

That should have helped. I talked to the therapist myself — the same one that you had gone to, thinking maybe she could help me to understand — but all that I learned was the brute indifference of the universe. There was no grand story here, no drama. Nothing to overcome, nothing to slay. Just banality that could still reach up and snuff you out, no matter how precious you were to me, nor I to you.

I blamed myself because it was easier than accepting the truth, that there was no one *to* blame. But more than that, I just missed you. I couldn't imagine a world without you, and I didn't want to live to see one. I said before that I didn't kill myself because I was afraid that there was only more pain waiting for me on the other side of death, but that's only part of the truth, if any of it. Let me be honest now, with myself at least, and with you, whatever part of you is still here, whatever part I'm talking to. What stayed my hand, more than anything, was the thought that taking my own life because I couldn't live without you would cheapen the tragedy of your death, somehow.

So instead I drowned myself in drugs and booze and repetition, until the day I realized that I was still killing myself, just a lot more slowly. That's when I came here, to Basin Springs, where I tried to lose myself, for a few hours a day, in the games in the arcade, in food that was bad for me, in this place that I found myself still able to love, even after all my love seemed to have abandoned me.

Like the drunkard in the game, I saw you waltzing away, in the embrace of oblivion, and I turned to drown my sorrows. In drink and pills and solitude, then in games and simplicity. In a strangely soothing new routine, one that required little of me.

"Was there anything I could have done?" I asked the therapist at my second-to-last visit, and she shook her head.

"There never is," she said. "Not really. We do our best, but sometimes, in spite of all of our efforts, love and will are not enough."

Friends and family encouraged me to pursue some legal recourse. After all, the change in your prescription had been what drove the blade, surely I could sue someone for malpractice. But I knew then that it wouldn't bring you back, that I couldn't stand there in front of a lawyer, in front of a judge, and see you picked apart, see you taken to trial.

"She had tried it before," they would point out, and I couldn't disagree. I could never make them understand how special you were, and no settlement, no money, nothing but you could ever be a replacement. So I walked away, and I hid in my own version of the bottle, the grave, the flames.

The beginning of the final level is obviously modeled on the French Cabaret of the Inferno, with its angry demonic visage framing the door as our drunkard enters through the mouth, which then promptly closes behind him, sharp teeth coming together with a crunch that shakes the floor. Inside it is initially dark, and then flames spring up to illuminate the goings-on within.

How to describe them? They are a Bosch painting come to life, an animated version of the stereoscopic clay sculptures of hell that were popular in France in the 1860s. The floors and pillars that hold up the level are wreathed in flame, and in the background, emaciated devils torment sinners with hot pokers, with bellows which they jam into their mouths or anuses and pump furiously, with other implements of torture that I cannot begin to understand or explain.

The enemies in this level are sometimes these devils themselves—striding forth on legs that are far too long, their beaked faces peering down as they jab at the drunkard with pitchforks; bouncing forth on round bodies with no discernable legs at all, the faces in their stomachs burping out balls of blue flame that hover in the air and don't dissipate, turning every inch of the level into an infernal obstacle course—and sometimes their animated devices of torture. An iron maiden bursting up from the floor, spilling open to reveal a bloody skeleton which stumbles several paces forward before collapsing into a pile of red bones. As the drunkard approaches a body being broken on the wheel, suddenly the wheel itself separates from the rest of its apparatus and comes bouncing toward him through the flames.

Everywhere in this level there are perils, and power-up bottles are few and far between. Not much comfort in Hell, I suppose, not even for the very wicked. Giant devils stomp back and forth in great iron boots and swing gigantic hammers. Helmets cover their heads, which must be knocked off before they can be destroyed, and once they *are*, the demons' movements become much faster.

Enormous worms tipped with gigantic pincers—larger versions of the maggots from the second level, perhaps—burst up from the flaming ground. When they're destroyed they disgorge a mass of zombie-like sinners who stumble forward, half-melted. At other times, balls of sinners bound together come rolling through the halls of Hell. When they're struck, sinners go flying off and the ball decreases gradually in size until it is gone completely, and only a skull remains, coming to rest on the ground and standing still.

At the end of the level, the drunkard enters a room and the doorway behind him is shut by a curtain of fire. At first, the background of the room is darkness, but then a throne is illuminated. On it sits a skeleton, a crown perched crookedly on its head. It has partly collapsed into dust, and I wonder, for a moment, if this is the monarch of Hell.

But no, the room is illuminated further, and I see the power behind the throne, the devil that the drunkard has come here to vanquish. It is huge, literally filling the room, so that there is virtually no space left to maneuver, and even then it is hunched, bent almost in half, so that its overlarge head both brushes the ceiling and nearly rests on the floor. It looks like a skeleton, the skin desiccated and stretched taught across the bones, but also like a puppet, somehow carved, its joints not quite right. On its head is a crown, perched against malformed horns, and in its hand it holds a long, crooked sword, the blade stained red with blood.

This is the final boss, and it moves back forth in the room something like an ape. At times it brings down that enormous sword in a blow that, as near as I can tell, is impossible to avoid. At other times it simply works its jaws soundlessly, as though chewing something invisible—a traitor, perhaps, for that would fit with Dante's account—and reaches out its long arm, its empty fist, to strike at the drunkard or at the air, if he has managed to vacate the premises.

I only defeat this final boss once, and even now I can't quite say how. By the skin of my teeth, I know that. With nothing left in the tank, all of my "health" depleted, no more quarters in my pocket or stacked on the machine, and only one more blow left between me and GAME OVER. And yet, I strike that final blow, and the huge skeleton devil puppet begins to shake, and the whole room begins to shake, until it shakes itself apart.

A strange wind comes up, and the dust and bones on the throne are blown away, one pixel at a time. The drunkard approaches the throne, and lifts the only item that remains, the crown, up onto his head, placing it atop that ridiculous knight's helmet. The screen fades to black, and a message appears:

*Is it better to rule in Hell than to serve in Heaven?*

## BONUS STAGE
## LES AMOUREUX

That is not quite the end of the game. The credits roll, but I feel, somehow, like I need to watch all of them, and at the end, I am rewarded with a final cinematic. Or, no, not a cinematic, because it doesn't move. Just a single image, of the same gravestone from the end of level three, with that name carved into it, the one you always called me.

The grave is no longer open, no stairs descend into the underground. Now there is a mound of earth, and a battered knight's helmet, and someone has left a single white flower. I wonder if it was the blonde-haired girl who was dancing with the dashing gent, or if, perhaps, the drunkard had someone else in his life who cared more for him, someone he didn't think of as he descended into oblivion.

It is pouring rain outside when I beat the game, and I stand in the archway of the arcade, considering the walk back to the apartment. The rain is hammering on the concrete roof of the arcade, and I think about staying, but I'm out of quarters, and have no cash that I could change for them, even if Janice were still in the booth, which she isn't. According to my watch it's after midnight. The place is pretty much deserted, except for a few young townies who are messing around with the skee ball machines. The food vendors up and down the street are all closed and dark. Everything is closed. There's nothing for me to do but walk home in the rain.

Home, is that where I'm headed? The tiny apartment that reminds me of ours, where I keep the handful of things that I still have to remind me of you? Is that home now?

Difficult as it is to believe, I haven't had a drop to drink since I came to Basin Springs. In our house I was well on my way to drinking myself into the grave, just like in the game, but here, something else replaced that addiction. Still, tonight I think about it. There's an all-night liquor store near the highway. It's a long walk in the rain, but I can see the gleam of the neon, and I've made longer.

By the time I come up the steps to the apartment, I'm soaked through, and still haven't completely talked myself out of turning around and heading for that neon sign. I drip water onto the hall carpet as I fish for the keys in my pocket, and then push open the door.

Inside, you're waiting for me, as I somehow knew you would be. Moth-pale and dressed all in white, you are radiant, and I think, as you must have wanted me to think, of our wedding day. You're smiling now, as you were smiling then, and I remember watching you walk up the aisle. How you glowed.

You were so happy in that moment, the happiest that I had ever seen you, and the best feeling that I ever had in my life was knowing that I had helped to make you that happy. Your smile was so wide, and I could tell that you were trying to tame it, to break it down so that you would look dignified for the wedding photos. I could see you fighting the desire to cover your face with your bouquet. I could never explain to you—then or later—that it was not the whiteness of your dress or the light streaming in through the stained glass windows that made you shine so brightly that day. It was that smile; the happiness so great that you couldn't hold it in.

Your smile tonight is the same, but different. Your hair is uncut, your bangs have fallen over your eyes, hiding your face in shadows save for that smile, and it is growing *too* big, stretching too far, creeping past the edges of your face. Your dress is white, white as a scar, white as the edges of your wounds when I found you that day, and you are dripping wet, as though you, too, have just stumbled in from out of the rain.

My first instinct is to run to you, no matter what. Angel, ghost, devil, death. Whatever you are, it's you, and that's all I care about, all I want. But I don't run. I walk, slowly. Your hands are cupped together, and you extend them out toward me, holding something in your palms.

They are full of water, and beneath the water are two eyes, closed now. The eyes that should be in your face, but up close I see that they aren't. Maybe the water isn't water at all but tears, leaking out from around their edges.

Floating atop the water is something I recognize. It's a straight razor, one that you got me for our second anniversary. As a joke, more than anything, because I always cut myself shaving even with regular razors, and I'd always said that with a straight razor I would inevitably slit my throat. It had a handle made of horn, matching a comb that you had inherited from your grandmother. You bought it for me from an antique shop. I sold it in the auction, along with everything else, and yet here it is.

Gingerly, I pick it up. The water in your palms is cold, and when the straight razor is gone, the eyes there open, and they are bright yellow, like molten gold. You hold your hands up to the side of your face, your smile growing ever wider.

Slowly, I open the straight razor.

I know what you want me to do. I remember the puckered skin around your wounds, how strangely bloodless it looked, given how much blood there was everywhere else. The doctor said that it was quick, that you'd taken pills to numb the pain, that it hadn't lasted long. This won't last long either, I know. I'm cold already, so very cold, but you're even colder. It comes off you like the air from inside a freezer.

You reach out a hand to take my wrist, to guide me, to show me where to cut, and how, but I step back, outside of your reach. You make a sound, a gasp that's also a screech. You know that something is wrong. I raise up the straight razor so it's between us, held up like a talisman, and then I snap the handle from the blade, and let both clatter to the floor.

The reaction is immediate. You expand, your dress suddenly flying up on either side of you as if in a gale, and then it's a dress no longer but long, diaphanous wings. And your smile is no longer a smile, it's a maw, filled with shining teeth. And what's more, I know that it isn't you, that it never was. And it makes a sound like weeping as it collapses in upon itself, all the fabric of the dress disappearing into a black hole the size of a half-dollar in the middle of the room, and then into nothing.

In its absence, the room seems warm and close and strangely silent. I can hear the water drip off my clothes and onto the carpet. I pick up the two pieces of the straight razor, which are still there on the floor, and carry them over and drop them into the trash.

I'm sorry that I ever thought it was you, there for me in my apartment tonight. Maybe it was the same thing that drove the razor along your skin, looking now for another victim. But I know that is something that you would never have asked of me.

I once feared what was waiting for me on the other side of death, but not anymore. I can't say what it will be any more now than I could then. I hope that it will be you, but I have my doubts. I think maybe that death is a vast ocean that drags us down and drowns us, and that whatever emerges on the other shore probably won't even know who I ever was, and that's fine. Maybe that's for the best.

There was a time when my fear was the only thing that kept me from welcoming death, but that's gone now, too. On the off chance that you *are* waiting for me there, beyond the veil, I know that you will still be there if I'm a little late in following. In the meantime there are rolls of quarters in the old cigar box by the door, and plenty of games still left to play.

## AUTHOR'S NOTE

Like the narrator of this story, I am married to someone who has struggled with suicidal ideation for most of her life. Many of the details of the narrator's history are drawn from the events of my own marriage, including the catastrophic near-misses that can come when something goes wrong with medication.

In the wake of one of those near-misses, I felt like I needed to write something that not only confronted what it means to live in that shadow, but that attempted to imagine a way forward if that unthinkable eventuality ever came to pass. Leave it to me to turn a story for a video game anthology into one of the most personal and difficult things I've ever tried to write.

Basin Springs is based on the real-life town of Manitou Springs, Colorado. Like my narrator, I visited it once as a kid, and it left a big mark, though I've never actually gone back. It was fun to return for a while, even if only in my imagination.

The titular video game is inspired by *Ghosts 'n Goblins* and its assorted permutations, but even more by the various *Ghosts 'n Goblins* imitators that have cropped up over the years. Specifically, I was inspired by a game that I've never played and that may not even exist. I saw a few sprites for it years ago on some website or another, and my memory tells me that it involved a hunchbacked cemetery caretaker battling monsters, but I can't remember a title and have never been able to find it again. Chances are it was some kind of homebrew thing, or I just made it up whole cloth.

The "Drunkard's Dream" penny arcade diorama is a real thing, and you can find video of it online, but I wrote the story based on my memory of a description of it in, I think, Neil Gaiman's *American Gods*. Sometimes inaccurate memories make for better inspiration than immediate reference. The knight-helmeted drunkard owes a more than minor debt to the swashbuckling protagonist of Gary Gianni's delightful *MonsterMen* comics. Jumble all that together for a few thousand words and, as Mike Mignola says, there you go.

## ABOUT THE DEVELOPERS

**ADREAN MESSMER** is a bisexual, gender dysmorphic horror writer living in Tulsa, Oklahoma with a tiny human she put together from some spare parts and a technowizard husband. She has too many cats and a dog who's really a magician. When she was eight, she asked her mother to read Stephen King's *It* to her as a bedtime story and her mother actually did it.

**SEAN M. THOMPSON** is the author of *Hate From The Sky*, a novella in the bizarro genre, from Eraserhead Press. He's cohost of the comedic horror/weird fiction podcast *Miskatonic Musings*, along with Charles Meyer and Leeman Kessler. You can find him on Twitter @SpookySeanT and at his official website SpookySean.com.

**JULIE K. GODARD** is a writer, web content producer, and editor living in the green-tinted morass that is Denver, Colorado. She loves to write about anything intriguing, including the nature of the human mind in various stages of cognition, horror, emotional torment, and especially confusion. She has been published in numerous anthologies and a few online magazines, including *Spooklights* and *Bust*. Her first love is short fiction, with coming-of-age stories and children's stories coming in a close second. Julie writes on every topic you can think of, with recent and successful ventures into the world of cannabis, hemp, and medical writing. Julie loves the foothills and mountains of Colorado and spending time exploring them with her husband and two daughters. Red Rocks Amphitheatre is her church.

**JONATHAN RAAB** is the founder and editor-in-chief of Muzzleland Press. His books include *Flight of the Blue Falcon*, *The Hillbilly Moonshine Massacre*, and *The Lesser Swamp Gods of Little Dixie*. His short fiction has appeared in *Lovecraft eZine*, *The Book of Blasphemous Words*, *Letters of Decline*, *A Breath From the Sky*, and *Turn to Ash Volume 2: Open Lines*. His nonfiction has appeared in the *New York Times* At War blog, CNN.com, *Stars and Stripes*, and others. He lives in Colorado.

**RICHARD WOLLEY** was born and raised in Southeast Idaho, but currently resides in Portland, Oregon. He lives there with his wife and new little critter they made together. He is currently a slave to this baby, and understands how his character feels. His favorite food is currently bean burritos. It used to be grilled cheese sandwiches and tomato soup, but he has a scary association with them now.

**J.R. HAMANTASCHEN** is the author of the 2011 collection *You Shall Never Know Security* and the 2015 collection *With a Voice that is Often Still Confused but is Becoming Ever Louder and Clearer*. He also co-hosts the semi-popular weekly podcast *The Horror of Nachos and Hamantaschen*.

**WILLIAM TEA** thought monsters lived in the dark when he was a child. So when the lights were out, he snarled and spat and twisted his hands into claws, trying to blend in with the things that went bump in the night. He's been friends with the monsters ever since. Today, William lives in the Northeastern Pennsylvania Coal Region. He has had stories published in anthologies from StrangeHouse Books and CLASH books, with more forthcoming from Dynatox

Ministries and Weirdbook Magazine. Find him online at www.WilliamTea.com.

**BRIAN O'CONNELL** is a fifteen-year-old author of horror and weird fiction. He runs the weird fiction review website the Conqueror Weird (conquerorweird.wordpress.com) and is assistant editor at Electric Pentacle Press' *Ravenwood Quarterly*. He enjoys the rain, the beach, the forest, and the smell of a crumbling church on a damp morning. You can find him online at devilcoven.wordpress.com.

**MATTHEW M. BARTLETT** is the author of *Gateways to Abomination*, *The Witch-Cult in Western Massachusetts*, and *Creeping Waves*. His short stories have appeared in a variety of anthologies, including *Resonator: New Lovecraftian Tales From Beyond*, *High Strange Horror*, *Lost Signals*, *Nightscript 2*, and *Year's Best Weird Fiction Vol. 3*. He lives and writes in a small brick house on a quiet, leafy street somewhere in Northampton, Massachusetts with his wife Katie Saulnier and their cats Phoebe, Peachpie, and Larry.

**AMBERLE L. HUSBANDS** is a writer, artist, aircraft mechanic, and native-daughter of the Okefenokee. Her short stories have appeared in numerous magazines and anthologies, including the Muzzleland Press anthologies *High Strange Horror* and *Spooklights*. Her first poetry collection, *Horseflesh*, is available from Maverick Duck Press and her novel, *See Eads City*, is currently available for order through Amazon and Barnes & Noble—other Eads City stories appear in the Pulp Heroes series of anthologies (vol. 1 & 3) by

Alchemy Press. For a complete list of her published works, or just to chat about books, look for Amberle's page at Goodreads.com.

**JACK BURGOS** is a 33-year-old author of transgressive, speculative fiction living in Tulsa, Oklahoma. He was born in Miami, the son of Colombian and Cuban immigrants. He graduated from Tulane University in New Orleans, Louisiana, in 2007 with a B.A. in English and a B.A. in Philosophy. He graduated with an M.A. in Clinical Psychology from the University of Tulsa in 2013. Jack co-founded the writing critique group Nevermore Edits in 2012. His work has been published in *Happy Days, Now Playing in Theater B, The Book of Blasphemous Words* and more. He edited the anthology *Broken Worlds*, published by A Murder of Storytellers. His series Stormborn debuted in 2017 with its first book, *13 Hearts to Start a Storm*. Jack also serves as the webmaster for the Oklahoma Writers' Federation, Inc. and as the Treasurer for Nevermore Edits. When he isn't engaged in writing-related activities, Jack proudly works as a home-based counselor in Youth Services of Tulsa's CARS program.

**AMBER FALLON**, formerly known as Alyn Day, lives in a small town outside Boston, Massachusetts that she shares with her husband and their two dogs. A techie by day and a horror writer by night, Mrs. Fallon has also spent time as a bank manager, motivational speaker, produce wrangler, and apprentice butcher. Her obsessions with sushi, glittery nail polish, and sharp objects have made her a recognized figure around the community. Amber's publications include *The Terminal, The Warblers, Daughters of Inanna, Sharkasaurus, So*

*Long and Thanks for All the Brains*, and many more. Please tweet her @Z0mbiegrl or visit her blog at www.amberfallon.net and listen to her podcast, *It Cooks*, on Project iRadio.

**THOMAS C. MAVROUDIS** is a Denver native, husband, and father, and possesses an MFA from the University of California, Riverside, where he studied under Stephan Graham Jones. He is the co-founder of the serial fiction blog Saturday Morning Serial (saturdaymorningserial.net) and his publishing credits include *Crosscurrents*, *Dreaming in R'lyeh*, and *Turn to Ash*.

**ALEX SMITH** is the author of *Hive*, published by Muzzleland Press. His fiction has appeared in *Theaker's Quarterly Fiction* and *Black Ink Horror*. His poetry has appeared in *Sink Review* and *Catch-up Louisville*. His poem book *BLOWN* was published by Superchief Press. He was born in Washington, DC.

**ORRIN GREY** is a skeleton who likes monsters, not to mention a writer, editor, and amateur film scholar who was born on the night before Halloween. His stories have appeared in dozens of anthologies, including Ellen Datlow's *Best Horror of the Year*, and he's the author of *Never Bet the Devil & Other Warnings* and *Painted Monsters & Other Strange Beasts*, as well as *Monsters from the Vault*, a collection of columns on vintage horror films. He doesn't play video games as much as he used to, but when he does, he prefers that they have ghosts or monsters in them. You can visit him online at orringrey.com.

Made in the USA
Columbia, SC
31 August 2017